A Future Fairytale

By Pauline Jones

Foreword.

According to BBC online 5th October 2007, when we eventually travel into space as tourists we will be using a new, purpose made and expensive currency called the quid. The currency, which will be equivalent to 6.25 English pounds, is used extensively by the characters in this book.

ISBN: **978-0-9556800-0-7**

Chapter 1.

Once upon a future time when dreams no longer come true there will live a beautiful but sad Princess.

But enough about her; let's get on with the real story.

The first rays of the morning sun lit up the spaceport that lay on the edge of the planet Bella's capital, Florien City. For the first time in living memory it had been turned over to civilian use.

Litter from the previous night's long awaited cease-fire celebrations blew around the feet of a serving girl as she ran up the steps and hammered on the door of an old space plane called the Genghis Khan.

No one came.

She pounded it with her fists; "I know you're in there, Open up pleeease!"

The door opened a crack, "You'd better move away, we're cleared for launch," a voice from inside said.

"I want you to take me with you; please I need to get away from here."

"Well you can't join the circus, we're not hiring."

"I didn't say I wanted to join, I just want you to drop me off wherever you're going."

"Why do you want to leave your planet now that the war is almost over?"

"Because I don't trust the peace treaty; it'll leave us wide open. The men of Bellus will use the Princess's forthcoming marriage as an excuse to enslave us all."

"That's who you remind me of... you're the Princess."

"No I'm not."

"Yes you are."

"No I'm not."

"There's a definite resemblance."

"That's because I'm a look alike, I sometimes get work impersonating her; you probably don't know this but when you see the Princess at official engagements it isn't really her, it's a decoy; someone expendable, like me."

"We're not licensed for passenger transport so you still can't come with us; now if you'll excuse us we'll be late for our gig on Astros."

As the door started to close completely the girl held up a fifty-quid note.

"Where did you get that?"

"Danger money, you don't think I would risk my life playing decoy for free do you?" The door swung open and a very tall, very thin man bent over and took the money out of her hand as she walked past him, "I'm Lydia," she said.

"My name's Jerome," the man led her through the ancient spaceship and onto the bridge; eleven faces stared at her as she walked in.

"You can have Freddie's seat, he's on Zreem getting treatment for his problem."

"Problem?"

"Keeps getting nasty boils; can't sit down."

"And you expect me to sit where his boils have been?"

"All the other seats are taken."

"You can have my place Mistress," a very short man; almost as wide as he was tall unstrapped himself from his own chair and settled himself in Freddie's questionable one.

"Thank you sir, thank you," Lydia gratefully settled herself into the dwarf's tattered seat.

"Take off in two minutes, please fasten your seatbelts; make sure that your tray tables are stowed and that your seats are in the upright position," a deep voice in front of them announced.

"Who's that?" Lydia ventured to ask.

"Geraldine she's our mechanic, and our pilot, and our tattooed lady."

"So this is a freak show?"

An older woman's voice came from the back row, "No it's a circus of special people who are also good performers; which you would know if you had visited our tent during the festivities."

"Sorry I was busy, but don't they have treatment these days for er... special people with problems?"

"Yes they do," Jerome told her. "But firstly it costs an arm and a leg and the only person who has a leg to spare is Jerry our three legged man and secondly we are all very talented people but no one would come to see us if we weren't special and thirdly it keeps us safe from planetary conflicts."

"Of course... as registered entertainers you have political immunity as long as you stay neutral," Lydia said.

There was no more time for talk because the engines roared and the pot-bellied space plane started to pick up speed; as they took off they could see the ground below out of the cabin windows.

"Hey there's the river and the town and the castle where I... where I was serving wine last night and there's the site of the old mansion house, the Bellusian ambassadors want to rebuild it and use it as an embassy once the peace treaty is finalized."

"How do you know that?" the old lady asked.

"Well I... well it's amazing what you hear when you're working behind a bar."

"Which bar did you work at?"

"The Cross Eyed Cobra."

"I thought that was bombed."

"It was; that's why I was at the castle."

When the air got too thin for the jet engines, the rockets fired. The Gee forces were so great that they all blacked out and when they woke up they were weightless until Geraldine turned on the artificial gravity. She started up the graviton engines and as they built up power she set course for Astros. After that the 'Fasten seat belt' sign went off and everybody unstrapped.

"I'm hungry," Jerry said.

"You always are," the old lady told him, "I'm sure that every one of your legs is hollow."

Lydia followed the others to the back of the vessel where there was a galley with a big, rectangular table that had been scrubbed so often that most of the artificial wood grain had been rubbed off. They all sat down hoping to be fed.

"Bunion how long till breakfast?" the old lady asked.

"I should go and check on the creatures first," the little man that had given up his seat for Lydia said.

"I'll send Jerry down to do that; you feed the humans."

Jerry left the table and went down below while Bunion went off into the galley and clattered some pans.

"You have animals?" Lydia asked.

"Actually we prefer the term creatures. Some of them are genetically modified, mostly failed experiments; we rescued them."

"So they're freaks too?"

"Not the ones in the petting zoo."

"But the rest?"

"They're special like us, Bunion how much longer?" the old lady turned to Lydia, "I'm Clarissa the two hundred year old woman by the way."

"Wow that's really old."

Bunion clattered more pans.

Jerome stood up, "In case any of you are wondering, everyone this is Lydia, she's a fare paying passenger."

"Hello Lydia," everyone said.

"Hello," Lydia replied.

"You look like the Princess," a man with a long face like a weasel told her.

"She has been working as her decoy Natter."

"That must have been exciting," Natter said.

6

"It was stressful and dangerous but it was how I got the money for my fare."

"And where are you planning to go Lydia?"

"I'm not sure yet, I just knew I had to get away."

"I thought the war was ending," Grumpus the strong man said.

"Doesn't it seem just a little bit strange to you that we have been warring with Bellus for a hundred and fifty years and now suddenly it's over, just like that? There's going to be a treaty; all our Princess has to do is marry their Prince and blam we have peace, it's easy… too easy."

"So you think this peace they speak of is an illusion?" Mr. Mystery the illusionist said.

"I don't know what hold the Bellusians have over our Chancellor but he is suddenly willing to give them access to our planet without restriction. Our Princess could be murdered on her wedding night and the Bellusians could take over the whole of Bella and there would be nothing we could do to stop them."

"It doesn't bear thinking about," Annie, one of the conjoined twins who were billed as the two headed woman said.

"Bunion, where's our breakfast?" Clarissa said.

More clattering; Grumpus's belly rumbled loudly.

"I have an idea," Natter spoke up, "Lydia may only be a serving wench but she bears a powerful resemblance to the Princess, can't we keep her?"

"You mean, include her in the show?"

"Looking like someone famous makes you kinda special; you remember when we had Joe Clotter working with us?"

"He looked like Frankenstein," Clarissa said.

"I think that someone as beautiful as Lydia would draw in the crowds."

"Our takings have been dive bombing lately," Grumpus said.

"Astros has been Disastros for the last couple of years," Jerry agreed.

"We do need a change, our takings at all venues were down an average of ten percent over the last year, but on Astros we grossed only two hundred quid, which barely covered our expenses; three years ago we took five times that," Josephine the cone headed woman said.

"I think people are getting bored with our show," Natter said. "We need something different; once you've seen one three headed cow you've seen them all."

"We've never had anyone pretty in our act before, how am I ever going to get a boyfriend if she's around?" Rosie, the other conjoined twin complained.

Clarissa spoke up, "I agree with Natter, we've lost our way lately, we haven't been keeping up with modern trends; something new could turn things around for us."

"We could stage mock weddings and marry her off at every performance, I don't mind playing the part of the Prince," Froggie suggested.

Jerome stroked his long chin, "I'm sorry Froggie but I don't think that even you are quite ugly enough for a Beauty and the Beast scenario."

"Bunion," Clarissa called out, "I've got a job for you."

"I'm not sure I want to be a part of your circus," Lydia said

"Have you got somewhere better to go?"

"Well... no...."

"Tell you what, you play Astros with us; see how it goes; if it works out you can stay and if it doesn't you'll be free to move on."

"Well I suppose...."

"You'll get the standard wage."

"What's that?"

"An equal share of the takings after expenses."

"Oh."

"If we do well, you do well," Clarissa said.

It took ten days to get to Astros and by the time they arrived they had worked out a script, rehearsed it and made the costumes. Astros was an agricultural planet that grew almost nothing else but wheat; it was the breadbasket of that small part of the Galaxy and the dough fair was the biggest event on their calendar. The Astrosissians were very proud of their dough; they produced many different varieties and at this fair the best ones won prizes. The competition was so intense that it was hard to tear people's attention away from dough related subjects and onto something more entertaining. But as Clarissa Clarke's Traveling World of Wonders set up in its usual position near the entrance to the grounds they knew they had a chance.

This year they did not advertise the fish headed woman or the flying trapeze dogs or even the Tyrannosaurus Rex (He wasn't with them long; they had to give him to a zoo on account of the fact that he nearly wrecked the space ship). This year, on banners larger than usual they invited people to witness 'The Royal Wedding.'

Clarissa was not only the troupe's decision maker, she was its chief costume maker; she had fashioned a flowing silken wedding dress for Lydia and a massive pink, short sleeved, multi-layered bride's maid's dress for Geraldine, the biggest, most tattooed woman that Lydia had ever seen.

"It's so beautiful... but my hair, what am I going to wear in my hair?"

"I found you a pink tiara that matches Lydia's white one," Clarissa told her as she was getting them ready. Geraldine had very short, very red hair but when she saw the tiara she looked visibly relieved.

It was Annie's job to do the makeup, "Stop it," she told her sister.

"I'm not doing anything," Rosie said.

"Yes you are; you're jerking my hand."

"I can do what I like with our hand."

"Not when I'm doing Lydia's make up you can't."

"She should be wearing greasepaint like the rest of us."

"Clarissa told me to make her as beautiful as possible."

"Can you do anything for me?" Geraldine asked.

Annie turned and smiled at her, "I will do my best; if my sister will allow me."

"Perhaps Rosie would like to be made up too."

"Me? You think I could?"

"You have a very pretty face."

"Do I?"

"You are a beautiful person and I know that one day someone will come along who appreciates you."

"You really think I have a chance?"

"Of course you do," Geraldine smiled.

"Thanks Geraldine, it's nice to know that someone is on my side around here."

With her makeup on, Lydia looked more beautiful than ever and Geraldine looked as demure as a mountain of tattooed muscle could look.

Clarissa came in to check on Lydia's costume, she looked flustered, "I got the dimensions for Bunion's suit wrong."

"Oh," Lydia said.

"It fits him."

"Sorry?"

"It looks good; it was supposed to be too small."

"Eh?"

"There has to be as much contrast between the two of you as possible, you have to look beautiful and he has to look... well ugly, as ugly as possible."

"Aren't the Bellusians going to be offended by this performance?"

"We just won't do any shows too near Bellus, besides no one knows what Prince Jason looks like, there are rumors that he's ugly."

"Yes I've heard those rumors too."

"So we can say that we are trying to be authentic can't we."

Lydia looked doubtful, "Isn't this whole performance in rather bad taste?"

"Don't worry," Clarissa assured her, "I've been at this game for a long time; I know what's acceptable and what isn't."

"Two hundred years?"

"Actually I'm only a hundred and seventy but don't tell the customers. As a matter of fact I was there when the Bellusian war started."

"When Lord Fopwais was killed?"

"Even before that, when Lord Fopwais challenged Lord Murmot to the duel over the Lady Sylvia."

"Really?"

"Remind me to tell you about it sometime... are you nervous?"

"A little."

"Now remember to do it just the way we rehearsed, you don't actually have to kiss Bunion, we'll close the curtains before you get to that."

"Okay."

"Are you ready?"

Lydia nodded.

"Then let the show begin."

The circus tent was packed. Clarissa had unearthed bunches of slightly battered silk flowers from one of the boxes deep in the dusty hold and tied them around the tent poles. Silken ribbons draped the chairs, and Froggie, the backdrop artist had made up an authentic looking stained glass window. Grumpus was dressed as a Cardinal, Clarissa played the Queen and Jerome was the King.

Rosie and Annie went up and down the rows selling souvenirs and ice creams, and Mr. Mystery, who was dressed in his best cape, sold scratch cards.

The wedding march began; Lydia took a deep breath and gathered her thoughts before she started walking up the aisle on Jerome's arm. Geraldine walked behind them; her massive hands clutching a bunch of dusty, silk, miniature roses. Lydia waved and shook hands with all those within reach. She looked radiant.

Queen Clarissa sat on her throne on the stage crying, the way that all mothers do at their daughter's wedding.

When Lydia got up to the front she looked around and took another deep breath, and then with one more look at the audience she started her speech, "Where is my husband? I have never seen him before, what does he look like?"

At this point Froggie and Natter, dressed as best men,

dragged Bunion on from the side of the stage. He wore a black suit and there was a black veil over his face.

"Please may I see the face of the handsome prince that I am about to marry?"

Bunion shook his head.

"We'll let you look at him after the ceremony," Natter said.

"But I wish to lay my eyes upon my Master."

The crowd cheered; Bunion shook his head again; the crowd clamored to see him. Bunion tried to leave the stage but Froggie and Natter wouldn't allow him.

Grumpus in his fish shaped hat called the crowd to order, "Dearly beloved we are gathered here together to witness the joining of this man and this woman in holy matrimony. If anyone has any objection to this marriage let him speak now or forever hold his peace."

The crowd all objected.

"Any legally binding objections?"

Jerry played a little wedding music while it was established that there were none. "Now I would ask these young people to take their vows, do you Princess Stephanie the Beautiful; take Prince Jason the... er never mind... to be your lawfully wedded husband?"

"Do I have to?" Lydia/Princess Stephanie asked.

"You do," the Cardinal insisted.

"Are you sure?"

"Yes you do."

"But are you absolutely sure?"

"Yes now just say, 'I do.'"

"I suppose I do."

"And do you Prince Jason take this woman to be your awful dreaded wife?"

"But..." Bunion/Prince Jason said from under his veil.

"Come on now."

"I'm not sure."

"Yes you are."

"But... but...."

"Get on with it, just say, 'I do'."

"I do," he said.

"Then I have the privilege to pronounce you both husband and wife; you may kiss the bride."

At this point Bunion was supposed to take off his veil.

"May I remind you Princess Stephanie that our church does not allow for divorce."

Froggie and Natter stood behind Princess Stephanie so that she couldn't escape while Prince Jason backed out the other way.

"Stand still," the Cardinal said. "Reveal to us who you are."

The audience started a slow handclap, Mr. Mystery stood behind Prince Jason blocking his exit; he slowly lifted the veil a little way up his face... then he let it fall again. The audience jeered; he did it again, building up anticipation, letting his hand fall again; the crowd jeered louder.

He pushed Prince Jason over towards Princess Stephanie who tried to back away. Slowly he lifted the veil from off the prince's face, Lydia screamed with genuine shock when she saw the realistic warts that Annie had added to Bunion's already questionable features.

Prince Jason pursed his lips into a kiss but Princess Stephanie broke free and he chased her screaming around the stage. The Queen burst into floods of tears.

The curtains closed.

Lydia ran offstage; she held her head in her hands and leaned over a chair as if she was going to be sick.

Clarissa followed her, "That was magnificent; I was so worried that you wouldn't know what to do but you behaved like a seasoned professional."

Some eerie, recorded music introduced the next act, which happened to be Mr. Mystery and His Amazing Illusions.

"How could you do it? I mean how could you demean yourselves? How could Bunion let himself be humiliated like that?"

"It's what we have to do my dear; it's the way we

survive."

"But how could you choose to… I don't understand."

"We make the audience laugh and they pay us."

"But they're ridiculing you."

Bunion came running up to them looking agitated, "Clarissa, the crowd won't settle down, they want the kiss!"

"Oh… I'd better go and have a look," Clarissa ran off and took a peek at the audience from the wings. She was soon back, "Those people are very agitated; if we don't do something there'll be a riot."

"I'm sorry Mistress, I didn't expect this," Bunion told Lydia.

"You'll have to give them what they want," Clarissa said.

Lydia shook her head, "I can't."

"It's only a stage kiss; not a real one."

"You don't get it do you? It's not the kiss that bothers me, it's the reason for the kiss; you're playing to the most degraded desires of the crowd, desires that you created, I didn't understand that before, but that's what you do."

"I think we should leave the philosophical discussions for later, right now we need to calm that crowd down," Clarissa said.

"You want me to kiss Bunion?"

"There's no alternative," Jerry ran up to her, "believe me I've seen audiences like this before."

"Give them all their money back."

"It's not their money that they want; quick you'll have to do something; Mr. Mystery is being crucified out there."

Bunion stared down at the ground, "I know that it will be repugnant to kiss me; I am sorry Mistress."

"Repugnant and distasteful Bunion but not for the reasons you imagine."

There was a huge roar from the audience followed by a shriek from onstage.

"You'd better get out there before they turn into a lynch mob," Clarissa said.

Lydia took hold of Bunion's hand, "Let's get this over

with."

They ran back onto the stage as if Prince Jason had been chasing Princess Stephanie all around the fairground. The floor was slippery from the bits of rotten dough that were hailing down on top of them.

Lydia deliberately fell into Mr. Mystery's arms crying, "No... don't make me do this."

Bunion looked up at her with his lips pursed but he slipped and fell badly on the rotten dough.

"Oh no, my husband has been injured," Lydia shouted, making it up as she went along. She bent down over Bunion, "Are you all right my husband?"

"I think I have broken both my legs and my pelvis."

"Then I will have to kiss you better."

The crowd roared.

Lydia bent down, slowly getting nearer to Bunion's face, she turned to smile at the crowd, egging them on; playing them the way Clarissa wanted her to.

Then finally she pecked Bunion on his lips.

But the people wanted more.

She kissed him lightly; they still wanted more.

She kissed him romantically; they wanted more.

She kissed him slowly; the crowd cheered and threw the rest of their dough onto the stage.

Some of it splattered onto Lydia's dress, but she had to keep kissing Bunion.

Some of it splattered onto her arms, but still she had to keep kissing him. At last some of it splattered onto their faces covering their noses and cutting off their air supply. Finally she was able to let go.

The curtains closed and as soon as they did Lydia stormed off, "Never ask me to do that, ever again."

"No Mistress," Bunion hung his big head in shame.

Clarissa ran over to them, "That was magnificent, look at the crowd, they're leaving, they're happy, they don't even want to see the rest of the show. I guarantee we'll be full for the next performance, no matter how much we charge at the box office. I think we should keep it just like that... Lydia where are you going? Lydia?"

Lydia stormed off back to the Genghis Khan. She sat in her small bunkroom, her eyes red with tears, cleaning off the dough that caked her face.

There was a timid knock; she tried to ignore it.

The knock came again; Lydia opened the door and Bunion stood there. He was covered from head to toe in rotten dough; he hadn't even taken the false warts off his face, "I wanted you to know that I'm sorry," he said.

"Sorry for what?"

"I... I'm sorry that you had to kiss me."

"Bunion, I'm not upset because I had to kiss you, I'm upset because I don't understand how you can put up with the humiliation."

"Mistress?"

"If Clarissa told you to do that again you would wouldn't you?"

Bunion nodded.

"Even though it makes you feel really bad?"

"Yes Mistress."

"And you see nothing wrong in that?"

"Clarissa is a good person; she takes care of us."

"People jeer and laugh at you."

Bunion looked down at the floor, "People have always laughed at me Mistress."

"Why don't you get the treatment? Your condition can be put right."

"It costs four thousand, two hundred and forty three quid Mistress."

"And you haven't got the money?"

"I have two thousand Mistress."

"So? You're nearly half way."

"It has taken me ten years to save that much Mistress."

"I still don't understand how you can give up your dignity so easily."

Bunion stood behind her and looked into her mirror, staring at their contrasting images, "There is no dignity to lose."

Lydia shook her head, "I know you think that it's easy for me to talk about dignity and self-esteem when I obviously don't have your problems, but I truly believe that such things come from inside you. I won't always be young; one day I'll have gray hair and wrinkles, but I hope I'll still have my self-respect."

Bunion sighed, "When you grow old you'll still be normal," he turned around as if to leave.

"Bunion, it wasn't the kiss that upset me, it was the fact that the crowds wanted to see both of us humiliated; they lusted for it and you gave them what they wanted; you allowed it. That's what a freak show is all about; you embrace other people's derision. You let them debase you and on this occasion you allowed them to debase me too."

"It's a shock isn't it? I remember my first time," Josephine stood at Lydia's door. "Clarissa found me on Zeltros Prime begging in the streets. No one would employ a freak even though I had taught myself to read and write and even then, although I was only twelve years old, I knew far more than anyone else did. They accused me of being a witch and it was hard to get anyone to put even a small coin into my begging bowl."

"Clarissa rescued you too?"

"Yes," Josephine said.

"And are you saving up money for treatment?"

"There is no treatment for me, if there was, believe me I would know about it. There's no treatment for Clarissa either; there's no cure for old age. She has money, she could retire and live comfortably off her savings but she lives for us, she is our mother."

"Did she send you here to plead her cause?"

"No I came of my own accord and so did Bunion."

Bunion nodded.

"Surely there must be a better life for you than this?"

"Not for us but there is for you, you can go home and be normal."

"I would gladly do that if I could be sure that the peace treaty is genuine."

"I understand your fear; I have heard that there are many others on Bella who feel like you"

"Five hundred and seventy million people have been killed in this senseless war. In fact we've been fighting it for so long that we've lost sight of what we were fighting about."

"So many lives lost for the love of a woman."

"If Lord Fopwais had not been killed, the war would never have started; but no one can turn back time."

"Unfortunately the law does not allow for it, all the technology was destroyed a thousand years ago."

Lydia sighed, "I know that the temporal laws were created to prevent the disastrous consequences of unauthorized time travel, but why should they bar us from going back and preventing bad things from happening?"

"Because it is believed that any interaction with the timeline will bring unknown consequences."

"Nevertheless if I had the opportunity to go back and change things I would," Lydia said.

"You'd risk a mandatory death sentence?"

"That wouldn't matter, not if I could save people's lives."

"I have heard rumors but they're probably not true."

"What kind of rumors?"

"They say that a time machine still exists on Zertza."

"Really?"

"But it can't be possible," Josephine said.

"But if it was and I could somehow get hold of it maybe I would be able to go back in time to prevent the war."

"The time machine has never been found."

"Surely searching for such a thing is illegal."

"Searching for it isn't illegal, but finding it would be."

"I wonder if I...."

Bunion who had been standing quietly in the corner as he often did when no one was talking to him suddenly spoke up, "If you are going to Zertza I will go with you Lydia."

"Why would you want to do that?"

"It would not be safe for a woman to travel alone."

"Are you volunteering to be my protector?"

"Yes," Bunion said.

"The whole thing would be a waste of time," Josephine insisted.

"That wouldn't matter if it was only my own time I was wasting, I don't have anything else on my agenda at the moment. But you're not coming Bunion."

"I will accompany you Mistress."

"I won't let you take the risk."

"It is my choice," Bunion said.

"But Zertza is in the Beta quadrant," Josephine said

"Then I must find a transport that's heading in that direction."

Clarissa appeared at the door, "Are you planning to leave us?"

"I think I've just decided to go to Zertza to search for the time machine."

"Hmm, there is no direct route to Zertza, you would have to go via the Arabica system and the Nierniss star; it would be costly and pointless."

"But I deserted my people."

"You were escaping from danger."

"Nevertheless I need to do something; anything is better than just running away."

"If you agree to perform the wedding scene three times a day for the rest of the dough festival, I'll take you there myself."

Bunion looked down at the ground.

"Your trip to Zertza wouldn't cost you anything and it would be a direct flight."

"Give me some time to think about it," Lydia said.

"Don't make it too long, the next performance starts in an hour and that dough has to be cleaned off first," Clarissa walked away.

Josephine left too and Bunion turned to go but then he turned back, "I'll understand if you don't want to do it; I don't blame you for not wanting to kiss me," he told her.

Lydia looked down at him, "Bunion how can I get it through to you? There are many reasons why I think that this whole thing is wrong but you are not one of them."

She held his face in her hands and bent down and gently kissed his lips. Bunion colored up and ran off to his room. He stared into the chipped mirror that hung on his door, surprised that he still looked like a big, fat, dough covered bullfrog.

Because inside he felt like a Prince.

Chapter 2

Zertza, population: seven million.

Capital: Love City.

Principal export: fine builder's sand.

Principal industry: sand art in all its forms.

Principal attraction: it's isolation. Zertza's principal attraction had always been the fact that nobody wanted to go there.

Zertza had started out as a haven for hippies, it was a place hanging on the edge of life, but it was cheap, in fact it was rent free and as long as you lived simply, catching fish in its one warm ocean, growing coconuts and doing a bit of art every now and then, you could live life away from the rat race and the cares of the rest of the Galaxy.

"Reason for visit?" the official said.

"Isn't it obvious?" Clarissa said.

The space plane had a large, red clown painted on the side and even though at present there were no clowns in the circus it gave observers a big clue as to who was on board; if that was not enough, the words 'Clarissa Clarke's Traveling World of Wonders' emblazoned underneath it should have sealed the deal.

"You should have rung ahead."

"I thought you were a minimum paperwork planet."

"Yea but if I had known you were coming I would have told my kids, they've had nothing to look forward to for months."

"We're welcome then?"

"No one ever comes here and there's nothing to do, we're glad of any break from routine."

Clarissa decided that since they had traveled so far they might as well do a couple of gigs while they waited for Lydia to find out about the time machine.

Suddenly they were swamped. They were turning people away; they were popular once again. They did their old show, the one where Natter in his weasel costume, ran up the giant trouser legs. On every other planet that performance was old and lame. But nobody ever came here; these people had never seen it before.

Now Lydia was the one selling the scratch cards and the ice creams. But she was also searching for information; how could she do that without looking obvious?

The mall; Love City's only mall was situated in manmade caves below ground so that you could shop away from the heat of the sun. It was a pleasant place with flowing streams that irrigated the crops that grew in the fiber optic light on a big stretch of ground between the two steep walls of a large rectangular cavern. The shops were built into the rocky sides.

There was sand art everywhere. Sand statues hardened with resin, murals made of multi-colored sands; even the benches at the coffee shop, which were made of sandstone, were covered with resin hardened sand art.

Lydia ordered her coffee. It cost her five quid... five quid for a cup of coffee? Even on Bella where there had been rationing and severe shortages, coffee had never cost so much.

"It's because it's imported, all the imported goods cost more," the bored looking girl behind the counter said.

"Do you have to import much stuff?" Lydia asked.

"Luxury items, tea, coffee, soap, things like that. So you come from that circus do you? Everyone is overjoyed to see you; you're the most sensational thing to happen around here for months, how sad is that?"

"So... while we're here is there anything for us to see or do? Any local beauty spots?"

"No," the girl said.

"Nothing?"

"You've come to the most boring place in the universe."

"What about those mountains to the east? They look quite picturesque."

"Don't go there."

"Why not?"

"They're dangerous, there's no water and anyway it's illegal."

"Illegal? Why's that?"

"Because of that time machine thing."

"Time machine thing?"

"Yea, people believe that there's a time machine buried up in the hills somewhere; you must know the story about two joy riders from the past who landed in the hills?"

"Well no actually I don't," Lydia told her.

"They were running from the Time Guardians and they had to bury the time machine deep in the mountains and then they died of thirst before they could get to safety."

"And you say that nobody's found it yet?"

"We used to get expeditions from other worlds coming here regularly until they were banned. You should have seen some of the men, they were hunks."

"Why did the authorities stop them?"

"To protect us from the outside world they said, I ask you could they make this place more mind-numbingly tedious? As soon as I've saved enough money I'm getting off this rock."

At that point another customer, an older woman dressed in the flowing style that passed for fashion in those parts came up. Lydia found herself a seat. There were plenty to choose from in the nearly empty coffee shop. Nevertheless the woman came to sit by her. "I couldn't help overhearing," she said. "If you want to go to a place of interest, I know one where there are some very interesting fish."

Lydia had to admit that the fish were extremely interesting. The pink Zertzan manta ray was as big as a light aircraft and very intelligent. It allowed Lydia; dressed in scuba gear, to hold onto the straps that had been attached to its back while it took her for a tour of the local coral reef, which was beautiful. The tour cost fifty quid; it took most of the money that she had earned at the dough festival, but it was well worth it. The day ended with dinner on a jetty that overlooked the harbor.

Interestingly seafood was not on the menu.

"Many people find it distasteful to eat the beautiful creatures that they have just seen swimming happily around the reef," Blue Pool, the waiter explained.

"This has been a really enjoyable day, I'm surprised that Zertza doesn't get more visitors," Lydia told him.

"The planet has a tradition of keeping people away, though I saw your circus last night and I thought it was really good, but all you did was sell ice creams, what was that all about?"

"I'm a Princess Stephanie look alike; we do a whole routine based around her but we're so far from Bellus and Bella that we didn't think you would have heard of them."

"We watch the news like everybody else; Princess Stephanie's gone to a monastery on the Mountains of Contemplation to be instructed in the wisdom of the monks hasn't she?"

"So I hear," Lydia said.

"And Prince Jason is still nowhere to be found, you do a routine about that?"

"Yes but well, everyone seems happy enough to watch the show as it is so maybe we'll save that one for later. In the meantime are there any other sights I should see whilst I'm on Zertza?"

"This is pretty much it," Blue Pool told her, "people around here used to make a lot of money taking visitors on trips to the mountains to hunt for the legendary time machine but there's nothing now."

"Did a lot of people come time machine hunting?"

"Too many that's why the council banned it; personally I would have added a theme park and made the most of it."

"So did they ever find anything?"

"Nope but that didn't stop people coming, they must have explored every inch of those mountains, except for where Crazy Jones lives of course, but they never found anything. The whole story's a myth; you would have thought that people would have figured that out, especially as it's so dangerous."

"Dangerous?"

"The whole of those mountains are magnetic, they can scramble your electronics; you have to use internal combustion ground vehicles and there's no radios if you get into trouble."

"Oh."

"If you're thinking of going, don't."

"I, I wasn't thinking of anything, it's like you say what would be the point if there's nothing there anyway?"

"Exactly."

"Em… who is this Crazy Jones?"

"So you're saying that the only place the time machine could be is on land belonging to a man called Crazy Jones?" Josephine said.

"He's a hermit who owns a whole valley in a remote part of the mountains, he's supposed to have been there forever, it sounds as if he's even older than Clarissa," Lydia explained.

"And you say that it's not possible to use any vehicles with electronics?" Clarissa said.

"They don't work."

"We don't have an internal combustion car, and if we tried to hire one we'd immediately raise suspicion."

"So what do we do?" Lydia asked Josephine whom Clarissa had billed as the most intelligent human in the universe.

"Um… er… um…."

"Camels," Bunion, a less intelligent human suggested.

"Camels?"

"Bertie and Gertie the triple humped camels."

"Have they ever been ridden?"

"They're performing camels; they used to work with the clowns who left us to join Enery White's Amazing Emporium of Magic and Illusion, on Stasos. Well I suppose that when you have a new baby to care for you have to think about settling down," Clarissa said.

"Are camels easy to ride…?" Lydia asked.

Two days later Clarissa Clarke's Traveling World of Wonders relocated to the Peace Plains where there was a settlement of sand artists eager to see the show. The spacecraft flew around the mountains, dropping the camels off as near as possible to the towering peaks.

You don't really ride camels, at least Lydia didn't; she just sat in her chair on the middle hump and wobbled from side to side as the beast made its way slowly forward, "Isn't there any way to make them go faster?" she complained.

"No," Bunion said.

"It would be quicker to walk."

"Save your energy," Bunion said.

"It's hot."

"Yes."

"I'm thirsty."

"Drink some water Mistress."

"Why do you keep calling me Mistress? Are you a slave?"

"No Mistress."

As the sun grew warmer, Lydia fanned herself and poured water over her head, "I'm so hot.

Bunion said nothing.

"Is it going to get much hotter?"

"Probably Mistress."

"Are you hot Bunion?"

"Yes Mistress."

"You don't complain much do you?"

"It wouldn't change anything Mistress."

"Do they have scorpions on this planet?"

"I don't know Mistress."

"I bet if they do there are some hiding under those rocks."

"Yes Mistress."

"Or there could be snakes."

"Maybe there are, Mistress."

"Rattle snakes do you think?"

"I don't hear any rattling Mistress."

"That's true, well maybe there's something else just as deadly."

"Possibly Mistress."

"I'm glad we're up on these uncomfortable camels, I wouldn't want something to jump out from behind a rock and attack me."

Bunion said nothing for a while.

"You don't talk much do you?" Lydia said.

"No Mistress."

"Is that because you don't have anything to say?"

"Nothing that would interest others Mistress."

"Go on, try me, what are you thinking about right now?"

"I am wondering what made you come on this quest Mistress."

"What do you mean?"

"Not many humble serving girls would do what you are doing."

"Of course they would they just don't get the opportunity that's all."

"Excuse me for saying so Mistress but most of the serving girls that I have had the chance to observe are usually intent on flirting with their better looking customers or maybe on avoiding work when their master isn't looking."

"Well obviously you don't know many serving girls; come to think of it there can't be many dwarfs who would be willing to go on a dangerous quest for the sake of dead people."

"Perhaps you don't know many dwarfs Mistress."

The camels plodded along until midday and then after Bunion had ascertained that there were no snakes, scorpions or spiders under the local rocks Lydia climbed out of her seat, stretched her legs and let the animals rest.

"So, tell me about your life," Lydia asked Bunion as they sat down to eat their lunch, "how long have you known Clarissa?"

"She has always been my mother."

"Do you remember your real parents?"

"No."

"Not anything?"

"Clarissa said they loved me and wanted the best for me, but they could do nothing for me."

"Why not?"

"Clarissa said they were very poor and they had other children to worry about."

"So she took care of you?"

"Since I was two years old Mistress."

"And now you're taking care of me?"

"Yes Mistress."

"You don't actually think we're going to find a time machine do you?"

"Time technology has been banned for a thousand years."

"Do you think that altering the timeline would affect you Bunion?"

"It would affect everyone Mistress."

"How?"

"No one can foresee that Mistress; that is why time travel was banned."

Bunion said little at the best of times and he clammed up for the whole of that blistering afternoon. Even as they led the complaining camels up almost sheer inclines and across slippery scree Bunion didn't open his mouth.

Mouths can be useful however. If it wasn't for Lydia's mouth and her beautiful flashing eyes that had mesmerized Blue Pool the waiter the day she toured the reef, they wouldn't have known where to go.

By the evening they were exhausted. Bunion checked under the rocks and then took care of the camels while Lydia laid out the sleeping bags. They drank their fill of the water they had brought with them and fell instantly to sleep.

It was Lydia who shook Bunion awake in the middle of the night just as the three swirling moons were rising, "I'm cold," she said.

"Deserts get cold at night Mistress."

"So why are we traveling through the day when it's hot and resting at night when it's cold?"

"Do you think we should travel at night Mistress?"

"Yes."

Bunion hauled himself out of his bedroll. They ate some dried dates and roused the camels who surprisingly enough did not object to having their sleep cut short.

They started up the mountain once more, "So let's go over the plan." Lydia said.

"I won't take the camels into the booby traps," Bunion told her.

"I wouldn't expect you to."

"But we must go ourselves," Bunion said.

"Not necessarily, we could just stand on the border of Crazy Jones's land and wave; he probably has binoculars; if he sees us he might let us in."

"We would make ourselves an easy target."

"You think it's too risky?"

"No more risky than the booby traps Mistress."

"Is there another option?"

"I shall take the risks Mistress."

"Not gonna happen."

"Mistress?"

"Why should you take all the risks and not me?"

"I wish to protect you Mistress."

"I am going to stand on the border of Mr. Jones's land and do the waving, I think that's the safest thing to do," Lydia said.

"Why Mistress?"

"Because Crazy Jones is a man and I'm better looking than you are Bunion."

When the day got hot they found a cave to sleep in, "This is so uncomfortable," Lydia said.

Bunion said nothing.

"You never complain do you? You always accept everything."

"All the wishing in the world will not get me a mattress."

"That might be a profound thought Bunion but it doesn't make this ground any softer."

Bunion climbed out of his bedroll and carried it over to Lydia, "Put this underneath you," he said.

"I can't take your bedding."

"I will be all right," Bunion moved over to where the camels were sitting and snuggled into them.

"But Bunion…."

"Go to sleep Mistress."

A big fly buzzed round around Bertie's nose but the animal was not perturbed and he and Bunion dozed away together. Lydia did not expect to sleep but the heat caught up with her and she slumbered through the lazy afternoon.

The moons were up again before they were ready to start off. They stood at the mouth of the cave and looked down at the dark valley that they had recently crossed. "Tell me what you're thinking now," Lydia said.

Bunion pointed to a group of stars in the blue-black sky, "They look like a long stemmed rose."

"Really? That's very imaginative; I thought you would say something more down to earth like, 'if we hurry we could be at our journey's end by sun up.'"

"I was thinking that too," Bunion told her.

They turned the camels up the hill and through a pass between the peaks; Blue Pool the waiter's directions were remarkably accurate.

"Many other people must have been here before us."

"Yes," Bunion agreed.

"What would make them take such a risk?"

"Money; a time machine would be a very valuable thing."

"You think that someone would want to buy it?"

"Yes."

"Even though it means the death sentence if they're caught with it?"

"That is what makes it exciting Mistress."

They reached the top of the pass and looked down at the valley on the other side. It was in shadow, "From now on we must be wary of traps," Bunion warned.

Coming down was harder than going up, "This journey would have been so much easier without Bertie and Gertie."

"We needed them to carry the food and water Mistress."

"Why don't you ever say much?"

"My opinions are of no consequence."

"Do you have opinions Bunion?"

"Yes Mistress."

"Are you telling me they're not worth anything?"

"No one asks for them."

"Bunion you don't have to say something profound and earth shattering every time you open your mouth, you can just converse, chit chat, talk about the weather."

"The weather is what it is."

"But everyone has something to talk about. For instance what's your favorite color?"

"Blue is nice… red is nice… green is…."

"Yes green is nice but what's your favorite?"

"You want me to choose one color above all the others?".

"Yes."

Bunion was silent for a minute, "I can't; they all have their own beauty."

"Okay let's leave that one for a moment, what's your favorite type of music?"

"I don't know Mistress."

"Well who is the most beautiful girl you've ever seen?"

"You are Mistress."

"Apart from me."

"Girls do not allow me to get close."

"You must see them when you're performing."

"They laugh at me but they don't want to speak to me and they don't consider my feelings. You are the only girl who has ever done that."

"What about the conjoined twins? Rosie is looking for someone special."

"I am not special," Bunion said.

They stood on a ridge and rested for a few moments. The moons were setting now and the valley was growing darker. But Lydia had sharp eyes and she spotted a ramshackle dwelling down in the distance.

Inside the ramshackle dwelling an ancient man looked through the scope on his missile launcher; he could see two camels silhouetted against a starry sky. There couldn't have been a more perfect shot, "Gotcha," he put his finger on the trigger.

Just then a figure moved out from behind one of the camels. By the shape he guessed it was a young woman. Amazingly enough she was waving.

"Humph," he said.

He pushed his eye up to the lens of his scope in order to get a better look.

She began to walk down the ridge toward him. It was too dark to see her weapon but there was no need to ask if she had one, they always did.

He kept his aim on her.

Normally the people who tried to approach him were men in mid-life crisis, armed to the teeth, dressed in khaki, convinced that killing a defenseless old man would be just the thing to make them feel better about their own ageing process.

She was different and so was the creature that was running behind her. She waved it back, but whatever it was it just kept coming; it was short and wide like a gorilla and as faithful as a dog.

The old man rubbed the stubble on his chin, not sure what to make of them.

As the strange pair stumbled across the rocky landscape, he kept his eye on them through the scope. The girl nearly fell over a small boulder because one of the camels snorted and she looked back to see if it was all right, but her companion caught her just in time and saved her.

He could now see that the little being was actually human. The girl was still waving and the dwarf held her other hand in case she stumbled again. That meant that three of their hands were occupied, but what about the fourth?

They were quite near now and yet the dwarf still swung his free arm by his side. The old man could not take chances, he pulled a lever and the strange couple suddenly disappeared from view, down an eight-foot hole.

"Aaahhh," Lydia landed awkwardly at the bottom.

"Are you all right?" Bunion asked.

"My foot, I think I broke my foot."

"Can you wiggle your toes?"

"What?"

"If you can wiggle your toes your foot's not broken."

Lydia lifted her foot up, "Ahh," she shouted.

"You did it, I saw them wiggle."

"It hurts."

Bunion lifted Lydia's foot into his hands and ran his fingers down from the ankle to the toes.

"There, ow yes just there, that's where it hurts the most."

"Hmm, you have a badly sprained ankle," Bunion started to massage it, "There is that any better?"

"Yes, yes thank you."

"Be careful when you try to put your weight on it."

A light appeared above them, "Ha! I got ya."

Bunion and Lydia looked up to see a scraggy old man holding a crooked, burning stick; he had a rifle slung over his shoulder, "What's your business here?" he growled.

Lydia struggled to pull herself up and Bunion lifted her arm around his shoulder to support her so that she could stand on one foot, "We are looking for Mister Jones," she called out.

"Crazy Jones would that be?"

"Is he the man who owns this farm?"

"You stupid? 'Tisn't a farm, you see any cows around here?"

"I'm sorry; I meant to say the gentleman who owns this land."

"And what dy'a want with him?"

"We need his help."

"Where's your guns?"

"We don't have any."

"Grenades? Bombs? Swords? Spears? Venomous snakes?"

"No sir we don't have any weapons at all."

"You must be mad; I thought when I saw you from a distance that you were from a freak show but then you girl, you looked normal. So it's your brain is it? You're crazier than me."

"Are you Mister Jones?"

"And what if I am?"

"We would like to talk to you."

"I'll have to check you for weapons."

"We mean you no harm Mister Jones."

"Huh."

"If you let us out of here we could explain everything."

"You can stay in there and tell me. Sit down and rest your leg and don't expect me to provide refreshments or anything."

Bunion lowered Lydia onto the ground.

"So go on then tell me what was so worth risking your worthless hides for?" Crazy Jones sat on the edge of the hole dangling his filthy bare feet.

"We are seeking…."

"Don't tell me… a time machine."

"How very perceptive of you Mister Jones."

The old man stuck the stick, which had already burned halfway down, into the ground and started to scrape something cheesy out of his thick, long toenails.

"As I was saying we need a time machine…."

"There's nothing like that around here, the whole thing's a myth; two joyriding teenagers hijacking a time machine? If you were them and you could go anywhere in time and space would you come here?"

"We don't need it for ourselves…."

"They never do, it's always for some noble cause."

"We want to prevent a war; my planet, Bella has been in conflict with its neighbor for a hundred and fifty years and…."

"Now I know who you are, you're that Princess Stephanie; I saw a picture of her once. You're supposed to marry that ugly prince from Bellus; got cold feet have we?"

"I'm not Princess Stephanie, I'm a look alike," Lydia told him, "anyway does it matter who I am? The important thing is to get the time machine and prevent that terrible war."

"And you expect me to give it to you just because you asked? Well sorry to disappoint you but I don't have one, I never did, the whole thing was just made up to bring in the tourists. So if I were you I would go home and stop worrying about things that can get you into a lot of trouble."

"But what about all the stories?"

"There are stories about beasts with two heads but that doesn't mean they really exist."

"We have a three headed cow," Bunion told him.

Crazy Jones laughed, "I am going to let the ladder down and I'll give you a ten second start before I commence firing my gun."

"Mister Jones, we're serious, we need a time machine; if we can only prevent the war we can save over half a billion lives."

"The Time Guardians would kill you."

"It's a risk we're willing to take."

"Well if I had a time machine I'd let you take it, but I haven't so scram and leave me in peace," the old man lowered a rickety old ladder down into the hole.

"But sir," Lydia said.

"Sir? Did you call me sir?"

Lydia nodded.

"I like that, you speak respectfully to your elders; that's a rare quality in young people nowadays, you've just earned yourself another five seconds."

"But Mister Jones we need a time machine."

"Try Fettuccia they're always boasting about theirs."

"Fettuccia? I've never heard of it."

"It's in the Omega quadrant, tourist district; it's a long way from here."

"Have you ever been to Fettuccia?" Lydia asked Bunion.

"No," Bunion said.

Crazy Jones raised his gun, "One… Two…."

Lydia tried to get to her feet, "Ahh my ankle."

"Steady," Bunion said.

"Three… four…."

Bunion supported her as she hopped over to the ladder and tried to climb up it using her knee instead of her foot.

"Five... six...."

"Mistress, please try to hurry."

"Mistress? Why does he call you Mistress? Is he your slave or something?"

"No sir, he just thinks he is."

"Seven... eight...."

Lydia reached the top of the ladder.

"Nine... ten, time's running out, I suggest you do the same."

Bunion took Lydia's weight in his arms and carried her away as fast as he could.

"Eleven... twelve... ha, ha, thirteen," Crazy Jones raised his gun, "fourteen... fifteen," he fired.

The bullet grazed Bunion's ear making it bleed; the next one ricocheted off a rock and landed just in front of them. The third fell out of range but Bunion kept running in case Crazy Jones tried to catch up with them.

The old man went back to his rocket launcher. At least he could still shoot the camels. But by the time he was in position they were gone. They had heard Bunion's whistle and were trotting down towards him. Lydia climbed gratefully onto Bertie's back; Bunion climbed up on Gertie and grabbed Bertie's lead.

A rocket zoomed past them, exploding into the ridge and sending bits of rock everywhere. Another one whizzed past the other side of them and the camels took off in panic. Bunion tried to steer them down the ridge to where the footing was a little firmer but they were too scared to obey instructions and rushed in the opposite direction.

A light appeared in the western sky; it was almost time for the sun to come up. But this was not the sun.

A rocket exploded just short of their position, showering them with pebbles. Bunion didn't need to ask the camels to go quicker; bats couldn't have flown out of hell any faster.

The searchlight in the sky got rapidly closer.

Crazy Jones watched through his scope. He could see the camels cresting the ridge. This would be his last shot but it would also be his best.

The light in the sky was almost over them now and they could hear the sound of rotor blades. The old man aimed at Bertie's rear and fired.

Bunion noticed a wisp of smoke as the rocket sped towards them; he yanked the speeding Gertie to one side and pulled Bertie after them. The rocket grazed his tail but passed on up into the sky towards the light and the spinning blades.

The helicopter swerved; Crazy Jones watched from a distance and laughed.

"Jones you complete idiot, cut that out or I'll arrest you," a voice boomed out of a megaphone. "This is the County Sheriff, stand still and put your hands up."

"Is he talking to us or to the old man?" Lydia asked.

"To us I think," Bunion tried to pull Gertie up to a standstill but the poor creature was much too frightened. She hurtled downhill on the loose scree with Bertie following right behind.

"Stand still or I'll shoot," the voice from the helicopter said.

"If they start firing at us we'll never get the camels to stop," Lydia shouted.

But they needn't have worried. Gertie lost her footing and slid onto her backside and Bertie, who was too scared to carry on without her, stopped too. Bunion jumped off; he helped Lydia who was hanging awkwardly, half out of the seat, to climb off Bertie's back.

"My foot, mind my foot... that man could have killed us," Lydia screamed.

"It's all right, you're safe now," Bunion held her till she calmed down; then he ran over to the shaking, complaining camels, stroking them gently and checking them for injuries, "It's all right, you're safe now."

"I wouldn't use the word, 'safe,' too freely if I were you," the sheriff said as he walked over the ridge with his gun pointed at them. "Arrest them Young Raindrop."

The sheriff's sidekick slid down the bank, cuffs in hand, "You don't have to say anything coz we caught you dead to rights and y're gonna have to pay the fine."

Lydia was crying loudly by now.

Crazy Jones appeared over the ridge, he seemed delighted at the arrest.

"Please tell me, what's going to happen to the camels?" Bunion said.

"I'll take care of them," Crazy Jones said, "haven't had any decent meat for a very long time."

"No, please no," Bunion pleaded.

"You got any way of persuading me not to hand them over to this man whose privacy you have so flagrantly invaded?"

"I... I... have money."

"We take credit prints," the sheriff said.

Bunion held up his thumb, "How much do you want?"

"Two hundred will do," the sheriff took his thumbprint reader out of his jacket. "Key in your pin code," Bunion keyed in his code and allowed the sheriff to take half a year's savings out of his bank account. "Right, you're free to go but the girl has to come with me."

"How much for her?" Bunion asked.

"Hmm, I haven't decided yet, come to my office when you get back to town and we'll discuss it then."

"But sheriff...."

"You haven't got enough money to buy her back."

"I have money."

"My office as soon as you can and I suggest you move your animals away from here before Jones remembers how much he likes the taste of camel meat." The sheriff called over to Young Raindrop and pointed to Lydia, "Get her into the helicopter."

"But I can't leave Lydia," Bunion cried.

The sheriff raised his gun.

"Please Bunion I'll be all right," Lydia said.

Bunion watched the rotors rise into the air before he raced Bertie and Gertie back down through the hills to where Clarissa would be waiting to pick them up.

Sometime later back at the sheriff's office, Lydia stared out of the barred window at the desert outside.

"Are you listening to me?" the sheriff said.

"Hm?" Lydia said.

"You don't seem to understand the seriousness of the charges against you."

"Aren't I supposed to have a lawyer present or something?"

"You are charged with the attempted acquirement of a time machine; do you know what that means?"

"It means nothing, if I had a time machine, then it would mean something but not acquiring one doesn't mean anything."

The sheriff laughed, "You mean like trying to kill someone but failing isn't attempted murder?"

"Well you would have to prove your point and the only witness you have is completely mad and isn't likely to be taken seriously by any court."

"The Time Guardians could think differently about that, Mr. Cheesemaker Jones can act sanely enough if he wants to."

"You wouldn't," Lydia said.

"I am only obligated to inform them if the law hereabouts isn't satisfied with the outcome of the situation."

"What do you mean?"

"There's a fine."

"How much?"

The sheriff stroked his stubble in consideration, "I would say that two-thousand-five-hundred crisp, green notes would help resolve the situation."

Lydia sank down in her chair, "You can't possibly expect...."

"If you don't pay up, your whole little theatre group will be reported to the Time Guardians."

"But I don't have...."

"Not my problem, I'm not the one who accused one of our fine, upstanding citizens of owning an illegal time vehicle."

"But where am I going to get that kind of money?"

"Like I said that's not my problem. Pay up by tomorrow morning or I'll inform the Time Guardians. I'll leave you to think about it; don't be too long," the sheriff left her alone.

What was Lydia supposed to do? She couldn't expect Clarissa to get her out of this jam. She sat there for a long time rubbing her sore ankle and staring through the bars at the swirling dust that blew across the road.

The sheriff sat down and put his feet up on his desk. Young Raindrop, who up to that point had been snoozing in his chair, opened his eye and tilted back his hat, "How much dy'a ask for?" he said.

"Two and a half thousand."

Raindrop whistled, "You sure that isn't a bit too much?"

"Nah, they'll find it somehow, that dwarf said he had money and I guess from the pleading look in his eye that he's soft enough on the girl to part with it."

"You sure he's got that much money?"

"Well if he ain't he'll have to ask his friends to help."

Lydia lay on her bunk. It was dark now and still no one had come. She couldn't blame them, she had only been a passenger on their ship, it's not like they owed her anything, certainly not two and a half thousand. So that was it; she had tried and failed. Five hundred and seventy million people would have to stay dead and now she would probably die too; Zertza's moons waxed and waned before she fell asleep on the dusty bunk and the sun glared in the window before she woke up again.

There was some kind of noise in the sheriff's office; people's voices.

"The fine's two and a half thousand quid," the sheriff said.

"We don't even have a thousand, let alone what you're asking for," Clarissa told him.

"I have money…" Bunion said.

"I'll do the talking Bunion," Clarissa turned back to the sheriff, "That was some show your man put on there, tell him I congratulate him."

"It weren't no show; Crazy Jones would have killed them if I hadn't turned up."

A huge tattooed woman looked the sheriff in the eye, "I couldn't find any electromagnetic shielding on your helicopter."

"Well it's there, ask my mechanic."

"I already did, he said it was never fitted. So how come your vehicle didn't ditch as soon as it got into the field?"

"How should I know? I'm not a technician."

"I did my own analysis of the electromagnetic properties of your geological structures and I found that the field is much weaker than you advertise. I also found evidence of a signal jammer, no wonder the radios don't work."

"So?"

Clarissa smiled, "We checked out your Crazy Jones character, it seems that records of an old man living in the hills, scaring the life out of everybody, go back a very long way, nearly three hundred years. I'm billed as the two hundred year old woman and I'm in a freak show, what does that tell you Mister?"

The sheriff backed away a little, "I'm still the law around here and the fine still stands."

"It's a strange fact that when you make something illegal it immediately becomes more desirable... and expensive, You must make more money out of your time machine legend now, than you did before."

"The legend is genuine."

"What if your little scam got out? What would the Time Guardians have to say about that?"

"Are you threatening me?" the sheriff said.

"No, I'm offering you a deal. You release our friend and I will give all members of the law enforcement agency and their families, free tickets to our show."

"We've already seen your show."

"I don't mean that show, I mean the real show."

"The real show?"

"The Royal Wedding," Clarissa said.

After they had gone Young Raindrop tilted his hat and laughed, "You handled that real well, you didn't get a penny out of them."

"I want you to find the number of the Time Guardians."

"You gonna report them? But they're on to us."

"We'll wait until they leave and send an anonymous tip."

"So we get to see the Royal Wedding first?"

The sheriff ignored his question, "Nobody gets one over on Sheriff Persimmon P. Raspberry," he said.

Chapter 3.

Josephine announced the crew's takings from the performances they had given on Zertza, "Three hundred... each."

Everyone at the meal table cheered.

"Josephine I owe Bunion two hundred, could you please make sure it goes into his bank account?" Lydia asked.

"No," Bunion dolloped potatoes onto white plates, "I paid that money not you."

"But if it wasn't for me you wouldn't have had to."

"No."

"I won't have you break into your savings on my account."

"Take the money," Rosie said, "she owes you."

"No," Bunion indicated that the conversation was at an end.

Lydia decided not to pursue the matter any further; she could make a private arrangement with Josephine later.

She changed the subject, "Where's Fettuccia?"

"Fettuccia? What's that? A type of cheese?" Annie asked.

"Pasta you fool, everyone knows that Fettuccia is a pasta," Rosie told her.

"Actually it's the name of a planet."

"It's a long way from here; it's in the Omega quadrant," Clarissa said.

"How would I get there?"

"A liner from the Galliah exchange."

"And how would I get to the Galliah exchange?"

"You'd have to get a transport from Coraopolis."

"And how do I get to Coraopolis?"

"Well I suppose you could probably get a transport from Queem."

"And how do I get to Queem?"

"We can get you there, it's on the way to the fishing trials at Kokorak City on Zenobulus 7; we're due there in three days." There was a groan from the table and it wasn't because Bunion was piling stewed cabbage on their plates. "Look I know you don't particularly like going there, but they're expecting us; we've performed there every year for the last ten years."

"Working Zertza was fun," Natter said, "we got great audiences."

"And we made a nice profit," Josephine added.

"But the Zenobulan fishermen have seen us so many times that the audiences can be dismal, you remember that one time last year when we had to run through the whole thing for three people?"

"We made a loss of exactly twenty three quid."

"I'd rather go to Fettuccia," Grumpus said.

"No, you wouldn't," Clarissa said.

"Is it dangerous?"

"Yes."

"What sort of danger?"

"The worst kind, traveling entertainers never go to Fettuccia."

"But why not?"

"Because it's too expensive."

"What? Is that all?"

"You don't understand; they have taxes for everything; I wouldn't be surprised if they tax the air."

Josephine picked up a computer tablet and accessed the Fettuccian database; she scrolled down the lists, "Hmm... most of the taxes are illegal, they contravene the laws of the Omega quadrant but the local government is allowed to get away with them because the planet has no natural resources and has to survive on tourism. The inhabitants are naturally wary of traveling entertainers as they see them as a threat to their livelihoods. They do their utmost to discourage anyone from coming in."

"Do you still want to go?" Clarissa asked.

By now Bunion was serving bean pie; everyone went quiet.

"It could still be worthwhile," Josephine said.

"How do you mean?"

"I just scanned the brochures; do you know what they are charging for a show?"

"How much?"

"Sixty quid a ticket."

Everyone said, "Wow."

"Yes but that would be for an amazing extravaganza with a full orchestra and all the special effects."

"Some of the shows are like that, but they're also offering Shakespeare's plays, which would have to be relatively simple."

"How much do they charge for those?"

"About the same."

"If they charge those kinds of prices it must be a high class place," Annie said.

"Too high for us," Clarissa insisted.

"I've never been anywhere like that before," Rosie's eyes glazed over as she dreamt of the possibilities.

"I could bring out my greatest illusions to please the crowds, if Lydia would consent to be my beautiful assistant," Mr. Mystery said.

"Well I suppose I could."

"I could sing," Rosie said, "I haven't had an opportunity to do that in a long time."

"I could play my harp to accompany you," Annie offered.

"I can dance as long as it's old fashioned stuff," Grumpus said.

"We haven't put the blue tigers through their paces for a long time; me and Bunion could do that," Froggie suggested.

"I could do the Chinese shadow figures routine," Jerome said.

Bunion poured lumpy gravy generously over everybody's dinners but said nothing.

"It won't be easy, the small print says that we would have to take an entertainer's exam and we'd have to have all the animals inoculated and we'd have to join their union and there are certain taxes to pay in advance," Josephine warned.

"Sounds to me like they need a bit of a shake up," Jerome said.

"You're dead right there," Froggie agreed.

"Do you all feel this way?" Clarissa asked.

There was a resounding, "Yes!" from the table.

"It's a big risk; we could lose a lot of money."

"Well Kokorak City is a dead cert; we know we're going to lose money there," Natter said.

Bunion took his place at the dinner table having finished serving the meal. Lydia looked at him, "What do you think Bunion?"

Bunion looked up, "I will go wherever you go Mistress."

"It seems I'm outvoted," Clarissa said. "Geraldine, as soon as you've finished your dinner could you please change course?"

Geraldine got up out of her seat. "I'll do it now."

Everybody cheered.

The Genghis Khan was a Mark Three, Lightening Wing design. She had been cutting edge in her day but that day was long past. She had been old when Clarissa had bought her twenty standard years before. And there was twenty year's worth of dust and junk in the cargo holds because Clarissa never threw anything away. That was how she found a tuxedo for Grumpus at the very bottom of a musty box. She cleaned it and then carefully let it out as far as it would go but that wasn't good enough so she found an old corset that would squeeze Grumpus in as far as he would go.

She made a flowing robe out of a bolt of red satin that she had picked up cheap ten years before for Geraldine who was going to be his partner and she gave her a long, blonde wig to go with it.

Clarissa found an old sequined leotard and some fish net tights for Lydia's performance as Mr. Mystery's assistant. A faraway look came into her eyes as she carefully washed them, "I wore these myself many years ago when I did a tap dancing routine with the clowns; but times change and one gets old."

She unearthed a striped suit for Natter; he was going to play the banjo and Jerry would play the flute.

Bunion spent a lot of time with the menagerie; he loved them and they trusted him and responded to his commands. He had already practiced some simple routines with the blue tigers. They would have to wear electronic stun collars in case they threatened to get out of hand but he knew that there would be no problem.

Rosie could sing; she had a very fine soprano voice. Jerome was a tightrope walker and he and Josephine worked up a ballet routine to some recorded classical music.

By the time they approached Fettuccia they had the makings of a classy show.

"Where do you think we should land?" Clarissa asked Josephine.

"That depends on how much you want to pay."

Josephine handed over a computer tablet with a long list of charges on it; Clarissa ran her eyes quickly down the page, "Hmm we were expecting the vet's bills and the exam fees and the license fees, and the union fees but an administration tax on top of administration charges, that's a new one... what's this? The total's ten thousand quid!" Clarissa nearly choked.

"That's the Roslyn City price, if you look further down the page you'll see that if you are willing to go to some of the less popular destinations you can get the same package for less."

"Chaiza Island eight thousand, that's still too much."

"Keep going."

"Saint Ingram's, it says here that it's up in the Southern Mountains, that's five thousand quid; that's still a big chunk of my retirement fund."

"What about Hagarovsky village? That's described as up and coming."

"It's still four thousand five hundred."

"Well there's always Scarab's End, that's only two thousand."

"There's no description, oh well a scarab was a sacred, ancient Egyptian…."

"Dung beetle."

"Oh," Clarissa said, "If I invest in that place I'm going to lose my two thousand aren't I?"

Josephine nodded.

"I think we had better turn around."

Bunion had been standing in the background as he often did without moving or saying anything. "I will put up the money," he said.

"No Bunion, that's all you have in the world."

"Lydia needs to go to Fettuccia."

"No Bunion," Josephine told him.

They all gathered around the dinner table while Clarissa told them the bad news.

"But we've worked too hard to back out now," Grumpus insisted.

"I want to sing," Rosie said.

"I want to play my harp," Annie said.

"What if we put in two hundred each?" Froggie suggested.

"Two hundred and fifty, then we would have enough to cover unforeseen expenses," Mr. Mystery said.

The vote was unanimous; they all put their money together and opted to go to Scarab's End, the cheapest place on Fettuccia.

It was hardly surprising to find that the landing strip was in the middle of a desert. The empty spaceport stood alongside some crumbling fake pyramids and a fiberglass sphinx. As soon as they touched down an official demanded permission to come aboard; he looked the spacecraft over critically. "I need either a deposit or your thumbprints."

"But we paid the two thousand," Clarissa said.

"This is for the hotel."

"We don't need a hotel."

"You're all booked into the Scarab Grand, that's standard practice when you don't indicate a preference."

"But we always sleep on the spaceship."

"Can't let you do that madam, it's a fire hazard."

"Fire hazard? That's preposterous; we live on the spaceship."

The official shrugged his brown uniformed shoulders; he stank of stale sweat, "The wiring must be old," he said.

"Our ship is thoroughly maintained, there's nothing wrong with it," Geraldine insisted.

"The décor is very out of date."

"The décor?" Clarissa said.

"It gives the wrong impression to paying guests."

"Well the paying guests are not going to be allowed on board to see it and anyway I haven't seen any guests here, the place is deserted."

"Regulations are regulations madam, if you want to remain on this planet your craft will have to have a makeover from one of our officially registered decorating agencies."

"You know I don't think we'll be staying long enough to have our décor adjusted, in fact I don't think we'll be staying here long enough to sleep at your hotel, just give us a launch window and we'll be gone."

"But you can't do that."

"Why? Do we have to pay to leave?"

"You're booked to do the entertainment at the hotel tonight. The usual performers are down with food poisoning and the agency couldn't send replacements in time."

"I thought we had to get a license and pass an entertainer's exam before we were allowed to perform?"

"You paid the two thousand didn't you?"

"You wouldn't let us land until we did."

"Then your license is issued automatically and your entertainer's exam will be scheduled in due course. In the meantime the job is yours if you want it, until the Hunchbacks are out of hospital."

"What do the Hunchbacks do?" Clarissa asked.

"Heavy metal, there's a crowd coming in from Sampson's forge tonight. They've been mining an asteroid for six standard months. They'll be a bit of a rowdy bunch but they pay well."

"But I thought this was an upper class..." Clarissa sighed. They were merely getting what they had paid for. If they had coughed up the ten thousand they could have expected a little more quality; but this was work and they needed the money. "Do we set up a tent or is there a venue?"

"The venue is in the Scarab Grand. My cousin is the taxi driver, he'll take you there."

The taxi driver also stank of sweat and he charged a lot but the hotel itself was much better than they expected. It was situated some way from the spaceport on the edge of a dried up lake and its architecture was a little confused. It had Grecian plinths, Roman columns, Egyptian murals and chic twenty third century Mutton style furniture but somehow all the styles blended together to make something that was quite pleasing. The floors were of polished marble and the ballroom, which was the venue, was magnificent.

And they were to be paid two hundred quid a night for a two-hour show. Admittedly the bill for their room and board came to one hundred but they were still going to make a clear profit of a hundred per night.

Clarissa was able to acquire the use of the hotel van to bring over the costumes and equipment. Grumpus, Jerome and Bunion did most of the moving and all the others helped set up. Bunion had to go back to the Genghis Kahn to take care of the menagerie but he was spared his usual efforts to feed the humans as they were all treated to a delicious meal in the hotel.

The show was to start at nine and finish at eleven, at which point the DJ would take over while the crowd was still sober enough to recognize what they were dancing to. The men from Samson's Forge piled into the hotel at six o'clock local time. By five past they had started drinking and gorging themselves at the dinner table and by nine they staggered to their seats with foaming mugs of beer and pockets full of ammunition to throw at the stage.

The opening fanfare played, the curtains parted and Clarissa walked on in her finest satin dress, "My Lords, Ladies and Gentlemen...."

"There's no Gentlemen here," someone from the crowd shouted.

"And there's no ladies either, except Nozzer over there."

"Who are you calling a lady?" Nozzer shouted getting up out of his chair ready to do damage.

"Welcome to our classical extravaganza," Clarissa carried on.

"Classical? I hate classical."

"Where's the heavy metal?" someone yelled.

"Yea where's the Hunchbacks?" Nozzer shouted, taking a break from pounding the man in the seat next to him.

"Well actually heavy metal is even older than what we are about to present to you today. Please sit back and relax...."

Boos came from the audience.

"And enjoy the closing aria from the twenty second century opera, Hitachi's 'The Fan and the Waistcoat'."

Something whizzed past Clarissa as she left the stage rapidly.

Rosie and Annie walked on; they turned to the audience and bowed ever so slightly. All at once the missiles stopped raining.

They walked over to the harp and Annie who was controlling their arms plucked a few strings to make sure it was in tune. The audience fell silent.

Rosie filled their lungs and sang, "Oh what a beautiful day this is though clouds bedarken the sky. My true love comes from a land far away and to him I must fly."

Her rich, full, soprano voice filled the ballroom; she sang three verses while Annie accompanied her on the harp; it was truly a beautiful piece.

The spellbound audience craned their necks to get a closer look. Clarissa watched from the wings; she had seen this reaction many times before. When they had finished, the audience went wild and Rosie and Annie had to do an encore.

Clarissa went backstage and found the rest of the troupe, "They've never seen a two headed woman before. Richard (That was Mr. Mystery's real name, his second name was Pargeter.) Richard do your Dracula routine, have you got your fangs?"

"Here, I always keep them in my pocket."

"Good now do the same illusions but don't forget the blood sucking thing. Lydia I know you haven't rehearsed this but just play along."

"Are you sure this is what you want?"

"Yes now go; get into position."

Lydia and Mr. Mystery stood in the wings waiting for Rosie and Annie to finish their performance. Clarissa could see Richard quickly explaining to Lydia what she would have to do.

"Good," she looked at Grumpus, "take off your girdle; that tux has to look three sizes too tight. And can you remember the sweeping her off her feet routine you and Geraldine used to do?"

"Yes of course," Grumpus told her.

"Do that," Clarissa said.

"Okay, you're the boss," Grumpus ran off to relieve himself of the very uncomfortable corset.

"Now Natter…" Natter's turn didn't come till nearly the end of the show. "Take the van back to the ship and get your trouser leg equipment and bring Daisy the three headed cow and fetch the gear for the wedding scene, we're going to give 'em a show they'll never forget."

Lydia did well as Dracula's victim. She screamed in all the right places and even managed to chase Mr. Mystery around the stage with a conductor's baton that looked reasonably like a stake from a distance.

"Well done," Clarissa said when she and Mr. Mystery had finished.

"Thanks but I think we'll rehearse it before we do it again," Lydia told her.

"The audience likes us."

"Do you really think so? They look pretty rowdy to me; they're worse than that first audience on Astros."

"We need to give them a good finale, something they'll really love."

"Natter's going to do his ferret up the trouser leg piece isn't he?" Lydia said.

"Well... yes...."

"But?"

"We need more."

"You want us to do the wedding sequence?"

"Yes."

"No."

"Yes."

"Bunion, tell her."

"Lydia doesn't want to kiss me Clarissa."

"Bunion, you know it's not like that...."

"Your performance could make a great difference to us; we don't want to make that crowd angry," Clarissa said.

"They won't even have heard of Princess Stephanie and Prince Jason."

"They won't care as long as you kiss the dwarf."

"The dwarf has a name you know," Lydia said.

"It'll make this show a hit."

Lydia sighed.

"There are two thousand quid riding on it...."

"I know," Lydia understood full well that she would have to comply even though Clarissa was using emotional blackmail.

"Bunion, please ask Annie where she keeps the fake warts."

The wedding finale was a hit; the whole show was a hit. The next day they put on two shows; the day after that they had to do three.

The day after that the Hunchbacks came back and so did the Hunchback's agent, "Sign up with me and I'll get you a gig at Salvation Fortunes tonight, you'll make two hundred and fifty for the full performance... and I'll only take ten percent. My name's Hugh by way."

"Where's Salvation Fortunes?"

"Up near the mountains."

"Do we have to pay any more for the right to perform there?"

"No it falls into the Scarab's End charging zone."

Salvation Fortunes was a worn out mining town where the biggest intact structure was the Ferris wheel and the only inhabitants were tourists who came panning for gold; they did two performances there.

"I can get you a well paying gig at Hagarovsky Village, just sign here," Hugh told them when they got back.

"But isn't that in another charging zone?"

"Give me a look at your receipt and I'll calculate how much extra it'll cost you," Hugh perused the receipt that the official at Scarab's End had issued.

"Hmm you haven't been on the entertainer's course yet?"

"No."

"And you haven't had the redecorating done; it would have been a lot cheaper in Scarab's End."

"Oh."

"You got all the inoculations though?"

"The vet came last night."

"What about the doctor? Have you had your broad spectrum shots for all the local diseases?"

"We always do that as soon as we land."

"Good, well then it comes to an extra seven hundred quid."

"That much?" Clarissa asked.

"We've only made seven hundred and eighty seven so far," Josephine said.

They all sat round the dining table.

Froggie offered his opinion, "It's a step up."

"Maybe the audience won't be as drunk," Geraldine said hopefully.

"It might be a bit classier," Rosie said.

"Yea, let's do it," Natter decided.

Hagarovsky village was a small seaside town which relied on fishing more than tourism. There were nets drying along the sea front and the smell of dead fish pervaded everything. Nevertheless they were booked into a large hotel with a casino and a theater at the back. There were two shows a day and they got three hundred quid per performance, and since they were going to be there for five days they opted to do the first module of the entertainer's course, which was on basic showmanship, all of which they already knew. They also had the local team redecorate the Genghis Khan.

"I see blue in here," a thin young man in a red, satin frock coat said. "My name's Justin by the way."

"I don't want blue, I want something comforting and warm," Clarissa told him.

"Hmm I see you've only signed up for the basic package. Well it's going to be a challenge...."

"I'm sure that someone with your talent will think of something."

"Well perhaps, perhaps, this craft is old so it will have to be something retro; fortunately retro is in this year."

"I'm glad to hear it."

"Red... yes a rich warm red... or maybe a tropical orange...."

"Don't ruin my spaceship," Clarissa warned him.

Justin had minions, people who actually did the work while he stood there and fussed, "If there had been more money in the budget we could have had prints."

"There is no more money," Clarissa told him.

The frustrated genius soldiered on despite the many privations that a limited budget brought him. He decorated the bridge and the galley on the upper deck and the cabins and the storerooms on the middle deck. The chipped paint was covered in tasteful colors, there were interesting geometric designs stenciled around the light fittings, and the bunkroom walls were painted to match the new bed linen. To Clarissa's relief there was no obligation to have the storage areas or the animal pens on the bottom deck redecorated.

The result wasn't perfect, but it wasn't bad. They had cupboards with shelves low enough for Bunion to reach, the living areas took on a fresh, clean look and despite his complaints Justin managed to find a couple of cheap pictures that they all felt they could live with to hang on the walls. It took him the whole of the five days to achieve the effect that he wanted and all they actually took down when he left was a pair of garish drapes that gave the impression that there was a window beyond them when really there was only the spaceship hull.

Clarissa was pleased, "We've made fifteen hundred quid."

Fifteen hundred quid was exactly what they needed in order to go on to Saint Ingram's in the Southern Alps. It was a ski resort.

"They're never going to want to watch a freak show here," Clarissa said nervously.

Rosie was overjoyed because this place was classy.

They adjusted their act accordingly and flopped, "Why aren't you doing the wedding sequence?" Hugh asked Clarissa over the radio.

"We didn't think anyone would want to see it," she told him.

"Try it at your next performance."

Clarissa made them revert to their original act, fangs, trouser legs and wedding scene included. They made two thousand quid.

This was exactly what it cost to go to Chaiza Island where Hugh had negotiated a well paying gig. Chaiza Island was in the tropics; a sun drenched paradise. It was beautiful; the ideal playground for the rich and famous. Clarissa wanted to change the performance again but the hotel management told her not to.

They were there for a week and when they were not performing, they were able to stretch out on the sand and drink fruit juice out of hollowed out pineapples with little umbrellas in them. Rosie was able to employ a voice coach, Geraldine got fat busting injections, and beautiful women gave Froggie and Natter soothing massages. Jerry got his for free because they had never seen a three legged man before.

There were zoological gardens where Clarissa's creatures spent a wonderful week in sumptuous surroundings lazing in the sun while people paid to look at them.

They all took time to review the entertainer's course materials and on the last day they took the exam and passed with flying colors. By then the little freak show had made a cool three thousand quid. This was just what they needed if they wanted to perform at the venue that Hugh had found for them in Roslyn City.

Roslyn city was white; all the buildings were made of magnificent, pure white, shining marble. White peacocks displayed in cool, fountained gardens around white, marble pools. The city reeked of designer perfumes; it was the home of the ultra rich.

Stafford hall was next to the library; it was round and white and held two thousand people. "I booked it for seven days, with the option of another two weeks if that's what you want," Hugh said over the radio.

"What's the price?" Clarissa asked him.

"Well that's the best part, if you agree to do all the cleaning yourselves you can have it for two thousand a night; in advance."

"You've committed us to this?"

"Yes but don't worry it's only the equivalent of one dollar a seat, the rest is all profit. What have you got to lose?"

Clarissa shook her head.

They all gathered around the table while she told them the situation.

"We need another two thousand?" Natter said.

"Plus our hotel bill, plus Hugh said that we're not allowed to appear in public unless we're dressed properly, no one is permitted to lower the tone of the place."

"We don't have to go out in public."

"Someone's got to handle the publicity," Jerome reminded them.

"Couldn't Lydia do that?" Froggie suggested. "She could dress up like Princess Stephanie and go and advertise the wedding."

"We'd have to buy her a dress," Clarissa said.

"So how much do you think we'll need?"

"About twelve thousand all together, that's two thousand for the rental of the hall, eight thousand for the hotel bills and an estimated two thousand for the dress."

"Josephine, if we all put our savings together, excluding Clarissa's retirement fund how much would we have?" Froggie asked.

"Around ten thousand."

Everyone went quiet for a minute.

Natter spoke up, "We stand to make fifty thousand on the first night; that means that even after we paid back everything we owed, we would come out with a profit of thirty-eight thousand for one performance."

"And if no one comes we could lose it all," Clarissa said.

Nobody was listening to her.

"If we took the three week option... at two performances a day... let's be realistic; say we only make an average of thirty thousand at each performance that would be..." Natter scratched his head.

"One million two hundred and sixty thousand, less Hugh's ten percent," Josephine calculated.

Everyone gasped.

"We've hit the jackpot," Jerry shouted.

"At last we'll have the money to get ourselves separated," Rosie and Annie cried out together.

"I could get my legs straightened; I think I would keep the gills though, they come in useful sometimes," Froggie said.

"I could get cosmetic... everything," Geraldine cried.

"I could build a big house for my wife and fifteen children," Jerome shouted.

"I could get my wife out of prison," Grumpus rejoiced.

"I could spend the rest of my life sipping pina coladas on Chaiza Island," Jerry dreamed.

"I could get a girlfriend," Natter said.

"You could lose everything," Clarissa warned them, "and anyway you still don't have enough money to get started."

"All the eyes around the table looked beseechingly at her, "Please Clarissa."

Clarissa sighed deeply, what could she do? She nodded her head.

"Let's print some flyers," Natter said.

"Something artistic," Rosie suggested.

"I have ideas," Mr. Mystery told them.

The meeting broke up on a tidal wave of enthusiasm.

The Hotel they stayed at was white, reflecting the bright Fettuccian sunshine in the polished marble of its walls. The enormous, flower bedecked rooms were called suites; there were mints on the pillows, the most beautifully scented body washes and shampoos in the gleaming bathrooms, and holo-TVs that could receive any channel in the known universe.

Froggie and Natter thought they had died and gone to heaven when they were offered foot rubs by the most gorgeous women they had ever seen.

"We're totally outclassed," Clarissa said, "what kind of a show can we possibly put on here?"

Lydia went shopping; every designer in the galaxy was represented in the exclusive boutiques that populated the long white streets. Lydia, who was dressed in the best that Clarissa could provide, went from one fashionable boutique to another but she very quickly became aware that there was nothing that she could afford.

And then, in a little, very select place at the end of Paris Avenue it happened; she fell in love... with the perfect dress. It had a high bodice and flowing lines, and it shimmered and sparkled like something out of a fairytale; it fitted perfectly like it had been made for her. However after the young assistant told her the price, all Lydia could do was shake her head and reluctantly take it off.

But how could she walk out of the shop without it?

She approached the black suited man at the gleaming, glass counter, "That dress...."

"Gown Madam."

"Gown."

"Shall I charge it to your account Madam?"

"I only have two thousand quid."

"Two thousand quid would not even get you the accessories for that gown Madam," the man looked down his nose condescendingly.

"I will have the rest of the money tomorrow."

"Then you may return for the gown tomorrow."

He signaled to the young assistant to bring the garment over to him so that he could scrutinize it. He flicked it with his white-gloved hand as if she had dirtied it somehow.

Lydia was angry for a split second. But anger would not get her that dress... er gown. She straightened her back and smiled, "Well done, my man; did you know that sometimes when I tell people that I can't afford to pay for something the assistants actually offer to give me credit, can you believe it?"

"No Madam I can't."

"But you, you respected my privacy, not a flicker of recognition, I like that."

"Madam?" The man shot his eyes over to the security guards by the front door.

"But it's okay I just got the all clear from my bodyguards on the street, they say everything's secure."

"Really Madam, well that's as maybe but I'm afraid...."

The security men by the front door gestured to the white-gloved man.

"How clever of you to know that I came here to buy my trousseau."

The man looked down his nose at her as if she was a piece of dirt, "Actually madam I'm afraid I'm going to have to ask you to...."

One of the security guards ran over to him and held a computer tablet up to his face; he looked at it and then at Lydia and then at the screen again and then at Lydia again.

He seemed confused, "Princess Stephanie I...."

"Shh, I don't want anyone to know I'm here. I'm supposed to be communing with the monks on the Mountain of Contemplation but I ask you, when am I supposed to do my shopping? Do they think that looking good at my wedding is going to happen all by itself?"

"No indeed Madam."

"I'm going to need a whole new wardrobe."

"Of course Madam," the man bowed slightly. He checked the computer tablet for a third time because he was not quite able to come to terms with the un-princess like way that Lydia was dressed. But Princess Stephanie came from a different quadrant; perhaps dressing down was in fashion there.

"You know you were right about that gown, I probably could do better."

"Do you want to try it on again?"

"No I don't think so; actually I'm not sure that there is anything in this fine boutique that would be quite suitable."

"But Madam...."

"But thanks anyway for your discretion. With three standard months still to go to my wedding and the final wording of the peace treaty not yet agreed upon we are technically still at war. It would be in the interests of certain factions to have me assassinated."

"I understand completely Madam but are you sure there is nothing we can do for you?" the man asked.

She walked towards the door but before she got there, she hesitated. "Well perhaps I could take one more look at that little gown," she looked at the man as if she were just humoring him.

Lydia didn't wave any banners or put out any flyers; she walked to the theatre district in that gown and approached people who were standing near the ticket offices looking as if they were not sure what show they wanted to see and gave them business cards; white on black.

They read: Royal wedding preview, Stafford Hall eight p.m.

When she had distributed all of them and could do no more she walked back along the perfect, white streets to the Stafford Theatre. Bunion was standing at an upper window, he smiled as saw her approach looking dazzling in that gown; she stood out radiantly in a town full of people who were all struggling to be noticed

Five hundred people came to the performance; Lydia told Clarissa to charge them fifty quid each and to serve them champagne and exclusive chocolates instead of ice creams and scratch cards.

The next day they were able to pay back the twelve thousand and hire the hall for another night and pay for the gown. That night seven hundred came to the performance.

Clarissa Clarke's Traveling World of Wonders actually made money.

"I can't believe it," Clarissa said as they were cleaning the auditorium on the third day, "I thought that rich people would be above this kind of entertainment."

Froggie collected the rubbish from the bins, "I think we should consider doing matinees," he said.

"Good idea," Natter agreed as he polished the arms and legs of the green and gold chairs.

Jerome dusted a crystal chandelier, "Don't you think that's a little premature?" he asked.

Bunion walked past on his way to clean the toilets, "What about the time machine?"

Everybody looked up, Bunion usually moved around so quietly that they didn't even notice he was there.

"The time machine... I had forgotten," Natter said.

"Me too," Rosie said, she and Annie were mopping the floor.

"I hadn't," Annie told them, "I just haven't seen any indication of one anywhere around here."

"Well we wouldn't see anything would we, we never leave the building."

"Lydia does but she's never says anything."

"The best place to look to find out if there is a time machine would be the library," Josephine said.

"That's next door isn't it?"

"When Lydia comes back I'll ask her to go and enquire."

It cost a thousand quid a week to belong to the library.

Lydia climbed the wide, white, marble steps into the cool, white foyer, past the gold framed paintings that hung on the wall and up to the most fashionable librarian she had ever seen. She bought a ticket that would entitle her to use the Library's information portal for one week and took it back to Josephine who linked it to a computer tablet and keyed the words 'Time Machine' into the search box.

There were three thousand, one hundred and ninety two results. A few of these were located in the science fiction section where there were cheesy adventure stories about people saving worlds, rescuing doomed maidens, finding ancient buried treasure, solving mysteries and opening restaurants using ancient recipes from a time when humans really knew how to cook.

But the vast majority of the references were in the archive section.

"Interesting," Josephine said, "it seems that they do have a time machine after all and they're very proud of it. Apparently a time tourist saved the whole planet. In his day Fettuccia was a ball of dust and debris because a huge asteroid had destroyed it. He wanted to see what the planet had been like before the calamity so he went back in time and fell in love with a beautiful woman who had come here to flee from persecution. Instead of just saving her he deflected the asteroid by hitting it with laser cannons. He pushed it far enough off course that it traveled safely past. The local frontiersmen were so grateful that they called the planet after him. His name was Roberto Fettuccia and the woman he was in love with was called Roslyn."

"Like the name of the city," Annie said.

"The strange thing is that he won't be born for another thousand years," Josephine told them.

"That doesn't make sense," Rosie said, "if he hasn't been born yet, this whole planet should still be space dust."

"No because he deflected that asteroid nearly eight hundred years ago, so it never hit."

"But if the planet isn't space dust now, when he is born it will be a thriving planet. And if it's a thriving planet he won't go back in time to save it," Rosie said.

"But if he doesn't go back in time and save the planet, it will be space dust and if it's space dust he will go back in time and save it," Annie said.

"Yes but if he saves it, then it won't be space dust and he won't go back in time and the asteroid will destroy it and the planet will be space dust...."

"And then he will go back in time and save it."

"That's what is called a temporal paradox," Josephine told them, "it's one of the reasons that time travel was outlawed so long ago."

"So could the planet disappear from beneath our feet?" Rosie asked.

"I think if it was going to do that, it would have happened by now."

"So what's the answer to the paradox?"

"I have no idea; maybe in the days when time travel was a legitimate activity they understood how such things worked but that knowledge has long since been forgotten," Josephine said.

"So does that mean that if we were ever able to go back into the past and prevent the war between Bellus and Bella, we've already done it?" Lydia asked. "Or does it mean that because history hasn't changed, we're never going to do it?"

"I have absolutely no idea."

"This is very depressing," Lydia said.

"What happened to Roberto, did he marry Roslyn or did he go back to his own time?" Natter asked.

"It says here that he was eventually executed for his good deed. Nevertheless there is a big annual festival to celebrate the saving of the planet, and guess what they parade around the streets of Roslyn City?"

"A time machine?" Lydia said.

"Exactly so."

"A real one?"

"The original one."

"I thought all the real time machines were destroyed."

"So did I but for some reason the Time Guardians allow this one to exist."

"When is this festival?"

"Six month's time."

"Oh."

"Hmm."

"Where is the time machine kept for the rest of the year?" Bunion asked.

The room was dark, lit only with muted blue lights. It was the middle of the night at the headquarters of the dreaded Time Guardians on the planet Tempus. A computer screen flashed a red warning and the operative called his supervisor over.

"We have a hit sir."

The supervisor looked down at the virtual monitor, "Clarissa Clarke's' Traveling World of Wonders; where have I seen that name before?"

"We had a report from Zertza several weeks ago sir."

"From that crackpot Sheriff Raspberry, I remember now. But what are they doing on Fettuccia?"

"They travel sir; they're a troupe of entertainers."

"Yes but what are they doing searching the library for information on time travel?"

"What do you want me to do about it sir?"

"Put a man on it, I want a full report; I want to know what their intentions are."

"The boss is already in Roslyn City, I could ask him to investigate sir."

"Tell him to give this one top priority; the integrity of the timeline must be preserved at all costs."

Chapter 4

"The Roberto Fettuccia Museum of Arts and Artifacts," Josephine said, "that's where the time machine is."

"Does the library have any information about the museum?" Lydia asked.

"Yes look, there's a virtual tour, there see? The time machine's situated in the Grand Hall... oh no actually it isn't, that one's just a replica, it says here that the real one is kept under tight security in a strong room in the basement."

"I think I should go there tomorrow and take a look around; I'll take the business cards with me."

The white on black business cards now read: "Royal wedding Preview, Stafford Hall, two p.m. and eight p.m."

Lydia stood in the white, high vaulted Grand Hall, handing out cards to all who showed an interest.

She had picked up a map of the building. On the right hand side of the Grand Hall was the room devoted to the Mother Planet. It contained curiosities from Earth that ranged from Indian arrowheads, to a Roman suit of armor, to a replica of the lunar module that was used the first time man set foot on another planet.

On the left hand side was the Exploration Room; it charted man's progress through the stars.

Behind the time machine exhibit was the Strange Worlds Room with its holographic images of some of the less than earthlike planets that exist in the galaxy.

There was also a reading room that displayed some important historical documents like the actual hand written log in which the legendary Adriana Tomlinson recorded her missions of discovery through uncharted space. There were also many of the notes and observations that Doctor Timothy Juniper had made when he was designing the standard terra-forming packages. Those packages were so good that they were used for centuries with very little change.

There was of course the exhibition of the dead, mostly bodies that had been interred in space before it was realized that this turned them into space junk and made them a danger to passing traffic. Captain Tomlinson and several other famous explorers were there, frozen in glass cases for all to see. Trian, the giant rodent who had guarded the Temple of Fear for over a hundred years was also there.

If Roslynians had gone in for children, they would have loved that room.

Above them was the huge Fettuccian room. It showed what life had been like for the first settlers; how they had faced the giant storms, how they were nearly overwhelmed by disease, how they came to control their environment and how in the end they began the tourist industry by offering the rest of the galaxy a peaceful hideaway from the problems of life.

The time machine exhibit was an interactive experience; Lydia paid her fifty quid and took her place in the queue.

It was very interesting. Actors played the parts of Roberto Fettuccia and his girlfriend Roslyn and the whole story was played out in all its emotional detail. They even reenacted Roberto and Roslyn's death. It was a little known fact that Roslyn's father was executed with them.

A shiver traveled down Lydia's spine when she saw them lined up against a wall, blindfolded. This was what happened to people who defied the Time Guardians. She shook her head to get rid of any negative thoughts.

After the presentation had finished, their holographic host asked if anybody had questions. People wanted to know why Roberto had to die even though he had done something good.

What followed was a long explanation about the unknown and dangerous consequences of attempting to change the timeline. Even actions taken with the best of motives could end up with disastrous results.

Most people did not agree that Roberto should have suffered such a severe punishment, he had done something beneficial, not disastrous and they wanted to know if anything could be done for him.

"The Corps of the Time Guardians was set up a thousand years ago; its sole purpose was and is to preserve the timeline. It has the authority to take any steps necessary to protect history from temporal abuses and it does a magnificent job. It would be wrong to question its methods," the interactive host said.

"Where is the real time machine?" Lydia called out.

"I am not authorized to answer that question."

"How do you stop people from stealing it and changing history?"

"The machine is held in an airless vault made of six inch thick titanium. There are pressure pads on the floor inside and out and motion sensors that will detect the presence of something as small as a fly, and besides that of course there are security cameras everywhere."

"Why is the vault airless?" Lydia said.

"It is in a vacuum to guard against corrosion. The Fettuccian time machine is in almost as good a condition now as it was in Roberto's day."

"Thank you," Lydia had all the information she needed and it was time to distribute more business cards.

"I want to join the circus."

Clarissa looked surprised, "Usually there are lots of kids in our audiences but there haven't been any here. You're the first one we've seen."

"So? Can I join or not?"

"No. Go home to your parents."

"They're in the solarium on Palm Street; they locked me in my room."

"Are you telling me you're an experienced escapologist?"

"I'll do anything," the boy was about ten years old, fat and freckled. Clarissa guessed by the expectant look in his eyes that he was used to getting his own way.

"Our life is not easy; it involves a lot of hard work."

"I don't mind; I'll do anything to get away from those dictators."

"Well if you feel like that you're hired; Bunion, come here," Bunion came over carrying his cleaning materials in a bucket. "You can be Bunion's assistant; you're almost the same height as he is."

"What do you want me to do?"

"Help him clean the toilets."

Half an hour later the boy was ready to go home.

"I'll call your dad," Clarissa said.

His father arrived within fifteen minutes, "Thank you," he said.

"It's no problem; it must be hard being a kid in this town."

"Yes indeed."

"Maybe you would like to bring your son to this afternoon's performance of our show? Here, I'll give you some complimentary tickets; you get free admission into our creature exhibition as well. You'll find some of the animals fascinating."

"Thank you."

"My name's Clarissa Clarke," Clarissa lifted her hand but he didn't shake it.

"I am Joseph Bridefield."

Mr. Bridefield and the boy left; they got into a car and drove down the street but when they were out of sight Bridefield stopped. "Here's your hundred quid, meet me back here in two hours, you must come to the matinee with me, I want to see these people again; they're hiding something and I want to know what."

"I'm supposed to be on another job this afternoon."

"This takes priority," Mr. Bridefield insisted.

There was no time to go back to the hotel for lunch so they ordered in. While they were sitting around eating Lydia made her report, "I got a very favorable response to the matinee this afternoon, a lot of people said they would come."

"What about the time machine?" Bunion asked.

Lydia told them everything she had found out.

"We're not going to be able to steal it from a titanium vault," Froggie said.

"How are you going to open the vault door?" Natter asked.

"I have no idea, but one thing I do know is that none of you are going to be involved; I saw Roberto's execution, this is not a game we're playing here. This is my problem and I will take the consequences, not you."

Mr. Mystery breathed deep, "Every system has a weakness."

"What do you mean?"

He put his hands on his head and removed his hair.

"You're bald," Rosie said, "I didn't know that."

"Observe," he lifted a fleshy pad from off the top of his head.

"Your head's coming apart," Annie cried.

Mr. Mystery's head was no longer smooth and round like a head should be but it had a deep dent in the middle like a valley between two mountains.

"Yuck," Rosie said.

He held up the fleshy looking pad, "This is merely an implant; a prosthesis. I was a test pilot for the space industry, but unfortunately because of my refusal to steal certain secrets from our competitors I made some powerful enemies. They arranged for me to have an 'accident.'"

"But you didn't die?" Rosie said.

"I lost half of my brain."

"Did you lose your memory?"

"No, the frontal cortex was intact; this device replaces my motor functions and my speech centers; without it I can neither move nor speak. It does have some interesting side effects however; as you can see I can take off the prosthetic device for cleaning and maintenance and it will still work because the signal can be boosted to operate over distances of up to five hundred feet."

Mr. Mystery turned his face towards Bunion and he disappeared.

"How do you do that?"

"It is a simple interference pattern, I am jamming Bunion's signal so that it does not reach your brain and you cannot see him. I discovered this function during my convalescence."

"Oh…" Rosie was not much the wiser.

Mr. Mystery turned his head again and Bunion reappeared.

"Is there anything else you can do?" Lydia asked.

"Watch Josephine's computer screen."

"You're hacking into my computer; how do you know my passwords?"

"I bypass them; the brain is so complex that it can tell that the input from the prosthesis is artificial and tries to reject it. So there is a program running continuously in the background that is designed to fool it into thinking that the signals are natural. It is related to anti-encryption technology and I found that I could easily adapt it so that I can get access to files that would normally be forbidden."

"Can you hack into security systems?"

"Yes of course, when I recovered from my accident and I had to make a decision as to which career to take up, I considered becoming a spy."

"Why didn't you? It must be better paying than this."

"I decided that the life of a traveling entertainer would be the safer option."

"So you became an illusionist?" Natter said.

"It seemed to be the wise choice at the time."

"So are you saying that you can help Lydia to get into the time machine vault?"

"Yes."

"I won't let you risk your life for me," Lydia insisted.

"That is my choice," Mr. Mystery said.

"What if you get caught? Wouldn't we all be in trouble?" Clarissa asked.

"You could claim to have no knowledge of it. Lydia has only been with us for a few weeks, we could say that she did it behind our backs."

"You want to break into the museum and steal the time machine?" Clarissa asked Lydia.

"Not steal it, borrow it, I don't want to physically take it away; I just want to use it and return it to the vault when I've finished."

"I'll come with you," Bunion said.

"Do you have a plan? I mean to say, if you did get hold of the time machine, when in history would you go back to? Would you stop the bullet that killed Lord Fopwais?" Rosie asked.

"I'm not sure," Lydia answered.

"Who did the Lady Sylvia eventually marry?"

"No one; she was one of the first victims of the war. Lord Fopwais' family blamed her for his death and swore revenge," Clarissa said.

"When did she meet Lord Murmot?"

"After she and Lord Fopwais had had an argument over money. Lord Murmot was the official ambassador representing Bella. The royal family invited him to a brunch in their famous gardens and they met under an apple tree."

"Did the Lady Sylvia and the Lord Murmot fall in love?"

"They had only just met when Lord Fopwais, who came late to the party, arrived to find them sitting close together laughing and talking. Naturally he assumed the worst and challenged Lord Murmot to a duel there and then. Lord Fopwais was always was a little rash."

"How come you know all this?" Jerry asked.

"I was a serving maid in the Bellusian Royal household at the time."

"You're Bellusian?" Lydia said.

"No I'm Zenebrian, but there was a terrible drought on my planet so I had to work off world; it was my great privilege to be employed by the royal household."

"So what you ought to do Lydia is go back in time and stop Lady Sylvia meeting Lord Murmot," Annie said.

"No, you ought to go back and prevent Lady Sylvia from having the argument with Lord Fopwais," Rosie said. "And Clarissa should be the one to go with you; so she can tell you where to go and what to do."

Lydia looked up into Clarissa's wrinkled face, "I'll go alone."

Bunion spoke up, "I'll go."

"Bunion will stand out," Annie warned.

"I'll be all right on my own," Lydia said.

"What happens if you fail?"

"The secret of success is good intelligence," Mr. Mystery said.

"Then just tell me what I need to know," Lydia said.

"No, too many lives depend on this; if you are to have any chance of success I will have to go with you," Clarissa told her.

They played two shows that day and made sixty thousand quid.

Mr. Bridefield brought the boy to the afternoon performance and after it had finished he came backstage with a huge bunch of flowers. But there was something sinister about the way he stared too long into each of their faces. "Thank you, my son found you show interesting," his mouth smiled but his eyes did not.

"Well thank you for the flowers." After he had gone Clarissa said, "There's something scary about him."

"He gives me the creeps," Rosie and Annie shivered together.

"The secret of illusion is misdirection," Mr. Mystery stated. "If you try to enter the museum at night you will be looked upon as an intruder but if you enter it during the day you will be called a visitor."

Clarissa and Mr. Mystery had to buy outfits worthy of Roslyn City but money was no longer a problem. "This is just wonderful, it's been so long since I've been able to choose something without looking at the price tag," Clarissa said, "but Richard you're not going to buy that, are you? It looks a little dreary."

"We must not stand out in the crowd; this is ideal for the purpose."

73

They decided to arrive the next day at five o'clock, after the matinee performance, when the museum was most likely to be crowded.

"Good," Mr. Mystery looked at the throngs in the great hall, "we shall easily blend in."

Clarissa looked at him, "Can you hack into the security system?"

"Do you have some money with you?"

"Yes of course."

"Then we must get some coffee."

They walked through the crowds to the cafeteria where Clarissa, who should have been used to it by now, nearly died at the price of a cup of coffee.

They had to wait for a table to be cleared before they could sit down. Mr. Mystery took a sip and closed his eyes, "Yes the signal is strong, wait please."

Clarissa looked at her watch; there were only two and a half hours until the next performance was due to start.

Mr. Mystery sat in a trancelike state.

"Are you all right?" Lydia said after a while.

"Don't speak to him, you'll break his concentration."

Several times Mr. Mystery shook his head vigorously and then he suddenly he opened his eyes, picked up his cup and drank.

"Are we allowed to speak to you yet?" Lydia asked.

"Yes of course," Mr. Mystery said.

"So...? Did you do anything?"

"Everything is arranged, we will not be detected on the security cameras. I know where the vault is located and I have created an interface so that I can control the security systems when I get there."

"Are there any guards that we need to worry about?"

"There are guards but they are easily dealt with."

"I don't want any violence."

"The guards will not see us."

"So, if this is going to be so easy why are we still sitting here?"

"I am waiting for that guard over by the door to make his report before we move out."

Lydia looked up, "I never noticed him."

"Do not worry he suspects nothing, but he does keep looking in our direction." They concentrated their attention on eating their muffins and looking ordinary; eventually the guard lost interest and stared at somebody else. "There is an entrance to the lower level in a corridor off the Strange Worlds Room."

They got up and moved nonchalantly out of the café.

The security guard in the Strange Worlds room was so bored that he was entertaining a bunch of tourists with gory stories of people who had mistakenly landed on planets covered in sulfuric acid.

Lydia, Clarissa and Mr. Mystery easily slipped past him into the corridor where Richard unlocked the electronic door and led the way downstairs to the part of the museum that the visitors never saw.

The basement was built, not of white, polished marble but of gray, concrete blocks. Lydia wondered if the basement of the hotel that they were staying in was like this too but she couldn't bring herself to believe it. There was a maze of rooms, most of which provided storage for specimens that had been gathered from all over the Galaxy. Mr. Mystery led them quietly forward. The corridors criss-crossed and they quickly passed through three open security doors.

Too late they heard the tapping of a woman's shoes on the hard floor as she walked around the corner, with her two male companions in white coats following along behind her. "What are you doing here?" she asked.

Clarissa held out her hand, "Clarissa Clarke, exo-biologist and these are my assistants Lydia and Richard. I'm doing research into extra-cranial consciousness but I rather think we've lost our way, you couldn't point me in the direction of the experimental mosses could you?"

"I'm sorry we're on our way to astro-physics but there's a security person down the hall, I'm sure he could direct you," the woman and the two men passed on.

"Extra-cranial consciousness? I've never heard of that before," Lydia remarked.

"Neither have I," Clarissa told her.

"What are we going to do when we come to the guard in the hall?"

"I will boost the interference pattern like I do when I am on stage, so that no one will be able to see you and no instrument will be able to detect you, but once you are past the guard you must stop and wait because you will not be far from the motion sensors and the pressure pads," Mr. Mystery said.

The little group moved forward, Clarissa leading the way. They got past the guard with no problems and turned into the corridor leading to the vault.

Then they stopped dead.

There were two sentries with guns cocked, standing outside the round vault door, which would have to be opened in order for them to get inside. Mr. Mystery pulled them back around the corner, "I will cause a distraction."

The two women walked unseen up to the sentries and stood beside them; Mr. Mystery closed his eyes and turned the pressure sensitive pads back on. He ignored the sudden blaring of the alarms and released the electronic lock on the vault door. The guards ran straight past his invisible self, searching for whatever had set the alarms off.

The pressure inside the vault leveled off and the heavy, round door slid open. They crept inside where there was no light except for the tiny amount that shone in through the crack in the door. "I can't see anything," Lydia said.

"It's dark," Clarissa pointed out.

"No I mean look around you, let your eyes adjust, what do you see?"

Clarissa scanned the room. The walls were smooth, the floor was smooth; the ceiling was smooth. There was nothing to interfere with their view of the whole room, which was in fact completely empty!

Mr. Mystery followed them in.

"There's no time machine," Clarissa said.

Lydia looked around the room in frustration and disbelief, "It's not here; they're guarding an empty room."

"Why would they do that?"

"I do not know," Mr. Mystery said, "but I recommend that we vacate the premises as quickly as we can!"

Up in the central security booth Mr. Bridefield watched the infrared holo-images of the vault.

"There's nothing in there sir," the guard reported.

"Nevertheless I want you to close the door."

"But what for sir?"

"Just do as I ask."

The guard went to manual override and the door began to close.

"Look, the door's closing, quick, run," Lydia shouted.

They were too late; the crack of light disappeared and the door shut tightly, trapping Lydia, Clarissa and Mr. Mystery inside. As soon as it had locked, the pumps activated and began sucking the air out of the room, "Richard, do something!" Clarissa cried.

"I'm trying to but I cannot get control of the door; they're overriding me."

Richard cancelled the interference pattern that had rendered them invisible; it was pitch black anyway so it wasn't needed. He concentrated on overriding the manual override.

"Richard, please, I'm an old woman; my lungs are not what they were."

Meanwhile in the security booth Mr. Bridefield studied the virtual screen; someone was trying to manipulate the door controls to the vault, "We have them, they are trapped," he said.

"Sir the intruders have only ten seconds of breathable air left."

Mr. Bridefield said nothing.

"Sir are you gonna let them die?"

"What they are doing carries an automatic death penalty; they are going to die anyway."

"I can't breathe," Clarissa gasped.

"Please Mr. Mystery don't give up now," Lydia said.

"It's no good, I can't," he slumped onto the floor.

Lydia's lungs felt like they were being sucked out of her chest and were about to burst through her nose. Clarissa staggered and Lydia lowered her gently to the ground; black clouds replaced the blackness of the room; she felt comfortable and at peace; she knew she was dying but it didn't matter.

Then suddenly the door swung open and air rushed into the vault. Mr. Mystery gasped; his chest heaved as he gulped oxygen into his lungs. As soon as he was strong enough he staggered to his feet and switched the interference pattern back on, thereby rendering them all invisible again. Clarissa was too weak to move so he and Lydia dragged her behind the door.

Men rushed in firing their lasers into the air.

"There's nothing here sir," one of them reported over his radio.

"Continue firing," Mr. Bridefield ordered.

The guards did as they were told.

Mr. Mystery and Lydia quietly carried Clarissa out into the corridor where the alarms were still sounding loudly; they dragged her down the passageway to where there was an electronic door, which Richard unlocked and let them through. Meanwhile the guards concluded that there really wasn't anyone in the vault and turned their gunfire onto the corridor.

Mr. Mystery locked the security door behind them and changed the code at the same time, "That should slow them down for a while."

They hurried down three more passageways and through two more security doors, which Richard locked as soon as they had gone through, but the guards were closing in. "It's no good, we'll never get out of here."

"What do you mean?" Lydia said.

"They're tracking our progress, every time I open an electronic door they can detect it and they know exactly where we are; there are guards behind us and I suspect that when we get to the exit they will have guards waiting for us there too."

"We'll be caught in the crossfire."

They had no choice but to keep going forward; the guards who were behind them blanketed the empty corridors with laser fire hoping to hit the fugitives by chance.

They came to the stairs that led up to the Strange Worlds Room but between them and freedom stood half a dozen security men that had been called from all over the museum and were glad of a little action at last. The invisible threesome crept forward until they stood two feet in front of them. To their rear the guards who had been chasing them opened the last security door and ran forward firing their weapons.

They stopped in front of the stairs.

"Anything to report?" one of the security men asked.

"The intruders have not been sighted sir."

"That's because they're invisible you fool."

"Yes sir."

"They could be standing in front of us right now."

"Yes sir."

Clarissa took off a broach that she had been wearing and threw it exactly between the two groups of men. It chinked onto the floor. Both sets of security guards raised their guns and blasted it to nonexistence, scorching a big patch of floor in the process. Meanwhile Lydia, Clarissa and Mr. Mystery used the distraction to slip past them all and through the door to freedom.

They stumbled out of the corridor into the Strange Worlds exhibition and made their way towards the Great Hall.

Mr. Mystery staggered forward, his invisible forehead ran with sweat, "I am sorry Clarissa but I don't think I have the strength to control the interference pattern much longer."

"Then we had better find somewhere to reappear inconspicuously."

They quickly found a blind spot under one of the surveillance cameras in the Great Hall. Clarissa rematerialized looking exhausted and gray.

"Are you all right?" Lydia asked her.

"I... I will be."

Mr. Mystery reappeared looking exhausted and green.

"Are you all right?"

"I think so."

They made their way to the front steps as quickly as their trembling bodies would allow. "I don't understand it; surely the guards would have seen us on surveillance, why is nobody chasing us?" Clarissa asked.

She soon had her answer.

All at once Mr. Bridefield stepped out in front of them as if from nowhere; he stared at them with his dead eyes, "What is your purpose here?"

"We came for the time machine," Clarissa said.

"Why?"

"We wanted to do something good with it, but since it doesn't exist, that won't be possible. Still there can be no accusation of illegal possession of a non-existent time machine now can there, Mr. Bridefield?"

"You have crossed the line Miss. Clarke."

"Good day Mr. Bridefield."

They hurried away.

"He let us go," Lydia said.

"He must have something else in mind," Richard said.

"Decontamination, he let us go because he wants to wipe us all out but he doesn't want to do it in public."

They hailed a taxi and drove back to Stafford Hall as fast possible. When they got there Annie and Rosie ran outside to meet them. "Did it work? Did you go back in time?"

Clarissa shook her head; she hurried through the grand front doors and into the theatre.

Geraldine greeted them; she was bouncing with excitement, "Clarissa you'll never guess, Bunion was searching through a book of ancient recipes and he found something amazing."

"Never mind about that now, we've got to get out of here."

"But he found a set of instructions."

"He can improve his culinary skills later; right now we have bigger fish to fry."

"It wasn't a recipe; it was a blueprint for a time machine and it looks genuine."

"But it disappeared," Bunion said.

"It just faded off the screen like someone wiped it out while we were reading it."

"Did you see much of it?"

"Yes I managed to memorize all the general principles."

"That makes things even worse. The Time Guardians must have detected the file as soon as you activated it, they'll assume that we've all been infected with the information."

"What do you mean?"

"They're going to decontaminate us!"

Grumpus had been in the military; he knew what decontamination meant, "Everybody back to the spaceship, now!"

"But what about the performance?" Jerry asked.

"No time; go!"

"But what about our things back at the hotel?"

"If you don't stop arguing and get going right now the Time Guardians will destroy us all!" Grumpus said.

Chapter 5.

By the time the van screeched to a halt outside the Genghis Khan Clarissa was on the videophone deep in negotiations.

"What do you mean exit tax? Yes, yes and how much to take care of the animals until we can make it back?" Clarissa took a deep breath, "How much? That's just a deposit? No, no you'll have to do better than that... then you'll just have to take them to the canned food factory, send me the bill for that."

Bunion looked at Clarissa, "Please... you can't."

Clarissa pressed the privacy button, "I'm not really going to let them hurt the creatures, I'm just negotiating a better price that's all." Bunion sighed with relief. "What do you mean we're not cleared to leave until we've paid the exit tax?"

They all piled onto the spaceship and Geraldine started the jet engines; she taxied forward without doing any pre-flight checks.

"Hey wait a minute I'm not strapped in," Jerome said.

"Then you'd better do it quickly because a big armored van with a flashing red light has just turned round the corner of the terminal building and it's heading straight for us!"

"Yes, yes all right we'll pay, now give us that launch window," Clarissa said.

Geraldine revved up the jet engines, "Flight control, this is the Genghis Khan, clear the runway, we're leaving now!"

"Genghis Khan you do not have permission to take off."

"You'd better clear the runway; I'm not going to stop," Geraldine switched off the radio and put her big foot on the throttle.

The armored vehicle fired a missile straight at them but Geraldine swerved onto the taxiway and the rocket blew the tail of an Axon 950, a very valuable executive jet. She swerved the craft around onto the runway and picked up speed. The van released another missile, forcing her to push the engines to their limit.

The rocket just missed the fuselage.

The armored vehicle hurtled up the runway after them and let off two more missiles, one after the other. The jet engines screamed as the ungainly space plane made it to take off speed. Geraldine pulled back the joystick and the Genghis Khan left the ground.

"Geraldine lookout!" Rosie screamed.

A huge transport ship on final approach loomed up in front of them; it filled the cockpit window. Annie screamed. Geraldine pulled the Genghis Khan up into a steep bank around to the left; its stubby wingtips nearly scraped the ground. The two vessels missed each other by less than the breadth of a human hair. The two missiles skimmed the incoming ship's underbelly, avoiding contact by less than a centimeter; but miraculously the pilot managed to land the ship safely on the ground.

"Let's get out of here," Geraldine pulled the juddering spacecraft out of the maneuver and headed upwards at maximum power.

Everybody puked. Annie and Rosie both puked even though they only had one stomach, "There's going to be some cleaning to do if we ever get out of this," Annie said.

Then the rocket engines took over from the jet engines and everyone stopped puking in favor of blacking out.

Geraldine, who woke up before the others, activated the start up sequence for the graviton engines and switched on the artificial gravity. Then she laid in a course for the Knotted Tree Nebula, a globular cluster full of small bits of debris, where there might be somewhere to hide. Then suddenly she saw something on the main monitor and her eyes opened wide. A big, dark craft was swooping down on them from the blackness of space.

"Time Guardians!"

The others started to come round.

"What's happening?" Clarissa asked.

"We've got company and I can't engage the gravity bubble; the graviton engines are only up to fifty percent."

"So what can we do?"

"Dunno they're nearly in range."

"Give me the comm." Clarissa picked up a microphone, "This is Clarissa Clarke's Traveling World of Wonders, we have entertainer's immunity; you have no right to apprehend us, cease your pursuit now!"

"You are in contravention of temporal laws 362 and 470 sections C, D and Q, sub paragraph 18. It is imperative that you give yourselves up," Mr. Bridefield said.

"Incoming!" Geraldine shouted as she moved the Genghis Khan into a higher orbit, "Oh no it's a heat seeker."

"Evasive maneuvers," Grumpus ordered.

"It won't do us any good. The missile will just follow us wherever we go."

"Just keep ahead of it, these types don't have much fuel; you should be able to outrun it."

"They've just let off two more."

"Just keep going," Grumpus said.

Geraldine kept going, she could outrun the missiles but the pursuing craft was fast, soon its lasers would be in range.

"How's the graviton engines?"

"Seventy-seven percent."

"How soon can you get the wormhole to form?"

"Not before ninety-five percent."

The spacecraft broke orbit taking them completely out of the Fettuccian gravity well. The Time Guardian's sleek craft followed them, firing its lasers. The Genghis Khan was not armed, so all Geraldine could do was use the maneuvering thrusters to make its movements so erratic that the Time Guardians couldn't get a lock. Grumpus was right about the missiles; one by one they ran out of fuel and could not follow the movements of the spacecraft.

But....

"They've locked on," Geraldine said.

"Can't you engage the gravitons?"

"They're only at eighty-eight percent," Geraldine told him.

"We're all going to die," Rosie screamed.

Geraldine wanted to tell her to shut up, but how could she when she knew it was true? She braced herself.

The Time Guardian craft fired all its lasers directly at their graviton engines in a continuous blast....

Geraldine closed her eyes never expecting to open them again. The hairs on the back of her neck stood up as the cabin heated up and sweat trickled down her forehead.

She breathed in and out, in and out, in and out, in and... "We should be... why aren't we dead?"

More breathing out and in, and out and.... She opened one eye and looked down at her pudgy hands still clutching the joystick.

The laser fire had completely stopped.

She opened her other eye and looked at the control monitor. "What happened? Where are we?" There was a planet below them but it was definitely not Fettuccia. She did a spectral analysis but there was no match with any planet in her database. The star patterns didn't have any equivalent either.

The comm. flashed; "This is Zedekiah Horatio Banes at your service."

Clarissa gasped.

"Hello, this is Geraldine."

"I expect you're wondering what you're doing here."

"I'm wondering why we're not all dead."

"H... how did you find us?" Clarissa whispered.

"I have been tracking you ever since I intercepted a message about you from Sheriff Raspberry of Zertza. I am sending you some landing co-ordinates; my drones are preparing dinner and if you will consent to share it with me as my welcome guests I can explain everything to you."

Geraldine turned around and looked at Clarissa, "This could be a trap," she warned her.

"Tell him we would be honored," Clarissa said.

"But we don't know anything about him."

"He just saved our lives; I'd like to know why."

"I'd like to know how," Geraldine piloted them down to the dark surface of the rocky, airless planet.

"Are you sure this is it?" Clarissa said as Geraldine powered the engines down.

"These are the exact co-ordinates."

The comm. flashed, "As soon as you're ready I'll bring you in."

Suddenly Bunion disappeared, he didn't even fade; he just popped into disappearance leaving his seat and his puke behind him. Then Natter did the same; then Jerry. One by one they all disappeared; Geraldine was last to go as she had to lock down the spacecraft and power off all the systems.

As soon as she had finished she disappeared too, suddenly finding herself squashed onto a long, green sofa between Froggie and Natter in an underground cave with white walls that had been painted with murals of desert palms and pyramids; the smell of food wafted into her nose.

Then a door opened and the distinguished figure of Zedekiah Banes entered the room. He had a long, gray ponytail, a neatly trimmed beard, a back as straight as a ramrod, twinkling blue eyes and a rakish tilt to his hat. "Welcome one and all to planetoid 32K01, I'm sorry for the rather abrupt way that you were all transported here but I felt that since you were about to die the matter was quite urgent..." suddenly his eyes fell upon Josephine; "Oh! Oh my... what do we have here?" He ran over to her and laid his hand on her head feeling its shape as if he wasn't quite able to believe what he was seeing. "Josephine? You can't be a Josephine that's not possible."

"How do you know my name?"

"But this is incredible; you shouldn't exist."

"What do you mean?"

"Your kind died out many years ago."

"My kind?"

"Don't you know what you are?"

"I don't understand."

"In archaeological terms you're a very rare find indeed."

"You're scaring me."

"Oh there's no need to be scared, it's just such a shock to see a living Josephine."

"Will you please explain yourself?"

But suddenly Zedekiah stopped looking at her; he had spotted Clarissa who was sitting behind the sofa on an old, brown, easy chair. He hurried over to her, searching her face for someone he recognized, "Isabella?" he cried.

"No, no, I'm not…" Clarissa looked down at the floor.

"No of, of course, my mistake; oh please forgive me but for a moment there you reminded me of… but no you couldn't be her; she died a long time ago."

"I… I'm sorry."

"How the mind plays tricks; may I offer you some wine Miss…?"

"Clarke, Clarissa Clarke," she held out her hand so that he could shake it but he lifted it up to his lips and kissed it.

"I am enchanted to meet you Miss. Clarke," he gave her a smile that was more rakish than the angle of his hat.

A glow appeared on Clarissa's cheeks and she had to cough to regain her composure, "Mr. Banes why have you brought us here?"

"Two reasons, firstly you were in need of my help and secondly I'm having problems with Zeno."

"Who is Zeno?"

"He's my assistant; it was he that constructed the vortex machine that I used to bring you here."

"And how can we help him?"

"Follow me; let me show you."

They all trooped after him as he led them down some stairs and along a natural tunnel made from a bubble in the volcanic rock. It opened out into a cavern, the walls of which had been painted white. Laboratory equipment stood on long tables and tools and strange looking spare parts lay on sturdy benches. Down the end was a computer station and a desk piled high with ancient papers, crystals, disks, and all kinds of eccentric little devices; some of which were obviously very old, and most of which were probably beyond repair. There were shelves lining the walls, with artifacts of all kinds piled onto them and there were boxes on the floor that obviously contained many more.

"Please excuse the mess, I wasn't actually expecting company and as you can see Zeno is in no fit condition to help me clean it up," Zedekiah said.

Zeno sat on the floor beside a pile of boxes, his eyes stared forward and there were traces of scorching on his face. "Zeno's a robot?" Rosie asked.

"Not just a robot, an artificial human," Zedekiah said

Geraldine bent down to examine him. "What happened?"

"I discovered him in the bowels of the lost museum of Argos, the miraculous thing was that he must have been there for five hundred years and yet he was in almost perfect condition."

"I have never heard of Argos," Clarissa said.

"It's in the beta quadrant near Honoria and like most planets in that sector it's no longer inhabited."

"And you restored him?"

"Colleagues of mine did the job; unfortunately they now have troubles of their own and are not available to repair him."

"So I take it that you are an archaeologist?"

"A temporal archaeologist."

Geraldine cleared the nearest bench and lifted Zeno onto it. She started looking around for tools, "What's a temporal archaeologist?"

"I track down and rescue the technology and research that has been lost since the temporal laws were put into place."

"What do you mean?"

"In the thousand years since the laws were enacted, there has been an atmosphere of fear among scientists; they are afraid to invent anything new in case it becomes outlawed by the Time Guardians and they have to pay with their lives. You probably don't realize it but the inhabited universe has been shrinking for all that time."

"You said a vortex machine brought us here, I've never heard of that before, is that lost technology?" Geraldine unscrewed Zeno's face.

"Portal Technology was developed over a thousand years ago. It was a spin off from the development of time travel and was about to be put into manufacture when the temporal laws were enacted. If people had been allowed to benefit from it, there would have been no need for spacecraft because you could have traveled from one planet to another simply by walking through a doorway."

"Cool," Froggie said.

"Sadly the technology was destroyed and believed to be completely lost until I unearthed an old data disc on Theta Seven. It was badly corrupted but I managed to rescue enough information for Zeno to be able to construct the prototype; he's a brilliant engineer."

"But now you need an engineer to repair your engineer."

"Exactly so."

"Mr. Banes is it safe to assume that you are not liked by the Time Guardians?" Clarissa asked.

"I am a wanted man even though what I am doing is not against the law and has nothing to do with time travel."

"Was it you who planted the time machine blueprint in the Roslyn public library?"

"A time machine blueprint?"

"Yes, Bunion here found it in an old recipe book."

"Is it genuine?"

"Geraldine says it should work, but she had to memorize the details because the file was deleted as she was reading it."

"Can you remember the name of the author?"

"No… sorry."

"Are you sure? Think carefully now."

"No, I wasn't taking any notice of that," Geraldine probed Zeno's neck with a phase tester.

"It was Bothus of Escobar," Bunion said.

"Are you sure?"

"Yes," Bunion said.

"Evidence is gathering that Bothus of Escobar may have been a pen name for Amos Narbandian."

"Who is he?" Clarissa asked.

"He was a fashion emperor who lived eight hundred years ago, people practically worshipped him but it seems that he could have been much more than just a style guru."

"You think he was secretly working against the Time Guardians?"

"There's no hard evidence as yet but if he really authored and effectively hid a book on time technology... are you sure this is genuine? Could you actually construct a time machine using the instructions you found in that book?" Zedekiah asked Geraldine.

"The principles are sound enough, but I would never be able to get the parts, most of them no longer exist and I don't know how to fabricate them."

"If you had the right components could you do it?"

"I suppose I could try," Geraldine unscrewed Zeno's flexible chest plate to check the memory cells that he carried instead of a heart and lungs.

Zedekiah jumped up with excitement, "Leave him for now; follow me." He ran ahead of them down more tunnels, "I have been collecting artifacts for such a long time."

Before long they came to a gallery carved in the rock; it overlooked a dark, echoing cavern. Zedekiah switched on the lights to reveal below them the biggest pile of ancient scrap that Geraldine had ever seen in her entire life.

"I don't know if there's anything here that might help."

"You actually want me to build you a time machine?"

"Yes," Zedekiah said.

"But why? What do you want to do with it?"

"A thousand years ago there existed a matrix called the Interference Project. It contained the whole of the accumulated knowledge of mankind up to that point. Tragically it was destroyed, completely erased by the Time Guardians because it contained research that could have led to the reinvention of time travel. I want to go back to obtain a copy of it so that I can give it to those who would know what to do with it. If I could do that my life's work would be complete."

Geraldine climbed down the stone steps that led into the huge cave. She picked up at random a purple, fluorescent box with rotten wires dangling out of it, "I wonder what this was, I hope Zeno is repairable because I have a feeling I'm going to need his help."

It was time for dinner so Zedekiah led them back to the main living area and sat them round a square of black tufa rock that served as a table. "I'm sorry there's not more variety but as you can see the only way I can grow food on this planet is underground in the heat of the thermal vents."

Robotic waiters of about the same height as Bunion served it up to them and considering its limitations the food was quite tasty.

Josephine opened her mouth to say something but Zedekiah beat her to it, "You were fleeing from the Time Guardians on Fettuccia, if it's not too intrusive, may I ask why?"

"We were hoping to borrow their time machine; we wanted to go back a hundred and fifty years to prevent the Bellusian war but I'm sorry to say that we discovered that they don't actually have one," Clarissa said.

"How were you going to prevent the war?"

"By avoiding the argument between Lord Fopwais and Lady Sylvia."

"Your purpose is admirable, I myself am Bellusian and I experienced firsthand the pain and suffering that war can bring when I lost my Isabella, perhaps we could find a way to fulfill both of our ambitions."

"You're talking as if you already have a time machine. I'm an engineer, not a miracle worker; I've got a thousand year old design that I'm supposed to reconstruct from memory with five hundred year old, worn out parts; it's probably not going to be possible to build anything," Geraldine said.

"I'm sorry, excuse me for getting so excited, of course you can't build it, I'm completely forgetting that if the Time Guardians found out about it you'd receive the death sentence."

"I guess we've already incurred that from the last little stunt. I don't mind trying to build your time machine; just don't get too set on the idea that I'm gonna succeed."

"Please Mr. Banes," Josephine said. Zedekiah turned around to her. "Please, you know my name, you told me that I shouldn't exist and then you left me dangling in the air and didn't tell me anymore; if you know who I am, tell me."

"The original Josephine design is over a thousand years old."

"I was designed?"

"The dome on your head houses a pseudo-brain, a kind of super computer, more efficient than any mechanical computer that mankind has ever devised; all the Josephines had them."

"All the Josephines?"

"The Josephines were clones, they were human computers owned by different corporations."

"What?"

"Haven't you ever interfaced with another computer, maybe a very old one?"

"No, Mr. Mystery does it because he's got a prosthesis in his brain, but I don't."

"Your pseudo-brain can do much more than his artificial brain will ever be capable of," Zedekiah declared.

"That can't be true; I've never even interfaced with the computer on the Genghis Khan."

"You probably can; you just don't know how."

"I don't understand this at all."

"I'm sorry, I shouldn't have said anything; this is too much for you to take in."

"But I've always wondered where I came from; please tell me everything you know."

"I can show you my research files on the computer if you like."

Josephine nodded in agreement and Zedekiah picked up a computer tablet and activated it. She wept when she saw images of her own kind, "I do have a family after all, but they lived so long in the past."

"It is thought that the last Josephine died out around seven hundred years ago."

"Then why am I here?"

"I have no idea," Zedekiah guided her through all the research he had ever done on the Josephines; she was still reading it when it was time to go to bed.

"I have always wondered if I had a family but I never expected anything like this."

"Do you want a sedative to help you to sleep? This must all be quite a shock."

"It is but I think I'll just stay at the computer for a while; Clarissa always billed me as the most intelligent woman in the universe but I knew that I wasn't. Now I find that I do have a purpose after all. I'm not sure what to think about it but I'd like to find out as much as I can."

"Your kind thrived at mankind's technological peak, when the Interference Project was compiled, just before time travel was outlawed."

"If it ever becomes possible to return to that time can I come with you?" Josephine asked.

"That would be very risky."

"I know but I really, really want to."

"Well you would certainly be a useful person to have around."

Josephine smiled, "Thanks," she said.

Zedekiah led them to the rooms that the housekeeping droids had hastily prepared for them. "We can start work in the morning after a good night's sleep."

"You don't have to do all this, we can sleep on the spaceship," Clarissa said.

"No, no I wouldn't hear of it."

"Well thank you for your hospitality," Clarissa hesitated, "I'll bid you goodnight then."

"Don't mention it." Zedekiah picked up her hand and kissed it again, "Sleep well," he said.

Clarissa smiled shyly at him.

"There's something about you... when I see you I can't help thinking of my Isabella, she promised me that she would marry me once the war was over but it never ended and she died and it was too late," Zedekiah wiped a tear from his eye.

"I... I'm sorry."

"It was a long time ago but I still miss her."

"I know how you feel; I miss someone from my past too. Well goodnight Mr. Banes."

"Goodnight Miss Clarke."

As soon as she was alone Clarissa took off her shoes, removed her makeup and her jewelry and changed into the night attire that Zedekiah had transported over from the spaceship. She found her favorite handkerchief before she lay down in bed and wept as she had grieved many times before, over the loss of her one true love.

It took three long days to fix Zeno, one of his hydraulic motors had burnt out, which wasn't a big problem in itself but it had scorched a nearby nerve bundle and it took Geraldine some time to figure out a way to fabricate a replacement. Finally all the repairs were finished and she was able to reboot Zeno's mental systems.

His eyes flicked open and he looked at Geraldine, "Who are you? What century is this? Where am I? Is Zedekiah still alive? If not how long has he been dead and where is he buried?"

Zedekiah ran over to him, "You did it, well done. Zeno you've only been down six weeks; Geraldine here repaired you."

"That's good because last time they reactivated me they told me that five hundred years had passed by." Zeno looked at Geraldine, "thank you for fixing me."

"Zeno, Geraldine knows how to construct a time machine," Zedekiah said.

"Really? I'll help," Zeno jumped off the workbench.

"Hey slow down, I want to clean the oil off you and run through a few diagnostics first."

"Okay," Zeno walked over to a computer station and plugged himself in.

Meanwhile all the others had been making themselves useful. After she had got over the initial shock of finding out who she was and was able to think of other things, Josephine studied the plans for the time machine that Geraldine had given her. She kept herself busy researching what engineering databases she could find for more information. She still couldn't interface with any computer but she tried to be aware of the activities of her pseudo-brain.

Clarissa gave Froggie, Natter, Jerry and Mr. Mystery the job of sorting through the scrap pile for any components that looked even remotely like the ones that would be needed. Jerome helped by taking the high things from the top of the pile.

Lydia, Bunion, Annie, and Rosie began to tidy up the mess in the laboratory-cum-workshop, filing all the papers and trying to put everything into some kind of order. Annie also volunteered to clean up the puke in the spacecraft, much to her sister's consternation. Rosie insisted on having control of one of their hands in order to pinch her nose.

Grumpus volunteered to fetch and carry anything that the others needed and Josephine started to design the software that would be needed if the time machine was ever going to work.

Geraldine stood with her welding torch in her hand surveying the weird and wonderful assortment of components that the others had piled up in front of her, "This is going to be the biggest bodge of all time," she said.

The first job was to fabricate the multilayered, egg shaped framework. It had to be constructed of polished, perfectly smooth steel with wafer-thin electromagnets embedded into it. There was to be nothing holding the layers apart but when the magnets switched on, each layer would repel the next.

Zeno was a mine of information; he knew all sorts of details about the components in the scrap pile and when he wasn't needed for anything else, he would tediously smooth and polish tiny areas of metal for hours at a time until they were just right. He also made sure that Geraldine had what she needed:

tools, equipment, cups of synthesized coffee and he would gently massage her neck at the end of the day.

"My makers didn't give me taste buds or scent receptors; I think they were trying to cut down on processing power. But they did give me touch sensors and I can feel the warmth of your soft skin. Why did you decorate it this way? Not that I don't like it, but I notice that other humans don't seem to have patterns on their skin as you have."

"It's a long story Zeno," Geraldine said.

"I have time."

"I don't like to talk about it."

"I would like to know."

Geraldine sighed; even though Zeno was only a machine he was easy to confide in. Maybe it was because she knew he wouldn't judge her in the same way that a human would.

"I come from Masagorian, it's an agricultural planet and as you probably know those are quite rare and so I was bred to be big and strong and to work on the land. All the people of Masagorian are big like me, but I was different. Masagorians are not bred to be thinkers, they are required to accept their lot in life and so they are generally not very bright. I was an exception and when my parents realized it, they sacrificed everything so that I could have an education. They wanted me to have a future away from the physical slavery that they had to endure. But ironically it was when I left my home planet to go to college that I realized just how different I was."

Zeno finished massaging Geraldine's neck and sat down beside her. He took hold of her hand and held it while she continued to talk.

"I found myself caught between two worlds. I was too well educated to fit into life at home and too big to be appreciated anywhere else."

"So what did you do?"

"I got a job as an engineer for an interplanetary trucking company. Their vehicles were very old and it was almost impossible to keep them space worthy but I still blame myself for the accident."

"Is that why you marked your skin?"

"It is a tradition on my planet to get one tattoo for every loved one that dies so that we won't forget them. The roses on the back of my hands are for my parents and my sister who were killed in the eruption of seventy-seven. The rest are for those who died in the accident, four hundred and fifty-seven people."

"I understand," Zeno put his arms around her, "we do not desire to do bad things but sometimes, against our will things turn out badly anyway."

Geraldine sighed and nestled into his cool, mechanical body. Somehow it helped her feel a little better.

"There's no way to test the time machine," Zedekiah said.

"But it's cobbled together from rubbish, something's bound to go wrong," Geraldine told him.

"The Time Guardians will detect it as soon as you power up; they'll be on us in less than thirty minutes."

"If they come here we'll all be arrested," Clarissa said.

"There's an old bio-habitation complex on Parasque Minor, it was abandoned a long time ago by Corinthian pirates. The life support doesn't work anymore but it feels better than being outside. I was thinking that we could use the vortex machine to transport us there."

"I've heard of Parasque Minor; it's two sectors away, will the machine be able to send us that far?"

"The vortex machine has a surprisingly good range."

They agreed on a plan. If the time machine could be made to work, Zedekiah and Josephine would go back in time for the Interference Project. As soon as they arrived at their temporal destination, Zedekiah would program the machine to go forward again to pick up Clarissa, Lydia and Bunion, who would travel back to Bellus to prevent the war.

Once there, they would program the time machine to journey automatically to random co-ordinates in time and space to confuse the Time Guardians. It would return to pick up Zedekiah and Josephine once their mission was completed and after their return it would pick up Clarissa's team at a point five days after they had arrived on Bellus. They would then come back to Parasque Minor, arriving at a point just before they left so they could tell their other selves of any problems they might encounter.

If they got the timing correct they would be on Parasque Minor less than half an hour and they would be able to go back to Zedekiah's hideout using the vortex machine before the Time Guardians caught up with them.

That was the theory.

Zeno gave the machine one last polish.

"Everything's going to be all right isn't it?" Geraldine said.

"It'll be as good as we can make it.".

"Let's hope that's good enough."

Josephine checked and double-checked the software. She took a computer tablet to a seat beside one of the bubbling culture pools where it was quiet. Zeno was already there. "Did you come here to do some thinking too?" she asked.

"This is my favorite place; I get my best ideas here."

"I have never met a machine that has ideas before."

"Is that how you think of me, as just a machine?"

"I'm a machine myself, a human machine with a computer in my head."

"What is it like to be human?"

"You're not missing much."

"Surely if I was fully human I would have respect."

"Not all humans are respected."

"But if I was fully human I would have others of my kind."

"Not all humans have families; mine are all dead."

"If I was fully human I could find love."

"Some humans search all their lives for love and never find it."

"You are young, and you are fully human, love will come to you."

"People don't always get what they wish for Zeno."

"We really, really need to do tests," Geraldine told Zedekiah.

"I've already told you; they can't be done."

"Well we're taking a big risk; an untested time machine could chew you into little bits and spit you out all over the temporal landscape."

"That's a chance I'll have to take."

"It could even leave your head in one century, your legs in another century and your body suspended between the two."

"I'm an old man and I'm on the Time Guardian's most wanted list. I have two choices. Either I end my days cowering here or I risk losing the small amount of life that's left to me and maybe accomplish something good; which would you choose?"

There wasn't much left to do; a few final checks and everything was ready.

It was time.

"What if you don't come back Clarissa? What will we do then?" Annie asked.

"You'll be all right Annie; you're stronger than you think. Anyway if this goes well, we may all suddenly find ourselves in a different and better universe."

"And if you fail?"

"We can't afford to think about that," Clarissa said.

They hugged each other before those that were leaving put on their space suits and screwed down their helmets. Then Natter activated the vortex machine and Clarissa, Bunion, Lydia, Zeno, Geraldine, Josephine and finally Zedekiah stepped through the portal. An instant later they walked into the old habitation dome on Parasque Minor and Grumpus pushed the time machine through the portal behind them.

"I suggest we get this over with," Zedekiah said.

Geraldine climbed into the shiny, egg shaped machine. She switched on the power and checked the readouts. Everything had to be precisely right. Once she was satisfied she climbed out and Zedekiah and Josephine climbed in and closed the door.

There was a buzzing sound as the power began to build up; after several minutes the magnetized shells separated from one another. When they were in the right position, Clarissa checked the time on her helmet display.

"I'm activating the photon emitters," Geraldine said.

"And I'm activating the photon accelerators," Zeno said.

"We have a twenty-five minute window, starting now," Clarissa told them.

The power continued to build and the shimmering time machine began to disappear. Geraldine nearly crushed Zeno's metal hand in excitement; he smiled back at her, "It's working," she said.

But suddenly there was a loud crackle and the little machine solidified again, Geraldine opened the door and yanked Zedekiah and Josephine out of it. She scrambled in and with her pudgy fingers trapped in the ungainly gloves of the space suit she adjusted the power to the photon emitters. It was difficult work and when it was done Zedekiah and Josephine climbed in again.

The machine powered up and faded to the point where Geraldine's helmet lights could shine straight through it. But it didn't disappear; it just hung there suspended between two points in time.

"I think we should adjust the angle of the photon accelerators," Zeno said.

"We can't do anything about them now, we'd need to strip down and rebuild."

"What if we just did the outer shell with a big magnet; we only need to move them the width of a few molecules?"

"Good idea, wait there," Geraldine turned round and ran back through the portal.

"What's happening?" Natter asked as soon as she appeared on the other side.

"Tell you later," Geraldine grabbed an electro-magnet and a big battery from the stores and jumped back through the portal.

She and Zeno connected them and lined them up very carefully before switching them on; the pull of the magnet was very strong.

"Is anything happening?" Zedekiah asked.

"Give it a few seconds."

Zeno watched the readouts on the monitor in front of him, "That's as good as we're going to get it, you can switch off now."

"You've had fifteen minutes; there's only ten to go," Clarissa warned them.

Zedekiah and Josephine stepped back into the time machine and shut the door. It powered up again; this time the egg shaped vehicle almost disappeared.

"We're so close," Geraldine said.

Zedekiah and Josephine got out again and Geraldine took the big electro-magnet inside; she tried to influence the angle of the photon accelerators from the inside of the craft. It was hard to tell if anything was happening.

"That's it; it isn't going to give us any more."

Geraldine climbed out of the time machine and Zedekiah scrambled back in, "This is the last attempt; there won't be time for another one, so I don't want you coming with me," he told Josephine.

"What? But why?"

"We're cutting it too close, this is dangerous; you go back through the portal, in fact all of you go back through the portal; go back to safety."

"But Zedekiah…" Josephine pleaded.

Zedekiah closed the door. The time machine powered up again and faded into a thin mist. All at once a flash of laser light hit the bio-dome. "That's the Time Guardians, they're early!" Clarissa shouted as another, brighter flash made the glass of the dome fizz, "Everyone, through the portal now!"

"But what about Zedekiah?" Lydia asked.

"He knows; he's powering down," Josephine said.

Bunion caught Lydia's hand and pushed her through the portal. Next he grabbed Geraldine's hand and pushed her through too. Zeno and Josephine jumped through together. The time machine materialized and the door opened just as Bunion caught hold of Clarissa's arm and jumped through the portal with her. He turned around to go back for Zedekiah.

On the other side Zedekiah took one last look at the failed time machine as a laser blast smashed the dome completely and poly-plastic glass began to rain down upon him; he prepared to jump... but there was nothing to jump through.

The portal had closed!

Meanwhile, on the other side of the void Geraldine struggled with the vortex machine, "It's failed," she said.

"Get it back," Clarissa yanked off her helmet.

"I'm trying to but the central processor's offline."

"Then get it back online."

"Let me get me my tools and take a look."

It took twelve hours for Geraldine and Zeno to strip down the machine and figure out what to do. None of the scrap components that they used to replace the processor worked, so eventually they soldered the original part carefully back together, hoping that it would do.

"This isn't a good repair; it could fail again at any moment and after twelve hours you can't realistically expect Zedekiah to be there," Geraldine said.

"Nevertheless I want to go."

"But it's very risky."

"I must see for myself."

Clarissa suited up and stepped through the portal. It was immediately obvious that there was no need to stay. The bio-habitation area was completely devastated and the time machine had gone. There was no sign of Zedekiah. Why should there be? The death sentence would have been carried out straight away.

She walked back through the portal just before the vortex machine failed again. Clarissa shook her head; everyone was devastated; they stood in Zedekiah's cave, not able to take in the fact that he was never coming back.

"What are we going to do now?" Annie asked.

For once in her life Rosie had nothing to say.

Bunion, breathing deeply, walked into the kitchen and started clattering pans. In some peculiar way it was comforting to be subjected to his familiar if dubious culinary skills, even if they had no clue as to the origins of the soup he served up to them, or the green meat loaf, or the brown mash for that matter.

They sat around the black stone table eating in silence until finally Clarissa said, "How much money do we have?"

"Two thousand quid plus what we started with," Josephine said.

"What? Where's all the money we made on Fettuccia?"

"It stayed on Fettuccia."

"How come?"

"They debited our bank account as we departed."

"They can't do that, that's robbery, that's against the law," Natter said.

"I told you that the Fettuccians make their own rules," Clarissa pointed out.

"They charged us a hundred thousand quid in exit tax, and then there were the stabling fees for the creatures that we had to leave behind, and the fines for the illegal activities that we carried on when we were on the planet," Josephine said.

"But all that money...."

"We did try to steal a time machine."

"Borrow it," Mr. Mystery said.

"What we did was against the law."

"We're outlaws aren't we?" Natter said.

"The Time Guardians see us that way."

"So what are we going to do now?"

"You can all stay here if you want to, this place has everything necessary to sustain your lives," Zeno said.

"What about you?" Geraldine asked. "What will you do now that Zedekiah is gone?"

"I shall continue his work."

"You don't have to, you're not his slave."

"I choose to, it is a noble undertaking, I wish to use my existence for good."

"Couldn't you have another stab at building a time machine so that we could travel back to before we became fugitives and tell ourselves not to do it?" Jerry asked.

"I don't have the right materials, I can't do the tests, and I've already used all the good components," Geraldine said.

"Even if we could, it would be too risky with the Time Guardians always on our backs," Jerome added.

Everyone was quiet for a moment as if they were not sure what to say.

Jerome looked up and sighed, "Let's face it we're in a mess. If we leave here the Time Guardians will find us, but if we stay we can't work, we can't make any money and we did it all for nothing because we still don't have a time machine."

"We're worse off than when we started," Rosie said.

"There must be something we can do," Natter said.

"I'll never get my wife out of prison," Grumpus sighed.

The comm. bleeped and Zeno, who wasn't eating anything anyway, got up to answer it.

"The Time Guardians must have some sophisticated technology if they could detect and respond to us so quickly," Grumpus observed.

"Unfortunately they are keeping it all to themselves," Mr. Mystery said.

"If we want to find mankind's lost knowledge, the Time Guardian's data base would be a good place to look."

"That would be far too dangerous," Clarissa said.

Zeno came back to the table, "Geraldine would you please assist me? I need to repair the vortex machine; I have just received information from the Keepers of Knowledge about an archaeological site that has been discovered in the desert of Avia on Karmos in the Polmic system. They say that the site is technologically rich and they need Zedekiah's expertise. He taught me everything he knew; I would like to go in his place."

"Karmos? Isn't that the planet that's supposed to be inhabited by giant, fire breathing dogs?"

"That's right, it's said that they can detect your scent from a thousand miles away."

"I'd like to help but I'm not sure that it'll be possible to repair the vortex machine," Geraldine said.

It took three days to confirm her suspicions. They tried everything, but the central processor was dead and it was going to take lot more than a few blobs of solder to resurrect it.

"Sorry, I wish I could have done more."

"I know you did your best," Zeno told her.

"But you won't be able to get to your archaeological site."

"Well I don't know about you," Natter said, "but I was getting cabin fever here anyway."

"You mean you think we ought to take him there?" Froggie asked.

"We don't all have to go; I could pilot Zeno to Karmos by myself; there's no need for anyone else to take risks."

"But Geraldine, if something goes wrong and you don't come back we'll lose our spaceship and be condemned to live on this airless rock for the rest of our lives whether we like it or not."

"And there's no escape route if the Time Guardians ever catch up with us," Grumpus said.

"So are you saying that you don't want me to go?"

"Well I for one was thinking of coming along for the ride," Natter said.

"Me too," Froggie said.

"How risky is it?" Rosie asked.

"The Polmic system has not been inhabited for four hundred years," Zeno said.

"So it isn't exactly in the thick of things?"

"The Keepers of Knowledge place great value on their secrecy."

"It should be possible to chart a route that would keep us well clear of any inhabited systems," Josephine said.

"So what's it to be? Do we go off into the totally exciting unknown? Or do we or do we sit here doing nothing for the rest of our lives?" Natter asked.

Even Clarissa had to admit that staying put was a dead end. Rosie had a few misgivings but in the absence of anything better to do they all voted to go to Karmos.

"Do you have to contact them to let them know that you're coming?" Annie asked.

"No, quantum communications can be traced, the message that I just received has probably been bouncing around the galaxy for several months."

There was a lot to do. Geraldine double-checked all the ship's systems, making sure that the Genghis Khan was thoroughly space worthy after the Time Guardian's attack, while Josephine worked out a route that took them around the Prion System, through the Hibiscus Nebula and past the Gideon sector, all of which were thought to be uninhabited. The others gathered supplies and refueled the craft.

The journey took several weeks. Time dragged. Natter told jokes while Bunion tried out some ideas for recipes that he got from the ship's database. The problem was that he only had half the ingredients, so at best his efforts were only half successful.

Geraldine ran some overdue diagnostic routines and Mr. Mystery and Josephine tried to design ways of cloaking the Genghis Khan in order to make it undetectable by the Time Guardians, but they weren't very successful.

Clarissa and all the others used the time to work on a completely new performance. Lydia suggested that they could tell a story instead of presenting a series of disjointed acts and Clarissa agreed that it should be something different from anything they had done before.

Rosie insisted that there should be singing in it and Annie said there would have to be musical accompaniment. Froggie maintained that it should be funny and Jerome decided that there should be dancing and acrobatics. They talked and argued all the way to Karmos.

Zeno watched them when he wasn't helping Geraldine. He had programming which was supposed to help him with relationships, but human behavior was hard to quantify. From the way they kept arguing there were times when it was hard to tell if these humans even liked each other; and determining which relationships had romantic undertones was harder still.

It was evident that Bunion spent a lot of time gazing quietly at Lydia and that Rosie spent sixty percent more time talking to Natter than to her sister. Interestingly they all treated Zeno like a full, sentient human, like one of themselves; even though he wasn't. When no one was paying attention he made a tiny hole in a minor line in the Genghis Khan's hydraulic system.

Full humans had free will but he didn't; all he had was programming.

Chapter 6.

Finally they arrived.

Karmos had reverted to desert. It had been terra-formed in the early days and farmers had settled there but they didn't stay because it was too hard to make a living. The few that didn't leave tried their hands at manufacturing, which was quite successful for a while until transport costs eventually made it uneconomical.

After that the research laboratories were established away from the immediate gaze of the Time Guardians. In reality though, there was no new research, just the putting of old knowledge to use in new ways. They prospered for a while but eventually faded away. In the end the delicate ecosystem disintegrated and the deserts expanded until there was nothing left and the desolate planet was abandoned.

The Genghis Khan entered orbit.

"Let me hail them, I know the frequency and the passwords," Zeno said.

Geraldine gave him the comm. and he transmitted the security protocols. There was a pause and then it lit up, "Confirmation Alpha one, what is your personal code?"

"Zeno 7235/PR7."

"This is Karmos Station; Zeno this is Aristotle, you should have been here two weeks ago, have you had problems?"

"We lost Zedekiah; he was captured by the Time Guardians."

"Oh… I'm sorry, Zedekiah was a good man."

"The vortex machine failed and is beyond repair so I came in a spaceship."

"What is the identity of the craft you are using?"

"This is the Genghis Khan; it is a Mark Three, Lightening Wing."

"And how did you obtain it?"

"Zedekiah's friends own it, when they realized my predicament they volunteered to bring me here."

"You mean there are people on board with you?"

"They were Zedekiah's friends, he trusted them and they themselves are fugitives from the Time Guardians."

"Nevertheless this is a serious violation of security protocols."

"I am sorry I did not know what else to do."

Clarissa took over the comm. "This is Clarissa Clarke, proprietor of Clarissa Clarke's Traveling World of Wonders…."

"Entertainers?"

"Zedekiah Banes saved our lives."

"Clarissa Clarke you said?"

"That's right."

"We intercepted a report from Zertza about you from a Sheriff Raspberry."

"Is there anyone in the galaxy who didn't intercept that message?"

"It was on an open channel; there was no attempt to encrypt it."

"We are requesting permission to land," Zeno said.

"That will not be possible, I'm sorry."

Geraldine took the comm. "I'm uploading the blueprints for the construction of a time machine; if you study them you will see that they are genuine."

There was a pause and then a deep breath and then another pause.

"Where did you get these?" Aristotle asked.

Geraldine told him the story of the cookbook.

"Why weren't you decontaminated?" there was a different voice over the comm.

"We came close; if it wasn't for Zedekiah we wouldn't have survived."

"How do we know that these plans work?"

"They don't, we built the machine but couldn't test it, the general principles are good but there need to be more refinements."

"Who am I speaking to?"

"I'm Geraldine the ship's engineer, and who are you?"

"You may call me Plato," Plato said.

The comm. went quiet for a while.

"This is Archimedes," another voice said, "Zeno can you vouch for these people?"

"Yes I can," Zeno told him.

There were muffled voices at the end of the comm. "We have decided that we can allow you to drop Zeno off at the co-ordinates that we shall upload to you. Unfortunately we cannot invite you to share our hospitality."

"We understand, we know you have to be very careful."

Geraldine entered the co-ordinates into the flight computer and as soon as she was ready she took the Genghis Khan down into the atmosphere.

"Hmm..." she commented.

"What's wrong?" Clarissa asked.

"Something doesn't feel quite right, the wings don't seem to be feathering normally." She ran through the readouts on the monitor, "It's the hydraulics, they're not quite...."

The spacecraft began to shake.

"What's wrong?"

"We're going too fast; I'm losing control."

"What's happening? This isn't normal," Rosie cried.

"I can't...."

The Genghis Khan juddered wildly for a few seconds and then it turned into a steep dive. Almost instantly the hull began to glow red.

Annie screamed.

A loud groaning noise came from the back of the fuselage.

Rosie screamed, "We're all going to die!"

"It's a bit too soon to say that," Geraldine fired the maneuvering thrusters to level out the nose and regain some control.

"I'll have nightmares about this if I survive," Grumpus said.

The spacecraft juddered and rolled, "I don't want to die this way," Rosie wailed.

"Will you all just shut up and let me concentrate?" Geraldine started the jet engines and put them in reverse to slow the craft down.

"Is there anything I can do?" Josephine asked.

"Just keep everyone quiet."

"The hull temperature is at critical."

"See? We are going to die," Annie shouted.

"Let Geraldine do her work," Natter yelled.

"Yea, she'll get us out of this," Jerry cried.

"Everybody, shut up and let me concentrate," Geraldine used the booster rockets to adjust the angle of the dive.

"I feel sick," Froggie moaned.

"We're losing altitude really fast," Josephine warned.

"That's obvious," Jerry said.

"I'm really hot," Rosie complained.

"So am I," Annie said.

"We're going to burn up aren't we?"

"Shall I send out a mayday?" Clarissa asked.

"We're too low; this planet has no magnetosphere," Zeno told her.

"What's he talking about?" Rosie asked.

"The atmosphere won't carry radio signals except in line of sight but the rendezvous point is half a continent away, over the horizon."

By some miracle Geraldine managed to level off the flight; she breathed a sigh of relief and headed the vehicle towards the all important horizon.

But it didn't last long.

"The undercarriage is stuck, I'll have to wind it down manually, Josephine you take the controls, just keep her as stable as you can."

"I can't, I don't know how to fly."

"I'll do it," Grumpus offered.

"I need you with me," Geraldine said.

"I'll try," Lydia volunteered.

"Have you had flight training?"

"Our planet was at war; we all had to spend time in the simulators."

Geraldine threw off her seatbelt and squeezed herself down the emergency hatch, Grumpus followed behind her. They ran through the lower decks and into the cargo hold where they heaved several large packing cases out of the way and yanked the cover off the mechanical wheel housing.

As the hull door hatches opened, a blast of hot air rushed in. They had to crank the landing gear down manually and for once in her life Geraldine was grateful for her immense strength.

"The drag from the wheels is slowing us down," Lydia said over the comm.

"Good," Geraldine said.

They could see the ground now, a rocky, dusty plateau coming up towards them fast. As soon as the wheels locked Geraldine raced back up to the bridge and took over the pilot's seat. She used the rocket boosters to bring up the right wing tip, which was threatening to smash into the ground.

Now it was a matter of keeping the craft as straight as possible and doing anything she could to control the speed. An outcrop of rocks appeared in front of them and Geraldine fired the nose thrusters to gain enough height to avoid them.

The spacecraft juddered through pockets of hot air.

"Crash positions," Geraldine shouted.

They all clutched each other's hands and bowed their heads in silent prayer. She fired the rocket boosters one last time straight downwards to give them as gentle a landing as possible.

The ungainly craft hit the ground, lurched and rebounded back up into the air and then slammed back down again only to bounce once more. Finally the space plane made a shaky touchdown and the jet engines reversed, roaring loudly. The ground was very bumpy and the Genghis Khan creaked and groaned and shook and banged all the way to a halt.

There was a breathless silence.

Then Geraldine heaved a giant sigh, "Abandon ship," she shouted.

"But why, everything's all right now?" Rosie asked.

"Standard procedure in case of fire; come on let's stick to the rules."

Everyone unbuckled and got shakily out of their seats.

Josephine checked the instrument panel in front of her, "It's hot outside but the air's breathable and I don't detect anything harmful."

Clarissa opened the door and let down the steps. Scorching air blasted onto her face but nevertheless she led the way down and would have kissed the ground if she hadn't been worried that it would burn her lips.

"How far short of the co-ordinates are we?" she called back to Josephine.

"About eighty-five miles."

They all blinked at the brightness of the sun as one by one they followed each other out of the spaceship. Geraldine stepped out last to the applause of all the others.

"You saved our lives," Rosie said.

"Don't be too quick to praise me, I was the one who was responsible for the ship's maintenance, I obviously didn't do my job good enough."

"Can the spaceship be repaired?" Clarissa asked.

Geraldine checked the outer hull, "If it's only the hydraulics, all I have to do is track down the leak but..." she spotted something, "everybody move away, move away from the spacecraft now!"

"What is it?"

"Jet fuel leak; it's hydrocarbon based and in this heat it could ignite at any second!"

They ran away from the stricken ship and huddled, panting behind a big rock.

"I can go and get help, I do not suffer from the heat like humans do and I can travel fast," Zeno said.

"Y..." was all Clarissa got to say before Bunion interrupted her.

"We go together," he said.

"Bunion?"

"We stick together," he was so insistent that Clarissa, who wasn't accustomed to hearing Bunion's opinion on anything, let his decision stand. "We'll need water and supplies," Bunion headed back into the dangerous spaceship.

The open rocky plane sizzled under their feet. "There you go," Natter adjusted Rosie and Annie's backpack for about the seventh time.

"I'm glad we didn't die," Rosie said.

"Me too," Annie said.

"Strange isn't it?"

"Makes you think."

"Life is... you know."

"Yea."

"I was going to say precious."

"Absolutely."

"Despite its disadvantages."

Grumpus led the way without a word. He had taken over the leadership of the expedition. He didn't have to explain himself to Clarissa who would not have had the strength to lead an overland trek; she knew that he had done it to take the pressure off her.

"What a time to have an accident, as if we didn't have enough to worry about," Lydia told Bunion as they trailed at the rear of the line.

"It wasn't an accident," Bunion said.

"What? What do you mean?"

"It was Zeno."

"You think so? Why would you say that?"

"Think about it. Why did the main component in the vortex machine fail just at the most crucial moment? Why did the time machine almost work but not quite despite all Geraldine's efforts? And why did the spaceship crash despite the fact that Geraldine had spent two weeks of flight time checking all the systems over and over again? Too many coincidences."

"And you think Zeno is involved?"

"Yes."

"Can't we just, you know, switch him off?"

"If we do they'll know."

"They?"

"His masters, the Time Guardians."

"Do you think we're in danger?"

"He's going to betray the Keepers of Knowledge to the Time Guardians and he's using us to do it."

"What can we do about it?"

"Warn them."

"But if that's true why did he sabotage the spaceship? He could have killed himself."

"Because Bridefield regards us as dangerous."

"Us?" Lydia asked.

"We've already made two attempts to get hold of a time machine when most people are too scared to even think about making one. Just imagine what would have happened if we had succeeded; others might have found the courage to copy us and that would have been a serious challenge to Bridefield's power."

"I hadn't thought... that puts us in a lot of danger."

"Yes," Bunion said.

They struggled on as the sun scorched the landscape out of a brassy sky, and the wind blew hotter than a hairdryer, and giant tumbleweed scudded across their path. They tried to push forward but had to take frequent rests wherever they found the shade of a rock.

As they walked Froggie took it upon himself to run around everyone making sure they had enough to drink; Natter and Jerry helped the women to keep up. Jerome helped Mr. Mystery, whose movements were very slow because of a malfunction in his artificial brain owing to the heat. He didn't talk because he needed to route all the processing power he had to his legs. The trek across that shimmering crucible seemed to last forever.

The evening didn't come for two standard days by which time Clarissa was seriously wondering why she had allowed Bunion to persuade her into this. Once the sun's strength had left the sky it became easier to walk, fireflies swarmed through the air producing their own light show against the backdrop of the slowly setting sun.

"Are we nearly there yet?" Annie asked.

"We've only traveled about twenty-six miles," Josephine told her.

"What? That's only thirteen miles a day. That's got to be wrong after all that effort we put in," Rosie said.

"Now that it's cooler we should be able to walk a lot faster."

"Clarissa can't go any faster, she's worn out."

"I was thinking I could carry her," Geraldine said.

"No, no I'll manage, don't worry about me."

"Sorry Clarissa you'll slow us down, let Geraldine carry you; Zeno can help."

"Of course I'll be happy to," Zeno said.

Grumpus was now able to lead them through the scrubby landscape at a strict march. Karmos's six moons appeared one by one, illuminating the scene. The troupe rested only as much as they had to before Grumpus marched them onwards through the cold night.

"Did you see that?" Lydia asked Bunion as she pointed downwards. Big plants with round, leathery leaves were slowly pushing their way up above the ground looking like upturned sombreros. "They must have been hiding from the heat of the sun."

Eventually they were too tired to go any further and there was no choice but to huddle together on a piece of sandy ground and try to get some rest.

"I'll stand guard," Zeno said.

"Is that wise?" Lydia whispered to Bunion.

"He won't let anything happen to us until we have led him to the Keepers of Knowledge."

Very quickly every one of them fell into an exhausted sleep. The air got colder and white frost glittered in the starlight.

Grumpus was the first one to wake up; he and Zeno sat on a rock with the night scope binoculars watching the horizon.

Clarissa woke up shivering; her old bones could not take the cold of night; she looked up, "Grumpus have you been awake all this time?"

"We're being watched," Grumpus pointed to a distant ridge.

"By whom?"

"I don't know; they're too far away."

"What are we going to do?"

"Move on," Grumpus said. "Get everybody up."

The temperature dropped further but no one except Clarissa felt the cold because they were traveling at speed now.

"Do we have to go through those hills; isn't there another way round?" Clarissa asked Josephine.

"It's a chain of mountains; it runs many miles in both directions."

"I can't see anything; are you sure there's someone following us?" Natter asked.

"Someone or something," Grumpus gave him the binoculars and pointed to the distant plain. For a minute Natter couldn't see anything unusual but then he spotted a shape moving in the far distance.

"Wow, whatever it is must be big if we can see it from this far away."

"It's matching our speed."

They pressed forward faster than ever, willing their tired bodies on and on. By the time the land began to rise, two of the moons had waned and the moonlight shadows were longer.

"What if there's more of those things in the mountains and we can't see them? We could be walking into a trap," Natter said.

No one answered him; they didn't have the energy to worry about it. Finally Grumpus stopped at the entrance of a cave. He and Lydia and Bunion checked out the surroundings.

"Some of those strange plants seem to have been nibbled," Lydia said.

"Look at this," Bunion pointed down to a huge, long depression in the dust.

"Is that a footprint?"

"Yes," Bunion said.

"Do you think it belongs to one of those fire-breathing dogs?"

"That's more like a really big man's footprint than a dog's."

"You mean there could be other giant creatures on this planet?"

"I don't know," Bunion said.

They checked out the cave using the night vision binoculars; it was sheltered from the wind and commanded a good view of the plain below.

"What's this?" Josephine held up long, green strands of hair in her hand.

Grumpus checked it out, "Animal hair and it's arranged like a nest."

"A big nest for a big animal," Josephine remarked.

"It stinks," Lydia said.

"I don't care what it's like, I'm so cold," Clarissa shivered.

Geraldine gently lowered her down into the fur and warmed her up with her great bear arms; the others all huddled in around her.

"Let's hope that whatever made that bed doesn't come back to claim it," Jerome said.

Grumpus settled himself down at the edge of the cave to keep watch.

Bunion climbed out and sat beside him, "You too Grumpus," he told him.

"Eh?"

"I'll stay here with Zeno; if there's trouble I'll wake you."

Grumpus slipped into the cave and Annie and Rosie moved aside and made room for him so he could get some warmth. They all fell instantly to sleep. Grumpus awoke a few hours later and took over the watch from Bunion so that he could have some rest. When the others finally woke up, they ate their supplies hungrily before climbing out into the cutting wind.

Their stalker hadn't moved.

They climbed upwards over the unstable ground and as they got higher the wind got even stronger. Two more moons slowly disappeared over the distant horizon.

"That thing's still matching our speed," Grumpus handed Bunion the binoculars, "you and me; how about we hide ourselves and ambush it?"

"Not yet," Bunion said.

Geraldine had rigged up a hammock with her jacket and Zeno's shirt as it was the easiest and most comfortable way to carry Clarissa; Grumpus and Bunion helped her.

The wind eased off a little when they reached the top of the hill; the last two moons were starting to set and the sky before them was getting lighter as dawn approached. Now they faced a climb down the other side of the mountain.

"Are we nearly there now?" Rosie and Annie asked.

"Ten more miles; we should be in line of sight though."

Josephine pulled a little portable radio out of her backpack and switched it on. "This is the crew of the Genghis Khan calling Aristotle and Plato do you read us?" The radio was silent, "This is the Genghis Khan, we had a mayday; we require assistance." There was no sound, not even a crackle.

"Are you sure it's working?"

"Yes I'm sure."

"Maybe we need to get a bit nearer."

"There could be something blocking the signal."

"We should keep moving," Clarissa said.

"Once we start climbing down the other side of mountain we won't be able to see whatever it is that's following us," Grumpus said.

"I'll stay; you take care of the others," Bunion said.

Grumpus nodded and handed him the binoculars.

Sliding down the gravel slopes was harder than climbing up; there was the constant danger of falling and breaking a bone. Jerome whose extra long legs proved to be very useful in getting across the rough ground and Jerry, whose third leg allowed him to keep stable, helped the others over the most treacherous places.

Meanwhile Bunion sat patiently behind a rock watching the movement of the distant creature as it ran four legged across the plain. Sometimes it stopped and grazed momentarily on a patch of the leathery plants, or it licked the frost off them with its long tongue. But it was soon bounding up the steep slope towards him, covering in minutes the ground that had taken them many hours of hard struggle to pass over.

The creature would have leapt straight over the rock that Bunion had been hiding behind if he had not moved out and stood in front of it. The monstrous animal stopped short and reared up onto its hind legs almost three times as high as the little man. Its wispy green hair blew freely in the wind.

Bunion looked up into its intelligent eyes. The two beings stood face-to-face, trying to decide what to make of each other.

Bunion looked at the creature's buckteeth and smiled, "You're a herbivore," he said.

The creature smiled back, "That assumption is correct."

"You must be Plato."

"Actually I'm Aristotle."

Bunion held out his hand and Aristotle bent down to shake it.

Meanwhile further down the slope a circle of rock like a rainbow rose out of the ground in front of them.

"What's that?" Froggie asked.

"It has to be manmade," Natter said.

"I think it's an entrance," Josephine commented.

"It's an archway not a door," Rosie told her.

"An entrance to what?" Annie asked.

"Maybe we shouldn't go through it; maybe it's a trap."

"I'll check it out," Grumpus said.

Aristotle and Bunion watched them from high up on the hill. Aristotle apologized, "We are sorry we had to put you through all this."

"You didn't know who we were," Bunion told him.

"The Time Guardians resort to many tricks."

"I know."

"We had to make sure you weren't being followed."

"You didn't make the crash happen."

"We needed to make certain that you didn't stage it so that we would feel sorry for you and come out of our hiding place to rescue you."

"Zeno caused it."

"The mechanical man?"

"Yes."

"But when our brothers restored him they thoroughly checked him out; they do not normally make mistakes."

"He also caused the vortex machine to fail, leading to Zedekiah's capture."

"Do you have evidence for what you are saying?"

"Zeno is not human, he cannot deny his programming."

"I am more inclined to think that it is you people that constitute a danger to us, not Zeno."

"We won't betray you," Bunion said.

"How can we be sure of that?"

"You can't be sure but nevertheless it is true."

"Zeno should not have brought you here, it is against procedure."

"It would be a dangerous mistake to trust him."

Aristotle's pointed ears pricked up; he could hear an ultrasonic message, "Plato says that your friends have been cleared through the deep scanner; here climb on my back, it is not far."

Meanwhile Annie shivered in the freezing wind, "What happens now?" she asked.

Suddenly a long, thin chink of light appeared in an outcrop of black rock nearby. As it became wider it revealed a very tall doorway, "Stay outside," Grumpus ordered.

"But we're so cold," Rosie moaned.

"Let me check it out first."

He walked through the doorway into a white walled corridor; in front of him stood a giant, green, furry creature at least two feet taller than Jerome.

"I am Plato," the creature said, "we have been waiting for your arrival."

"One of your kind has been following us," Grumpus said.

"To protect you; we mean you no harm."

At that point Aristotle arrived and set Bunion gently down onto the ground. Bunion introduced him, "This is Aristotle." He told everyone to come inside.

"Are you the Keepers of Knowledge?" Josephine asked.

"How do you know abou...," suddenly Aristotle stopped in his tracks, "are you a Josephine? How is this possible?"

"I don't know."

"But your kind died out seven hundred years ago."

"I don't know how or why I got here."

Aristotle ran his green, furry hand over Josephine's skull, "But you are a Josephine," he said.

"Yes I believe I am."

"What discoveries have you made that you wanted Zedekiah's help with?" Zeno asked.

"You must be the mechanical man."

"You've never met him before?" Clarissa asked.

"We were only informed of his existence when his services were deemed to be useful."

"So what do you want me to do?" Zeno asked.

"This planet has proven to be rich in technological finds; we need Zedekiah's expertise," Plato said.

"I carry much of Zedekiah's knowledge with me, where is the excavation site?"

"We will tell you everything in good time, but first, you must all be hungry, come let us get you warm and serve you some dinner. And perhaps afterwards if you would allow us Josephine we would dearly love to scan your pseudo-brain, we never expected to see one of your kind in this century."

They were introduced to Archimedes who served them from a big bowl of pasta that was flavored with a little dried tomato.

"Interesting," Plato stared at Froggie.

"What do you mean by that?" Froggie speared some pasta onto his fork, grateful for something to warm his insides.

"Karmos is where some of your ancestor's DNA was altered in order to adapt your body for its specific purpose. You are an amphibian Mr. Froggie; you were created for boggy worlds."

"I like wet places," Froggie said.

He looked at Geraldine, "And you were created for agricultural work, you were also modified here."

"And what about me, is this where I was adapted?" Jerome asked.

"Yes I believe it was; you were designed to live in low gravity."

"What about you? Are you human or something else?"

"We are humans but we are adapted to survive on this planet."

"People call you dogs; they say you breathe fire."

"And we let them think it, but only our bodies are changed, our minds and hearts are as human as any of you."

"But if we were all created for specific purposes how come we feel like freaks?" Natter asked.

"Because people treat you like freaks. They think of you as too different to have anything in common with original humans," Plato said.

"You could say that all the experiments that were carried out on this planet failed, not because they were not useful or that there was something wrong with the science, but because instead of welcoming the adaptations, mankind took them as an excuse for division," Aristotle added.

"My ancestors didn't come from here, my parents were ordinary humans, I remember them, I was kidnapped when I was a kid and turned into this," Jerry pointed to his strange pelvis and third leg. "They put me through some horrible tests and then told me that the experiment was a failure. They gave me money and set me free but I didn't know where I was and I couldn't remember where I came from. If it wasn't for Clarissa I don't know what would have become of me."

"Unfortunately there is such a thirst for new knowledge that a seedy underground has grown up and much money is being made by unscrupulous people. The human race craves new technology but people are afraid to do research openly," Plato told him.

"I like being an amphibian," Froggie said.

"So am I right in assuming that your purpose is to gather as much knowledge as possible in order to preserve it for future generations?" Josephine asked.

"Yes," Plato said.

"And for that the Time Guardians want to destroy you?"

"While we are known only as fire breathing dogs our identity is safe."

"Why did you choose to hide out on Karmos?"

"Because it is isolated and technologically rich."

"Will you help us to repair our spaceship?" asked Geraldine. "While we're here we're putting you in danger."

"If you leave you will eventually be captured and the Time Guardians will force you to tell them everything you know."

"We wouldn't betray you," Clarissa said.

"You would have no choice."

"The Time Guardians can read minds," Aristotle told her.

"So what do you want us to do? Do you want us to stay here?"

"It would not be possible for you to do that, we do not have suitable food for you."

"So we can't stay but you don't want us to go?"

"I am saying that we have a problem," Aristotle said.

"We don't want to be your prisoners."

"If we left where would we go?" Rosie asked.

"You will be at risk as soon as you pass anywhere near an inhabited world."

"So you're saying that we can't stay here and we can't leave; what do you expect us to do, commit suicide?"

"We'll have to keep to the uninhabited worlds," Annie said.

"We can't do that, how are we going to earn money? And how are we going to get food?" Froggie asked.

"I have a wife and fifteen children, how am I going to provide for them?" Jerome asked.

"My wife is still in prison," Grumpus said.

"Well there must be something…" Annie said.

"You tell me what," Froggie shouted.

"There's no need to shout at Annie, it's not her fault," Natter barked.

"I wasn't shouting, I was asking her a civilized question."

"Both of you stop shouting," Jerry shouted.

Bunion had been tucking eagerly into his pasta while listening to the pointless argument. Something moved at the edge of his vision.

"You're overreacting."

"They let us wander for days in that desert without lifting a finger to help; anything could have happened to us," Rosie said.

"They had to check us out, we could have been Time Guardians in disguise," Jerome said.

"Will you all just shut up; this conversation is not constructive," Jerry shouted.

Lydia noticed that three people had left the table and that there was still pasta on Bunion's plate.

Zeno stood outside in the light of the rising sun; he turned around when he heard Bunion coming.

"How much do they know?" Bunion said.

"Everything; the walls of the rocky chamber are shielded from quantum signals but as soon as I was sure that those creatures were Keepers of Knowledge, my programming forced me to look for a way to slip outside and send the signal."

"How long till the Time Guardians get here?"

"Twenty-six minutes and thirteen seconds; please you must deactivate me now, before I do any more harm."

Bunion pressed a button on Zeno's back and powered him down. He turned around to see Aristotle, who must have followed him as he left the dinner table, standing in the doorway.

"We must evacuate," Aristotle lifted Zeno onto his shoulder and hurried inside. He walked up to the dinner table and announced, "Zeno has betrayed us and the Time Guardians are on their way."

"But what are we going to do? We can't evacuate, our spacecraft needs repairs," Geraldine said.

"Follow me; we are well prepared for emergencies."

Bunion grabbed his plate of pasta and followed the others down a slope to a huge underground cave where a beautiful, metallic spaceship stood before them.

"Wow," Geraldine gasped.

"You want us to have that? But it's too much," Clarissa said.

"It is the only way; you must leave quickly."

"Treat her carefully; she is my favorite," Plato said.

The door of the craft opened and they hurried up the ramp.

"I don't know how to pilot this ship," Geraldine said.

"She is already programmed, hurry you do not have much time."

"Where are we going to go?" Annie asked.

"You may go wherever you wish but keep away from inhabited planets."

"Have we got to take him?" Rosie pointed to Zeno.

"Yes," Aristotle said.

"What will you and Plato and Archimedes do?"

"We have our own plans; it is best that you do not know them; now go and let us pray that we all survive until we meet again."

The roof doors of the hangar opened and everyone rushed to buckle themselves into the wide seats on the tall bridge. The sleek craft fired its rocket boosters and the spaceship shot into the air so fast that they all blacked out.

When they woke up, Karmos was no longer on the scopes. Geraldine looked down at the control monitor and saw that the graviton engines had automatically engaged, "The ship is taking us to the Andreas Expanse," she said.

"Do you think the Time Guardians will follow us?" Rosie asked.

"There's nothing on the scopes at the moment but it will be hours before we can be certain," Geraldine said.

With the spacecraft on autopilot, most of a warm meal inside them and the temperature in the cabin a little higher than they were used to, the exhausted crew, one and all, fell asleep.

The living areas of the spaceship had been designed for tall bodies with large fingers, which suited Geraldine just fine. The fuel cells were full, the ship was clean and shining, and the beds were big and soft and comfortable. There was just one problem, the only food on board was Karmosian; it was green and fibrous and totally inedible. There was nothing at all for regular humans to eat. Bunion examined the stuff closely but the truth was that no amount of pan clattering would make it fit to be eaten.

"If we go to the Andreas Expanse, we'll starve to death," Geraldine warned them.

"What are we going to do?" Annie asked.

"We'll have to find an uninhabited planet that grows food," Natter said.

"What's the nearest Earthlike planet you can find?"

Josephine searched the database, "There's one called Granary."

"That sounds hopeful," Natter said.

"Perhaps not, it says here that people tried to colonize it but conditions were too hostile and they failed."

"So there's not likely to be any food on it?"

"Huge green worms that feed on some weird type of cabbage is about all that's there."

"Anything else?" Geraldine asked.

"There's one here called Marmarand, it was an old agricultural planet that had many inhabitants until there was a gold rush. It says here that the whole population, one and all, moved to the Rings of Circa, hoping to make their fortunes in prospecting."

"So some food might still grow there?" Jerome said hopefully.

"Are you sure it's uninhabited?" Clarissa asked.

"We won't be able to tell until we get into orbit."

"How far away is it?"

"About three days."

"Three days without food?" Jerry groaned.

Josephine nodded.

"Ohhhh," he said.

They drank water, they rested, they argued, they rehearsed their ideas for the new show even though they could see no prospect of ever performing it. They tried to ignore the hunger pangs that plagued them when they were awake and interrupted their sleep. Then they argued again. Particularly they argued about Zeno.

"He betrayed us," Rosie said.

"He couldn't help it," Annie told her.

"I don't know why we don't just throw him out of an air lock."

"You can't do that he's a... a person."

"He's not a person, he's a machine; he's just programmed to make you think he's a person."

"You don't know that, how do you know that he doesn't have thoughts and feelings like ours?"

"You want me to forgive him just like that don't you? You'll be asking me to switch him back on again next."

"You don't understand...."

"I thought he was my friend," Geraldine heaved a deep sigh.

"It's his fault that we're all hungry," Froggie complained.

"We should leave him powered off, he isn't safe," Clarissa said.

Everyone nodded; that was one thing they all agreed about.

Chapter 7

The computer database was wrong; the old agricultural planet was inhabited. It was pointless even entering the solar system because they could see on the long-range scanners that there was traffic between at least three of the local planets.

They turned away.

Josephine searched again.

"Couldn't we just buy some food and move on?"

"We can't use our thumbprints or we'll be traced, and we don't have any cash," Clarissa said.

"We could put on a performance; sing for our supper."

"What if someone found out who we are? They might betray us to the Time Guardians."

"I'd take the risk; it's better than starving to death."

"So where can we go?" Rosie asked.

"There's a planet closely circling a red dwarf star; people used to live that far out but they don't any more. It's called Aqua; it should still be home to the basic carbon based life forms; seaweed, mollusks and fish," Josephine said.

"I could eat fish," Natter said.

"It's a water world."

"No land at all?"

"None at all."

"Well that won't necessarily be a problem," Froggie said.

"How far is it?" Jerome asked.

"Six days."

Everybody groaned.

"There must be somewhere nearer."

"I can't find anything."

"Are you sure your information is correct?" Mr. Mystery asked.

"I'm not sure of anything."

"Can you make the ship go any faster?"

"We've been traveling at maximum speed already."

"Six more days? How are we going to survive?"

It wasn't a problem for Mr. Mystery. He set the timer on his artificial brain and went to sleep. Everyone else had to cope. Grumpus was used to meditating before a performance but now he did it in earnest. Clarissa found spare bedding and a sewing kit. She started making costumes for the new show.

The only person that was happy with the situation was Rosie. "We should have done something about our figure a long time ago," she told Annie as she admired their body in the mirror.

Bunion eyed up the green stuff that the Karmosian humans ate, it had to be carbon based; he started boiling it. Then he decided to examine the bed linen that Clarissa was cutting up. It was made out of something organic so he shredded the off cuts and boiled them; then after hours of cooking he mashed the two ingredients together and baked them in the oven. Josephine analyzed the result and said that it wouldn't actually kill them. It tasted terrible but no one complained; anything was better than the pain of hunger.

Rehearsing for the new show helped take their minds off things but they felt weak and miserable and they slept a lot.

As they approached Aqua Josephine began scanning for data, "Good news, there's no radio or quantum signals coming from anywhere in the whole of the solar system." As they approached the planet she could confirm that there were no orbiting satellites and that there was a breathable oxygen/nitrogen atmosphere.

"Are there any fish?" Froggie asked, "I can't wait to go fishing."

"Oh," Josephine said.

"What? What is it?"

"Well I read vegetation and fish and big floating islands of something organic and... I don't like to tell you this but there are humans on the islands, and there are also humans under the sea."

"Are you sure about the readings?" Clarissa asked.

"Humans don't live under the sea," Jerry said.

"They do here; the people living above the water seem to be loosely surrounded by the people living below the water."

"Do they use technology?"

"There is limited electricity generation, mostly it runs from wind generators above the water to some kind submerged sensor network but there's no heavy industry and there's not even much mechanical transport, most of the ships are wind powered. It's strange though because I can see a few hot spots with a much higher grade of technology. It's like they use it but they don't like it."

"So if we touched down in some remote area would they detect us?"

"It's hard to tell."

"If we could just go somewhere quiet for a few hours, I could do a little fishing and we'd all feel a lot better," Froggie said.

"Perhaps you could help me search for a good spot."

The poles were too cold and there were several trenches in the oceans that were too deep, but the submerged mountaintops seemed to be considered prime real estate and there appeared to be some jostling for position at those points. It took Froggie a while to find a place that was not too deep and not too populated.

"Land there," he said at last, "but don't go anywhere deeper or I won't be able to stand the water pressure."

Josephine checked out the site that he had chosen; it was shallow and isolated, "Yes, I think we could take a chance there."

"Are there plenty of fish?" Natter asked.

"Yes there seem to be; it's strange that no one lives there."

Geraldine piloted the ship down to the watery surface of the planet. The spaceship was not designed to be submerged but it could float. Once they had landed they opened the hatch door to a blue sky and a sparkling sea.

Froggie wasted no time; he checked the temperature of the water, "Yea that's fine," he said.

Geraldine fixed a waterproof camera and a light to a band on his head. During their long journey Clarissa had unraveled threads from some spare bed sheets and spent long, hungry hours fashioning a fishing net, she now packed it onto his back.

When he was ready Froggie sat for a while at the door of the spacecraft doing breathing exercises and opening and closing his gills.

"I wish we could help you," Annie said.

"I'll be okay; I'm looking forward to this."

He stood up tall on the rim of the spaceship and dived into the clear, tropical waters; he swam downwards in the green sunlight; suddenly joyful to be in the environment for which he had been bred.

The dark shape of the spaceship hung comfortingly above him and silver fish, delicately tinged with yellow flashed in front of him; he pushed most of the air out of his lungs and watched the glistening bubbles float upwards towards the sunlight. He pointed the head-cam at the different varieties of marine creatures so that Josephine could identify them and tell him if they were edible.

After a while he headed down further to investigate a school of brown, striped fish that were feeding on some yellow weed that grew out of the rocks of the underwater reef. A thin, electric blue fish streaked past him, and then a school of speckled fish passed in the opposite direction. The marine life down here was abundant. Froggie sat on a rock running the water in and out of his gills, just enjoying the peace.

Josephine checked the database and came back to him with a list of the creatures that could be eaten. They had all been in the terra-former's standard tool kit fifteen hundred years before and on this planet they had thrived.

Froggie flipped his webbed feet through the water speedily filling the net and when it was full he headed back to the surface.

"Poor creatures, I wish we didn't have to eat them," Annie said when Froggie brought his plunder on board.

Bunion took some fish out of the net and hurried off to the galley.

"I'll go back for more," Froggie said.

"Not until you've had something to eat," Clarissa told him.

They sat on big chairs around the shining, high table while Bunion served them large helpings of dry fried fish. No one ate a bite until Bunion was able to sit down too. No one spoke during the meal. No one left anything except stripped bones. Everyone sighed when they were finished.

Eventually Froggie stood up and prepared to make another dive.

He got to work catching as many fish as he could. He was nearly at the surface with another full net when he heard the scream. Maybe, scream was the wrong word; it was actually a high-pitched, fast clicking sound. It vibrated through Froggie's body and although he had never felt anything like it before he didn't doubt what it was.

He kicked the last few feet up to the surface and handed the net to Jerome. "I'll be back," he shouted before he disappeared back under the water and swam down into the twilight of the depths below the reef where the pressure hurt his ears.

The sound, which was now becoming more frantic, emanated from a little further along the ridge. He swam as quickly as he could, and then suddenly the clear water became murky and mud and weed swirled around in front of him.

All at once he touched something warm and living, a small, fat, webbed hand. Froggie grabbed hold of it and pulled it towards him. A child, a boy with smooth, gray skin and wide pleading eyes appeared out of the turgid water. He made clicking sounds with the roof of his mouth, which must have meant something, but Froggie had no idea what. All he knew was that the boy was terrified of some danger very close by. He grabbed the child's hand and pulled him up the side of the reef.

Suddenly a black shadow cut out the sunlight; for a moment it wasn't possible to see anything and then all at once massive, white teeth appeared out of the gloom as the cold, unblinking eyes of a conga eel of nightmare proportions stared down at them.

Josephine saw it on the monitor in front of her. Rosie screamed; Annie screamed; Geraldine screamed, "What are we going do?"

Froggie dragged the boy downwards; it was the only way they could go even though the pressure on his ears was painful and the water got colder and colder. The monster followed them down; it curled around, preparing to strike. Froggie frantically searched for some kind of cover. He pushed the child under a ledge, shielding him from the colossal fish as it snapped at a big chunk of brittle rock with its massive jaws. The sound the boy made began to change frequency, becoming lower in tone. There was something wrong but it took Froggie a few seconds to realize what it was.

He was drowning; the child was an air breather; he didn't have gills.

Froggie blew the remaining air from his lungs into the child's mouth but it wouldn't help much. If he didn't get the boy to the surface he would die.

"We've got to kill that conga," Josephine said.

"Lasers won't work under water," Geraldine said.

"Torpedoes," Josephine said.

"They're heat seekers and the eel is cold blooded, the warmest things down there are the two humans."

"Couldn't we just make a big bang and scare it away?"

"There'd be a shock wave."

Josephine radioed Froggie, "You need to get to open water."

He couldn't talk back but he made a circle with his finger and thumb in front of the camera to show that he understood.

He needed to take the boy upwards towards the sun and the fresh, life giving air. But the only route open to him was further downwards into the dark abyss and water pressures that his body was not designed for. But he had no choice; he stuck close to the rocks and pulled the child further and further downwards. And then suddenly they came to a deep cave; Froggie's head lamp shone on the jagged walls as he dragged the child inside.

"Froggie we won't be able to help you if you go deeper; you've got to find a way to get back up to the surface."

Froggie waved his hand downwards; his gesture meant that what she asked was impossible.

"We have torpedoes here but they're heat seekers."

Froggie made a circle with his finger and thumb.

"He wants us to use them," Geraldine said.

"You want me to fire them?" Josephine said.

Froggie made the, 'Okay,' sign again.

"They'll come straight for you."

Nevertheless Froggie made the sign again. The boy had gone limp in his arms; there wasn't much time.

"I'm arming the missile now, are you really sure you want me to fire?"

Froggie stared at the massive snout of the eel as it rammed the entrance to the cave. He made the sign.

"Do you think he knows what he's doing? Maybe he's oxygen deprived."

Froggie made the circle sign again; he seemed to want them to hurry up.

"I don't like this," Josephine said but Froggie's gestures were becoming insistent.

She fired the torpedo.

The boy lay still in Froggie's arms as the eel pounded the rocks inches away from them; it jammed its massive head as far into the cave as possible.

Any second now.

As the torpedo impacted into the eel's head Froggie darted downwards shielding the child with his body. Water swirled around them with the force of a tornado. He hung on for dear life until its energy was spent and dim twilight entered the cave.

The current was still swirling when he swam, with the boy in his arms, through the cave entrance, past the quivering body of the monster and up towards the sunlight. He didn't stop till he broke the surface at the side of the spaceship. Jerry and Natter lifted them aboard.

"Can you increase the atmospheric pressure? We went too deep, we've got to decompress," Froggie asked Geraldine.

"I can isolate the higher pressure to within two bulkhead doors, say the dormitory section?"

"That'll do fine," Froggie carried the child with him.

Annie followed them, she took a look at the gray skinned boy, "I think he's still alive."

"Annie, I'm going to close the bulkhead doors so that Geraldine can raise the atmospheric pressure. If you stay you won't be able to leave again for a few hours," Josephine said.

"I'll stay, if that's all right with you," Annie asked Rosie.

"If you think you can help the poor child," Rosie looked down at his limp body.

The air vents hissed as Froggie lowered the boy onto one of the beds.

Annie checked him over, "He must be about ten years old don't you think?" she took his pulse. "His heart's still beating but I don't think he's breathing."

She straightened his airway and pinched his nose. "Brace your neck Rosie, this is going to be a little awkward," she bent down and blew air into his lungs. The boy's chest rose and fell but did not rise again.

She repeated the action but he still didn't breathe.

"Come on now…" she blew air into his lungs a third time.

"Please try… please."

The boy gagged and then coughed and wheezed as he drew oxygen deep into his lungs again and again. Annie sat him up and rubbed his back while he came round and his breathing returned to normal. He stared with wide eyes at the strange human with the two heads who was speaking gently to him.

"What's your name?" Annie asked.

"Kiii," the boy replied.

"Perhaps he doesn't understand universal," Rosie said.

"My name is Kiii," Kiii looked around him, "what have you done with my mother?"

"Your mother?"

"You are Xenons," Kiii said.

"No we are not from your planet."

"You are space travelers?"

"You know about space travel?"

"Many of us wish we could fly away from here."

"Oh."

"I want my mother, where is she?"

Josephine used the computer to do a scan; she found a gray skinned woman drifting several feet under the water not far away.

"I'll go and get her," Froggie said over the comm., "I'll use the emergency airlock, that way I can bring her straight in here."

"Froggie you can't do that, you haven't decompressed yet," but Froggie was already on his way through the door.

The woman was unconscious and could have been dead but Froggie didn't stop to find out, he dragged her back to the spaceship trusting Annie's skills to save her if anyone could. Jerry, whose third leg helped him balance where others could not, stood outside the airlock ready to help them in. "You shouldn't have done that," he told Froggie.

"I couldn't just leave her there, don't worry I'll be fine."

Froggie carried her in and laid her on the bed next to her son. She wasn't breathing and her heart had stopped.

Annie did compressions, "She's very cold; I'll ask Geraldine to turn up the heat."

"Is mama going to wake up?" Kiii asked.

"Wait a minute... I've got a pulse."

A few more breaths and she was breathing on her own.

"When is mama going to wake up?" Kiii asked.

"Soon," Annie assured him.

Slowly the woman's pulse and breathing stabilized and eventually her eyelids fluttered. Kiii made strange clicking sounds.

"I think he's telling her what happened."

"I'm telling her not to be afraid."

The woman coughed as if she had not used her vocal cords in a long time and she tried to open her eyes.

"Take your time," Annie said gently.

The woman squinted; not sure if she could believe what she was seeing.

"My name's Annie and this is my sister Rosie, we are conjoined."

"I am Amaak," the woman's voice was very hoarse.

"Here drink this," Annie held out glass of fresh water and Amaak drank deeply, "you were attacked by a monstrous fish."

"We should not have come this way."

"You knew about the giant eel?"

"We took a chance; many people are hurrying to A'arkak for work; if we do not get there ahead of them we will starve."

"Perhaps it wasn't worth the risk."

"We are poor people; we have few choices."

"You live in the sea; why can't you just fish for food?"

"The Xenons control the fish stocks everywhere but here, where the monster fish protect them. They have eyes in all places; they take everything there is and make us serve them."

"Where is the boy's father?" Rosie asked.

"The Xenons let him die; we have no protector and no provider."

The intercom buzzed and Josephine's voice came over it, "Bunion has cooked some more food, we'll leave it in the emergency air lock."

"Where is that sound coming from?" Amaak asked.

"The radio on the wall, you'll meet our friends when the air pressure equalizes, we had to put you into decompression; it'll take a few hours I'm afraid."

"Only Xenons decompress, we are like seals and dolphins we do not need to do that."

"You don't? Then you don't need to stay here, why don't you go and eat dinner with the rest of the crew, if you feel strong enough."

Annie informed Jerry over the intercom and when he came into the airlock to leave food for Annie and Rosie and Froggie, he waved at Amaak through the glass door and beckoned her to follow him.

"It's okay, Jerry won't hurt you, he'll introduce you to the others," Rosie said.

When the inner airlock door opened Annie and Rosie took the food and Amaak and Kiii hesitantly walked in.

"You'll be all right, you'll like the rest of the crew; they want to be your friends."

Amaak wasn't totally convinced but nevertheless she let the door shut so that the air pressure could be equalized. Then she and Kiii followed Jerry to the galley where everyone smiled and welcomed them.

Meanwhile Annie went to check on Froggie.

"Is he all right?" Rosie asked.

Froggie lay still and silent in his bed.

"He's fine; he's just asleep that's all; he must be exhausted poor thing."

Meanwhile Clarissa welcomed Amaak and Kiii, "Sit down and eat with us."

Bunion put two plates of fish in front of them and they stared at the food hungrily, "You eat cooked food, the Xenons do that sometimes," Amaak told them.

"The Xenons are the people on the islands?"

"Yes, your skin is the same as theirs but you have a different way of speaking and you look...."

"Unusual?" Clarissa prompted.

"Yes," Amaak said.

"You wear different coverings too," Kiii said.

"Why did you come to this place?" Amaak asked.

"We needed food, we hadn't eaten in nine days and our data base said there would be fish here; as soon as our freezer is full we intend to move on."

"Then please could you take us with you?"

"But there is nowhere for you to go."

"There must be somewhere that a mother and a child would be welcome."

"Are there many poor people like you?"

"The Xenons keep us hungry."

"But how do they do that? You are the ones that live down with the fish?"

"They use automatic guards to control all the good fishing grounds; all they leave us to live on is shell fish and weed, which makes us sick."

"When you say automatic guards, does that mean that the Xenons use technology?" Josephine asked.

"Yes they do, it is even said that they still have a spaceship hidden somewhere on one of their great, floating islands."

"So they could have detected our landing?"

"Yes but you are in a remote place; it will take many hours for them to get here."

Josephine checked the computer and to her relief there was nothing on the sensor screen.

"What are we going to do?" Natter asked.

"Get more food," Bunion said.

"But shouldn't we get out of here? We don't want to wait around for the Xenons to capture us."

"Bunion's right," Clarissa said, "we need as much food as possible, there's no way of knowing when we'll be able to pick up more."

"We can't send Froggie down again, he's exhausted and he's in decompression."

"I can catch fish," Kiii said.

"How many?" Bunion asked.

"We need a month's supply minimum if we're going to be sure of survival," Clarissa said.

"I can catch as much food as we need now that the monster is gone."

"I hate to rain on our parade but something's just appeared on the edge of the scopes, it's heading straight for us, I estimate by its speed that it'll be here in three hours," Josephine told them.

"Nobody can catch a month's supply of fish in three hours," Geraldine said.

"There must be a lot of meat on that conga," Grumpus remarked.

"It's down too deep."

"I can dive deep."

"No Kiii," Amaak said.

"I can do it mother."

"No, it is too dangerous."

"Not for me, you know that I am good at deep diving."

"Your mother's right, you've taken enough risks for one day," Geraldine decided.

"But you need food. Please mother let me dive."

Amaak was quiet for a while, and then she said, "If these people will promise to take us with them I will do the diving."

"You don't want to come with us, the Time Guardians are after us," Natter told her.

"Who are the Time Guardians?"

"Men who want to kill us," Clarissa said.

"If you leave us here the Xenons will accuse us of fraternizing with aliens and will execute us anyway," Amaak said.

"When you say aliens do you mean us?"

"Yes, the Xenons do not welcome visitors from space; they do not want them to provide an escape route for us."

"What if we let you out now? You could swim away before they get here."

"This is the territory of the monster fish; there is danger everywhere."

"If you come with us we cannot guarantee your safety."

"We will take our chances, death may be a possibility with you but it is a certainty if we stay here."

"So you say you can help us get food?" Bunion said.

Geraldine found a long reel of steel wire attached to a space anchor in one of the utility boxes and Grumpus secured it to a supporting strut on the bridge.

He ran his hands over his shiny, bald head. "It's the weight of that fish that's bothering me; we'll have to cut it up."

"Can't someone put on a space suit and go down with Amaak to help her?" Jerome suggested.

"We shouldn't let her go down alone," Clarissa agreed.

"I will go," Bunion said.

"I'll go, it's going to take some strength to cut up that eel," Grumpus said.

It was just as well that it was Grumpus who volunteered because the spacesuits were made for very tall Karmosian humans. He was swamped but he filled it better than most of the others would have.

While he suited up Bunion searched the tool cupboards for cutting instruments. He found plenty of power tools but none that would work under water; however he did discover a variety of handsaws. He chose the sharpest one along with the biggest kitchen knife and he tied some of the other heavy tools securely to Grumpus's waist to weigh him down. When all was ready, Grumpus and Amaak slipped under the water.

It took Grumpus a few seconds to orient himself before he could check the heads up display on his helmet.

So far so good; they started to sink down into the gloom and Grumpus paid out the wire, which he just hoped would be long enough. Beautifully colored fish began to appear all around them.

It was hard to swim in the space suit which was far too buoyant and there were no flippers to help with propulsion but Amaak pulled him along the edge of the reef to where the ground dropped away into darkness. The water got murky as they sank down past sharp rocks and dirty weed. It was eerie this far down and Grumpus found himself wondering if there were any other giant eels down here.

Finally their feet touched something. It wasn't rock; it was smooth and pliable and it twitched. Grumpus shone his helmet lights on it, "We've found it and it's… it's enormous," he said over the radio. There was no way that they were going to just be able to tie the eel to the wire and haul it up, "We're going to have to cut it into pieces."

He took the saw off his belt and Amaak grabbed the knife. They started at the head end where the ratio of meat to bone was the highest and Grumpus trimmed off the damaged part of the skull that was still attached. Then he found a place along the back and started sawing while Amaak worked from underneath cutting the underbelly flesh. She stripped out the internal organs and sliced upwards while Grumpus cut downwards.

It was slow work but time passed quickly. Eventually they had what was in effect an enormous fish steak. Amaak helped Grumpus secure the wire around it and then they let the others haul it up.

Amaak followed the big chunk of fish up to the surface so that she could take some breaths and could retrieve the line before going down again. Grumpus started on the next piece; the intense water pressure was painful but he was not called a strong man for nothing.

He carried on.

They worked hard and eventually they were ready to send another steak upwards.

"We're running very short on time," Josephine warned him over the radio.

"We've got time for one more piece."

They chose a point further down the spine so that this piece would be the biggest of the three and they started cutting furiously; by now many small fish had joined them to take advantage of this unexpected feast.

"The Xenons are only fifty miles away."

"We can make it," Grumpus said.

By the time they had the third enormous steak attached firmly to the wire it really was time to move.

"You've got less than five minutes," Josephine said.

"We understand," Grumpus detached the tools from his waist in order to make himself buoyant. He signaled Amaak who squeaked in agreement and shot up out of view, heading for the surface. He caught hold of the wire that held the eel steak, "Ready," he said and those on the surface hauled him and it up as fast as they could. He could see the precious light above him; any minute now he would be able to breathe fresh air again.

And then suddenly the wire stopped moving.

"Sorry Grumpus, the Xenon's boat has long range weapons; we didn't see them until they fired."

"What?" Grumpus said.

"It's okay we destroyed the missiles with our lasers."

"Get me out of here fast."

"We want you to pull yourself up the wire at the same time that we're pulling you in, Natter says he thinks he's spent enough of his spare time at the shooting galleries at all those fairs we visited to be able to keep them at bay for now but we need to get you out of there as quickly as possible."

Grumpus whole-heartedly agreed. As he hurriedly pulled himself up the wire, his mind went back to the last time he had been under fire; it was when he was in the military. He had never told anyone why he joined the circus.

Clarissa had not checked his résumé; she hired him because she liked his face. He told her that he had been in Earth Defense and that he had been a fitness instructor. She had never seen the words 'Dishonorable Discharge' on his military papers.

He had been good at the theory of war and was an excellent physical instructor, but when his captain ordered him to fire his weapons he couldn't do it. His family had been in the military for generations and by his refusal he had let them all down. He had disobeyed orders because in his heart he was not a warrior. No one suffered because of his refusal, in fact it turned out that there had been a misunderstanding and that the vessel that they were aiming at was not part of the secret drug running operation they were targeting, but a similar looking one full of children on a school trip to the moon. He didn't get an award for saving their lives however; rather he got a court marshal for disobeying orders and with it came the realization that he could never be a good soldier.

Grumpus's helmet broke the surface only to see the Xenon vessel circling the spaceship at close quarters. Geraldine quickly pulled him out of the water, letting go of the wire.

Grumpus grabbed hold of it again.

"What?" Geraldine said.

He gave her back the wire and indicated that she should keep hauling while he took his helmet off. "We need the food; it's so near the surface, if we pull together…"

"Grumpus you've got to decompress, you'll get the bends."

"Later," he and Geraldine pulled with all their strength.

"What are you doing?" Josephine shouted as a missile whizzed past them. "Natter's not as good a shot as he thought he was; we need to get out of here now!"

"One more minute," Grumpus's face and head were red with the strain.

The eel steak broke the surface and they heaved it on board. As soon as it was safely inside the spacecraft, Josephine closed the door and Geraldine ran onto the bridge to start the engines. Grumpus ran around to the airlock and climbed into the dormitory section while Josephine turned up the atmospheric pressure again.

"Nothing's happening," Geraldine shouted.

"What do you mean?" Clarissa said.

"The engines won't start, this craft is vertical takeoff and the jets are underneath the water."

"Why didn't you think of this before?"

"Because the Genghis Khan's engines are multiple-atmosphere, they work in all kinds of environments, even liquid ammonia, but these engines are modern technology, they're a lot simpler than the ones I'm used to working with."

"What about the rocket engine?"

"Not big enough, they're only designed to be supplemental engines; you'd need a very light gravity in order to take off from the surface with them."

"The shields are taking a battering," Natter called out, "and well, when I hit that one missile I think it must have been a fluke because this is a lot harder than it looks."

"Isn't there any way to get this craft to move?"

"We could use the rocket boosters to push us along the surface for a while, that would give us some thinking time."

"Do it," Clarissa said.

The almost round spacecraft had integral wings molded into the underside of its body; it wasn't the right shape for slicing through the water.

"Where are we going?"

Josephine looked at the charts on the monitor, "We'll just head south for now; habitation is scarce for a while."

"I need someone else to pilot so I can concentrate on clearing those engines," Geraldine said.

"I'll do it," Lydia offered.

Bunion gave her a quiet look and then walked away. He had to process that conga eel before it killed everybody with its fishy smell.

It felt good to be actually fleeing from the Xenons; Geraldine redirected some of the main fuel to the maneuvering thrusters so that they would run for longer and then sat down to try to figure out how to clear the jet engines. "What idiot would design spacecraft engines that only function in an earthlike atmosphere?"

"Some nerd who works in an office and has never been off world in his life," Josephine said.

"I don't know how the Keepers of Knowledge got hold of this ship but apart from the living quarters, the design is a basic Follux 140," Geraldine said.

"It looks good but you only get what you pay for."

"Yea."

"We've got more vessels heading in our direction," Josephine warned, "I think we can keep them busy for a while but don't be too long, there's a craft coming up from the south and we're running out of alternatives."

It took a while for Geraldine to unsuccessfully exhaust all the options and conclude that there was only one thing to do,

"Flip her over," she said.

"What?" Lydia said.

"It's the only way. Josephine and me have worked out a simulation. You get up to full speed and then turn suddenly like so," Geraldine ran the mock-up on the screen. "That'll drain the water out of the engines."

"But we won't get any lift if the engines are on top," Lydia said.

"When we get them working we push them up to speed and then we use them to flip the spacecraft back over again, if we're going fast enough we should take off instead of settling back onto the water."

"What if you can't get them working?"

"There's nothing wrong with them, I've checked and double checked the manual, they should work fine once they're out of the water."

"And what if something goes wrong?"

"Well at best we just flip over onto our backs again."

"And at worst?"

"We hit the water at the wrong angle and break into pieces."

"And you want me to pilot you through this?"

"You seem to have the skill Lydia."

"You're a far better pilot than I am Geraldine."

"I'll be busy with the engines and Grumpus, who is the only other one with flight experience, is in decompression."

The southern settlements were getting all too close and time was running out.

"Tell everyone to buckle up really well," Lydia did a few practice runs in order to confirm the angle of the turn, "is everybody ready for this?"

No one looked as if they were ready.

"Go for it," Geraldine said.

Lydia realigned all the boosters; she chose a part of the sea that was relatively free of pursuing vessels and ramped up the power. The craft gathered speed and when she swung it around it stood up on its side and teetered for a second before falling onto its back. Everyone found themselves hanging upside down from their restraints.

"I'm too old for this," Clarissa groaned.

The spaceship came to a halt because now the maneuvering thrusters were under water and wouldn't work.

"So far so good," Geraldine tried to start the jet engines but everything was too wet. She increased the fuel flow but there was not much response.

"I don't like to tell you this but we're surrounded; you'd better hurry up," Lydia was trying to look at the monitor from her upside down position.

"Give me one more minute," Geraldine increased the throttle.

The engines caught but quickly died.

"They just need to drain a little more... " a loud bang sounded on the hull of the spacecraft.

"They're attaching a line," Lydia shouted.

"Yea, just gimme a few more seconds..." the engines coughed, "come on, come on."

A clank reverberated through the craft. "Let me guess, another line," Clarissa's stomach was hurting where she dangled in the restraints.

The engines coughed louder, "Come on... come on... you can do it..." Geraldine willed them to start.

The spaceship started tipping on its side, "They're turning us back over," Annie cried.

"That's pretty obvious," Rosie said.

The engines stuttered as the spaceship wobbled on its edge.

"This really hurts," Jerry and the others hung suspended in a very awkward position.

The engines coughed once, twice, three times before they finally caught; Geraldine pulled back the throttle and began to feel a surge of power.

But it was too late, the spacecraft fell back into the water the right way up and the engines died once more. There was silence for a moment and then a great whirring sound, which indicated the grinding of metal.

"Fire the maneuvering thrusters," Geraldine ordered.

"I'm trying to but nothing's happening, I think they're water logged," Lydia said.

The grinding got louder, "Open the door or they'll cut a hole in the hull and we'll never get this ship back into space."

Lydia released the door catch.

"What are we going to do? I don't want to be killed by the Xenons," Rosie shouted.

"I have absolutely no idea," Clarissa said.

Chapter 8.

The musty smell of damp reeds pervaded everything. The mat of reeds beneath their feet was hundreds of feet thick and it was added to regularly from the floating reed beds that grew all around the artificial islands.

"We are a troupe of traveling entertainers, our regular spaceship is in for an overhaul so they gave us this courtesy vehicle while we were waiting," Clarissa repeated. In front of her stood an ordinary human that had not been enhanced in any way that she could detect.

"What were you doing on the Veringarious Reef?" their interrogator asked.

"I already told you, we were fishing; we didn't realize when we accepted this vehicle that there were hardly any supplies on board. We had to find food somehow."

"Why didn't you request permission to land?"

"We were under the impression that you were not a technological society; we didn't think it was necessary."

"Why did you have two Aquans on board?"

"We rescued them from a giant conga eel; they said they were taking a short cut looking for work."

"The Veringarious Reef is a very dangerous place."

"So we found out."

"Why did you come to this planet?"

"We're trying to expand our customer base."

"Then why did you fire at us when our ship came to examine you?"

"Because someone launched a missile at us, I have to say that we were shocked at your response, usually people are pleased when the circus comes to town."

"This is all a pack of lies."

"Don't you believe us?"

"No I don't."

"We're good entertainers, if you let us perform for you, we can prove it," Clarissa said.

The man frowned.

"You don't get much amusement around here do you?" The man frowned again.

"I didn't mean to insult you; it's just that yours doesn't seem to be the type of planet that would be accustomed to our form of entertainment."

The man walked abruptly out of the room.

"Clarissa what can we perform here? We don't have any props or costumes," Jerome reminded her.

"I was thinking of the new show," Clarissa said.

"But it's not ready yet, how are we going to rehearse all that in time to put on any kind of performance?"

"If we use the general outline of the new act and the bits we have rehearsed we could add in some of the older material to bulk it out."

"But we haven't got a finale."

"I thought we'd do the wedding scene."

"But Natter's the hero of the new piece, if there's a wedding at the end he's the one who should be getting married," Jerry pointed out.

"Yea," Natter said, "I don't mind doing the kiss."

"Look this is how I see it..." Clarissa proceeded to outline her ideas to them and by the time their interrogator returned, the vision had taken on a solid shape.

"The elders have decreed that you are to perform before them and the town dignitaries at thirty hundred hours tonight."

"Thirty hundred hours, you have a long day here don't you?" Natter was cheered by the thought that at least they would have plenty of time to prepare.

"It is now twenty seven hundred; you have three hours."

"And what about the venue?" Clarissa asked.

151

"You will perform on the parade ground in front of the prison."

"We'll need access to our spacecraft in order to get our costumes."

"I will arrange for an armed escort."

Three hours was nowhere near long enough to get everything ready, they rushed as fast as they could; they even practiced their lines at top speed. They rehearsed, worked out the choreography, finished off the costumes and made backgrounds out of bedding material and reeds.

Froggie made crude screens out of reed matting so that they could have some kind of an off-stage. Geraldine got out her welding torch and fabricated a framework and a tightrope out of spare struts and some of the wire they had used to salvage the eel. And since there was no backing music they decided that Rosie would do the singing and at the end they would have an audience participation number called, "Love's Young dream," the words of which Froggie wrote out on a big computer tablet.

Since there was no harp, Annie took some of the pans from the galley and made them into a makeshift drum kit and because Jerry didn't have his flute he decided to improvise with a comb and paper.

"Now it's essential that you all look professional," Clarissa said wearing a dress that she had cleverly made out of bed sheets.

Annie mixed some cream that she found in the first aid box with black ash made from burnt reeds in order to make up people's eyes; however she had to be sure that it didn't actually touch the eyeball as it stung quite badly. But there was no lipstick, and no flowers for the wedding scene, and no sword for the giant; and even the beanstalk would have to be imaginary.

Jerome discovered some stiff, hollow reeds lying in a corner just by the jailhouse. He cut them carefully before blowing over the top of them; but they weren't right so he fiddled with them a little more, taking time that he should have used for rehearsing his own act. "Jerry I made this for you," he said once he had finished.

"Pan pipes?"

"They're not quite the same but I think they'll do."

"They're great, how did you think of that?"

"Well I guessed that you could do with something a little better than a comb and paper."

"I wonder what they did with Kiii and Amaak," Clarissa hadn't seen them since they had been thrown in the jail; "I think I might try to find someone to ask." Soldiers brought chairs made of thick reeds into the square and people began to fill them. "Excuse me, I was wondering what happened to the mother and child that were with us on our spaceship," she asked one of them.

"Be careful, do not speak of the Aquans in public or you will have to pay the penalty."

"But they were in our care, I feel responsible."

"They are where they should be."

"What do you mean by that?"

"For your own sakes I advise you to say nothing more," the soldier turned quickly away.

Tall chairs made of sturdy reeds were set at the side of the square for the elders of the city. Geraldine rigged up two spare lights that she found in a toolbox on the spacecraft but there were no microphones.

By thirty hundred hours everything was as ready as it could be. The audience stared silently at the makeshift stage; the sun was sinking low. It was time to begin. There could be no stalling because it was obvious that the Xenons believed firmly in punctuality.

"Well," Clarissa told the company as they prepared to start their performance, "we've played to some rough audiences and survived; we can play to this one too." They all slapped their hands together and took their places.

The lights came on and Annie rolled her drums. Jerry played a fanfare on the comb and paper and Clarissa walked out in front of the audience, "Ladies and gentlemen it is heartwarming to see so many of you here tonight. What we are about to perform is a new show in a format that you may not be familiar with. We invite you to sit back, relax and enjoy yourselves as we perform our version of the traditional tale, 'Jack and the Beanstalk.'"

Jerry changed to the panpipes and Clarissa left the stage as Rosie and Annie walked onto it to perform the opening number. In the background Lydia danced graceful steps to the cheerful tune.

If you had been to the places I've been,
If you had seen the things that I've seen,
If you could know the things that I know,
You'd see why my heart has nowhere to go.

For in this place there's magic,
And in this place there's joy,
And in this place there's laughter,
For every girl and boy.

A mystical kingdom,
A fairyland,
Come enter with me,
Come take my hand.

Chorus:
Of all the places in the universe,
Where I've laughed and shed a tear,
The most perfect place I've ever been,
Is here, right here, right here.

After Rosie had finished, Natter walked onto the stage.

Annie was the narrator; she said her first line, "Are you sad my boy? You look depressed and glum."

"I should be," Natter said, "I'm avoiding my mum."

Natter played the role of Jack and Clarissa played his mother. She scolded him for being lazy; there was no money for food so they would have to sell the cow. Jerry with three legs and a sheet played the cow, Jerome of course played the giant and Geraldine his long-suffering wife. Grumpus was the thief that stole the goose that laid the golden eggs. His plan was to clone it to get enough golden egg laying geese to generate the money he would need to hire henchmen to take over the universe.

Mr. Mystery played the private investigator that the giant hired as he and Jack joined forces to retrieve the goose, or geese if Grumpus's plan had worked. On their way they met a frog, played by Bunion who of course was in love with a princess. This gave Rosie the opportunity to sing some romantic songs while Jerome did his tightrope walk in the background and Josephine danced her ballet.

Natter as Jack now became Bunion's love doctor, showing him how to win the princess. This gave them even more excuses to sing romantic songs. Froggie who played Grumpus's side kick eventually saved everybody from being blown up by a big ball of reeds with a piece of wire sticking out of the top, representing a bomb. Eventually Clarissa came back as the Queen, who banished Grumpus to a monastery allowing him to come back as the priest in the wedding scene.

Annie couldn't find any warts for Bunion so she used some of the green, gunky food that she found in the spaceship's galley. After the wedding scene they all sang the final number. "Laugh 'Cos the Day is Fine." Froggie made sure that the audience could see all the words but no one joined in.

They had never played to silence before. They had played to crowds that had booed and jeered and threw things and they had played to crowds that had laughed and whistled. They had even played to crowds that had shouted and drank and vomited, but they had never played to a crowd that did nothing. As the performance ended they took their bows but there was no applause.

They did their encore anyway and took their final bow.

Everyone but Clarissa quickly made their exit; she stood in the middle of the stage and looked up at the elders in their row of high seats, "I know you have probably never seen anything like this before but did you like it?"

The elders all turned to one another and whispered and then the nearest one faced to Clarissa and said, "Yes we liked it."

She stood there for a few seconds longer but it was evident that he was not going to say any more so she bowed again and left.

Half an hour later the whole troupe was back in the cell. It was almost dark but no one brought them a light. "That was the hardest performance of my life," Natter declared.

"Me too," Rosie agreed.

"No one said anything, they didn't even move," Jerry said.

"They didn't join in any of the songs," Froggie said.

"There was no applause, none at all, not even when I sawed Geraldine in half," Mr. Mystery looked mystified.

"I saw one person who actually looked disappointed when he realized that she wasn't dead," Lydia told them.

A guard walked in and pushed some platted reed baskets under the jail door, "Food," he grunted.

It was raw fish.

"Did you enjoy our performance?" Clarissa asked.

"I didn't see it."

"Do you know what happened to the child and his mother who were brought in with us?"

"The Aquans?"

"Yes."

"They'll be in the holding cell."

"Holding cell? Where's that?"

"Just by the quay of course, we like to keep them wet and fresh on their last night."

"What do you mean by... last night?"

"It turned out that they were wanted criminals even before they got here, they stole some Dukruth from a Xenon."

"What's Dukruth?"

"Personally I don't like it, it's very cheap bread and apparently it was stale. The complainant says he was going to throw it to the birds when these two Aquans actually had the audacity to climb up out of the water and ask for it. Well as you can imagine he told them to go and eat seaweed. He said they went away but they came back later when they thought no one was looking and took it from his ground."

"What is their punishment?"

"Execution of course, we can't allow dirty Aquans to steal our food or who knows what they'll be doing next? Well enjoy your dinner," the guard left.

Nobody ate a thing.

"We've got to do something," Annie said.

Grumpus had been examining the walls of the cell, "I wouldn't have believed it if I hadn't seen it for myself, this cell may only be made of reeds but it's really secure."

The bars were thicker and tougher than bamboo. Geraldine grabbed hold of one and started pulling, "Help me Grumpus."

Grumpus grabbed the bar with both of his hands and they pulled as hard as they could. The bar bent a little so that there was a bigger gap between it and the next one but there was no way that it was going to break.

"What if one of us gets one bar and pulls one way and the other one gets the other bar and pulls the other way?"

They took two bars next to each other and pulled in opposite directions; a gap appeared, "Someone, try to squeeze through that."

Lydia had a go, "No it's not possible; can you pull it any wider?"

They strained as hard as they could and Lydia tried to help by pushing the bars outward as she attempted to pass through them but it was no good. "Not gonna happen," she said.

Geraldine and Grumpus sat on the floor panting for air.

"Couldn't we try digging our way out?" Jerry asked.

Despite the fact that it was almost dark they did their best to find a weak point in either the floor or the walls but the reeds were matted and twisted into strands that were stronger than rope.

"A sharp knife would have helped," Froggie said.

"We could try to make a hole in the roof," Natter suggested, "roofs are always weaker than floors."

Grumpus lifted him up onto his back and Natter started digging into the thatch with his long fingernails. Dry bits of reed rained down on them as he scrabbled his way through the dusty reeds, "This is easy," he said. But the first layer of reeds turned out to be superficial; after that came another, much more solid layer. "I take that back; this is going to take hours."

"Can you do it before sunrise?" Clarissa asked.

"That depends on when sunrise is and how many layers of this stuff there are."

"Is there anything we can do to help?" Lydia asked.

Jerome was so tall that he could reach the ceiling by himself, while Lydia had to climb on Geraldine's shoulders. They dug their fingers into the twisted, iron like reeds. "This is going to be really difficult."

The door to the cellblock creaked and Lydia and Natter instantly jumped down before the man who had interrogated them walked through it. "The council of elders has decided that you will provide entertainment for any who wish to see it," he said.

"Oh really? So they did like our performance then?" Clarissa said.

"Elder Bracken told you they did."

"Ah yes, so he did, so what are we to be paid for our services?"

"You will keep your lives."

"Oh, well in that case, how about doing another performance right now?"

"In the dark?"

"That's not a problem, if you'll allow us to go back to the spaceship we can rig up more lights. We'd be happy to do it if anyone wants to watch. We just love performing; can't get enough of it."

"Wait there," the man walked out of the room and closed the door.

They all sighed with relief; it was only because it was so dark that he hadn't seen the loose reeds covering the ground and the dent that was appearing in the ceiling.

"What did you have to promise him that for? We've only got the two spare lights and we're using them already," Geraldine said.

"Well get creative, I would say that having someone unlock this door for us is a far simpler way of getting out of this cell than digging a hole through the roof," Clarissa said.

Eventually the man returned and told them they could perform for the insomniacs.

They were allowed to go back to the spacecraft to get their stuff. When they got there they saw that it had been hauled up out of the water.

"They're going to strip it, I knew that's what they wanted, hey look they've already started," Geraldine pointed out some of the storage bins that were lined up alongside the quay in the moonlight.

"But the ship's out of water; doesn't that mean that the engines will work?" Clarissa said.

"Yea, but we'll have to get to her before they strip the heart out of her."

"Shh, not so loud we don't want the guards to hear."

"We've got to figure out where that holding pen is," Froggie said.

"It's in the water somewhere."

"I was thinking, if Natter could help Jerry with the accompaniment for Rosie on the first romantic number."

"You mean 'I wish I was in Love?'" Natter said.

"Yes, that's the one; I could sneak away and have a look around."

"I could sing a few extra songs, perhaps I could do some classical stuff; that would give you longer," Rosie suggested.

"Good idea," Froggie said.

"If I asked Mr. Mystery to lengthen his act there would be a nice little segment in the middle of the show where you wouldn't be missed, it might just work," Clarissa said.

Geraldine had to strip the light fittings from the bedrooms to provide enough illumination. When they started the performance the seats were only half full and the guards looked very tired.

"These people seem to go to sleep as soon as the sun goes down," Clarissa remarked.

"We can use that," Josephine said.

Clarissa told everybody to drag out their acts; it was easy to make them lack luster because this audience, like the last, didn't clap or shout or sing or applaud or respond in any way. Clarissa's aim was to bore them all to sleep. It took four long hours before the last guard dozed off and the last one of the tired audience snoozed in his seat. By then the performers were also exhausted; they took their final bows.

"Ladies and gentlemen thank you for your attention; we wish you a safe journey home. We are now going to return our belongings to the spacecraft," Clarissa announced.

Nobody moved; several people snored. They all picked up what gear they could manage and began heading back to the spaceship. "Did you find the holding cell?" Clarissa asked Froggie as soon as they were out of earshot of the audience.

"Yes, it's by the dock near some warehouses, not far from the spaceship. It's well guarded though."

"Let's go and investigate."

They used the faint moonlight to guide them over to the area of the docks and sure enough there was a group of tired looking sentries standing at the water's edge obviously guarding something.

Clarissa walked up to one of them, "Excuse me, could you help us take our gear back to the spaceship? We're very tired and we don't have the energy to do it all ourselves, I hope you don't mind." The man yawned but didn't move; the other guards looked at her with sleepy curiosity, "Could you tell me what the time is?"

"Four clocks past sunset."

"Oh my goodness, is it that late? Well then please could you and your men render us some assistance?"

"We can't leave the prisoners," the guard tried to look grim but his yawns spoiled the effect.

"You do know that we are traveling performers don't you? Will you be coming to see our show?"

"If we are ordered to."

"You have to be ordered to have fun?"

"Fun?"

"Yes you know, having a laugh, enjoying yourself."

"I'm sorry my universal isn't as good as it should be."

"Fun... you know ha, ha, ha?"

"Oh, oh yes I understand. We will come if we are ordered to."

"Tell me, why don't your people applaud the performers?"

"Applaud?"

"Yes, you know clap your hands?"

"Why would we want to do that?"

Clarissa sighed, "Look, since you might not be ordered to come and see our show would you like Rosie here to sing you a song so that you can get some idea what it's like?"

As the guard yawned again Froggie slipped into the water unnoticed. Geraldine had given him a pair of cutters that she had found in a tool kit that the Xenons hadn't raided yet. He didn't bother with the complicated series of knots and tangled fibers that made up the lock but went straight for the hinges, which were a lot simpler, and sliced through them.

There were twenty Aquans sleeping at the bottom of the cage; they would rise to the surface to take a gulp of air whenever they needed it, before sinking to the bottom again. The door swung open and Froggie woke Kiii up. Between them they stealthily shook the rest of the prisoners awake and sent them on their way.

Froggie led Amaak and Kiii back to the spaceship.

"Well we really must go," Clarissa said as soon as Mr. Mystery had produced the last of the bunches of fake flowers that he had up his sleeves, "perhaps we'll see you at one of our performances."

The guards refused to leave their posts to help them drag the armfuls of costumes aboard the spacecraft.

"There's no way I can start the engines," Geraldine said, "they've taken all the starter relays and most of the batteries are missing."

Josephine switched on the computer, "They've been downloading the stellar database; this probably isn't the first spacecraft to land here and be stripped."

"Someone has to go and retrieve the battery that we used for the lights."

"What about the rest of the costumes?" Natter asked.

The sentries who were guarding the empty cage nodded their heads sleepily. Bunion and Natter and Froggie and Jerry crept back to the jail to find that some of the audience was still there, resting peacefully in their seats or lying on the floor of reeds. They collected everything they needed and slipped back to the spaceship.

"Is everybody on board?" Clarissa said.

They did a head count; everybody was present and correct. Geraldine turned down the lights and the temperature controls in order to save on battery power.

"Where's Zeno?" Annie wondered.

Zeno had been packed away in a locker like a man-sized doll in a toy box. They had all had so much on their minds that they hadn't noticed that he was gone.

"They must have unloaded him."

"We can't leave him here, they'll dismantle him," Geraldine said.

"He betrayed us, why should we worry about him?" Rosie said.

"If they reactivate him the Time Guardians might get a fix on us."

"I'll go," Bunion said.

"No, not on your own."

"You can't go Geraldine, you have too much to do here," Clarissa said.

"I'll help," Froggie offered.

"Me too," Natter said.

"Where do you think they've taken him?" Annie asked.

"The same place as all the other stuff they helped themselves to," Rosie said.

"But where would that be?"

"It wouldn't be far."

"I'll find out," Lydia said.

"And how are you going to do that?"

"Watch me," Lydia sauntered down to where the men were guarding the reed cage, "Excuse me gentlemen but I seem to have lost my necklace."

The men looked at her through sleepy eyes, "We haven't seen anything like that around here."

"I left it in the spaceship but a lot of our stuff has been moved."

"That's our salvage rights."

"Oh don't get me wrong, I'm not complaining about that, it's just that this particular necklace belonged to my dead mother, it's the only thing I have to remember her by," Lydia looked at them pleadingly with her beautiful, blue eyes.

"Well, em, everything was moved into warehouse number one, over there, but there won't be anybody there now except the sentries; you'll have to come back in the morning."

Bunion who had been standing in the shadows moved off to tell the others.

"That's all right, I can wait, it's just that I would be so disappointed if I lost it. "By the way did you know that I play a very important role in our little performance," Lydia tossed her hair carelessly.

The men didn't see Bunion, or Froggie, or Natter slip past them as they headed for the well-guarded warehouse, taking cover behind some packing cases made out of reeds so that they could survey their target.

"Half of those guards are asleep," Natter whispered.

"Not the ones by the doors," Froggie said.

"There's a window over there and none the men guarding it seem to be awake," Bunion said.

"Yea but that part of the wall is lit up by the moonlight, if any of the guards by the doors turn their heads at the wrong moment they'll see us."

"I'll distract them," Bunion walked out of the shadows and up to the guards, "I've lost my necklace," he said.

Froggie and Natter crept forward.

"You'll have to leave; this is government property."

"But I'm looking for my necklace…."

Froggie and Natter climbed in the window.

"It was my long lost mother's."

"Well it's ours now."

"But you don't understand…."

"Go away little man, scram."

"I'm from the traveling circus," Bunion said.

The warehouse was full of objects made of reeds. Thick reeds, thin reeds, the fluffy cotton that grew from the tops of the reeds, clothing made from the stringy threads that came from the roots of the reeds, roasted reed seeds, reed seed oil, even a kind of coffee that came from the seeds of one highly sought after species of reed. It was dark in the warehouse; the only light was from the moonlight that streamed gently in through the unglazed window.

"I wish we had a torch," Froggie whispered.

"They'd spot us if we did," Natter said, "let's go down there."

"You can see?"

"No, but there's nothing up here so whatever we want must be down there."

They crept past a row of reed baskets.

"Look… there."

"I can't see."

"Over there, are those our spare computer tablets?" Froggie took a risk and switched one on; the light from the screen allowed them to see what was around them.

"Look what they've done to Zeno," Natter said.

Parts of Zeno lay all over a reed table. Tools from the spaceship were arranged beside him; obviously someone had been using them to take him apart.

"They haven't reactivated him."

"We still can't leave him here."

"Grab a big basket and throw the pieces in, I'll get another one, Geraldine will need those tools, and some of this other stuff, ah look I think I can see the starter relays."

Froggie and Natter climbed out of the window with two fully loaded baskets and two heavy fuel cells.

Bunion was still distracting the guards, "Do you know what part I play?"

"No and we don't want to, now go away."

"I have to kiss the Princess."

"And you want us to be impressed by that?"

"She's beautiful."

"We're not interested, go away."

"Come and watch our performance and you'll see for yourselves."

Froggie and Natter crept past them, and past Lydia who was teaching the other set of guards how to sing a romantic song. "That's the most I've ever heard Bunion say," Natter said as soon as they made it inside the spacecraft with their booty.

Geraldine looked at Zeno, "How could they do that to him?" she said.

Bunion annoyed the guards by trying to sing to them whilst standing on one leg and juggling some reeds that he had found on the ground and knotted together. Eventually they drove him off and he was able to return to the spacecraft. However he didn't go inside but ran over to where Lydia was still entertaining the other guards.

"Clarissa wants you to come and help," Bunion said.

"Who's this?"

"My husband," Lydia said.

"What?"

"In the show, he's the one I marry."

"But you're not really married to him are you?"

"No of course not; now I'll see you boys later," Lydia and Bunion walked off hand in hand towards the spaceship.

Meanwhile outside the jail the only people left in front of the makeshift stage were sound asleep....

That is until a particularly big mosquito bit one of the soldiers. The man slapped his thigh so hard that he woke himself up. He yawned in the darkness and fidgeted to get comfortable. This was not the first time he had fallen asleep on duty, but nothing ever happened so it didn't matter. Then he remembered, they were supposed to be guarding those off-worlders whose show would have been enjoyable if it hadn't gone on for so long.

He opened half an eye to check where they were.

Then suddenly both his eyes were open wide.

The performers had disappeared!

He woke up his patrol leader, "Sir, the prisoners...."

Back at the warehouse the guards nodded their heads and wished they were in their comfortable barracks, sleeping like babies on their reed beds until suddenly the sound of pounding feet broke the monotony and soldiers appeared out of the shadows.

"Those entertainers have you seen them?"

"They went back to their spaceship; be careful though, if you say the wrong thing they'll burst into song."

"Come and help us; they're trying to escape."

"They didn't appear to be running away."

Nevertheless all the guards from the warehouse and all but one of those guarding the cage followed them.

Meanwhile inside the spacecraft: "How are those starter relays coming along?" Josephine asked.

"Yea well if I wasn't so tired..." Geraldine muttered.

"You'd better hurry, a big bunch of guards has just showed up, they're running around outside."

"Just give me...."

The patrol leader tried to open the door but it was locked; he banged on the hull but no one answered. He banged again but got no reply, "We'd better get the equipment," he said.

Inside the spacecraft everyone was panicking, "Geraldine we've got to go now!" Josephine shouted.

"Okay I'm working as fast as I can."

A whirring sound reverberated through the hull, "Did you feel that?" Natter shouted.

"It's a cutter and it's not made of reeds," Jerome said.

The spaceship jerked, "Geraldine, they're pulling us back to the water," Grumpus warned.

"I'm nearly ready," she twisted the last few wires together and tried to start the engines but they only coughed. "These stupid, cheap, pathetic, useless...."

She tried again and the engines reluctantly spluttered.

The whirring sound got louder and the spaceship began to tilt as the Xenon soldiers hauled it over the side of the dock.

"If they tip us up any more we're going to end up in the water again and the engines will get wet," Clarissa said.

"Come on you worthless bits of junk..." Geraldine kicked the control panel. By now the spacecraft was teetering at ninety degrees on the edge of the dock. The engines puttered, then growled and then suddenly they caught. Geraldine throttled up quickly, revving them as hard as they could go. "Hold on tight!" She pulled the throttle right back and the spaceship lurched forward, righting itself at the same time. Then it tipped its nose up and shot upwards into the darkness like a bullet out of a gun, "I just hope we have enough fuel to make it into orbit," she said.

But they were still in low atmosphere when the jet engines cut out and Geraldine had to fire up the rockets. They all blacked out because of the high Gee forces. When they woke up they had gravity, which either meant that the artificial gravity had switched on automatically or they were still in the planet's atmosphere. It didn't feel as if they were falling, but your senses can deceive you when you're in flight.

Geraldine took a look at the monitor in front of her to confirm their status, "We made it," she cried.

Everybody cheered as she started up the graviton motors.

"Is anybody following us?" Annie asked.

"Of course not; you can't make a spaceship out of reeds," Natter told her.

"I'm not so sure, they're very clever with those reeds," Jerry said.

"I hate to tell you this but there's something behind us, it just appeared out of nowhere and it's huge; I don't think it belongs to the Xenons though," Geraldine said.

"Oh no let me guess."

"It's the Time Guardians!"

Annie screamed, "We're all gonna die!"

"The shields aren't working, I activated them but they're not working," Josephine cried.

"That's because the Xenons removed the relays for them too. They must have a thing about relays."

"So what are we going to do?"

"Put as much distance between us and the Time Guardian ship as possible."

"How did they find us?" Rosie asked.

"The Xenons must have told them."

"What if we pretend that we know something that they don't? They'll have to keep us alive so they can get it out of us," Grumpus suggested.

"Oh yes wonderful; I always wanted to be tortured before I died," Rosie said.

"We'll both feel the pain," Annie said.

"It won't happen anyway, they don't need us, all they have to do is reactivate Zeno and they can get all the information they need from him."

"They're gaining on us," Geraldine said.

"Why did the Xenons report us to the Time Guardians?"

"They don't want us to escape; they're too used to getting their own way."

"Or it could have been that terrible performance we put on, maybe they were trying to punish us for it," Natter suggested.

"They liked it," Amaak said.

"How do you know?"

"They said so when they came to sign our death warrants."

"Really?"

"Yes," Amaak said.

"But they didn't clap or cheer or show any sign of approval."

"They told you they liked it and that was enough."

A laser blast dissipated on the hull; "We're almost in range," Geraldine shouted, "I estimate that we've got less than a minute."

"This really is it then?" Natter said.

"The graviton engines won't be up to full power in time."

"I suggest that we each do what we need to make peace with the universe," Clarissa said.

Everyone unstrapped themselves from their seats and hugged each other. Grumpus and Jerome sent messages of love to their families using the very expensive quantum communicator; well it wasn't like they were going to be around to pay the bill.

Natter held Rosie's head in his hands, "There's something I should have done that a long time ago," he bent down and kissed her.

For a split second Rosie looked surprised but then she smiled and kissed him back.

"They're powering up their cannons," Josephine said.

"I can't do evasive maneuvers; the rocket fuel's gone," Geraldine said.

Bunion squeezed Lydia's hand.

"They're nearly in position."

They held onto each other and bowed their heads, "It's been a privilege knowing you all," Clarissa said.

They all closed their eyes.

The Time Guardians bombarded the ship with laser fire.

Static electricity crept up their backs and made their hair stand on end. The temperature rose and their skin got hot. The structure began to creak and there was a whining in their ears that got higher and higher....

Chapter 9.

Suddenly there was silence; a long silence that carried on and on and on. Geraldine opened her eyes. The navigation monitor was still there but all that was below them was a huge banana shaped asteroid. There was no sign of Aqua or the Time Guardians. The air was already cooling. The comm. bleeped and Geraldine put it on loud speaker.

"It seems like I'm always getting you out of trouble."

Clarissa inhaled sharply.

"Zedekiah? Is that you?" Geraldine said.

"In the flesh."

"But we thought you were dead."

"Are you a ghost?" Annie asked.

"No I don't think so; sorry about the timing though, it took me a while to triangulate your position."

"Where are we?"

"A long way from the Time Guardians, you can be sure about that."

"But how did you survive?"

"Well now, it would have been very foolish of me to carry out a dangerous experiment on a remote planet without a backup plan wouldn't it?"

"Did you have another vortex machine?"

"No I didn't but the Keepers of Knowledge did."

"Did Zeno know anything about it?"

"No, why do you ask?"

"He was programmed to betray us to the Time Guardians."

"But that's impossible; I would have trusted him with my life."

"How did you find us?"

"I intercepted the call from Aqua to the Time Guardians. I've been looking for you for some time."

"We went to Karmos."

"You've got a different space ship."

"It's a long story."

"I'll direct you in and you can tell me everything."

They landed in the center of an asteroid that had been hollowed out by mining, and they disembarked as soon as the spacecraft was in the landing bay and the space doors were shut.

Zedekiah stood outside, waiting to greet everyone as they came out.

Clarissa was last in the line, "I've missed you so much," tears escaped her eyes and they fell into each other's arms.

"This place is amazing; you've installed artificial gravity," Geraldine said.

"I'd like to take the credit for that but I can't, this whole place was lent to me by the Keepers of Knowledge. You should see their gardens they're bursting with fresh vegetables, please follow me."

Geraldine stopped to examine the second vortex machine, the one that Zedekiah had used to bring them here, "This is far better than the one Zeno built."

"The Keepers of Knowledge constructed it."

"Which sector of the galaxy is this?" Josephine asked, "I couldn't find the star configurations on the computer anywhere."

"You're not supposed to and it's better if you don't know."

"I do not understand, I thought we were going to die," Amaak said.

"Please be my guests, we shall eat and then I can explain everything to you."

"Great I'm starving," Jerry said.

Their hunger made the food taste even more wonderful than it actually was. Amaak and Kiii had never had anything like it before; but they couldn't understand why everything had to be cooked. In the sea where they lived, there could be no fire, so all their food was eaten raw. Natter took his normal place beside Rosie and Annie; Rosie colored up and looked away from him.

By the end of the meal, they had explained so many things to Amaak that her head hurt. They had also told Zedekiah everything that had happened to them since they had last seen each other.

"My next mission is to go to the temple of Amos on Candice; the Keepers of Knowledge have discovered an ancient text that indicates that there might be secret information stored there. Even back then, only two hundred years after the temporal laws were enacted; it was obvious that the influence of the Time Guardians was impeding mankind's technological progress. Although I would hardly have expected Amos to be the person to have done anything about it," Zedekiah said.

"Perhaps he was secretly a Keeper of Knowledge," Mr. Mystery suggested.

"He was a very public figure; it would have been difficult for him to do anything in secret."

"Misdirection is the key to illusion," Mr. Mystery said.

"Do you want us to go with you?" Josephine asked.

"I could use your help if you're willing."

"Yea why not," Natter said.

"I'd like to see the place," Jerry agreed.

"Me too," Geraldine sounded enthusiastic.

"It's not like we have anything better to do," Rosie said.

"It's not inhabited is it?" Jerome asked.

"The last person left many, many years ago."

"Then there's no reason why not," Clarissa said.

"Can we use the vortex machine to transport us to this temple of Amos?" Froggie asked.

"That's exactly what we're going to do," Zedekiah said.

They were all exhausted so they slept in their beds on the spacecraft that night preferring to leave the preparation for their trip till the next day.

The following morning they refueled and started loading food, tools, flashlights, magnetic scanners, ropes, pulleys, and even scuba gear into it.

That evening when they were around the dinner table they discussed their mission, "Why did Amos need a temple?" Annie asked.

"It started out as a retreat; he always claimed that the inspiration for his greatest achievements came to him while he was on that planet. But people flocked to it and Amos had to accommodate them so he built what constituted a fashion theme park. Even the toilet cleaners had to wear designer clothes and you could be refused entry if you weren't wearing the right gear," Josephine explained.

"How do you know all this?" Geraldine asked.

"It's on the computer; I've been looking it up. Look at the fashions; this is my favorite design so far," Josephine handed round a computer tablet.

Geraldine studied it closely, "It's wonderful."

"Wow," Rosie and Annie gasped together.

"Wow," Lydia said

"And this is what he looked like."

It was obvious that Amos had been a very courageous man. The image that Josephine brought up on the screen depicted him wearing a frosted pink suit with a pink Panama hat. Some men would have looked insipid in that color, others would have looked effeminate and still others would have looked downright ill. But maybe it was something to do with the way he held himself or maybe it was how the color looked against his shining, black skin.

Amos was absolutely....

"Gorgeous," Annie gasped.

"Wow again," Lydia said.

"He was some handsome man," Clarissa whispered.

Amaak made strange whirring sounds like a dove with a sore throat.

"He's really, really..." Geraldine drooled.

"Yes, he really is."

"Do you realize we're swooning over a dead guy?" Lydia reminded them.

"Yes but what a dead guy," Josephine brought up pictures of him in outfits of baby blue, ultramarine, and hot orange.

"Perfect."

"He was an absolute genius."

"Pity he's dead."

"He committed suicide in his prime."

"A lot of geniuses do that," Annie said.

"People said at the time that it must have been because he wanted to bow out at the height of his career. But his girlfriend disagreed; she never accepted his death."

"I smell a conspiracy theory," Natter said.

"There were plenty of them but nothing was ever proved."

"I'm sorry to spoil your fun ladies but we are wasting time here; we need to be reviewing the schematics of the temple if we are ever going to figure out where Amos might have hidden that secret information," Zedekiah said.

Reluctantly Josephine brought three-dimensional plans of the Temple up onto the screen. It had been a glorious stone edifice surrounded by an extensive complex of buildings, all of which were pink because the stone that it was constructed of contained an unusual mixture of calcium and iron.

"It must have been massive," Froggie said.

Amos had been into the whole body approach to style. There were luxurious gymnasium facilities where personal trainers were available, hotels that only served the healthiest of foods, salt-water pools, seaweed baths, meditation pools, holistic and genetic therapy centers. There were life control courses, educational facilities, artist's workshops and tranquil gardens designed to create a sense of well-being. All this as well as great halls dedicated to fashion and design with personal advisors trained by Amos himself. The whole thing was magnificent.

"Why would someone want to commit suicide when he had all this?" Annie asked.

"I'll go with the conspiracy theory," Rosie said.

"This complex is no place to hide secret information," Zedekiah told them.

"Why not?"

"It's too accessible to the public."

"We could search the schematics of the temple's utility systems," Josephine searched the database but didn't come up with anything useful.

"Hm," Zedekiah scratched his nose.

"What are you thinking?"

"There must have been some secret rooms."

"What about his private apartments and his meditation room?"

"I doubt if they would have been private enough."

"I agree," Natter said, "so where could you incorporate a secret hidey hole into that design?"

"It would have to have been integrated from the beginning; it's not something you could add on later."

"But that means that his builders would have to be in on the secret."

"I wouldn't trust anybody would you?" Josephine said.

"Where else would it be?" Zedekiah wondered.

Josephine told the computer to search for any anomalies in the building plans; anything that would indicate an unassigned space but it came up with nothing.

Natter nibbled his strong, black fingernails.

"What are you thinking?" Rosie asked.

"If I were him I'd dig downwards."

"Yea well you always think that way because you were designed to be a miner," Geraldine told him.

"No, he has a point," Zedekiah said, "anything above the ground has public access but if you built a tunnel below the ground you could design it to have only one way in and out and that's much easier to control."

"When we get there I'll take a look around if you want," Natter said.

"That might not be as easy as you think; six months after Amos died, a freak earthquake destroyed the place."

"A freak earthquake?"

"This whole continent is geologically stable; it should never have happened."

"Well that proves it was a conspiracy," Rosie said.

"I'd still like to have a look," Natter said.

The next day, when they were ready, Zedekiah powered up the vortex machine and entered the co-ordinates before strapping himself into a seat on the bridge of the spacecraft.

Geraldine piloted the vessel out of the asteroid to a spot some three kilometers away.

"Prepare for the count down, ten... nine... eight... seven... six... five... four... three ... two... one...."

Suddenly the view on the navigation control changed and the asteroid disappeared. But Candice was not below them; the sky was above them because the vortex machine had placed them on the ground right beside the famous temple.

It was the depths of winter here and before they could go out they had to wrap themselves up in blankets to keep warm. They walked slowly down the steps of the spacecraft taking in all that they could see around them.

"It's a strange place," Annie whispered.

"But it's beautiful," Rosie said.

The temple itself was completely ruined; the pink stone blocks were piled randomly upon each other where they had fallen when the earthquake had shaken the buildings apart. There was a slight dusting of snow on top of them as they lay beneath a pale, violet sky.

"It reminds me of a huge bowl of Turkish Delight," Jerry said.

Amaak and Kiii purred; they liked the cold. Natter ran off around the perimeter, squinting at boulders. "What are you supposed to find in these ruins?" Froggie said.

"I won't know until I see it."

Annie bent down and picked up a tiny glass bottle that she found lying on the ground in the shadow of a rock where the snow had not fallen. "I wonder how many people were here when these buildings came down."

"One thousand three hundred and twenty," Zedekiah said.

"Did anyone survive?"

"Only a handful."

"Oh that's terrible." Annie said.

Natter ran back to where they were standing, "Let me have another look at the computer," Josephine handed him a computer tablet and he carefully studied the pictures of the temple. "So the central tower was there."

"Yes and the gymnasium was to the right."

"Okay so that meant that the salt baths and the hydrology center were to the left."

"Why do you want to know?"

"Because they must have used a lot of water, which came from somewhere and went somewhere; also I want to know where the electricity was generated."

"You're thinking about the places that the public wouldn't go?" Zedekiah said.

"The stone that the temple is made of doesn't match that the rocks around here, this pink stuff must have been imported."

"And is that significant?" Lydia asked.

"Yes of course, you see it means that the local rock structure is probably impervious to water, which means that we should see streams above ground, but we don't and that means that the rock is fractured or badly worn and that all the water is below ground and that indicates that there are probably caves down there too," Natter said.

"But couldn't that all have happened during the earthquake?"

"I don't think there was a true earthquake, I'll have to do more checking but it seems to me that the bedrock hasn't moved for thousands of years."

"That's weird," Annie said.

"It looks more like the place was blown over by a strong wind."

"Or maybe some kind of explosion?" Rosie suggested.

"I haven't had time to check it all out properly, but it wouldn't surprise me if that temple was destroyed deliberately."

"Wow," Annie said.

Josephine studied the computer tablet, "It says here that all the drinking water came from a pure source deep in the bedrock.

If your theory's correct it should still be there. The location's on the map here."

Natter examined the computer screen carefully, "They must have drilled a well through those rocks there."

"I can send a remote camera down if the way is clear," Zedekiah said.

Natter climbed over the ruins of the temple towards where the saltwater baths would have been. He stood there scratching his head, his eyes darting back and forth over the rocks, sniffing the air. However for some reason he didn't look satisfied; he shook his head, moved over a bit and started again.

"What's he doing?" Annie asked.

"He told me he has a very sensitive sense of smell; he actually thought it was normal until he found out that other people don't have it," Rosie said.

"I don't remember him saying that."

"You were asleep at the time."

"Do you often talk to Natter when I'm asleep?"

"Sometimes… lately."

Natter called over to them, "The waste water was treated at that building in the distance over there, so it wasn't pumped back down into the substructure," he headed over to check the layout.

At lunchtime Bunion made vegetable soup followed by a salad with hot potatoes and cold meat. At least it was warm in the spacecraft. Everybody had been shivering outside. Bunion poured hot coffee into mugs.

Zedekiah had spent a long time poking a remote camera down the fresh water pipe but there was not much to report, the water was still flowing and there was no visible earthquake damage. "Natter was right, that pink rock isn't local; it's probably not even from this planet."

"It must have cost millions to import," Rosie said.

"We're pretty sure that there are caves somewhere under the temple. What we can't figure out is exactly where."

"Can I help?" Amaak asked.

Suddenly Lydia screamed.

"What's wrong are you hurt?" Bunion had just put a plate of salad in front of her.

"There's a... there's a creature...."

"I'm sorry mistress," Bunion picked up a lettuce leaf; it had something gray, slimy and alive sitting on it.

Zedekiah looked over at it, "Oh good you found one of our slugs."

"What did you call it? How can that be good?"

"We grew it inside that barren asteroid, think about how difficult that was; an ecosystem capable of supporting genuine mollusks is a real achievement."

"Don't they have slugs on Bella?" Froggie asked.

"I've never seen one," Lydia said.

"Do you mind... if you're not going to eat it?"

Amaak croaked.

"You want some?"

"No, no I do not need...."

"Look you take it, it's the nearest thing to natural food you're gonna see for a long time."

Amaak thanked Froggie shyly but she didn't eat it; she gave it to Kiii.

"Yeuk that's disgusting," Rosie said.

"Oh I don't know," Natter commented, "they're okay once you get used to them."

Kiii chewed on his treat while his mother told the others of her abilities, "I am sensitive to the presence of water and I can tell many things with my sonar."

"Can you tell if something in the ground is soft like maybe it's filled with mud, or hard like rock?" Natter asked.

"Yes."

"Great, that would really help me with my digging."

After they had eaten, Amaak, Kiii, Natter and Zedekiah went outside. The others stayed in the warmth of the spaceship. Zedekiah got out his geophysics gear and they climbed over treacherous rocks surveying the area until the sun lost its strength and the cold set in.

By the time they came back inside Bunion had prepared some more hot soup and some warm rolls. Bread was one thing that he was actually good at making. There was also hot apple pie, which tasted good because all he had to do was defrost it.

Zedekiah displayed the results of the geophysical survey on a large computer tablet, "As you can see it's a little bit patchy because of the unevenness of the ground but you get the general idea," he showed them various straight lines which he said were foundations and then he pointed to two fuzzy, gray features on the screen. "The temple is built on bedrock; these two sites are the only places where the ground is soft."

Natter and Amaak studied them carefully, "There's water in this area, I could smell it," Natter said.

"That one goes straight downwards but quickly becomes narrow, it's a natural fissure in the rock," Amaak told him.

"What about the site without water?"

"That one is quite wide and goes down further than my sonar can track it."

"According to my instruments it's dead square and goes straight down like a shaft. It's very unlikely to be natural."

"My senses still tell me that it's the other one we want," Natter said.

"If there's water, there could be flooding."

"Well I suppose we could try the dry site first and if it comes to nothing we still have the other one."

"Aren't there huge blocks of stone all over that area?" Josephine asked.

"That's where me and Grumpus can help," Geraldine said.

After they had eaten their meal they all went to bed in order to get an early start in the morning.

When the sun rose Geraldine and Grumpus went over to examine the problem.

There was only going to be one way to remove the stone blocks. They found the rope and wire that Zedekiah had packed before they left the asteroid and wrapped it around one of the offending rocks so that they could attach it to the spacecraft.

Then Geraldine started the jet engines and taxied away, dragging it clear. It took all morning to move three stones.

Bunion cooked a nourishing stew with extra hard dumplings for lunch.

"Are you sure you want to start digging today?" Zedekiah asked. "Wouldn't you rather wait till tomorrow so you can get a good run at it?"

"It won't make any difference, we'll just work till it's dark and then we'll stop, and then tomorrow morning we'll carry on again," Natter said.

Zedekiah insisted on going with them even though Natter said it wasn't necessary. He volunteered to carry the shovels.

Before they left the spacecraft Rosie came up to Natter and handed him something, "It's a jacket, I made it out of some bedding while you were surveying the site, I thought it might keep you warm," she said shyly.

Natter put the jacket on, "I didn't know you could sew," he smiled at her.

"Clarissa's been teaching us for some time now, during the long trips between planets, she told me she could do with some help making costumes."

"Well thanks Rosie, thanks Annie."

"It wasn't my idea it was Rosie's," Annie told him.

"Are we ready to go?" Zedekiah asked.

"Be careful," Rosie said.

"Don't you worry about me," Natter bent down and kissed her.

Rosie turned the color of beetroot as he headed out of the spacecraft door.

"He really likes you doesn't he," Annie said.

"I think he must," Rosie sighed.

"I'm happy for you," Annie said.

"Do you think he'll be safe? What if the earth caves in on top of him?"

"He's an experienced miner, don't you worry; he knows what he's doing."

Everyone watched the screen as Zedekiah, Amaak and Natter picked up the shovels and started to dig. The first few inches took a long time to hack out because the ground was frozen, but Amaak turned out to be stronger than she looked; she chirruped as she worked and after they had dug their way through the hard layer, the dirt soon piled up beside the hole. When they had gone down about two feet Amaak used her sonar to check the depth. The sound waves traveled over ten feet down into the soil, which meant that there was no rock so far.

While she labored Amaak sang a strange and eerie song whose melody would have traveled many miles under water. Natter twitched with delight to be digging again, he looked at his nails and hoped they had not been weakened by inactivity.

Zedekiah didn't fare so well, "My back," he groaned.

"Your back hurting?" Natter asked.

"I'm afraid I'm a little too old for all this physical activity."

"Go back to the spacecraft and relax."

"Are you sure? I want to do my bit."

"Don't worry we've got this covered."

Inside the craft everyone was getting bored of watching a screen where not much was happening."Can you teach me to cook?" Lydia asked Bunion as he headed towards the galley to prepare another meal.

"I'm not very good at it," Bunion said.

"Then maybe we can help each other."

Meanwhile outside Natter put his shovel to one side and got down on his hands and knees to sniff the ground, "This dirt must have washed in here over the years since the earthquake."

"I like the color of the sky, it reminds me of home," said Amaak, completely ignoring his comment.

"Your home under water?"

"Yes, at certain times of the day you could actually see the pink light from the sun as it mingled with the blues of the ocean, those were the times I always liked the best."

"Were you born in the sea?"

"I took my first breath on the surface of the Violet Ocean; I remember how awesome I thought the world was."

"You remember your first breath?"

"Yes of course, don't you?"

Natter paused for a minute, "You know I think if I could just...."

"You want to burrow?"

"Yes."

Amaak climbed out of the hole, "I will watch the sunset."

Natter flexed his sharp, black nails and then suddenly he was away, using his hands as scoops, not clearing all the material right to the walls but making a little tunnel through the dirt in the center, compacting earth into the sides of the hole and throwing some on top.

Josephine watched him on the computer screen. "How does he do that?" she asked.

"He'll need a good wash when he comes back inside," Rosie said.

"No I don't mean that. How could he stand that enclosed space?"

"He was bred to it."

"I couldn't do it, even the sight of it makes me claustrophobic."

If Bunion was surprised that Lydia really couldn't cook he didn't show it; and Lydia realized that he wasn't as bad a cook as people thought. It was just that he had so much work to do that he couldn't watch all the pans at once. He should have asked for help long ago but it wasn't in his nature to complain. Lydia learned how to hold the knife when peeling vegetables.

"Always point the blade away from you," Bunion said.

"Like this?"

"Yes but don't take off so much skin or there'll be nothing left to cook Mistress."

"Bunion about you calling me Mistress, I know you're just being respectful but could you just stop please?"

"Why?"

"Because I'm not your Mistress," Bunion looked up at her questioningly, "Bunion I am not your Mistress."

It took a while to get used to holding the knife blade at the correct angle but even so Lydia found that she could be a help to Bunion. The dinner was cooked on time and with a second pair of eyes watching the sausages, they weren't as burnt as usual.

Natter, who after working till sundown, had cleaned himself up and put on fresh clothes, was ravenous, "I didn't realize how much I missed this work," he said cheerily.

"Have you found anything yet?" Lydia said.

"No, not so far, we're down to fifteen feet and Amaak tells me that there's nothing but dirt for the next ten so I'll start again at first light tomorrow; if I get the whole day at this pace I should be down near the forty foot mark by the end of it."

The next day Lydia learned how to make bread and she also found out how the dough could be made into a base for pizza.

By sundown Natter had dug a hole thirty-eight feet straight down. Grumpus and Froggie and Jerry and Jerome had been hauling earth away as fast as they could, sweating even though it was very cold because they were having trouble keeping up with him. Occasionally they would lower Amaak down into the hole on ropes and she would make the strange sonar clicking noises that allowed her to tell the condition of the soil below them.

"No rocks yet," she said.

Josephine watched on the camera from the warmth and safety of the spaceship; she shuddered every time she looked at that confined space.

Natter wanted to rig up lights and carry on digging, but the night would be short enough on this rapidly spinning world and he was ordered to bed.

On the third day Lydia learned how to make pancakes; she even figured out that what was wrong with the way Bunion made them was simply the fact that they were too thick. He made thinner ones and they tasted just fine.

Natter got down to sixty-eight feet, he had dug thirty feet in one day and that was a record even for him. But still there was nothing but earth for the next ten feet.

On the fourth day he got down to eighty-one feet before Amaak announced that there was rock below him, "Can you tell if there's anything else down there?" he asked.

Amaak double-checked, "There is something at the bottom of the shaft; something made of metal."

Natter dug down the last ten feet and then burrowed into a corner where he uncovered a metal box. It was a steel safe in remarkably good condition and it was bolted down into the rock. "I'll need some tools if I'm to retrieve it," he said.

"No," Mr. Mystery told him, "do not do that, I have seen that design before, do not touch it; it could be booby trapped."

"Surely after eight hundred years the explosives couldn't still be live."

"That is possibly true but I do not want you to take the chance."

"So what do we do?"

"I will open it," Mr. Mystery said.

Natter didn't need to be hauled up the shaft, he just wedged his feet and arms onto the sides and quickly ran up to the top; but Mr. Mystery did have to be lowered down.

"Be careful Richard, if that thing goes off it'll bring tons of earth down on top of you," Clarissa said.

Mr. Mystery attached wires and batteries to the safe and put a listening device up to the door, "It is a pity that I do not have my quantum x-ray device, I would have been able to tell what is inside."

He very carefully cleaned, brushed and oiled the frozen dial; it took a lot of effort to get it to turn at all. Eventually he was able to crunch it backwards, and then forwards, and then backwards and forwards again.

"One more digit and the combination is complete."

"Can't you open it by remote control?" Clarissa asked.

"It is a manual safe; it has to be operated by hand."

"So if you get the combination wrong, you're dead?"

"I have taken risks before."

"Please be careful," Clarissa said.

Everyone crowded around the monitor as Richard clicked the stiff dial backwards. He heard the tumbler drop and nearly let go but something told him that he had not done enough. He pulled the dial outwards but that did nothing, so he pushed it in and the door crunched and grated and creaked open. A split second too late Mr. Mystery realized that he should have pulled the dial back out again to complete the action.

He closed his eyes and braced himself.

Nothing happened.

He looked into the safe and sure enough an explosive charge lay just inside the door. It was a crude device but if the volatile substances had not evaporated over the centuries he would not be looking at it now.

"Are you all right Richard?" Clarissa asked.

"Yes perfectly."

"Can you see anything? Is there anything in there?"

Mr. Mystery pulled out a pile of brittle, brown paper; Clarissa could see it on the monitor. "Money?" she asked.

"Hardly legal tender in this day and age."

"Is there anything else?"

Mr. Mystery felt around inside the safe, "There is a secret compartment..." he pulled out a little package, something that had been carefully wrapped as if it was precious. Everyone cheered when they saw that it was a memory crystal.

Zedekiah rubbed his chin, "After eight hundred years in the ground I doubt if this is going to yield any information, to be honest I'm a little disappointed, I was hoping for more."

Natter, who was exhausted, had a long shower, a good meal and went to bed. His part of the job was over; now it was up to Zedekiah and Josephine to see what information they could extract from the crystal.

The crystalline matrix of the ancient recording device was remarkably stable but the contacts had corroded and disintegrated. Zedekiah looked at it carefully, "That might not be a problem, this is a TR7; you can download the information directly from the crystal if you have the right receiver."

"But how is it powered?" Josephine asked.

"Photonic energy, you can activate it by shining a strong light onto it."

"So do we have a receiver?"

Zedekiah pointed to Josephine's cone shaped head, "It should be compatible."

"You think I could read this crystal?"

"You should be able to tune yourself to the right frequency and upload the data to the ship's computer."

"Well I suppose I'll give it a try."

Meanwhile Lydia had been studying some recipe books that she found in the ship's database, "This one looks simple enough."

"If they don't like it they'll complain," Bunion warned her.

"Look, I'll prepare the vegetables and you cook them; that way if anybody doesn't like the food I can say that it was my fault."

"But Mi...."

"Don't call me that Bunion."

"But...."

"Just call me Lydia."

Bunion shook his head in a way that worried Lydia. She was glad that he didn't say much and that what he did say was not always taken seriously because she had a feeling that Bunion understood not just more than everyone else, but everything.

For dinner they made stir-fry vegetables in an extra special sauce. "Mmm, we've never had this before, where did ya get all these vegetables?" Geraldine asked.

"Zedekiah's garden," Lydia told her.

"They're really nice," Froggie said.

"Excellent," Jerome agreed.

"Did you find any more slugs?" Amaak licked her lips.

"Bunion did the cooking; I just helped him with the preparation."

"Let me have a taste," Annie said.

"But it's my turn to eat today," Rosie reminded her.

"I only want a taste."

"You remember our arrangement? Two heads—one body, one eats one day and the other the next."

Annie looked disappointed.

Rosie laughed, "Here, try these they're really nice."

"Don't wind me up like that."

"Sorry I just couldn't help it, it's so easy."

Meanwhile Zedekiah had explained to Josephine that the pseudo-brains of her ancient sisters were able to tune in to the dedicated interface nodes that were incorporated into every device of their day, even though they did not exist on modern computers.

To Josephine's amazement as soon as she shone a strong light onto the crystal, a visualization of its node appeared in her mind. She spent some time working out how this had happened and discovered that she could control the crystal with her thoughts. After she had got over her astonishment she suggested that they try to create a software interface node for the computer by manually copying the one on the crystal. It turned out to be a straightforward operation and by the time the others had finished their dinner she was ready to test it.

Natter woke up hungry again; he came wandering up to the dining table stretching his arms. Bunion got up and brought him a plate full of tasty vegetables.

"Have I missed anything? Has anyone deciphered that crystal yet?" he asked.

"Josephine's still working on it, oh here she is now," Jerry said.

Josephine and Zedekiah walked in carrying a computer tablet.

"Let's hope this works," Josephine said.

Everyone crowded around the computer tablet and Josephine handed the crystal to Natter, "Here you should be the one to hold this; shine the light onto it," she gave him a powerful torch.

Natter held the light and the crystal the way that she showed him.

"Ready?" Zedekiah said.

Josephine nodded; she took a deep breath and closed her eyes.

Everyone waited.

"Something's happening," Annie said.

Big squares of color appeared on the screen; they got smaller and smaller until they resolved into the words 'The Amos Narbandian Corporation.' There was a picture of Amos himself to the left of them and there was a picture of the temple to the right.

"I can see all these images in my mind, it's just amazing," Josephine started scrolling through the pages of text that followed, running the words faster and faster until no one but she could read them. At last she stopped and opened her eyes.

"I did it; I interfaced with the crystal and the computer," she shouted.

Everyone hugged her.

"Well done," Zedekiah cheered.

"It's not what you were hoping for though was it?"

"No."

"I checked for secret encryption and piggybacked messages, I can do it really fast, but there was nothing."

"So the secret information is a second set of books?"

"What does he mean?" Annie asked.

"He means that the Amos Narbandian Corporation had been hiding a percentage of its profit so that it wouldn't have to pay so much tax."

"I can't believe that Amos could do such a thing."

"To be fair these records start after his death, he can't have known anything about them."

"Can I put this torch down now?" Natter asked.

"Yes of course," Josephine said.

Natter looked over at Amaak, "Tomorrow morning?"

She nodded and chirruped.

Josephine looked at him questioningly.

"Tomorrow I want to start digging at the other location."

"Do you think it's really worth it?"

"Well we won't know until we try."

Natter's hole didn't have nicely carved straight sides. It was a natural fracture in the earth and most of the time he found himself scrabbling through mud, not soft earth. At times he wondered if he and Amaak were going to get stuck between its stone cliffs. It was hard work but however difficult it got, Amaak would keep telling him that there was another ten feet of earth still ahead of them. So he would continue to excavate while Grumpus and Geraldine hauled the mud to the surface.

It took four exhausting, mind-numbing days.

Then suddenly there was no more earth; Natter broke through the ground and found himself hanging in space. If it wasn't for the rope that was tied around his waist he would have crashed headlong down onto the rocks below. He shone his helmet lamp around, "I knew it; it's a cave and look there's running water at the bottom."

Everyone crowded around the computer screen as Natter pointed his head-cam downwards. Sure enough, some distance below him they could just make out an underground river.

"Can you see anything?" Josephine asked.

"Not from here but if Grumpus can lower me down to the floor of the cave I'll take a look around."

A few minutes later Amaak landed beside him; she chirruped at the sight of water and bent over the side to taste it, "Not enough salt," she said.

"Is it good drinking water?" Natter asked.

"Yes it is," she gazed at it longingly, "can I? Can I just get my skin wet?"

"Won't that be dangerous? It's dark; you won't be able to see where you're going."

"I have my sonar to guide me."

"Well if you're sure... yea why not? It'll take me some time to investigate this cave."

Amaak slid silently into the cold water and disappeared below the surface while Natter examined every crack and crevice in the cavern. There was a high ceiling, dripping walls, strange rusty patches at one end and rows of sharp ridges at the other.

Eventually Natter had to admit, "There's nothing unusual here."

"After all that effort," Rosie was disappointed.

"It doesn't seem fair," Annie sighed.

"I should go down and help him look," Froggie said.

"There doesn't seem to be much point," Zedekiah sighed.

"It's just a regular cave, plain and simple, I'll wait for Amaak to come back and then we'll return to the surface, I'm hungry," Natter sounded let down.

"Shouldn't she be back by now?"

"Is my mother all right?" Kiii asked.

"She'll be fine, she just wanted to swim for a while that's all," Natter said.

"Me too, my skin is all dry and sore."

When Amaak didn't show up Grumpus lowered a sandwich down to Natter. The sun dipped low in the sky.

"When is my mother coming back?" Kiii asked.

"Oh soon I expect, she's probably just enjoying herself in the water," Josephine tried to sound dismissive.

"I think I should go and take a look," Froggie told Clarissa out of Kiii's hearing.

Clarissa nodded.

Geraldine rigged up a waterproof headlight for him since he didn't have the benefit of sonar. She also fitted a multi-atmosphere camera and remote microphone to his headgear before he slipped away from the spacecraft. He climbed over the pink rocks in the twilight and Grumpus tied him to a line and lowered him down into the hole.

Froggie wasn't fat by any means but there were times when even he found it hard to fit himself between the two rocky sides of the fissure. It was muddy, cold and damp, but he didn't mind those things, he had been bred to tolerate them, it was only the claustrophobia that bothered him. He was glad at last to be able to drop through the roof of the cavern and land on the floor below.

"Any sign of Amaak yet?" he asked Natter.

Natter shook his head.

"I'll go and look for her," Froggie jumped into the freezing water. He realized at once that this must be melt water from the snow on the mountains that they could see in the distance. But that wouldn't worry Amaak; she had a layer of blubber to keep her warm.

He dived down to the bottom of the river where the current was swift, and he swam around but Amaak wasn't there. He didn't know which way to go, upriver or down so he turned to go down river thinking that maybe she had followed the current as it flowed through a big gap in the rocks. Then suddenly he felt a vibration run through his body. The noise came from Amaak and it came from upstream.

Froggie put his head up above the surface, "I can hear her, she's all right, I'm going after her now," he said.

He blew the air out of his lungs and swam down to where he could see an opening in the rocks. The current was stronger here but he kicked his webbed feet and swam upstream. Amaak chirruped again; it was hard to tell how far away she was but he kept going. Suddenly the walls of the stream opened out and when Froggie put his head above the surface of the water he could see that he was in another, smaller cavern. Seconds later Amaak appeared by his side blowing air out of her nose.

"This way," she said and she swam off again.

It was all Froggie could do to keep up with her while she negotiated the current in the river. She chirruped and croaked so that he could follow the sound of her voice. Eventually they came to a huge cavern that was fed by three small streams.

Amaak disappeared down into a hole in the rock and Froggie had no choice but to follow her gray, flippered feet for what felt like a long time, first of all downward and then upward again through a narrow tube.

Finally they broke the surface.

Again Amaak blew through her nose, "It took me a long time to find this; I nearly got lost several times, but look over there," she said.

Froggie followed the direction of her finger as he shone a light into the cave for the first time in eight hundred years.

"Oh… we must tell the others," he gasped.

Chapter 10.

"It's a chair," Froggie told them over the radio.

"A what?" Natter asked.

"It's a stone chair."

"Are you sure it isn't just a pile of stones that happen to look like a chair?"

"No, it's a real chair," Froggie zoomed the head cam in for a closer look.

"Tell him what else we found."

"Amaak found some kind of a door hidden in the rock; we wouldn't have known it was there if it wasn't for her sonar."

"Do you know what's behind it?" Natter asked.

"No, but it's not very big, it could be another safe; we thought it might be booby trapped so we didn't try to open it."

Mr. Mystery looked worried, "I cannot go down there; my prosthetic brain would not react well to freezing water."

"Everybody come back to the spaceship, we've done enough for tonight, tomorrow morning we'll arrange for an expedition; we'll get to the bottom of this," Zedekiah said.

"I thought you'd be eager to find out what's down there," Clarissa told him.

"No one works at their best when they're tired. It's been a long day; let's get a good night's sleep. Whatever secrets that cave contains, have been down there for eight hundred years; one more day won't make any difference."

If Zedekiah had known what the morning would bring he wouldn't have been so eager to go to bed.

The next day Bunion was the first up; he and Lydia had been working on the pancake recipe. Bunion's problem had always been lack of ingredients. He served bean pie when there was no meat, sometimes he had to serve pizza without the cheese, there were never any extra flavorings like herbs and spices and although Zedekiah had been able to supply them with fresh vegetables, which they had not seen in a long time, there was hardly any sugar left. He was going to try making fluffed up savory pancakes filled with shredded onions and reconstituted, powdered egg.

He yawned and stretched and wandered into the galley to boil water for a hot drink. If there was coffee he would drink coffee, if there was milk he would drink milk, if there was only water he would drink hot water. Today there was a small supply left of Zedekiah's coffee.

He took his steaming cup down to one of the soft chairs on the bridge so that he could drink it in comfort before starting work.

His gaze wandered over to the window and suddenly his eyes opened wide, "Oh," he cried. He ran to the dormitory section and banged on Clarissa's cabin door, "Clarissa wake up, there's a spaceship outside, please Clarissa wake up."

Clarissa opened her door; her thin, gray hair hung in wisps about her lined face. "What did you say Bunion?"

"There's a gigantic, pink spaceship parked beside us." Clarissa looked out of her bunkroom window. "Not that side, the other side."

Clarissa threw on a housecoat and followed Bunion up to the bridge. She stared out of the window. The spaceship was big and sleek and very, very pink and it had the name 'Arial' emblazoned on the side. It stood proud against the white clouds and the lilac sky like the Temple of Amos must have done so many years before.

"What on earth…?"

"What are we going to do now?"

Clarissa woke up Zedekiah, "Just tell them the truth, we're archaeologists and we've come here to survey the ruins."

"Look at us, do we look like archaeologists?"

"Oh… Well I suppose you've got a point there."

"We're entertainers," Bunion said.

Clarissa looked down at the little man, "Thanks for reminding me Bunion." She looked out of the window at the massive ship, "It makes me think of the type of craft we saw in the marina on Chaiza Island and yes we are entertainers, we should ask them if they want to see our show."

Ten minutes later Clarissa walked up to the huge, pink edifice and knocked on the door. Everyone else blearily crowded around the window to see what would happen.

"She's gone inside," Rosie said.

"Is she going to be all right?" Annie asked.

"She knows what she's doing."

They all stood and waited… and waited… and waited.

"Do you think…?"

"No…."

"But she's been such a long time."

"That doesn't necessarily mean anything."

"But…."

"Let's just be patient and not let our imaginations run away with us?" Zedekiah said.

After what seemed like a very long time the main door of the pink monstrosity opened and Clarissa walked out looking calm and carefree.

Everybody breathed a sigh of relief.

"What did they say?" Geraldine asked as soon as Clarissa got back.

"I know the captain, you remember the man that used to drive the space taxi on Olympia? His name was Herman Waters."

"That must have been ten years ago," Grumpus said.

"Fifteen actually, well he's come up in the world, he did some trucking for a while and then he drove a space limo and after that the company he was working for trained him on the luxury yachts."

"So that's what that is, a space yacht?" Jerry asked.

"Yes and it's full of very spoilt rich girls who are on a fashion pilgrimage to the place where it all started."

"So when do we get to meet them?" Froggie asked.

"They won't want to see us," Rosie said.

"Well actually they do, there's a small ballroom with a stage at one end on their ship; Herman showed it to me. He told me that the girls are bored because of all the long space journeys with nothing to do, so he said he would give them a day to drool over the Temple and then tomorrow before they start to realize that all they're looking at is a pile of old stones, we're booked to entertain them."

"And where are they now?" Froggie was torn between his desire to find out an eight hundred year old secret and to meet the beautiful girls.

"At the moment they're still asleep, they're on universal, not local time and so to them it's the small hours of the morning. Herman says that even when they do get up they'll want showers and they'll have to do their hair and their make up; it'll be well into the afternoon before we can expect to see any of them."

"So what are we waiting for? Let's mount our expedition," Zedekiah said.

It took some time to get things ready. Zedekiah wanted to accompany them so he took out his scuba gear and wet suit, Grumpus insisted on checking all the ropes and Mr. Mystery put together a selection of the tools that they were most likely to need.

Kiii wanted to go too but Amaak would not allow him, even though his skin was shriveling from lack of water.

At last they were ready and one by one, with Natter in the lead and Amaak at the rear they were lowered into the fissure. The gear came in after them and eventually Froggie, Natter, Amaak and Zedekiah found themselves standing on the floor of the cavern.

Zedekiah got into his scuba gear and Amaak took the lead. Froggie took the rear position so that he could help if Zedekiah got into any trouble. Natter was to stay in the cavern and wait. He had a computer tablet so that he could follow the action from the fiber-optic camera.

Froggie was worried that Zedekiah's air bottle would make him too wide and he would get jammed in the small tunnels. It turned out to be a hard squeeze and he only just made it.

At last they reached the small cavern with the chair in it and Zedekiah popped his head out of the water, "That really is a chair," he exclaimed.

It had a big, square, block base; a flat back and solid arm rests. Amaak smiled as she climbed out of the underground river; she showed Zedekiah the hidden door set almost perfectly into the rock.

Meanwhile back in the space craft Mr. Mystery studied the view on the control monitor and picked up the microphone, "Run your hand around the rock; see if you can feel any irregularity."

"There," Amaak pointed to a spot above the top of the door. "It's too smooth."

"Press it...."

Zedekiah pressed it but nothing happened.

"Push harder."

"It won't budge."

"Use the oil from the toolbox."

Zedekiah soaked the area in oil; then he and Froggie pushed together. They heard a click and in the middle of the door a hidden hatch creaked open to reveal a shining dial. "Whoever built this mechanism wanted it to last; all the mechanical parts seem to be made of gold."

"The dial mechanism is the same as on the other safe," Mr. Mystery said.

"Does that mean that there are likely to be explosive charges inside waiting for anyone who doesn't have authorized entry?"

"Yes; you must be very careful."

Zedekiah ordered everyone else out of the cavern.

"We can't leave you here alone."

"Too risky Froggie."

Amaak made a clicking noise, "I at least should stay."

"Sorry Amaak, I'll have to do this without your help."

The lock was as primitive as the one on the safe had been, and because it had to be operated manually it was also potentially deadly.

After everyone had retired to the first cavern, which Natter estimated would be safe enough even in the event of a big explosion, Mr. Mystery taught Zedekiah how to listen through the stethoscope for the dropping of the tumblers, and Zedekiah completed the first four operations successfully.

"Now comes the difficult part...."

Meanwhile back in the spaceship; Bunion couldn't make out the monitor because everyone had crowded around it and he was too short to see over their bodies. His eyes flicked over to the pink space yacht outside the window. Two stylish young women were standing on its steps looking curiously over to where Grumpus stood above the fissure holding onto the ropes.

They began walking towards him.

Bunion ran to the galley, grabbed a cup, raced out of the spaceship, hurried over the snowy ground and intercepted the two girls.

"Hey what a funny little man, who might you be?"

"I'm Bunion," Bunion said.

"How do you do? We are daughters of the Great Emperor Omar, Lord of the Twelve Continents of Acadia and the Seventeen Systems."

"Are you sisters?"

"We are all sisters, now what can we do for you little man?"

Bunion held up the cup, "I was wondering if you had any sugar."

Meanwhile from the Genghis Khan Mr. Mystery was guiding Zedekiah through the last operation. "When you feel the tumbler fall you will have to either push the dial in or pull it out. You'll feel a slight movement; go with it to relieve the pressure."

"You think this thing is airtight?" Zedekiah asked.

"If it is not, the contents will be worthless," Mr. Mystery said.

Zedekiah took a deep breath and turned the dial forward; the tumbler dropped, "I can't feel anything."

"Replay what you just did in your mind."

"There was noth... wait a minute I did feel someth..."

"Go with it now!"

Zedekiah pushed down hard on the dial and then pulled it out again straight away.

The door creaked open and there was a fizzing sound.

Zedekiah sighed with relief when he realized that it was air rushing back into the safe and not the sound of a bomb about to explode.

"What's in there? Point the camera inside the safe," Clarissa said.

Everyone crowded around.

"Is that all?" Rosie said.

There was a small, metal box, a miniature fission generator, and a headpiece, that was not shaped for a person with a normal head, or even for someone with a big Karmosian head. Rather it was shaped for someone who had a cone head!

Which meant that on the Genghis Khan Josephine was staring at the computer screen and starting to panic, "I... I can't go down there, I'm claustrophobic."

"You may have to, you're probably the only one who can interface with that machine; Zedekiah says that Josephines were standard hardware when Amos was alive," Clarissa said.

"Can't they bring it up here?"

"Through the freezing water? They risk damaging it if they do that."

"But you don't understand; I can't go down there."

Just then there was a knock on the spacecraft door. Jerry opened it to find Bunion standing there with a cup of sugar in one hand and a bag of coffee in the other, and three pretty, young women hanging on his arms.

"Hi, I'm Miranda," the young women smiled and before Jerry could reply all three of them walked in.

"My, my, what a quaint little craft."

Clarissa switched off the computer screen and turned round.

"Hi my name's Janine," the second girl said.

"And my name's Clarissa; can I get you anything? Would you like something to drink?"

"Do you have any iced tea?"

"Do we Bunion?"

Bunion shook his head.

"Well that's all right, how about fruit juice?"

Bunion shook his head.

"Then how about... oh, oh what an unusual child," Janine had spotted Kiii.

Kiii squeaked.

"What's your name?" the third girl asked, "I'm Samantha," Kiii tried to hide behind Clarissa's back. "What's wrong with your skin? It seems to be all wrinkly; is that normal for you?"

Kiii squeaked again.

"His natural habitat is water; his skin has been shriveling," Clarissa explained.

"Where's his mother?"

"She's em, gone for a walk."

Suddenly the girls noticed Rosie and Annie, "Oh wow, oh wow, oh wow..." Miranda cried.

"Yes absolutely, wow." Janine said.

"How did you do that? That is so... I wish we were all joined up like that," Samantha jumped about excitedly.

"How much did it cost?" Miranda asked.

"You mean us? We're conjoined; we were born like it."

"You are so lucky; you couldn't buy a unique look like that."

"Do you really think we enjoy being like this?" Rosie said.

"It's very inconvenient at times," Annie told them.

"Yea but worth it eh? What a way to get noticed."

"To think, we met you in the style capital of the universe," Miranda looked as if she was going to cry.

"What a privilege," Samantha said.

"Say why don't you all come over to us for drinks? We have everything. And did you say that this young man here needs to be in water?" Janine asked.

"Yes," Clarissa said.

"Good, well it so happens that our swimming pool contains salt water that was imported all the way from the green pools of Karelia."

"I'm sure that Kiii would love to swim in your pool."

"That's excellent, and while you're there you may as well stay to dinner; you can tell us all about yourselves."

"But there are sixteen of us all together; some of us are out er... walking."

"Tell them they are all welcome," Miranda smiled.

"Josephine can do that; she can stay here until the others return; the rest of us can come over now."

"We could leave them a note," Josephine said.

"Notes can be lost, I would rather you stayed and told them personally."

"So... have you ever seen a three legged man before?" Jerry asked as he walked out of the door.

"No," Miranda said, "you're amazing."

Jerry held out his arms so that the girls could grab on, "Let me tell you my story."

As soon as they were gone Josephine switched on the computer screen and informed the others of the situation.

"You'd better come now; we've got to get this done before those young women get too curious," Zedekiah said.

"Can't you do it?"

"We've all tried; the system seems to be working all right but we're not receiving anything."

"Maybe it wouldn't work for me either, it's eight hundred years old; it's probably broken."

"Josephine everything is working just fine, but the headpiece is shaped for a Josephine, I don't know where you came from but I'm very glad you're here because you're the only one who can interface with that machine. Please, we need this information."

Josephine put her head in her hands and rubbed her eyes. "Okay, okay I'll try." Very unwillingly she left the spacecraft and climbed over the snowy rocks towards Grumpus. The fissure was hardly wider than her own body; she stood above it shaking her head, "I can't, I can't, I just can't."

"Take your time," Grumpus told her.

Suddenly Natter's head appeared above the surface, "I'll lead you down."

"Please I can't…."

Grumpus grabbed her by the shoulders, "Pull yourself together woman, no one would be asking you to go down there if there was any other way."

"Close your eyes, now breathe deep, that's it, Grumpus will tie a nice, strong, secure rope around you and lower you down and I'll be with you every step of the way," Natter said.

Josephine closed her eyes and kept them closed throughout every long second of that cruel and harrowing journey, "It feels like the walls are closing in," she kept saying.

"That's impossible; you know that," Natter told her.

She relaxed a little when she landed on the cavern floor and could feel solid ground beneath her feet. She allowed herself to open her eyes but stiffened up again when she saw Zedekiah standing there holding the scuba gear.

"All you have to do is breathe; Froggie and Amaak will guide you along." Josephine struggled into the wet suit and Zedekiah put the heavy air bottle on her back, "Put your face mask on and breathe through your mouth; good, now bite on your mouthpiece, that's right. Breathe in… out… in… out, that's very good. Do you feel ready to get into the water?"

Josephine nodded and Froggie and Amaak helped her down into the stream. "Put your head under the water."

Josephine did as she was told… and panicked.

She pushed her head back up and dropped the mouthpiece, "I can't breathe… I can't breath."

"But you were breathing."

Amaak caught hold of Josephine's hand and made soft chirruping sounds until she was calmer.

"Close your eyes and relax, let Froggie and Amaak do the rest."

Josephine closed her eyes and put her head back under the water; it took her thirty seconds of sheer terror to realize that she could actually breathe.

Amaak still chirruped pleasantly; to her this black, underground prison was a place of freedom and adventure. She and Froggie moved Josephine along slowly against the current, guiding her through narrow rocky tunnels that she dared not look at or think about. It seemed to take forever; she wondered how much air was left in the bottle.

They got to the hole that went down and then up. She could feel her body touching the sides and was tempted to take out her mouthpiece so that she could scream, but she knew that if she did, she would drown. Instead she tried to concentrate on Natter's words: "Close your eyes, relax, relax, relax...."

The nightmare got worse as she realized that she would have to go through all of this in reverse, in order to get out of there.

Then suddenly it was over.

They popped up in a small cavern and through the mask she could see the stone chair and the headpiece that had been preserved in the airtight safe for over eight hundred years.

Amaak helped Josephine out of the water. Froggie took the heavy bottle off her back and she sat trembling into the chair. Slowly she took off the mask and replaced it with the headset. It lit up immediately. She closed her eyes once more but this time she leaned her head back and relaxed.

Then suddenly she opened them and leaned her head forward again.

"Didn't it work?" Froggie asked.

"Oh yes it worked, I mean it really did work, I could feel the data in my mind, I could see it, I didn't have to think about it, I just did it."

"But that was so quick."

"There wasn't very much there."

"Are you sure you got it all?"

"Yes absolutely; but it's okay because I know… I know what we have to do next," she took off her headset and put on her mask.

On the way back up to the surface, Josephine had something to take her mind off her fears. She burst out of the fissure and they all ran back to the spacecraft, which was empty,

"Oh I forgot; we've been invited to dinner."

They all cleaned themselves up while she uploaded the information onto the ship's computer and then they gathered around a monitor to look at the data.

"Is this all there was?" Zedekiah asked.

"Read it," Josephine told him.

"This is dated the day before Amos died."

"Notice the name he mentions half way down."

"'Bridefield suspects me but he doesn't know the extent of my secret organization. No one does, if he captures me, others will carry this mission on into the future. My only hope is to be able to store as much knowledge as I can in this secure place before I am caught,'" Zedekiah read.

"He *was* a Keeper of Knowledge," Froggie said.

"It's a tragedy that he didn't get to fill the database."

"But look at the information he did leave for us."

"The works of Plato, and Aristotle, and Archimedes, and Zeno of Elea, and Euclid, the ancient Greek masters; he was starting at the beginning."

"Yes but for some reason he also included this."

"It's a report about two young boys who walked into a time machine and activated it by accident and ended up on Zertza."

"Yes but that's not all, when they got there they were approached by some strange looking people who said they needed it… that's us," Josephine said.

"But those boys arrived on Zertza two hundred years ago."

"No, they didn't. The strange people sent them back to their own time and then programmed the machine to return to Zertza by remote control. The kids were interrogated by the Time Guardians but it turns out that although they had traced the time machine to its spatial location on Zertza, they didn't know when in time it had landed and for some reason the boys lied to the about the date. Sadly they were the first people to be executed under the new laws."

"So if the date they gave was the wrong one, what was the right one?" Zedekiah asked.

"Three days from now," Josephine said.

Zedekiah headed for the spacecraft door, "I'm going to tell Clarissa," he said.

There were fifteen daughters of Omar aboard the Ariel.

They told Jerry that there were another eighty-six at home but none of them could marry until the oldest one, Olivia chose a husband and she was unbelievably fussy.

Jerry regaled the girls with stories about the perils of the life of a traveling player with himself as the hero of course. Kiii's skin was nearly back to normal and Jerome had been entertaining them with some juggling. Bunion was sitting very uncomfortably on a comfortable sofa with a girl either side of him and two more on the arms.

"Bunny-Wunny you are so cute, I love your gorgeous, big, brown eyes," a petite, black haired girl was saying.

Samantha put her arms around him, "He's so cuddly," she said.

He stared over at Lydia with a pleading, "Get me out of here!" look in his gorgeous, big, brown eyes.

Lydia got up and squeezed in between him and a girl who was probably called Tara; she took hold of his hand.

Miranda smiled at them with a knowing look on her face, "Is there something going on between you two?" she asked.

Lydia frowned, "Bunion is a quiet, hard working man who never complains; he is intelligent, tenderhearted, generous and humble, how many men do you know that are like that?"

Miranda nodded, "Well I guess he would be quite a catch if... well you know."

"Bunion's a decent human being and he should be treated with dignity," Lydia frowned.

"So there is something going on."

There was a knock at the door and she got up to answer it.

The girls welcomed Josephine and the rest of their guests. They were fascinated with Froggie, "You have gills? Can you really breathe underwater?"

"I thought you had to be cold blooded for that system of respiration to work," a girl called Sadie said.

"Take no notice of her, she thinks too much," Miranda told them.

"I don't know how they work; I was just born this way," Froggie said.

"Can we touch them?" the girls wanted to know.

"Well, sure you can if you want, but be careful, they're delicate."

Josephine slid a small computer tablet over to Clarissa who read it carefully.

"We're so looking forward to your performance tomorrow," Janine told them.

"I'm afraid there isn't going to be any performance, we've been called away urgently," Clarissa said.

"What? You've got to go? No you can't do that, you said you'd do a show for us, you promised."

"But this is an emergency."

"An entertainment emergency?"

"Look, couldn't you just stay a while? You could still have dinner; after all you've got to eat sometime haven't you? And then you could put on your show and after that you could deal with your emergency, please..." Miranda said.

"Yes please," all the other girls cried in unison.

"But...."

"We'll pay you a thousand quid," Janine said coaxingly.

"A thousand quid for one performance?"

They all nodded.

Clarissa could not afford to pass up that kind of money; "Oh, well er I suppose it is only two and a half days to Zertza; perhaps we could stay a few more hours."

None of the girls ate very much at dinner even though the food was exquisite. They talked a lot though and they were fascinated when Zedekiah told them that he was an archaeologist.

"So what's a group of entertainers doing at an archaeological site?" a girl called Shauna asked.

"I needed transport and they said they would be passing near the system with a few days to spare. They promised they would wait while I did my survey."

"What kind of survey are you doing?"

"Oh, you know, where did they get their water? How did they produce their power? How did they process their waste? Things like that."

"It sounds pretty boring."

"Actually it's a fascinating site, when we first landed we found a little glass perfume bottle lying on the ground; just think, it belonged to someone who probably died in the earthquake eight hundred years ago, don't you ever wonder what those people were like? What their hopes and dreams were? What they thought about? What they feared?"

"She could have been just a girl, like us," Tara said.

"Tell us, what was Amos like?" Miranda asked.

For the rest of the meal Zedekiah entertained the girls with anecdotes about Amos and his life. How he was born a printer's son on a planet so primitive that virtual books were virtually unknown, how he played with the different inks from a young age and how the colors inspired his art. How he never received much formal education and yet everyone that met him came away feeling that he was a very wise man. How he met his girlfriend when she spilled some pink ice cream down his white suit at a fair, and how it all ended so sadly on the day they found him hanging in the kitchen of his private apartment with the suicide note in his pocket.

The girls wept when they heard the story, but the meal was over and Clarissa was anxious to get on with the entertainment. They had no proper costumes and little equipment and what had been acceptable on Aqua, a planet where everything was made of reeds would not cut it here on this gleaming craft. Nevertheless Rosie could still sing, Grumpus could still lift incredibly heavy weights, Mr. Mystery could still make things disappear and Jerome could still walk the tightrope.

And they could still do the wedding sequence.

"That's who you remind me of, Princess Stephanie," Miranda said.

"We were hoping for invitations to the royal wedding, since we are princesses ourselves," Samantha told them.

"You really look like her," Sadie said.

"Well I am from Bella, it's possible that I carry some of the royal genes from way back," Lydia said.

The girls laughed when they saw the improvised wedding dress made out of bed sheets that Lydia wore. But they wept when she kissed Bunion.

"I knew there was something between those two," Miranda sighed.

"It's so sweet."

"I hope I get a good man like him."

"It's so romantic."

Clarissa shook her head; she'd never had that reaction to her comedy before. The show finished and she instructed everyone to pack up as quickly as possible.

"But you can't go yet," Janine said, "we notice that you need... well help, so we've all decided to contribute some of our stuff, the stuff we don't use any more, if you'll accept it."

"Well, that would be nice," Lydia said.

"We don't have time," Bunion insisted.

"It won't take long, just a few more minutes, I'm sure I have some things that would fit you."

There was nothing to fit Geraldine but the girls gave her some jewelry, and some of their spare make up and some advice as to what to do with her hair.

"Grow it longer than you think it ought to be, wait until it really irritates you and then get it styled, I have a book here with some really good designs in it, and don't dye it red, red's out at the moment, use a honey wheat or a chestnut brown."

A girl called Laurie found Clarissa an expensive anti-ageing cream, "I use it all the time; it has actual gene therapy in it that can add years to your life."

"Oh well, thanks," Clarissa said.

"What are we going to do for you?" a girl called Terri looked at Amaak.

"You really need to lose some weight," Sophie urged her.

"It is blubber; I live in the sea."

"Oh, so what clothes do you wear in the sea?" Sophie said.

"We do not wear clothes for warmth or protection but we do wear them for modesty and decoration."

"That thing you have on now, you'd be better with something that doesn't hug the figure quite as much."

"All my people look like this, it is natural for us."

"When you're in the sea maybe, but on land..." Sophie went off and brought back a silk robe. "It's meant to be a housecoat but I never liked the color and it looks good on you, very good."

Amaak studied herself in the mirror, "I like it," she said.

They gave Josephine a jaunty hat, that hid her cone shaped head almost completely, and an outfit to match.

"It was always far too big for me, I told my mother not to buy it but she insisted, you know what mothers are like," Miranda said.

Josephine nodded even though she never had a real mother and didn't know what they were like.

Lydia was given three gowns and a pair of gorgeous shoes.

Rosie and Annie fitted into a long skirt and although because of their unique physiology they could not wear the top, they were given shimmering shawls.

"Shall I do your nails?" a girl called Tanya offered, "it's a skill I have; I do everybody's nails."

"She's a true artist," Janine said.

"But we really must be going," Clarissa said.

"Can't you just stay long enough to have your nails done? You'll arrive at your entertainment emergency looking really good."

Geraldine had never had clean nails before. She got extensions with white bits underneath them. She was overwhelmed; she couldn't stop looking at them except when she was wiping the tears from her eyes.

Even Clarissa had to admit that it was nice just to spend a little girl time.

The men were happy enough to wait, they were drinking brandy and eating chocolate, both of which they had not seen for a very long time; and they were sitting down in front of an all action-adventure, holographic film that one of the girl's boyfriends had left behind. It was easy to relax....

It was Bunion who noticed the time; he got up and went upstairs to the girl's apartments to find Lydia.

Tanya looked at him, "Hey little man you're not supposed to be in here."

"We must go," Bunion said.

"But you can't go yet, we're only just getting to know you."

"Lydia we must go."

"Yes you're right Bunion, I'm sorry we've allowed ourselves to get sidetracked."

She went to find Clarissa.

"How can you have an entertainment emergency?" Sophie asked. "So you don't turn up to your next show on time? Who is really going to worry?"

Bunion's gorgeous, big, brown eyes met hers, "Many lives depend upon us," he said.

"Really?"

"Yes," Bunion said.

"But you're entertainers if someone doesn't catch your next performance they're not going to die."

"Two and a half days from now a time machine is going to land on the planet Zertza. We hope to use it to take us back in time to prevent the Bellusian war. If we do, half a billion lives will be saved."

"But that's dangerous; you could be killed."

"Oh no," the girls said all together.

"We may never see you again," Sophie's tears smudged her make up.

"What if you die?" Janine said.

"Bunion should never have told you about our mission but now that he has please remember, that if you tell anyone else, you put our lives in danger," Clarissa said.

"We'll remember."

"Thank you for everything," Lydia said.

Amaak chirruped.

"Yes, thank you," all the others said.

"Try to stay alive."

"Here's my mailbox, if you survive, let us know," Miranda handed Clarissa a card.

"Mwa, mwa, mwa," there were kisses all round.

Clarissa backed towards the door, "Thanks for the clothes and the food and the money."

"We'll miss you," Miranda said.

"We really must go," Clarissa opened the door of the space yacht and stepped outside.

"Are you sure there's nothing we can do to help?"

"No, we couldn't let you become involved in this; it's far too dangerous."

"I hope Bunny doesn't die," Janine said.

"Hey what about me?" Jerry spoke up.

Sophie gave him an extra kiss on the cheek, "That goes without saying."

Bunion pushed Froggie and Jerry out of the door; they really didn't want to leave.

"Where is Kiii?" Amaak suddenly realized that he hadn't come out with them.

"I'll go get him," Jerry said.

"No you won't," Clarissa said, "Amaak, we'll all go over to our spacecraft and get ready for takeoff while you go back and get Kiii."

Kiii had eaten dinner with them and headed straight back to the pool; he was asleep on the surface of the water. Amaak picked him up, he was growing fast; he reminded her so much of his father. He didn't wake up when she carried him gently back to the spacecraft and strapped him safely into his bunk hoping that the take off would not disturb him.

Half an hour later they were in orbit around Candice where Geraldine set course for Zertza and engaged the graviton engines.

"Will we make it in time?" Zedekiah asked.

"If all goes well we'll have an hour to spare."

"Then let's hope that all goes well," Zedekiah said.

Chapter 11.

Zertza, population: seven million.

Principal attraction: a fully working time machine.

Geraldine touched down in the mountains but the electromagnetic effects were too weak to present any real danger to the spacecraft.

Crazy Jones's hovel was built on the exact co-ordinates that the time machine was due to inhabit but he was not around, no one had warned him to take up his post and expect visitors. The hovel was really only a piece of stage scenery and Grumpus and Geraldine were well used to moving such things.

Josephine could feel herself getting excited about going on the mission with Zedekiah; she longed to see the other Josephines, her sisters.

Lydia and Clarissa dressed themselves in some of the clothes that the daughters of Omar had given them, hoping that they would be good enough to blend into the royal court on Bellus. Clarissa had a one hundred and seventy year old silver dollar that had been given to her by her aunt when she was born. It was the only legal tender they had from the period.

Bunion packed some sandwiches, and some cold pancakes made with sugar, and a small bottle of water. With ten minutes to go they all lined up outside in the shadow of the spacecraft waiting for the time machine to appear.

"Does everybody remember the plan?" Clarissa asked.

"Keep the engines running," Geraldine said.

"We shall go first," Clarissa said, "but as soon as we get to our destination on Bellus we shall program the time machine to return to these co-ordinates. Then Zedekiah and Josephine will use it to take themselves back one thousand years so that they can retrieve the Interference Project. At that point Zedekiah will send it traveling randomly to different points in space and time to keep the Time Guardians busy until we have completed our missions."

"The time machine will return for us twenty-one hours after it left," Zedekiah said.

"Do you think that's going to be long enough?" Natter asked.

"I know it doesn't seem very long but we are going to a highly populated area at a sophisticated time in history, the chances of our being discovered are quite high; it's in our best interests not to be there longer than we have to."

"We shall need longer to complete our mission so we shall be on Bellus for five days."

They stood in silence waiting for the seconds to tick by. Then Lydia spoke out. "Look, none of you have to do this, you should all leave now while you can."

"I'm coming," Bunion said.

"This is my life's work," Zedekiah reminded her.

"You need me," Clarissa said.

"Then the rest of you, leave now, while you still can."

"If we don't wait, the Time Guardians will catch up with you and kill you," Geraldine said.

"That could happen anyway."

"I'll be waiting with the engines running and we'll engage the gravitons as soon as we're in orbit; we'll give them a run for their money."

"No one can outrun the Time Guardians."

"You don't know that," Rosie argued.

"We stick together," Jerome said.

"Yea," Annie agreed.

"We always have," Froggie said.

"That's how we survive," Mr. Mystery said.

"We won't leave you," Jerry told her.

"Are you all sure about this?" Lydia asked.

"Yea," everybody nodded their heads.

"How long now?" Clarissa asked.

"Six minutes."

"What's that sound?" Jerome remarked.

"What sound?" Froggie said.

"That sound."

"Oh, that sound, I hear it now."

"Sounds like an engine to me."

"A bit like a…"

"Helicopter."

A dark shadow approached over the landscape and passed above their heads and a voice blared down from above them, "This is the County Sheriff; move away from your vehicle and stand still with your hands in the air."

"What are we going to do?" Annie cried.

"Move over now or you will be fired on."

They all put their hands up and moved out of the shade of the spacecraft and into the hot Zertzan sun.

"What happens when he finds out it's us?" Annie asked.

"Someone will have to cause a distraction so that the others can get into the time machine," Grumpus said.

"I'm going to run," Natter said.

"Don't do that; they'll shoot you," Rosie cried.

The helicopter landed right next to the spot where the time machine was due to appear and Sheriff Raspberry got out, followed by Young Raindrop.

"You back for another performance?"

"Well actually we have been working on something new since we were here last, do you like Chinese shadow figures?" Annie asked.

Zedekiah looked at his watch; the time machine was due to appear in three minutes.

"You won't live long enough to put on another show, I don't know what you're doing here but it looks pretty suspicious to me, Young Raindrop, alert the Time Guardians."

"Ah but boss can't we watch their show first?"

"Do your duty Young Raindrop."

Young Raindrop stumped back to the helicopter.

216

Natter, whose movements were always jerky, looked from Young Raindrop to the sheriff, to the open desert before him. He broke out of the line and began to run.

"No... they'll shoot you," Rosie cried.

Sure enough the sheriff and Young Raindrop raised their guns and fired.

"Please don't kill him."

She needn't have worried, Natter was fast and he was soon out of range.

"Get him Young Raindrop," the sheriff shouted.

Young Raindrop ran after Natter but Sheriff Raspberry didn't; he headed towards the helicopter. "You didn't think that little distraction was going to keep me from doing my duty and contacting the Time Guardians did you?"

Clarissa broke ranks and ran after the Sheriff, "Please let us explain," she came to a sudden stop when the sheriff raised his rifle.

"One more step and...."

A dark shadow cut off the sunlight.

The sheriff looked up; above him was the pinkest space yacht he had ever seen. It drifted down and landed near the helicopter. Zedekiah looked at his watch; the time machine was due to appear in one and a half minutes. The door of the space yacht opened and fifteen of the richest, most beautiful young women in the galaxy stepped out.

"Excuse me," Miranda called over, "can you help us? We seem to be lost."

Young Raindrop stopped in mid-flight and changed direction; the sheriff hesitated as Janine waved over to him.

"Please, our pilot seems to have lost his way, we don't know what to do and we'd love you to come over for drinks."

Sheriff Raspberry lowered is gun and headed over to the Ariel

"My name's Janine, what's yours?"

"Where did they come from?" Jerry whispered.

"They must have followed us here," Josephine said.

"They're braver than I gave them credit for."

Rosie and Annie ran to meet Natter, who had noticed that he was no longer being pursued and was running back to them.

Five seconds after the sheriff entered the space yacht and the girls closed the door, a buzzing sound started to make the air tingle and a little egg shaped time machine began to materialize beside the helicopter; it solidified but the door didn't open.

"It's very small," Rosie sounded disappointed.

"It's not even as big as the one we built," Geraldine said.

"Well at least it works," Natter pointed out.

"When are they coming out?" Annie asked.

Josephine looked over the machine, "I think they're locked in, in fact I know they're locked in. This is weird; I can see the combination in my mind." She pressed some numbers that were etched into the shell of the machine; the door opened and two kids fell out, gasping for air.

"We couldn't breathe, I thought we were going to die," the younger one wheezed.

Kiii squeaked; one of the boys was not much older than he was.

"Where are we?" the older one asked.

"What were you doing in the time machine?" Zedekiah said.

"Time machine? No way, we can't be in a time machine."

"It was all his fault," the younger boy told them.

"How can you say that? It was your idea."

"So? I've been exploring in that place loads of times and nothing's ever happened before."

"What place? Tell us about it," Clarissa said.

"The old junk yard down on Main Street, they have some really interesting stuff there but none of it works."

"Well this thing evidently did, what did you do?"

"We climbed inside to see if we could tell what it was. There was this keypad."

"And you hit some keys and ended up here?"

"Yea, we did; where are we?"

"You're on the planet Zertza and you're a thousand years into your future."

"You mean that we've really traveled in a time machine?" the younger boy asked.

"Yes," Clarissa told him.

"Cool," he said.

"Not cool Mikey, time travel is against the law and if we get caught they're supposed to kill us."

"They wouldn't execute kids would they?" Geraldine asked.

"Paul, I don't like this; I want to go home," Mikey said.

"If you go home the Time Guardians will track you down and kill you," Josephine said.

Mikey started crying.

"We can't send them back; they'll have to stay here," Annie said.

"But if they do that they won't misdirect the Time Guardians and the whole Zertza time machine myth won't grow up and we won't discover the truth in Amos's underground cavern and we won't travel here, which means that when the boys arrive they'll either suffocate or be tracked down by the Time Guardians whichever comes first," Rosie pointed out.

"And half a billion people will stay dead," Lydia added.

"But we can't send them back," Annie said.

"Yes we can, we've got a time machine; we can do whatever we want. Once they've given the false information to the Time Guardians and the true information to the Keepers of Knowledge we can go back and rescue them."

"Yea," Froggie said, "of course we can; I wish I'd thought of that."

"Would you be willing to trust us?" Clarissa asked them.

"I hate to break up the party but if that time machine doesn't move soon the Time Guardians will get a lock on it," Zedekiah told them.

Josephine found that she instinctively knew how to program it. She didn't even need to touch the keypad or the remote controls.

Clarissa quickly instructed the boys as to what they were to do, "Don't worry we'll be back for you," she said.

Josephine closed the door and activated the time machine. She had programmed it to take the boys back to where they came from and then to return to Zertza on automatic. It dematerialized, but reappeared almost instantly. This time it was empty.

"Let's hope they got back safe," Clarissa said.

"History hasn't changed; we're still here, which means that we got Amos's message, which means that the boys said what they were supposed to say, which means that they must have got home like they were supposed to," Rosie said.

"Which means that they were executed after all," Annie wiped away a tear.

"Yes but the great thing is; that's the bit we can change."

Lydia and Bunion climbed into the time machine; it was a tight squeeze and Lydia had to bend her head down low.

"How are we all going to fit into that small space?" Clarissa asked.

"We'll squeeze up as far as we can go," Lydia said.

"Mind the control console, don't sit on any of the buttons," Josephine warned her.

"I think I just did."

"Don't worry I cancelled out what you did, just move over a bit more."

"Okay I'm in as far as I can go, Bunion you push yourself against that wall."

Bunion molded his body carefully to the side wall.

"Is that as much as you can do?"

"Yes," Bunion said.

Clarissa climbed in; she was taller than Lydia and had to bend over even more. "I can't do this, my arthritis..." she backed herself out of the door, "that really hurts; we're going to have to think of something else."

"How about if we move our feet over like so and you sit on the floor?"

They tried Lydia's suggestion but now she and Bunion were trying to grip their feet onto the smooth sides of the time machine and Bunion's top heavy body was threatening to fall down and crush Clarissa. She got out again.

"How about if you get in first and we squeeze ourselves around you?"

Lydia and Bunion got out and Clarissa got in but she couldn't bend down, "It's no good there's too much arthritis in my spine."

"Stand up in the middle at the tallest point."

Bunion got in and flattened himself against the side wall and Lydia got in and squeezed herself against the other side.

"I think we might do it this time, if only I can get the door to shut."

Clarissa was sweating with pain.

"Can someone help us close the door?"

Geraldine gave it a good yank.

"Ow, you nearly killed us," Lydia shouted.

"Sorry I was only trying to help."

"Oh my back; it's no good I'll have to get out again," Clarissa said.

"Well that wasn't going to work anyway, we just can't get that door to go the last couple of inches," Lydia said.

They all got out of the time machine again.

"You're cutting things fine, if you don't go soon the Time Guardians will get a lock on us," Zedekiah warned them.

"How about if Bunion gets in first? He doesn't need to bend his head."

Bunion positioned himself over by the back wall and then Lydia squeezed herself against the side wall, "Now you get in Clarissa."

Clarissa climbed in, "Haven't we tried this already? Now I have to bend over again, I'm too old for this."

"Whatever you're going to do, you'd better do it soon."

"Perhaps only two of us should go," Clarissa climbed stiffly out of the time machine and tried to straighten her back.

"No," Lydia answered her, "that would ruin our plans."

"I'll go," Bunion said.

"No Bunion you get out, Lydia needs my help."

"Lydia will need protection," Bunion insisted.

"But she doesn't know her way around the castle."

"There's no more time, you're putting us all at risk here."

"Bunion quick, get out," Clarissa said.

"Let them go," Zedekiah said.

"But Lydia needs my help."

"It's too late Clarissa they've got to go right now."

Josephine closed the door and activated the time machine.

It faded and then disappeared.

"I hope they'll be all right."

"Don't worry Clarissa; Bunion will take good care of Lydia," Zedekiah said.

"I know he will but who's going to take care of him?"

"Perhaps it's time you let him take care of himself."

The time machine reappeared; the door opened and again the inside was empty. Zedekiah and Josephine climbed in and Josephine set the co-ordinates; again the time machine disappeared.

"I'm going into the spaceship to warm up the graviton engines," Geraldine said.

"What about the Omar sisters?" Jerry asked.

"I would say that they are very capable of taking care of themselves," Clarissa said.

They all climbed into the spacecraft ready to fasten their seat belts. Amaak was the last one through the door and she was the only one to see the ominous shadow that cut off the rays of the sun. She let out a squeal of alarm.

A sinister, black machine that resembled a hungry bird of prey landed beside them.

"The Time Guardians, they've found us!" Clarissa shouted.

Chapter 12.

Lydia and Bunion stood in a cobbled courtyard that was surrounded by high stone walls.

"This was a really nice place before my people destroyed it," Lydia said.

"The castle on Bella survived?" Bunion asked.

"Actually it didn't. But every time it was destroyed, it was rebuilt."

"And Bellus didn't rebuild?"

"They considered it a waste of money and manpower," Lydia looked around her, "Where are we supposed to go?"

"Perhaps we should follow him," Bunion pointed to a man in a bright red hat with a big, brown feather stuck into it, he wore a red jerkin emblazoned with an official crest, and tough, leather pants.

"He's one of the Royal Guard, but this isn't right, they stopped wearing those uniforms five hundred years ago, do you think we made a mistake? Do you think we've landed in the wrong time period?"

Meanwhile Zedekiah stepped out onto polished plastic floor tiles that shone softly the way that plastic tiles in office blocks had shone for the past thousand years.

He looked around, noting to his relief that the corridor was empty; he scanned for hidden cameras; it was all clear. "Come on, quickly," he said to Josephine.

"I... I..." Josephine shook her head vigorously from side to side.

"What's the matter?"

"I'm in a network."

223

"Are you all right?"

"Yes, I think so."

"Good, you can tell me all about it once we're secure."

Josephine climbed out of the time machine.

"Quick, send it away before the Time Guardians trace it."

"I can't," Josephine held her head in her hands.

Zedekiah climbed back into the little machine and used the remote control to key in a list of random co-ordinates; he checked that it was programmed to return in twenty-one hours, threw the remote onto the floor and closed the door. The buzzing started and the time machine activated.

"That should keep the Time Guardians busy for a while."

"Zedekiah I saw the co-ordinates," Josephine told him.

"What do you mean?"

"Do you know where you sent the time machine?"

"No I just hit the keys as fast as I could so that it'll keep moving and the Time Guardians won't be able to trace it."

"Yes but do you know where you sent it?"

"No; does it matter?"

"The second destination was Fettuccia, two hundred years into the future."

"Amos's time?"

"Yes and also the time when the asteroid was supposed to hit."

Zedekiah took a step backwards, "Don't tell me…."

"The first co-ordinates were Omeros, Roberto Fettuccia's planet."

"You mean the time machine that he used to save Fettuccia was our time machine?"

"Yes that's exactly what I'm saying."

"But the Time Guardians captured him and Fettuccia claims to have his time machine…."

"It wasn't in the vault but then why would it be? The Time Guardians would have destroyed it."

"Perhaps it traveled on to the next co-ordinates before they could get their hands on it," Zedekiah said.

"I hope you're right because if not we're in real trouble!"

Rob Fettuccia was in his bathroom brushing his teeth when the time machine materialized in the bedroom of his dismal little apartment.

The fashion for wearing striped flannel pajamas had been in and out twenty times in the past two thousand years. At the moment it was out, but Rob didn't care, he was a poverty-stricken student who was more interested in killing his brain cells with beer than he was in fashion. He stared at the virtual clock on the grubby wall. Did it say three-zero-eight or was it eight-zero-three?

Did it matter? He yawned widely and staggered drunkenly towards his bed. He should have turned on the light but he had forgotten where the switch was and the landlord hadn't fixed the voice recognition protocols yet; still even in his condition he couldn't lose his bed in that small apartment.

He bumped into something.

It was about five feet high and egg shaped and there was a door in it, not that he could see it in the dark; he just fell into it and the door closed.

He was used to alcohol-induced sensations so he didn't notice anything strange when the time machine activated. A light came on in the tiny cabin and he tried a few times to get up but standing proved to be too difficult. He was thinking he must be trapped and was just settling himself down on the floor to wait for help or to go to sleep, whichever came first, when there was a little fizzing sound and the door swung open all by itself. He struggled to his feet and tried to step out over the rim, intent on heading for his bed, but he stumbled onto dusty ground instead.

He was so tired that he couldn't be bothered to figure out what was going on; he just lay down on the soft earth and went straight to sleep.

Meanwhile on Bellus the man in the leather pants was walking purposefully towards Lydia and Bunion and they could see that he had a crowd of people following him. They were all trying to squeeze through a narrow entranceway at once.

"Are you on the tour? Do you have your tickets available for me to check?"

"Er, where do we get the tickets from?" Lydia asked.

"The gatehouse of course, to the left as you come in, it's hard to miss."

Lydia and Bunion ran back in the direction he was pointing, through the narrow gateway and down a cobbled slope towards a booth where there were two other men in costume. The words, "Guided Tour," were written in Bellusian and in Universal, on a board at the side of it.

"How much for two tickets?" Lydia said.

"A dollar," the man said.

Bunion pulled the dollar that Clarissa had given him out of his pocket.

"This is an unusual coin; it's got the royal crest on it. Are you sure you want to spend it?"

Bunion looked at Lydia, "It's the quickest way to find our way around," he said.

Lydia nodded and the man issued them with two tickets.

By the time they caught up with the tour guide he was entertaining his hearers with the story of the hidden princes.

"Princess Alice had secretly married Lord Higham of Celosia in a ceremony which took place underneath our very feet in the old cellars, six hundred years ago. Her father, old King Nicholas didn't approve of the young man because of his flamboyant ways and wanted her to marry the Prince of Bella in order to secure an important trade agreement. But Princess Alice had been in love with Miles Higham since they had shared a tutor when they were just six years old."

"What happened when the king found out?" someone in the crowd asked.

"Well that didn't come about for some years, not until the day before her supposed wedding to Prince James of Bella when she finally had to confess. By then she had two children, the little princes Marcus and Steven, who had been living in the cellars all of their young lives."

"So what did the king do?"

"He was so angry that he took a laser pistol and went to find the children; he wanted to kill them. The guards had to restrain their mother who was distraught and screaming."

"What did he do?" a woman in a red dress asked.

"He searched the cellars for hours until eventually he discovered them trapped in a store room at the end of a dark corridor. He aimed his gun, intending to kill them but as he looked into his little grandson's big, round eyes all his anger faded away.

"Those little grandsons eventually made him proud. They grew up to be handsome and intelligent and all the people loved them. Marcus, the oldest brother eventually became our longest reigning monarch. In those days longevity treatment was more sophisticated than it is today and he ruled wisely for nearly two hundred years."

The Royal Guide whose name was William had many more interesting stories for the crowd as he showed them the Jewel room, the armory, King Peter's laboratory, which still contained replicas of the anti-gravity inventions for which he got into so much trouble with the Time Guardians. They also saw the accommodations where the royal family used to live, as well as the display of fashions through the ages. Everyone agreed that Queen Sarah's gown, the one designed exclusively for her by Amos Narbandian himself was absolutely magnificent.

"These are the old kitchens, as you can see it was possible to cater for thousands of people at each meal if necessary," William told them.

"Where do the royal family live now?" Bunion asked.

"Our tour doesn't cover the present Royal family."

"Yes but where do they live?"

"In the annex of course, the modern part of the castle; but don't even think of going there, the guards are trained to shoot on sight."

Zedekiah and Josephine hurried stealthily along the corridor, "All this input, it's overpowering," Josephine said.

"What exactly is happening to you?" Zedekiah asked her.

"It's hard to explain, all I can tell you is that I have my own brain, the part of me that controls my consciousness, but I also have another part which can communicate with all the computers... no not computers... something else. It's like there are lots of other brains out there that all carry the same hardware as me but they have different software, I can feel their communications but I can't access them, I know that I'm sensing the other Josephines."

"Have you found the Interference Project?"

"I know it's here somewhere but it's going to take some time to track it down."

A door opened in front of them and a woman carrying an empty coffee cup walked across their path. "Hello," she said politely before moving on.

"She had a cone head like you," Zedekiah remarked.

"Don't be surprised, I think you'll find that most of the people who work in this building have cone heads, it feels like I've come home."

"Kill me," Roberto pleaded as shafts of bright light stabbed into his head like knives.

"Excuse me?" someone whose face he couldn't focus on asked.

"The light, it's too bright."

"What are you doing here? You could have waited till we'd gone before you came to loot the place."

"Where am I?"

"On our property."

"I should be in my apartment."

"Where's that?"

"Charlotte Town."

"There are only two towns on this planet and neither of them is called Charlotte Town."

Rob squinted up through the cruel sunlight at the girl who was speaking to him, "What are you talking about? What planet is this?"

"110A/126."

"Eh?"

"This planet hasn't been named yet and it probably never will be; we're evacuating."

"Don't do that, I'd really like to get to know you."

"You're full of it aren't you?"

"You got anything to drink?"

"I would say you've had enough of that already."

"No, I mean water or something."

"Stay there, I'll get you some from the house."

The girl ran into the small, metal shack behind her. Roberto looked around the dusty paddock. Somehow, by some miracle that he didn't understand, he had been transported away from the life of a trainee lawyer that his father had chosen for him and that he hated from the bottom of his soul because he really wanted to be a musician, to some dusty heaven where he had seen a vision of the most beautiful girl in the universe.

He looked down at his hand; there was something in it. He didn't remember the landlord handing him a new remote control for the TV, or the sound system, or the personal transport unit, which should have been scrapped ten cycles ago, or the communications system. But there it was; a remote that controlled something. Perhaps it belonged to this dream that he was having. What did they put in his beer last night?

The girl reappeared, "Sorry about the chipped cup, all the others are packed."

"Thanks," Roberto sipped the ice cold water, "I'm Rob by the way; full name Roberto Fettuccia, trainee lawyer so if you are being forced off your farm for any reason, legal or illegal, I could help."

"You can't help with this, there's a huge asteroid heading for this planet and the Time Guardians won't let us destroy it in case we interfere with the future; it's going to smash it to smithereens so we've got to move on again."

"Why do you use the word 'again'?"

"We're always moving on. Dad gets himself involved with obscure political causes that are constantly getting him into trouble. He's a humanist; at present he's campaigning for equal rights for the Josephines."

Rob was listening to her truly he was, but politics didn't really interest him, no more than the law did. He started fiddling with the remote control.

"Eventually he got in trouble with the Time Guardians who as you know always want things their own way and they told him he would have to find a distant planet and live quietly or his daughter would no longer have a father."

"What's your name?" Rob said.

"Roslyn," Roslyn told him.

"Nice name."

"Have you been listening to anything I've been telling you?"

"Yes of course, but what do you mean by Josephines?"

"You know Josephines... the human computers... and will you please stop fiddling with that thing while I'm talking to you?"

"Sorry, I just discovered it, I'm not sure what it is, I think maybe the landlord left it in my apartment and didn't tell me."

Roberto pressed a few more buttons; the last one he pressed had the word 'Recall' written above it. There was a buzz but there were no insects.

Roslyn tried to ignore it, "Look you'll have to excuse me; I've got to get on with the packing."

The buzzing got louder and then something started to appear just behind Roberto.

"What on Earth is that?" Roslyn said, "Don't tell me... I've read about... no this can't be right... is that a time machine?"

"I don't know, is it? I've never seen one before; they've been banned for nearly two thousand years."

"Two hundred."

"Two thousand."

Roslyn looked at him quizzically, "Have you ever heard of Amos Narbandian?"

"Yea of course, I learned about him in history, he died ages ago."

"Well in my time he's the biggest sensation the galaxy has ever known; you've been in this time machine before."

"Do you think that's how I got here?"

"I'm pretty certain of it."

"It's not very big is it?" Roberto pulled himself stiffly to his feet.

"You'd better get rid of it before the Time Guardians catch up with you."

"How do I do that?"

"Well firstly you could figure out how to get back to where you came from."

"But there's nothing for me there, I'd rather stay here with you."

"Sorry I'm not interested."

"But I like it here; I like you."

Roslyn took in a deep breath, "If you like me so much you'll get rid of that thing as quickly as you can."

"But I don't know how it works; how do you open the door?"

Roslyn looked at the remote. "Here," she pressed the button that said 'Open.'

The door hissed open and Roberto put his head inside, "There's a keypad," he said.

"Well get in and see if you can figure out what to do with it."

Roberto climbed in; he examined the keypad, "There's two sets of numbers."

"One of these must control the temporal co-ordinates and one must be for the spatial co-ordinates."

Roberto scratched his head and looked at the remote and then at the keyboard, "I think I've found the numbers that refer to the date... or maybe not, maybe it's the other thing you said."

"Keep going; make it quick."

There was a hissing noise and the door began to close automatically. Roberto looked at Roslyn whose image was disappearing behind it. Where was that button on the remote that would open it? His eyesight still hadn't recovered from the hangover. He pressed something and looked again, was it the right button? The door wasn't opening.

The buzzing sound started and the time machine powered up. He pressed more buttons; he didn't want to leave the most beautiful girl in the universe without at least getting her number.

Roslyn breathed a sigh of relief when the time machine and its strange inhabitant faded away. How come it was possible that after another two thousand years of mankind's progress all they could produce was that?

Roberto had no idea where he was going and when the buzzing stopped, he hadn't a clue where he had landed. All he knew was that the door still wouldn't open and there was a warning light on the screen in front of him.

The door didn't open because Roberto had pressed one too many wrong buttons and the time machine was buried in solid rock. The red warning light was flashing because the solid rock was about to crush the little time vehicle.

Roberto hadn't moved anywhere in time, but he had traveled sideways in space. According to the data on the screen, he had landed slap bang in the middle of the asteroid that was due to hit planet 110A/126 in three day's time!

Lydia stood up straight; she took a deep breath and walked brazenly towards the guards.

"Stay back," one of them ordered her, "stay back or we'll be forced to shoot."

"Excuse me, I don't mean to disturb you but I'm looking for the entertainments manager, I can't find him anywhere."

"We don't have an entertainments manager."

"Well that explains it then. We're traveling performers, we got a fax; we're booked to do a show in the banquet hall tonight. Show them what I mean Bunion."

Bunion took three packs of sandwiches and the bottle of water out from under his jacket and juggled them while standing on one foot.

"Do you have any ID?" the guard asked.

"I have the fax, I think… somewhere. I'm sorry I probably left it on the space plane, look just radio in, it was a man by the name of Wentworth who booked us."

The guard spoke into his wrist, "There's a woman here, says she's been booked for the entertainment tonight."

A young man in a white suit studded with silver sequins walked up. Lydia thought for a moment that he must be part of the real entertainment. He held out his pass to the guards.

"No need for that Lord Fopwais we all know you."

"Ah Lord Fopwais what a privilege to finally meet you at last," Lydia smiled up at him.

"I'm sorry, do I know you?" Lord Fopwais asked.

"No but I know of you. It is said that you are the most eligible bachelor and the most handsome man in the four systems."

Lord Fopwais was flattered, "Well one does one's best, and who might you be?"

"I am Lydia de Beaufort of the Kingdom of Bella, and this is Bunion my assistant. We are performers, I was just telling these gentlemen here that we received a fax, booking us to do a show tonight in the banqueting hall, but I get the impression that we have been hoaxed. That would be the third one we've received this lunar cycle."

Lord Fopwais looked up at the guards but they shook their heads. "Well look there must be something we can do about this. We don't want you coming all this way for nothing do we?" he turned to the guards, "I'll vouch for them," he said.

The guards still looked doubtful.

"We're unarmed; you can search us if you like."

One of the men got out his scanner and ran it up their fronts and down their backs, "They're clear," he said.

"So is it all right if I take them in?"

The guards reluctantly nodded their heads.

"Thank you for your kindness Lord Fopwais," Lydia said.

"Call me Percy," Lord Fopwais said.

Nearly all the women who worked in the building were Josephines. It was Zedekiah who was out of place.

"This is amazing, these people are so like me that it makes my stomach turn over," Josephine said.

"Well at least we don't have to skulk around here in case anybody notices your unusually shaped head."

"Let's go to the canteen."

"You want coffee?"

"No I want to explore the network somewhere that we won't be noticed." She opened the door of the nearest office, "Excuse me I'm new here, where's the canteen?"

A cone headed woman who looked almost identical to her said, "Why it's in the same place that it is in all buildings."

"Sorry I was just checking."

"I can upload a map if you like."

"I would be grateful; I ought to know where all the fire exits are."

"They should have told you all that at induction."

"I haven't done my induction yet, this is my first day."

The woman transferred a small map of the building straight into Josephine's brain. "You don't have any software installed," she sounded surprised.

"I got reformatted when I left my last place; they didn't want me taking their secrets with me."

That seemed to satisfy the woman.

"Thanks for your help."

"You're a Josephine Mark Ten? I wasn't aware that anything higher than a Mark Two existed."

"I don't know of any others either," Josephine answered truthfully.

"Well I hope you enjoy working here."

"Goodbye Josephine," Josephine said.

She led the way to the nearest elevator and hit the button for the top floor. "It's like these people are my family, I could have cried, I just wanted to run up and hug her."

The canteen was built on the roof; it was situated in an orchard.

Zedekiah gazed around him, "I never thought I would see this; the functionality of the work areas contrasted by the pleasantness of the rest areas is unique to this period."

Below them and beside them was a rooftop landscape of gardens and parks. People were walking between the buildings on invisible force-field bridges. It was a wonderful place to spend your break time.

The Josephine they had just met went back to her workstation but she was puzzled. A bio-machine such as a Josephine Mark Ten should not exist, especially one with no standard software. She did a careful search but she couldn't find references to such a thing anywhere.

She had no choice but to report her concerns to the security network.

Josephine looked around her, "This must be where my people came from; I wonder what happened to us."

"The Josephines suffered from replication failure and died out about seven hundred years before our time."

"Oh... that's sad," Josephine breathed deep, "you never told me which planet this is."

"Earth, the administrative center of the galaxy."

"My people came from Earth?"

"All our people came from Earth originally."

Zedekiah and Josephine made their way into the canteen; it was a very pleasant place and its large windows took full advantage of the view. "Here, I brought some ancient money with me; I got it from a shipwreck on Achore Prime. I'll get the coffee."

The coins were dirty and battered and the woman at the checkout looked at them warily. But they were legal tender and she had no choice but to take them.

Josephine found a table. "You see that woman over there? She's a Josephine Mark One. Her serial code is 11240D."

"You contacted her already?"

"It's not a contact, it's an interface; I can access the computer in her head and I can read her identity and her serial code and I know what files she has. But I can't open anything; I don't have the software."

"How come you could open Amos's files?"

"Each company uses standard software but it adds its own encryption in order to prevent other Josephines walking into the building, integrating with the network and stealing sensitive documents. Amos's files weren't encrypted."

"Not even the ones on the crystal?"

"No," Josephine told him.

"Wouldn't that have been a little unusual?"

"Maybe the crystal was planted for someone to discover after the earthquake."

"You mean it might have been put there to discredit Amos's Corporation?"

"Obviously no one found it because those big rocks fell over the shaft."

"Part of the conspiracy?"

"I think so."

"So we need to find you some software that has this company's encryption so that you can open the Interference Project."

"I know where it is."

"Where?"

"On floor five."

Zedekiah took a drink from his coffee mug, "This is good stuff... is that security guard coming over to us?"

"Yes I think he is; what shall we do?"

"Don't run; just act normally."

The guard reached into his jacket and pulled something out.

"Hull stresses above accepted tolerances," the message on the screen read.

Roberto scratched his head and studied the remote control. The 'Open' button for the door didn't work so he tried pressing something else and a general menu came up on the screen.

He looked down the options.

Temporal co-ordinates.
Spatial co-ordinates.
Atmosphere control.
Properties.
Help
He pressed help.

A page of writing came up: "In order to set the temporal co-ordinates please press the hash button twice."

He scrolled down the page: "In order to set the spatial co-ordinates please press the star button twice."

A big red warning message flashed on the screen: "Hull integrity loss in thirty, twenty-nine, twenty-eight seconds."

Behind it he was reading: "If you do not know what temporal or spatial co-ordinates your require press F3 for a comprehensive stellar data base."

"I don't want to know any of this stuff, I just want to know how to stop this asteroid from crushing me to death," Roberto shouted out loud.

"In order to prevent hull breach arm defense mechanism," a soft, female voice said.

"You mean I've been struggling with this menu and all the time I could have just asked? Anyway where is the defense mechanism?"

"The defense mechanism is situated at F5 on your keyboard or number sixty-one on your remote control."

"Hull integrity loss in ten, nine...."

Roberto hit F5.

A message appeared on the screen: "Please state reason for arming the defense mechanism."

"I'm sitting in the middle of an asteroid and it's crushing me to death and I don't know what to do; can't you do something?"

"Five, four...."

"Do you want me to arm the defense mechanism?" the soft female voice asked him.

"Yes," Roberto shouted.

"Please confirm."

"Yes!" Roberto screamed.

"Defense mechanism armed."

"Two, one...."

There was a terrific explosion.

The shock wave hit Roberto in the head and knocked him out cold.

"This new part of the palace is completely different from the old," Lydia said.

"Well would you want to live somewhere as cold and drafty as that?" Percy Fopwais asked.

"It's so warm in here."

"They're not running the heating in the old part of the castle yet even though it is late autumn."

"How many people are living here in the private quarters?"

"What do you want to know that for?"

"Oh nothing sinister, I just wanted to know how many we might be playing to tonight that's all."

Lydia and Bunion followed Percy along a red-carpeted corridor with oak paneled walls. Suddenly a white missile whizzed past Lydia's ear, "Hey, your highness, be careful," Percy shouted.

"You shouldn't be in my way," a young man of about eighteen who was holding a golf club said.

"You might be well advised not to kill the entertainers."

"Entertainers? Percy, introduce me."

"This is Lydia de Beaufort and her companion er, what did you say his name was?"

"Bunion," Lydia said.

"And this is his Highness Crown Prince Thomas Dewberry Higham De Faye, son of King Theodore and Queen Miriam Dewberry Higham de Faye who are at present on a diplomatic mission to Raynis."

Lydia curtsied.

"So we have the place to ourselves; what kind of entertainment do you do? Do you sing? Do you play a musical instrument?" Crown Prince Thomas asked.

"I do neither your Highness; Bunion here juggles and does acrobatics."

"And what do you do?"

"I dance, I do comedy turns, and I foretell the future."

"Nobody can tell the future."

"I can," Lydia said.

"Give me an example; tell me something that's going to happen."

"Tonight you will enjoy our performance so much that you will invite us to stay for two weeks."

Thomas laughed; he gave his golf club to his attendant, "Hey why don't you join us for lunch? Cousin Izzy will be there, I'm sure she'd love to meet you."

Thomas ordered the lunch table to be set out by the pool in the huge conservatory, "I like to eat in here because if anyone displeases me I can have them thrown into the water."

"Do you wish me to bring you some drinks, your Highness?" the waiter asked.

"Anyone want anything to drink?" Thomas said.

"Do you have fruit juice?" Lydia asked.

"Oh come on you can manage something stronger than that."

"Well that's very kind of you but I...."

"How about a cocktail? Let's all have cocktails. Ah look here's Sylvie, a tropical sunrise all right for you My Lady?"

"Well yes, if that's what everyone else is having."

When Sylvia came over to the lunch table Percy smiled at her and caught her hand.

"Sylvie this is Lydia de Beaufort; Lydia, meet Lady Sylvia Dewberry Higham de Faye, daughter of the king's younger brother and therefore my cousin."

Lydia tried to hide her surprise as she stood up and shook hands with her. The Lady Sylvia had straw yellow hair that went down to her waist; she smiled at Lydia with innocent blue eyes. She was very pretty and very young. Lydia doubted if she had even seen her seventeenth birthday.

The black suited waiter cleared his throat, "Shall I serve lunch now your Highness?" he asked.

"Izzy's not shown up yet," Sylvia pointed out.

"She's always late and I'm hungry," Thomas said.

"Thomas is right of course," Percy told Sylvia.

The waiter clapped his hands and serving maids dressed in black, with frilly white aprons served soup out of a big, silver tureen.

"So how was the opera last night?" Thomas asked Percy.

"Oh it was fine."

"He hated it, he couldn't wait to get back to his late night poker game," Sylvia said.

"Do you sing opera?" Thomas asked.

"No don't worry, you and Percy are perfectly safe," Lydia said.

"Thomas says you're going to entertain us tonight," Sylvia said.

"Yes if you want."

Sylvia turned around and looked at Bunion, "Do you like the soup?" she asked.

"Yes Mistress I should very much like the recipe."

"Are you a chef as well as an entertainer?"

"Only a plain cook Mistress. When we are traveling we all have our jobs to do. Mine is to make sure that everybody is fed."

"Are there more of you?"

"Usually we travel as a troupe Mistress but today there are only two of us."

Lydia smiled; she liked Sylvia for her gentleness and for the way that she treated Bunion with respect.

Suddenly there was a commotion as the door to the conservatory opened and a young woman stumbled in dropping books all over the floor. "Oh there you are Thomas, sorry I'm late, it's just that I had a piano lesson and then I thought that you said that we were eating in your apartments and then when I was on my way to find you I met Magenta Oprey and you know how long it has been since I spoke to her and then I dropped my books and...."

"Izzy come over here and meet Lydia and Bunion, they're going to entertain us."

Izzy stumbled over to meet them. One of the servants took the books out of her hands as she sat down. Bunion stared at her.

"This is Isabella, my kind of Aunt. Dizzy Izzy we call her."

Bunion gaped at the young, blonde-haired, brown-eyed beauty.

"Is the soup any good?" Isabella asked.

Bunion nudged Lydia, "That's Clarissa," he whispered.

"Yes I can see why Zedekiah mistook the two of them," Lydia agreed.

"No," Bunion whispered, "that *is* Clarissa!"

Chapter 13.

The security guard pulled a stick of gum out of his coat, "Hello, my name's Alex, do you mind if I sit next to you?"

"No of course not, go ahead," Zedekiah could see that there were at least a half a dozen free tables in the room.

"It's just that I've never met time travelers before."

"Time travelers? I don't know what you mean."

"No need to be ashamed, if I could afford it I'd do it myself."

"You would?" Josephine said.

"You must be from the future; they haven't even released the Josephine Mark Three yet, never mind a Mark Ten."

"You don't mind that we're time tourists?"

"Well we would like to know what you're doing here of course, have you come back to prevent some kind of a disaster or something?"

"Well yes you could say that, I'm a temporal archaeologist," Zedekiah told him.

"What do you do? Dig up our bones in the future?"

"No I leave that to others, I salvage ancient technology."

"How ancient?"

"We come from over a thousand years in the future."

"Really? That far? What kind of ancient technology are you looking for? I've got an old car that I'd be willing to sell."

"We're hoping to obtain a copy of the Interference Project."

"What for? I guess it must be a quaint little artifact in your time."

"Actually we need it to fix some problems that have appeared in our own time."

"You mean the future needs us? That's hard to believe. But what I don't understand is why you didn't knock on our front door and ask? Why all the skulking about?"

"Because time travel will be outlawed in a few months' time and we didn't know if you would betray us to the Time Guardians."

"The who?"

"The Corps of Time Guardians will be set up for the express purpose of preventing people from traveling in time, even if their purpose is to do good; they will enforce the law with severity."

"Well I've heard various reports about some kind of commission being set up to study the effect of time travel on the temporal environment. But at present it's perfectly legal."

"Not for much longer."

"It sounds like the future is going to bring us a lot of trouble."

"If I can get a copy of the Interference Project, maybe a little less," Zedekiah said.

"Well if you want to come down to room three on floor five as soon as you've finished your coffees I'll make sure that my colleagues do their best to help you."

"I don't have any software, I'm going to need it if I'm to download the Interference Project," Josephine said.

"No problem, I'm sure we can help you."

Alex got up from the table and strolled off.

"Well that was easy," Josephine sighed with relief.

"Too easy," Zedekiah said.

"What do you mean by that? If he had wanted to hurt us he could have arrested us or even killed us right there on the spot."

"I still don't trust him.

They finished their coffee and made their way to the elevator, "Are you comfortable about doing this? We still have time to escape."

"Let's just get what we came for," Josephine said.

They found room three on floor five easily and didn't even have to knock on the door as a technician in a white coat opened it and greeted them, "Hello my name's James, please come in, we've been expecting you."

Zedekiah and Josephine walked into a pleasant but functional room; "Please sit here."

James led Zedekiah over to a sofa.

"Can I watch?" he asked.

"Of course, but there'll be very little to see," James led Josephine into the next room, which strongly resembled a dentist's surgery. Two other technicians, one male and one female were sitting at a desk filling in reports; they turned around and smiled at her.

"This is where we test all our units for faults, we'll do a system diagnostic while you're here to make sure that you're running at full efficiency, if you would sit in the chair please."

Josephine lowered herself into a full-length dentist's chair.

"Now I'm going to put restraints on you because there is just a very tiny, remote risk of an epileptic seizure the first time you're exposed to the programming. Is that all right?"

Josephine looked over to Zedekiah and he nodded, "I'll be here to make sure nothing happens to you.

After strapping her into the chair James attached electrodes to Josephine's chest and head, "These are just to monitor your vital functions. If there's any problem at all we will simply stop the operation." Josephine nodded and James lowered a helmet onto her head. "Your programs will be downloaded through this interface.

"I don't think I need it, I can detect the network without any help."

"But how can that be? You haven't even got basic software; anyway you'll still need to keep your helmet on so that we can scan your brain, those diagnostics are important."

"Are bio-mechanics a big thing around here?" Zedekiah asked.

"Of course they are, I would have thought, being an archaeologist you would have known that."

"Much useful information has been lost to the future."

"Well don't worry it's all there in the Interference Project; are you ready Josephine?"

"Yes," Josephine said.

"I'm switching you on now."

No strange sounds emanated from the chair and there were no whirling or flashing lights; instead Josephine began to groan, "Zedekiah, help me."

"What's wrong, what have you done to her?"

"Nothing's wrong, what Josephine is experiencing is a perfectly natural part of the process," James assured him.

"But you don't understand; my brain is emptying; everything is being taken away from me.

"Stop the machine; switch it off now."

"I'm afraid I can't do that.

The hairs on the back of Zedekiah's neck sprang up as he suddenly felt someone standing behind him, he tried to turn round but it was too late because that someone squeezed a hypo-spray into his neck and he dropped to the floor!

Roberto felt like a ten-ton mule had kicked his head in. For some time he stayed still, imagining that he had the mother of all hangovers. And then it came to him that since he was alive, the little time machine must still be intact and since he was floating weightless he must be in space, presumably somewhere near the remains of the big asteroid. In his mind's eye he could see Roslyn's beautiful face; her flashing eyes, her full lips, and her long, shimmering, hair. If he didn't get back to her now, he might never see her again.

The remote controller had buttons with numbers on them, plus a menu button, a power button, the recall button, the button that opened the door and arrows pointing up and down. On his TV remote if you pressed the down button you changed channel back to the one you were previously watching. What had he got to lose? He pressed the down button.

There was a familiar buzz and a familiar tickle in his ears and a familiar gagging sensation in the back of his throat. The next thing he knew, his mother of all headaches got worse as the door opened and sunshine blasted in, "Yes, yes I did it," he shouted.

Roslyn was lining up some packing cases outside the house; she came running over, "You fool, you idiot, what are you doing back here?"

"I just destroyed the asteroid," Roberto said.

"Good for you now go; if the Time Guardians track you down, we're finished."

"No, I won't leave you," Roberto dropped the remote and climbed out of the time machine, which started making noises again.

"Go away, we don't want you here, we're in enough trouble already without having to be responsible for you."

"But… but I think I love you."

It was too late; the door closed and the time machine powered up.

"Noooo…" Roslyn cried as it faded away.

A small, open backed jeep rolled into the driveway and skidded to a halt in front of them. "I just heard it on the news, the asteroid's been deflected or destroyed or something, anyway it's not going to hit and we don't have to move on." The driver, a middle-aged man jumped out of the jeep and gave Roslyn a big hug.

"Who's this," Roberto asked.

"My dad," Roslyn said.

"Oh, I'm pleased to meet you sir."

"Me too," Roslyn's father held out his hand to Roberto.

"No you're not, you're not pleased at all," Roslyn said.

A dark shadow moved slowly above the ground as a black craft shaped like a predatory bird swooped over them and landed in the paddock. The door opened and a troupe of armed men marched out with Joseph Bridefield in the lead!

The sandwiches had become warm and chewy in Bunion's jacket. Lydia had to persuade him to take it off so that they could rehearse. To give a satisfying performance when there was so little to work with and so little experience on Lydia's part was going to be a challenge. They had to get creative.

Lydia decided to recite a comic poem about a rabbit and she practiced several card tricks that Mr. Mystery had shown her. After that they rehearsed some of the routines that Bunion remembered from the days when Clarissa's troupe had included clowns. Also Bunion could play the spoons and Lydia, who was a good dancer, figured out a routine that could be done to their rhythm.

Bunion practiced his acrobatics and his juggling but Lydia could see that there was not going to be enough music so she decided to borrow a portable music player. She made up a comic routine in which she pretended to show Bunion how to ballet dance.

"I thought we were supposed to be searching for ways of keeping Lord Fopwais and Lady Sylvia together," Bunion said.

"I know that this looks like a waste of time but it's important that we gain these people's trust in order to be in the right position to stop Percy and Sylvia having their argument."

"Clarissa told us she was a servant."

"I know."

"Clarissa's Bellusian; she told us she was Zenebrian."

"I know that too."

"I've never known Clarissa to lie, why would she do that?"

"I don't know, but if we stick around long enough we might find out," Lydia said

They were invited to dinner that evening where they were to eat roast duck in orange sauce. "I'm so nervous I don't have much of an appetite," Lydia told Bunion.

"You must eat; we have four more days here and no money to buy food."

"I promised them a good performance."

"Don't worry we will make them happy."

After dinner they put on their show. It was a nice, intimate presentation because the king and queen had taken most of the adults to Raynis with them. The clown routines went down well, the juggling was well received and everyone enjoyed the acrobatics; even the poem made people laugh.

But there was something missing.

And they couldn't rely on the wedding scene this time for their finale. In fact they couldn't rely on anyone else; there were only the two of them. Bunion did a solo encore on the spoons while Lydia looked through the menu on the music player.

It was then that she had an inspiration born of desperation. As Bunion finished his rendition of Rosie's usual performance of the Fan and the Waistcoat, on the spoons, Lydia put on one of the few tunes she recognized....

Clarissa and the others assumed they must have been taken to Tempus but they had no idea what year they were in. They slept on the cold, hard floor of a prison cell for several long nights before the door clanged open and three more figures were thrown on top of them. The girl was crying and an older man was trying to comfort her while a younger man said he wished he hadn't gone out drinking on a weeknight. Everyone had to move over in order to make room for them.

Clarissa gasped suddenly.

"What is it?" Geraldine asked.

"I keep getting the strongest sensations; I think Lydia and Bunion might be changing history."

"How do you know?"

"I just got a memory which I can't have had before, because I would have known wouldn't I?"

"What's the memory of?"

"It's from when I was young, it must have been just before Percy and Sylvia broke up,"

"Don't keep us in suspense, what was it about?"

"I distinctly remember...."

"Yes?"

"I distinctly remember...."

"Yes?"

"I... I remember Lydia doing the chicken dance!"

"Wow what a brain," a female voice said.

"She could store the whole of the Interference Project and much more in that head," a male voice said.

"She's had no software installed and yet I found three files that she's already downloaded and read. And what's more she's been able to interface with our networking systems. She didn't even seem to know that she had cracked all the security codes," James said.

"She's some machine; do you think it will be possible to reverse engineer her?"

"Take a look at the readouts."

"Hmm, it won't be easy."

"We could do it given time,"

"We should do more tests, the cerebral configuration is very different from anything we've seen before," James said.

Zedekiah lay on the floor snoring.

"What are you doing to me?" Josephine said.

"Hey, she can still speak."

"What are you saying about my brain?"

"Look at the configuration of those neurons."

"Yea and look at amount of axons and dendrites, there's so many of them that the memory capacity of this machine must be bordering on infinite."

"Why do you keep calling me a machine?"

"Can you see?" James asked.

"No," Josephine told him.

He adjusted something on his control panel, "Better?"

"No... oh well yes, a little bit."

"Now?"

"Yes thank you that's much better."

James looked triumphant, "Well ladies and gentlemen, I think we have found ourselves a goldmine."

"Are you talking about me?" Josephine asked.

"Have you any idea what you are?" James said.

"What do you mean?"

"You're the most advanced bio-machine in existence."

"Am I?"

"Hello I'm Mandy, pleased to meet you. Are you aware that your pseudo-brain is writing its own software?" the female voice asked.

"Is it?" Josephine said.

"Hello I'm David, are you aware that you are creating your own firewalls?" the male voice asked.

"What?"

"Firewalls and hardware detection protocols."

"Really?"

"The diagnostic probe must have set off some kind of automatic reaction in your pseudo-brain."

"Has it?"

"Yes and on top of that somehow your designers have managed to separate your own living consciousness from that of the computer. This has never been done before."

"David we don't have time for chitchat, we need to get these tests done before anyone notices that we're not working in the lab."

"Yea Mandy, sorry."

"Just a minute I have questions. Where did I come from? Why do I live in the future when all the other Josephines are living now? Did we have parents… ever?"

"How far into the future do you live?" James asked.

"A thousand years," Josephine said.

"Well then I really can't answer your questions. All I can tell you is that you are far more advanced than all these other Josephines, they're clones; I don't know what you are."

Thomas invited Lydia and Bunion to stay on at his pleasure and after the performance they retired to the great room for coffee and brandy. Isabella had been playing the grand piano for a while and when she finished, she and Lydia went out onto the balcony to get some air. The sky was streaked with silver as the full moon shone brightly through the clouds.

"Father's angry with me," Isabella said.

"Why is that?" Lydia asked.

"I told him I didn't want to join the security forces."

"Why would he want you to do that?"

"It's a family tradition that's been passed down through the generations, back even beyond the time when people first came to Bellus. I'm the only child; I'm supposed to carry it on."

"I thought you were a member of the royal family."

"The Queen's grandmother is my grandmother's half sister, but my father has always been a military man."

"So what are you going to do about it?"

"I don't know."

"Perhaps you should talk to him."

"I did but he wouldn't listen."

"I mean did you talk to him properly? Did you discuss things with him or was it just a confrontation?"

"My parents never see things the way I do."

"Try to explain; perhaps they'll surprise you."

"Do you really think I should?"

"What have you got to lose? If you tell your parents how you feel and they don't listen, you're no worse off than you are now. And if they do listen you could be a lot better off."

"Father will be in town tomorrow."

"Talk to him; he loves you doesn't he?"

"Yes of course he does."

"Then go and see him," Lydia said.

They looked up at a flock of birds, whose shapes were silhouetted against the large moon; their lonely calls echoed over the frosty ground.

"They're flying south for the winter," Isabella shivered, "I'm cold, let's go inside."

Thomas, and Sylvia, and Bunion were playing cards by the fire.

"Where's Percy?" Isabella asked.

"Where do you think?" Thomas said.

"Now Thomas I don't own him; he's allowed to do what he likes," Sylvia said.

"With his own money, I hope you didn't allow him to take any more of yours to his poker game."

"He'll pay me back."

"I'll have him beheaded if he doesn't."

"You wish," Isabella said.

"Don't worry Thomas, I know you're only looking out for me, but I can handle Percy."

It was pleasant and warm playing cards in front of the fire and they stayed there talking well into the night.

"If we slice into her pseudo-brain sideways, we could tell much more about the way it's all put together," Mandy suggested.

"Keep away from me you... you murderer," Josephine said.

James laughed, "We're not going to kill you; we just want to scan you to see how your hardware is constructed."

"What I can't understand is why you didn't just knock on the front door and ask me if you could examine my brain."

"Well what we're doing isn't exactly legal. We couldn't take the chance that you wouldn't rat on us before we got a look at your wonderful noggin."

"Are you going to damage me?"

"No we just want to figure out how you're constructed."

"Why don't you just clone me?"

"Can't do that, your DNA's encrypted with a patent stamp; there's no easy way I'm afraid."

"How long is all this going to take?"

"Oh not long... really."

"And then are you going to load my software?"

"Yea sure, why not? It'll be interesting to see how much of the Interference Project will actually fit into that super brain of yours and how quickly it all loads up," James said.

"So how long is this all going to take?" Josephine asked.

"Oh, about three days should do it."

Clarissa tossed and turned. But it wasn't the hard floor that robbed her of her sleep or the fear of what Bridefield would do to her; it was her memories.

She sat up grasping her skinny knees with her knobbly hands. Annie put her arms around her as she and Rosie couldn't sleep either, "I've been remembering things; things about Lydia," Clarissa said.

"Well that's good isn't it? If you remember her, then she must have been there in your past," Annie told her

"She gave me good advice."

"That's a good thing."

"I went to see my father and we had a very productive discussion."

"That's good too isn't it?"

"Yes but...."

"But what?"

"When I got back to the castle, I was walking past the library when...."

Isabella was walking past the library with a smile on her face. She wanted to find Lydia to tell her what had happened when she spoke to her father.

Suddenly she heard Percy Fopwais' voice coming from behind the door saying, "You are the most beautiful creature that I have ever had the privilege to set my eyes upon." Isabella smiled, how sweet that Sylvia and Percy should be so much in love. "That's why I persuaded the guards to let you in."

"But you've already got a girlfriend," a voice said. The voice belonged to Lydia.

"Yes well, she's a sweet little thing but you're so much more than she is, you're a woman not a child, you can't blame me for falling for such a beautiful creature as you," Percy said.

At that moment Bunion came out of the pink room down the corridor, "Have you seen Lydia?" he asked Isabella.

"Lord Fopwais, how dare you? Get away from me," Lydia's voice came from behind the door.

"Lydia, don't reject me out of hand."

Just then Sylvia came bustling up the corridor from the other direction, sniveling into her handkerchief, "Have you seen

Percy? We had an argument, it's all my fault; I shouldn't have confronted him about his gambling, do you know where he is?"

Isabella opened her mouth but nothing came out.

"Get away from me," Lydia shouted from behind the door.

"But Lydia…" Percy pleaded.

"What are they doing in the library?" Sylvia asked.

"Percy you know this is wrong."

"I can't help myself."

"But I'm not interested in you."

"I'm down on my bended knee."

"Percy, no!"

Bunion and Sylvia pushed past Isabella and ran into the library. Sylvia screamed. Bunion rushed up to Lord Fopwais and hit him squarely under the chin, sending him down to the floor.

"Were you trying to kiss Lydia?" Sylvia shouted.

"No of course I wasn't, it's all a mistake; I can explain everything."

At this point Thomas came walking down the corridor looking for Bunion; he heard the commotion in the library and went in to see what it was all about.

"Oh Thomas I'm so glad you're here, he hit me," Percy pointed to Bunion, "and it really hurts."

Thomas stood there for a minute; then he burst into laughter, "Well done little man, Percy here has needed taking down a peg or two for a very long time. Actually I have an announcement to make, I was thinking of making Bunion our official court jester."

"We don't have three days," Josephine said.

"Do you know how long the Interference Project takes to download?" Mandy asked.

"And do you know what would happen to us if we were caught in here?" David added.

James looked at his watch, "Five minutes guys."

"We've got to get back to work," David said.

"And what am I supposed to do while I'm waiting?"

"Whatever you were doing before."

"We can't hang around in the canteen all day, they've already caught us on surveillance camera; they'll think it's very suspicious if I'm not doing any work."

"Don't worry about that, the security team were the ones that tipped us off, they're always looking for ways to make a few extra bucks."

"But I can't stay here for three days, our time machine will return to pick us up in sixteen hours... I hope."

"Well make it wait."

"We can't, what we're doing isn't exactly legal either; for our mission to succeed we have to be ready when it appears."

"Look, we can't discuss this now; we have to get back to the lab. Meet us here in three hours." James released Josephine from her restraints.

"What if I tell your supervisors what you're doing?"

"I wouldn't do that if I were you, they'd want to take your head apart literally. You don't realize it Josephine but you are worth a lot of money," he detached her from the headgear and walked over to the door. "Don't worry about your friend; he'll wake up feeling great."

"But I don't even have money for a cup of coffee."

"Here take this," James pulled some paper out of his pocket and threw it behind him on the floor, "don't spend it all at once," he said.

Percy had run off to look for something to staunch the blood from his nose while Isabella sat on the black, leather sofa in the library holding Sylvia in her arms so that she could ball her head off.

"Go on that's a girl, let it all out."

"Are you sure Lydia didn't do anything to lead him on?"

"No of course not, she was trying to fight him off," Isabella said.

"He's just a total scumbag," Lydia handed Sylvia a tissue.

"That's such a harsh word," Sylvia bawled.

"Not after what he did to you."

"I was going to make up with him, we argued about money, but I think I could have got over that...."

"How could he do that to you? I'm telling you now, you're better off without him."

Thomas edged his way towards the door, "Well Bunion I think we should leave all this to the girls, I need a drink, come let's go and play some cards." Bunion didn't move, in fact he edged towards Lydia. "Come on Bunion this is girl's business."

Bunion tapped Lydia on the shoulder.

"It's a good job you found out what he was like now, before your relationship got more serious," Lydia said.

"Lydia's right, what if you had married him?" Isabella said.

"He had several opportunities to propose but he never did," Sylvia sobbed.

Bunion tapped Lydia again, "What? Bunion, what do you want?"

"Mistress."

"I told you not to call me that."

"Lydia."

"What?"

"Don't forget why we're here."

"Oh," Lydia said, "the war!"

Zedekiah lay on the shiny, plastic floor with dribble coming out of his mouth and a smile on his face. Josephine had shaken him, pushed him, shouted at him and slapped him, but there was no way he was going to wake up.

She considered leaving him there and spending the paper money on coffee and whatever food they ate around here. But it probably wasn't a good idea to split up.

She looked up at one of the security cameras and waved, "If you're not going to help me I'll have to do it myself." She walked over to the computer screen by the examination chair and started fiddling with the memory, "Don't worry I'm not deleting anything."

Everything was strangely familiar; in fact it was so easy to use that it was almost instinctive. She already knew which menus to utilize and how to set it all up. By the time Alex the security guard arrived eighteen seconds later everything was in place.

"I'm going to load my own software," she said.

"Oh no you're not," Alex told her.

"I'm saving time."

"James probably has other tests and scans to do first."

"He can do them afterward."

"But what if they have to be done before you start?"

"Ask him, does he have a pager?"

"Wait there."

Alex was gone for ten minutes.

"Did you see him?" Josephine asked when he returned.

"Yes of course."

"What did he say?"

"He says that if you are thinking of loading the software you should have someone with you."

"I'll take the chance; you just make sure that nobody else comes in here for the next few hours."

"It's Saturday, everyone goes home early but I can't let you do anything until James comes back."

"If you're so worried, stay here yourself."

"I can't allow you to do this."

"You can't stop me, if you try I'll just hit this delete button here and all the data they have on me will disappear."

Alex reached into his pocket and pulled out some handcuffs, "I can't let you do that either."

"I don't have to use my fingers; I can control the computer with my mind."

"If you wipe the computer they'll have to do the tests all over again."

"They won't be able to because long before then I will have sabotaged it so thoroughly that it'll never work again."

Alex scratched his belly and yawned, "Okay I give in, what do you want me to do?"

"I'm going to sit in the chair now and attach the headset; you are going to watch the instruments."

When Josephine was ready she made herself comfortable, selected the operating system and started the installation.

"What war?" Thomas asked.

"Oh nothing, our friends, the rest of the troupe are in a war zone that's all, we were supposed to call them to see if they're okay," Lydia said. "Don't worry I'll do it later."

"Well come on Bunion, there's a game of cards and a bottle of wine with our names on them in the other room."

"You shouldn't drink," Bunion said.

"What do you mean my friend?"

"You drink too much."

"I only do it to help me relax."

"Don't rationalize."

"What?"

"Your highness, you drink too much."

"Do you think so?"

"Yes," Bunion was adamant.

They played cards in the drawing room and although Thomas only ordered fruit juice Bunion still won the game.

Alex didn't know much about computers but even he suspected that something unique was going on here. Josephine would select a program to install and it was as if the computer inside her head recognized it and instantly began to write improvements for it. It did it blisteringly fast and what was even more amazing was that she could talk at the same time about something totally different. She could grill Alex with questions about her origins, while controlling all the operations that were going on inside her pseudo-brain.

"You wouldn't get me a cup of coffee would you? And something to eat, do they have chocolate in this century, or scones or something sweet? I need some instant sugar."

Alex walked towards the door. It was obvious that the Josephine didn't need him so he may as well do as she asked.

By the time James and his cronies reappeared, she had installed a full suite of software, improved it significantly, uploaded the improvements back into the mainframe, checked all her settings and sat there for two hours drinking coffee and eating sweet angel cake while wandering around the galactic net looking for information on the history of cloned bio-machines.

"I didn't want to start on the Interference Project until you got here," she said to James, "it's all set up, just sit over there and watch me through it."

James did as he was told. He went weak at the knees when he saw how unbelievably fast the download was.

"You know I never understood why having all that extra brain didn't make me more intelligent than I was. My IQ is only a hundred and fifty. It didn't seem worth while walking around with an odd shaped head just for that," Josephine told him while everything mankind had ever learned about anything downloaded into her brain at the speed of light.

James scrutinized the computer not quite believing what he was seeing.

Then suddenly the door opened and a sour faced older woman in a lab coat entered the room. "What's going on here?" she said.

Chapter 14.

"Why didn't you tell them what we're really here for?" Bunion asked as he and Lydia walked in the castle gardens outside the conservatory early the next day.

"We can't, if we tell them that we're illegal time travelers, someone could betray us to Bridefield," Lydia said.

"That's not likely to happen."

"But we can't be sure; this mission is too important to take chances."

"We should tell them what's going to happen."

"Suppose they don't believe us? I'm from Bella; what if they decide to interpret our arrival here as some kind of attempt to spy on the royal family? That would only make the possibility of war even more certain; the point is that we should see this thing through properly, I want to be sure that the job is done before Bridefield catches up with us, otherwise it's all for nothing."

Bunion nodded his head, "Do you have a plan?" he asked.

"It should be fairly simple; all we have to do is prevent Sylvia from meeting Lord Murmot."

Thomas appeared from around the side of the house, "Hey, I've been looking all over for you, guess what Mason found for Bunion? Ta-da," he held a unicycle up in the air.

Bunion hadn't ridden a unicycle since he was a teenager when Clarissa had complained that he had crashed into one too many things on the Genghis Khan.

"Come to breakfast and I'll show you what else I got for you."

Lydia and Bunion followed Thomas into the conservatory.

"What do you think? I had these specially made. I was wondering if you would do some kind of performance for us tomorrow, we're having a brunch out in the garden if it's warm enough. The new ambassador of Bella will be there. My parents should have been back from Raynis but they've been delayed and all the invitations have gone out, so they told me I'd have to handle it all by myself. I've never done a garden party on my own before and I really want to show them that they can trust me. But I seriously need help." He handed some clothes to Bunion, "You'll make you a great court jester."

Bunion scrutinized the fool's costume.

"I had my seamstress replicate it from our best historical records. See? She made you the shoes with the curly toes and the bells; and look at the hat, isn't it great? It has horns and bells on too; we'll hear you coming from miles away."

The costume consisted of a half bottle green and half yellow jerkin with tights whose colors were reversed. The hat was half green and half yellow as well.

Bunion still didn't say anything.

"Em well yes it's… great," Lydia said, "I'm sure Bunion will be very happy to wear it. So are there many people invited to this brunch?"

"Only a couple of hundred, it's quiet at this end of the season. Bunion do you tell jokes?"

"No."

"Oh but I need…."

"No," Bunion insisted.

"But I can't have a jester who doesn't tell jokes."

"Don't worry, Bunion's just a little timid that's all," Lydia said. "He'll be all right on the night; or on the day so to speak."

"Oh, right well, and can he breathe fire?"

"Yes," Bunion said, "I can do that."

Josephine sat in the chair with her eyes closed.

"What are you doing here at five o'clock on a Saturday evening? Didn't you know that there's an emergency lock down scheduled for this weekend?" demanded the sour faced woman.

"That's just what I was about to ask them," Alex said.

"And what's this man doing sleeping on the floor?"

"Oh, well, that's Professor Chancery, he was visiting from the Bio-mechanics lab across town; he's been working very hard lately. We wanted to show him how our latest batch of Josephines was holding up and I was just getting this one ready when we turned around and found him asleep on the floor," James said.

"I've never heard of a Professor Chancery."

"He moved here recently from Cleveland after a messy divorce. I'm sorry Mrs. Clayton I had the impression that you knew all about this."

"What's his employee number?"

"1771 850 650, oh look his file's on the screen."

The woman walked over and checked the monitor, sure enough his employee file; photograph included was there. "Well yes I see, but I want you packed up and gone within the hour."

"Yes of course, that won't be a problem Mrs. Clayton."

The sour looking woman left the room.

Alex spoke into his wrist, "Jim, why didn't you warn me... the supervisor... what's he doing here? Oh okay I understand." He looked up, "Jim says that the supervisor's on their backs and we're on our own."

"How did you get that file?" David ran over to the screen to take a look.

"I found the nearest bio-mechanics lab, ran through the employee records, pulled up somebody's name and altered a few details," Josephine opened her eyes. "I also told James what to say."

"It's true, the words came up on the monitor," James said.

"What are we going to do? We have to be out of here in one hour," David said.

"Well I'm done; the Interference Project is now stored in my pseudo-brain and it takes up only three percent of my memory," Josephine said.

"Incredible."

"Unbelievable," Mandy whispered.

"Here, in this environment it's like I'm superhuman."

"You are," James said, "but how are we going to do all the tests if we only have one hour?"

"You told us we had three days," Mandy said.

"Well I didn't know they were going to lock the place down for the weekend," James told her.

"That's because you always slip out early so that you and Alex can reserve your stools in Murphy's bar."

"We have business to conduct that you benefit by."

"If you take a look in the mainframe data base you will see that there's a file marked 'Coffee and Angel Cake,' the schematics for my pseudo-brain are in there along with a few relevant facts that I copied from the Interference Project," Josephine said.

"Really? You've already done it?"

"Yes I have, so you can go to Murphy's bar with a clear conscience and leave us here to wait for our time machine."

"But you can't wait here," Alex said.

"Why not?"

"You heard the woman, there's a lock down."

"So? We'll find somewhere to hide until tomorrow morning."

"You don't understand, when they do a lock down they use a different security company. We don't know these guys; all we know about them is that they're very efficient and that if they catch you, you're in deep trouble," Alex said.

"Why did the robot cross the road? Because he was programmed to; that's pathetic, that's not even funny."

"Can you think of anything better Bunion?" Lydia said.

"I can't tell jokes," Bunion said.

"You'll just have to do your best."

"I don't like these clothes."

"I hate the jester's outfit too but you must wear it, Thomas lives on whims, he will only keep us here if you please him."

"What are you going to do?"

"I'll stick to Sylvia like a leech; under no circumstances is she to go to that brunch," Lydia said.

James and David picked up Zedekiah, "He's heavy," David said.

"He'd move under his own power if you hadn't shot that sedative into his neck," Mandy reminded him.

"I don't think we should hide him in the refrigerator."

"It's been turned off; you know it never works right."

"Will there be enough air?" Josephine asked.

"It's a big, walk-in one and anyway you'll have the door open a crack," James said.

"Isn't there anywhere more comfortable?"

"It's about the most secure place I can think of."

"Have you got anything to keep us warm?"

"You can have my jacket," Mandy said.

Alex walked out of the door and checked the corridor, "All clear," he reported back.

David and James dragged Zedekiah along the hallway and hid round the corner while Alex called the elevator. "All clear," he said again.

They carried the sleeping man inside the lift and hit the button for the top floor. On floor fifteen it stopped, the doors opened and two Josephines got in. They pressed the button for the ground floor and seemed surprised when the elevator took them up instead of down.

"We'll get out before the lock down won't we?"

"Of course," Alex assured them, "I'm sorry about this but we found the suspect drunk in charge of a test tube and we're going up to the cafeteria to revive him with coffee before we interrogate him."

"Oh," the Josephines said.

Josephine smiled.

One of the Josephines smiled back, "Are you part of our network? I can detect your pseudo-brain but I can't get through your security."

"I'm carrying top secret data," Josephine told them.

They got out at the top floor and the other two Josephines started their descent to the lobby.

Alex ran on ahead of them to see if the coast was clear but he was soon back. "There's still people cleaning the dining hall, we'll have to wait a few minutes."

They all hid round the corner. The canteen workers didn't leave till ten minutes to six. The last one was about to lock the canteen door when Alex approached him and said, "I'll take the keys, we've got a lock down this weekend; I just need to double check the security." The man handed the keys over and got into the elevator. Alex checked the cafeteria and the kitchens behind them to confirm that they were empty before going back for the others, "All clear," he said.

"Do we have to carry the old man up all those steps?" David complained.

"If you want to hide him, yes you do."

They dragged Zedekiah slowly up the stairs and into the canteen.

"Hurry up; we've only got five minutes till lock down."

"Someone's using the elevator," Josephine said.

"How do you know?"

"I've tapped into the surveillance system."

"People use the elevator all the time."

"Your uniform is blue; this is a man wearing brown."

"Oh no they're on to us," Alex said.

A man in a brown Securi-guard suit, the uniform of the other security company got out of the lift and ran up the stairs; he had orders to check out a disturbance in the canteen.

Sylvia sat red eyed and bedraggled on her bed. "What did I do wrong?" she sniffed delicately into a lace handkerchief.

"You did absolutely nothing wrong, he's the wrongdoer not you," Lydia insisted.

"I… I really thought he was in love with me."

"The only person he's in love with is himself."

"You should take a few days off, go somewhere in the country, get some peace," Lydia said.

"What? And make it look as if she's running away like she did something wrong? No I'd stay and face him. I'd demand the money he owes. It's he who should be leaving town not Sylvia."

"I agree; I would take a few days rest to get over the shock and then I'd come back and face him."

"He'll be at the brunch won't he?" Sylvia said.

"Yes, you should avoid that at all costs," Lydia said

"I don't think he'll even turn up, he'll be too ashamed of himself," Isabella said.

"But what if he does? How are you going to cope with seeing him again?" Lydia asked.

"You should look him in the eye and spit in his face."

Sylvia looked up at her two companions, "Yes I should, shouldn't I."

"But that's not a very dignified thing for a lady to do."

"Nonsense in this case I would say it's the most dignified thing that a girl who has been wronged could do."

Sylvia wiped her eyes with her handkerchief, "I really ought to thank you Lydia; if you had not come along I might never have known what Percy was really like."

"I'm sorry you had to find out this way."

"You know when I look back on it I have to admit that it was funny when your boyfriend knocked Percy to the floor."

"Oh Bunion he's not… well yes it was very funny."

"Come on dry your eyes," Isabella said, "we've got two hours to make you more beautiful than you have ever been in your whole life."

"Are you sure this is wise? If you see Percy there it might be too much for you; you could crumble."

Sylvia turned to Lydia. "You really are a kind friend but I don't want you to worry. I'm feeling stronger already; if you and Isabella stay with me I know I'll be able to cope with anything."

Alex led the way into the fridge while James and David carried Zedekiah in behind him. Mandy shoved a strangely reluctant Josephine inside as far as she could before squeezing in herself. She pulled the door towards them until it was just open the tiniest crack. They could hear the guard poking about in the kitchen.

"All clear," he said into his radio, "I'm returning to base, it must have been a false alarm."

They would have breathed out with relief if there had been room to do so.

"Oh wait a minute; someone forgot to close the fridge door."

They could hear his footsteps coming towards them; the door closed with a click; it was pitch dark.

"I… I'm claustrophobic," Josephine whispered.

"Shh, the guard will hear you," Alex said.

Zedekiah let out a loud snore.

"Keep him quiet too."

"I've been pinching his nose," David said.

"I'm going to panic," Josephine warned.

"He's really heavy," David complained.

"Will you all be quiet? Wait until the guard has gone."

"He'd better hurry up."

"It's really cold in here, I thought you said the refrigerator wasn't working properly," David said.

"They must have got it fixed."

"I think I've put my elbow into something sticky; hmm yes actually it tastes quite good."

"Could you please open that door," Josephine gasped.

Alex sighed, "He's probably gone by now, I guess it'll be all right. Everybody be quiet."

"Ow, that was my foot," David protested.

"I shouldn't have got in first; ah sorry was that your nose?"

"Just open the door," Josephine begged.

Alex ran his hands up and down the inside of the doorframe, "I can't find the internal handle."

"Are you sure that the refrigerator has one?" James asked.

"Of course I am, they all do, it's just that for some reason it's not here."

"But if it has one it has to be there," Mandy pointed out.

"Hurry up, we're going to run out of air; I'm struggling for breath."

"You're hyperventilating," James said.

Zedekiah snored on.

"How does he do that when I've got my fingers firmly clamped on his nose?" David said.

"He's dribbling on me," Mandy complained.

"Everything's going black," Josephine cried.

"That's because it's dark," Alex told her.

"Just breathe in and out, in and out," James said.

"Josephine, can you get into the network?" Alex asked.

"They've locked me out."

"Oh."

"Can't you get past the security systems?"

"I could if I could breathe."

Zedekiah snored very loudly.

"He's not having any trouble breathing," David remarked.

"You can breathe, just relax and take your mind into the network," James said.

"Yes, yes I can see it."

"Now can you look for ways to hack into the system?"

"Piece of cake, wait one minute... there I'm in."

"Right, now you want the building controls."

"Got 'em."

"Concentrate on finding the controls for the canteen."

"I'm suffocating."

"No you're not, come on concentrate," James said.

"I still, can't breathe."

"Just concentrate."

"Got 'em."

"Is there an electronic door lock on the refrigerator?"

"Yes."

"Can you open it?"

"No."

"Is it encrypted?"

"Yes but that's not the problem."

"What do you mean?"

"That guard's still here, he reported suspicious sounds coming from inside the fridge and there are six more security men coming up the elevator."

"Do we have a back up plan?" David asked.

"Let them in," Josephine said.

"What?"

"There isn't much oxygen left in here, if we don't get out soon we're all dead anyway."

"You're panicking," Alex said.

"I'm not I'm reading the gas exchange data on the system's control panel."

"You mean there really is a problem?"

"Yes, there's no choice, we have to give ourselves up."

"Well if we're going to do that, we'd better get our story straight," Alex said.

"I'm still not happy with your hair," Lydia told Sylvia.

"But you've done it three times already."

"I know but I think that on this occasion it has to be perfect. You want to knock them dead don't you?"

"It looks fine to me, Sylvia you look just lovely."

"There's something wrong with the hairstyle, I just can't put my finger on what it is, and are you sure that's really the right dress?"

"Why Lydia I almost think that you're more nervous for me than I am for myself."

"I am; I really think you shouldn't go down."

"You know what they say about falling off a horse; you should get back on immediately," Isabella said. "Come on let's go, the longer we hesitate, the more nervous we're going to get."

Lydia walked over to the window, "It's not very warm out there; I think you should get something to put round your shoulders." It was a crisp, sunny, late autumn day and as she looked down on the crowds she could see that most of them were wrapped up. Bunion had given up telling jokes and was riding in between groups of guests on his unicycle, juggling some soft balls. There was no sign of Lord Murmot yet but there was little hope that he wouldn't show up.

As they came out of the house they could hear musicians playing chamber music in a little pavilion on the lawn. Waiters wafted in and out of the crowds offering canapés and wine.

Thomas spotted the girls as they walked across the grass, "It's about time," he said.

"We wanted to look our best for you," Lydia told him.

"And that you do, come over here; let me introduce you to some of my friends, Lord Jack Kensworthy is really eager to meet you Lydia."

"Do you mind if I just dash over to Bunion first? I'll only be a minute."

"All right but don't be long."

Lydia ran up to Bunion, "How's everything going? I don't see Lord Murmot, is he here?"

"Yes he's in the house speaking to the Chancellor on business. You couldn't keep Sylvia away then?"

"No, Isabella persuaded her to come down."

"Clarissa you mean?"

"If she lied to us she must have had a good reason."

"That's what I think."

"Well she's unwittingly acting against us at the moment, she definitely doesn't know anything."

"So how are you going to keep Sylvia and Lord Murmot from meeting?"

"I might not be able to."

"Then what will you do?"

"Stick to Sylvia like glue, if she's never alone with Lord Murmot, Lord Fopwais can't accuse her of anything and there won't be a duel."

"But suppose she really likes Lord Murmot?"

"That probably won't happen but if it does we'll have to cross that bridge when we come to it."

Lydia ran back to Sylvia who was still in a group talking to Thomas and his friends. She laughed and joked with them while the waiters brought around bacon and egg rolls.

"This is unusual fare for a royal garden party isn't it?"

"What's unusual about it? Everyone likes it," Thomas said, "and it gives us energy for the dancing."

The chamber music stopped and the musicians made their way back to the house; two minutes later a different set of musicians carried instruments and equipment over to the pavilion.

"Now Lydia can show us all how to dance," Thomas said.

They spent the few minutes that it took for the band to set up, in idle conversation. Lord Jack Kensworthy liked to travel and was fascinated when he found out that Lydia was a touring player and had been to numerous planets.

Lydia told him what Aqua and Fettuccia were like. In fact she got so engrossed in telling him how the Xenons had reacted or more accurately, had not reacted to the troupe's performance that she forgot to look over towards the lawn.

But Bunion had seen him and he nearly hit an old lady dressed in purple feathers as he scraped past Prince Thomas heading for Lydia.

"Hey Bunion what's going on?" Thomas asked.

He bent his head down to speak into Lydia's ear, "Murmot's coming."

"What was that?" Thomas said.

"Oh nothing, he wanted to know if he should start his fire eating act yet."

"Yea, good idea." The band struck its first chord. "Hey Lydia show us what the galaxy is dancing to these days."

Lord Murmot had crossed the lawn and found a place next to Sylvia in the circle round Lydia, "I'm not going to do this on my own, Sylvia, Isabella, join me. Come on don't be shy."

They hesitantly stepped into the circle.

"Wow what a beautiful girl," Lord Murmot declared.

"You mean that one there? Sylvia?" Thomas said.

"Yes," Lord Murmot said.

"Sylvia's my cousin. You're the new ambassador aren't you?"

"Henry Murmot, your Highness."

"You're right Henry, I don't know what those girls did to her but she looks particularly pretty today."

Lydia could see Lord Murmot's eyes fixed upon Sylvia; she spoke to the band, determined that they would perform the dance that could strip away all of a person's dignity.

"Put your heads forward and scratch your feet like a hen; I'm going to teach you all, the chicken dance."

Josephine burst out of the refrigerator and hugged the startled security guard. "Oh thank you, thank you, I thought we were all going to die," she said truthfully.

"What were you all doing in there?" the guard asked.

"Looking for coffee."

"Our friend fell asleep and we wanted to wake him up," James told him.

"But why would it take five people to find one jar of coffee... in a refrigerator?"

"To tell you the truth we were trying to hide him, I know it looks very irregular but we didn't want people to see him like this; he's a good man and he would lose his job."

"Too much whiskey with his lunch," David said.

"His wife's just left him for someone half his age and I'm afraid he's not taking it very well," Mandy added.

"Who is he?" the security guard asked.

"Professor Chancery, you can look up his employee file if you want to."

One of the other men handed the security guard a computer tablet, he pressed the screen a few times and the file appeared.

"See? He recently moved from Cleveland. He left everything behind because his wife said she wanted to live here. Then she ups and leaves him. Life's not fair is it?"

"And it took all five of you to help him?"

"Yes, in the short time he's been here he has become a very dear friend."

The security guard moved away from them and started speaking into his watch.

"Do you think he believes us?" James said.

"I wouldn't and I'm not half as good as these guys," Alex said.

"I loved the chicken dance and all those other dances you showed us," Sylvia said.

"Good, I'm glad," Lydia wiped her forehead with the back of her hand.

"And I'm really happy that you two made me come to this party. But I'm so thirsty, I'll have to go and get a drink."

Lydia had been through the chicken dance, the chameleon dance, the dance of the manic robots, the dance of the fireflies, and several others that she had made up herself. Everyone had joined in, but like Lydia they were all beginning to tire.

"Time for something slower I think," Thomas decided and the band complied by playing a romantic waltz.

"Excuse me, could I have the pleasure of this dance?" Lord Murmot asked Sylvia.

"Sorry maybe later, we're very thirsty and we've got to get something to drink," Lydia started dragging her away.

"It's okay, you go, I'll be along in a minute," Sylvia stood transfixed by Lord Murmot's handsome, blue eyes.

Lydia took a good look around the crowd; there was no sign of Lord Fopwais. "All right then but don't be long, we don't want you dehydrating now do we?"

"This is a great party, my parents will be so pleased and those dances, they really livened things up, where did you get them from?" Thomas asked.

"Oh a friend of mine, Clarissa taught me most of them," Lydia gulped down three cupfuls of fruit punch and was starting her fourth when Lord Jack Kensworthy approached her.

"Would you like to dance?"

Lydia looked around but there was still no sign of Percy anywhere, perhaps her encounter with him had changed history and he wouldn't appear. "Okay," she said with a smile.

She danced two dances with Jack and one with Thomas who kept on about how much less boring this party was that the usual affairs and why wasn't Bunion eating fire yet? And she danced several dances with people she didn't know and then she danced another one with Jack.

Sylvia danced them all with Lord Murmot.

"You really need to go and drink something Sylvia; you were thirsty an hour ago."

"I'll go with you," Lord Murmot said.

Lydia followed them and got another drink for herself.

"You're tired," Lord Murmot said to Sylvia, "let's go and sit under that apple tree where we can talk."

"No…" Lydia started to say.

"Not dancing? Have all your partners abandoned you? Come let me rectify the situation." Thomas took Lydia's hand and started waltzing with her on the spot.

"Actually I…."

"What, you don't want to dance with me?"

"No but…."

"I'm the prince, the future King."

Out of the corner of her eye Lydia could see a familiar figure heading towards the drinks table.

"Percy looks as if he hasn't slept all night, where's Sylvia? Oh look she's over there with that ambassador fellow from Bella, under the apple tree."

Suddenly Bunion's unicycle blocked their view, he still had his striped tights and his curly ended shoes with the bells, but his muscular torso was naked and there was fire leaping out of his mouth. He crossed Lord Fopwais' path again and again, juggling batons that were burning at both ends.

"I've got to go," Lydia said.

Thomas didn't object; he was fascinated by Bunion's performance.

Lydia ran over to the apple tree, "Percy's here," she slid herself down to the floor and squeezed in between Sylvia and Henry Murmot.

"Ow, please there isn't room… and who's Percy?"

"Her boyfriend," Lydia said.

"Ex-boyfriend," Sylvia corrected her.

"As of yesterday, I think he's come to try and make up with you."

"I don't ever want to speak to him again."

"I think I'd better go," Lord Murmot said.

"No stay, he's not going to ruin my life."

"I think perhaps you ought to go and talk to him," Lydia said.

Reluctantly Sylvia got up, "Please stay, I won't be long."

"I'll be here," Lord Murmot smiled up at her.

Lydia watched as Sylvia walked over to where Lord Fopwais was. She saw him get down on his knees and beg forgiveness and she saw Sylvia hold out her hand and lift him up. They hugged each other tightly.

"I thought their relationship was over," Lord Murmot said.

"You must let Sylvia make that decision; she will never be truly yours if you don't," Lydia told him.

Sylvia dabbed Percy's eyes with one of her embroidered handkerchiefs. Then she told him something quietly.

He shook his head.

She told him again.

"No, no, you don't mean it, you're still angry that's all; when you calm down you'll change your mind."

"No Percy I'm sorry, I won't."

"You're toying with me, you know you're going to marry me eventually, your parents wish it."

"Percy you have to face facts, it's over between us, I'm sorry but what you did yesterday; I have forgiven you for it but I couldn't possibly marry a person who does such things."

"But I'll change, you'll see; it'll never happen again."

"When Lady Grace told me that you had tried to kiss her I thought she was just jealous of us."

"But that was nothing; I felt nothing for Grace."

"Then why did you do it?"

"Because I… I don't know, I don't know."

"Goodbye Percy."

"Sylvia, please."

"Goodbye Percy," Sylvia turned to walk away; by this time a crowd had gathered to watch the argument.

"Sylvia, don't go," Percy ran behind her and caught her by the shoulders.

Lord Murmot stood up.

"Let me go," Sylvia said.

"Lord Murmot, stay here; let them resolve their own difficulties," Lydia caught hold of his hand.

"But Sylvia, please...."

"Percy, you're hurting me."

Lord Murmot pulled away from Lydia and ran towards Sylvia.

Lydia ran after him, "Lord Murmot you don't know what you're doing."

"I can't let that beautiful creature be treated this way."

"But Lord Murmot you're going to kill him!"

Bunion jumped down off his unicycle and threw his flaming batons to the ground. He ran up to Percy and delivered a sharp uppercut under his chin; Percy fell backwards into the crowd.

"So this is how the land lies is it? This is why you won't forgive me? You've fallen for that, that thing... that ugly... you prefer that dwarf over me."

"Percy I have already forgiven you, I just can't have you back," Sylvia cried tearfully.

Percy stumbled to his feet and rubbed his painful chin, "We'll see about that." He turned to Bunion. "Pistols at dawn!" he said.

Chapter 15.

Josephine sat in a gray interview room at the opposite side of the table to a grim looking man. James, David, Mandy and Alex sat on a bench at the back of the room while Zedekiah lay on the floor still blissfully asleep. Men in brown uniforms guarded them all.

"Do you take me for a complete idiot?" the interrogator said.

"No certainly not," Josephine told him.

"Do you know why we had to lock down this weekend?"

"No."

"Because there are one too many Josephines in this building, that's why."

"Are you sure you counted them correctly?"

"We believe the extra one is you."

"But I work in wheat distribution on the seventh floor, room 3B; you can pull up my employee file if you want."

"I think I might just do that, what's your number?"

"757 351 792."

The man keyed in the numbers and a file came up on his computer screen.

"Now do you believe me?"

"I want to check your DNA patent," He ran a small probe over her skin; fortunately for Josephine she was able to interface with it and control the readouts.

"It's a match isn't it? See? You shouldn't be so suspicious. I'm sure if there had been any irregularity Alex here would have told you about it."

"He has been under investigation for some time and so have some of his buddies."

"Hey that's not fair," Alex said.

"Do you have any proof of your accusations?"

"Nothing concrete but we have enough suspicions to fill a whole file."

"Then officer…" Josephine reached over the table and peered at his name badge, "Jenkins, I suggest that you be careful of what you say."

Zedekiah snored.

"Why doesn't he wake up?"

"We suspect that somebody spiked his drink."

The door opened and a distinguished looking man walked in, "How is the interrogation going Jenkins?"

"Oh well enough sir," Jenkins said.

"Good, well now that you've softened them up for me I'll take over; get me a cup of tea will you?"

"Yes sir."

"And tell the people waiting outside to come in."

Jenkins walked out and a white coated man and woman entered the room.

The distinguished man stared into Josephine's face, "So you're the clone that's been giving us all the trouble."

"I'm no trouble sir; I was just in the wrong place at the wrong time."

"Well I hope you're willing to prove that, let me introduce myself. I am Inspector Smith; I will be your interrogator for the evening. This is Teresa Marshal, she's a doctor; she's going to give your friend there something to help him wake up. And this man here is Kenneth Andrews; he's an expert bio-technologist. He wants to take a look at you."

"What if you just don't turn up for the duel Bunion? Why don't we use the remote to recall the time machine so that we can get out of here?" Lydia said.

"No, we must see this through, if we go now, Lord Murmot might decide to defend Sylvia's honor in my place."

"But you've never shot a gun before."

"I have no intention of killing Percy."

"He could kill you Bunion."

"That is of no consequence Lydia."

"Yes Bunion it is of consequence; it's of a great deal of consequence."

"One life for half a billion?"

"There has to be something we can do."

"Do you have any ideas?"

Lydia shook her head.

Kenneth Andrews had thin, sandy hair and freckles. He was probably a lot younger than he seemed, but he looked like he didn't get out much. He peered at Josephine as if he was examining a lab rat, "The cranial structure looks a bit oversized to me; let me get my calipers."

"Leave me alone," Josephine said.

"I'd like to find out what's causing the anomaly," he took his calipers out of their case.

"Stop that, leave me alone, I don't want to be examined; this is an invasion of my privacy."

"Now you know as well as I do that Josephines don't have any privacy." He measured her head front to back and side to side and top to bottom, "There's a discrepancy of about four centimeters," he said.

Meanwhile the doctor had given Zedekiah a shot of something; slowly he yawned and opened his eyes; she helped him onto a chair.

"What's your name?"

"Zedekiah Banes."

The doctor typed his responses onto a computer tablet, "And what do you do?"

"I'm an archaeologist."

"Where do you live?"

"Oh nowhere in particular, my last base was in the heart of an asteroid in the Marango system."

"What are you doing here Mr. Banes?"

Zedekiah looked up; he had a wide-eyed expression on his face, "We came for the Interference Project."

Meanwhile Kenneth had set up a mobile scanner and was trying to put a helmet on Josephine's head, "Get that thing away from me."

"Now come on it doesn't hurt," Kenneth said.

"How do you know?"

Two menacing guards pointed guns at her so she had no choice but to sit still while Kenneth locked the helmet into place.

"Switch the scanner on," Inspector Smith said.

Kenneth did as he was told... and drew a very deep breath, "This is amazing, it's what I've dreamed of my whole life; this has to be military hardware."

"What does finding six people in a refrigerator have to do with a military Josephine?" Inspector Smith asked.

Zedekiah must have thought he was asking him because he answered, "We were hiding from you; we needed to finish our mission."

"What mission?"

"To copy the Interference Project and take it to those who will know what to do with it."

"Excuse me; did you give him a truth drug?" Josephine asked.

"Yes," the doctor said.

"You're conscious?" Kenneth said.

"My personal consciousness and my pseudo-consciousness are entirely separate."

"That's incredible; I never thought that was possible."

"Turn the scanner off."

"How did you get into the building Zedekiah?"

"We used a time machine."

"Did you come from the past?"

"No the future."

"Why would you want to take the Interference Project into the future?" the inspector asked.

"We need the information."

"These answers don't make sense are you sure the truth drug's working properly?"

"Yes sir," the doctor said.

"When is the time machine due to return?"

"Tomorrow at eight a.m."

"In this building?"

"The seventeenth floor."

"We shall be there to meet it," Inspector Smith said.

"When are you guys going to give us something to eat? You're not allowed to hold us here without feeding us, that's torture," David complained.

Inspector Smith ignored him, "If you needed the Interference Project so badly why didn't you just download it off the Galactic net?"

"The net version isn't complete because many things are patented and much information is in the domain of the military, or it is speculative and hasn't been included."

"Aha now we come down to the real reason you're here, you came to steal secrets from the military."

"I thought they were the military," Kenneth said.

"I suspect that what we are dealing with here is rogue military hardware, mercenaries willing to sell to the highest bidder."

"I'm not hardware," Josephine insisted.

"How far in the future do you live?"

"A thousand years."

"Don't give me that, by that time the Interference Project will be nothing more than an ancient curiosity. Something else is going on here, perhaps I should ask your four accomplices over there. Dr Marshal, prepare four more doses of the truth serum."

"But you can't do that, we were innocent pawns in their game." Alex said, "If we had known who they really were we would have reported them straight away."

"Everything you have told me so far is just a pack of lies. You know what I think? I think that you're just thieves wanting to make a few bucks by selling off military secrets."

"That's not right," Zedekiah slumped down in the chair, "I don't feel well."

"I'm not finished with you yet."

The doctor shone a light into Zedekiah's eyes, "The old man's had enough."

"Already? Can't you give him another shot?"

"No, I don't think he could take it."

"Then give it to the Josephine."

"Hey that contravenes my human rights," Josephine said.

"Josephines are not human; they don't have any rights."

Zedekiah rubbed his red eyes as if they itched badly.

"It's late; I should be tucked up in bed by now," David said.

"Can I get a message to my mom? She'll be worried sick," Mandy asked.

"Yea, can I get through to my girlfriend? She'll be wondering where I am," James said.

Zedekiah's shoulders slumped over.

"No messages to anybody till we get to the bottom of this. Administer the truth drug."

"You're not entitled to the information in my mind; it could do you more harm than you realize," Josephine said.

Zedekiah's eyes rolled in his head.

"Answer my questions."

"I can't, you know too much already, if I tell you more it could do untold damage."

"Excuse me if I don't believe you."

"She, she w… wants to protect you," Zedekiah slid down onto the floor unconscious.

"Inject her," the inspector ordered.

A mist rose up from the front lawn as dawn arrived. Waiters passed through the crowd serving bagels and coffee.

"Thomas, please for the last time; stop this."

"Lydia for the last time I can't."

"This is a stupid tradition."

"Are you calling our traditions stupid?"

"You know I don't mean it like that."

"Are you saying that a man should not defend a woman's honor?"

"No, I'm just saying that this is all a mistake, it isn't necessary; and who is he?" Lydia pointed to a man with a TV camera.

"He's the official recorder, we don't want any misunderstandings from the loser's relatives afterward do we?"

"Please Thomas, Bunion is a good man, he's never handled a pistol before."

"Really what was he trained on? Swords, rocket launchers, poisons?"

"No, none of those things; Bunion is a man of peace."

"He punched Percy under the chin twice in two days that's not very peaceful. Where are our two antagonists anyway? It's about time we got this over with, I'm getting cold and I want to go back to bed."

Lydia ran inside to Bunion's room. He was sitting on the end of the bed, "Where's the remote for the time machine?"

"In my pocket."

"Give it to me."

"No."

"Give it to me; let's get out of here now."

"We've changed the timeline; I'm not going to risk changing it back."

"But Bunion you could die."

"I used to do an act with a knife thrower; he wasn't very good; I learned to dodge."

"Knives are different, they're slower."

"I'll be able to see where he is aiming and get out of the way."

"You're not immortal and you're not superhuman."

"I know but I am a dwarf; I make a smaller target."

"That's not much comfort," Lydia said.

Bunion put his arms around her and held her tight, "You told me that we must see this thing through."

"Yes but I didn't think it would come to this."

A deep, bored sigh emanated from someone at the bedroom door, "Percy's there; are you coming?" Thomas said.

"I want…" Josephine said woozily. "I want…."

"What do you want?" the doctor asked.

"I want to go to the bathroom."

The corridor was a twisting, turning tunnel. She nearly fell onto the toilet and afterwards when she had emptied all the contents of her stomach, she had to squint hard to find the sink so that she could wash her hands. She cupped them and drank some water before swaying back into the interview room.

"Who do you really work for?" Inspector Smith asked.

"Clarissa Clarke's Traveling World of Wonders."

"Doctor, is she resisting the drug?"

"It's hard to tell."

"I'll repeat the question, who are you really working for?"

"Clarissa Clarke's Traveling World of Wonders."

"Where are they based?"

"They don't have a base, they move around all the time."

"How long have you worked for them?"

"Fifteen standard years; since I was twelve years old."

"Who do you work with? Come on I want names."

"Bunion, Jerome, Rosie and Annie."

"Those are all undoubtedly codenames," Kenneth said, "I'm inputting them into the computer now; I'll see if I can find any matches"

"What was your last assignment?"

"I had to get some information from Amos's cave under his temple."

"Who were you working with?"

"Amaak, and Froggie, and Zedekiah."

"So you admit that Zedekiah works with you."

"Of course he does."

"What is your next assignment?"

"I don't know; it depends on what Clarissa has us booked in for. I think it's probably the watermelon fair on Crespus."

"Have you got that?" the inspector asked Kenneth.

"Just entering it into the computer now," Kenneth said.

"Any results yet?"

"No matches found, but what can you expect with all this top secret stuff? Those military guys, you don't know what they'll come up with next."

"The drug's starting to wear off," the doctor told them.

"Already?"

"She's younger and stronger than the old man."

"Give her some more," Inspector Smith said.

The pistols were very ornate; they were old-fashioned replica flintlock, lasers. Lydia shuddered when she saw them. If they had contained real bullets or even if they had been modern weapons instead of fake ancient ones, Bunion would have had to face one bullet and that would have been all. But the lasers had a three second charge, which meant that if you missed your target you could keep firing until you found it.

Bunion picked up his pistol and a man dressed in black showed him how to use it. Percy looked much better this morning. He was clean, his stylist had done his hair and someone had manicured his nails.

"Make sure you film my silk blouson, blue suits me don't you think?" he confidently picked up his pistol.

Lydia stood by Bunion's side holding his hand.

Sylvia ran up to him with tears in her eyes, "Please don't hurt Percy, I know he's a fool but he doesn't deserve to die."

"I don't intend to hurt him," Bunion assured her.

"Thank you," Sylvia said.

"What if Bunion dies?" Lydia asked.

"Then he shall be forever honored as a Champion of the Royal House."

"She thinks Percy's life is worth more than yours," Lydia said after Sylvia had run off again.

"She is probably right."

"No Bunion she's dead wrong."

Isabella made her way through the crowds, "Sorry I'm late, I couldn't sleep, I just kept thinking about how either Percy or poor Bunion will have to die because of our ridiculous traditions; I must have fallen asleep just before dawn because my maid had to wake me. This isn't right, I wish there was something I could do about it."

"Sunrise is upon us, it is time to begin," the black suited man announced, "would all spectators please withdraw to a safe distance?"

Lydia held onto Bunion but he pushed her away, "Can't you just forfeit?"

He didn't reply but the stubborn look on his face told her that he was committed to this madness.

Isabella pulled her out of the way.

The black suited man stationed the two antagonists back to back on the grass. "You must take ten strides as I count them out, then you may turn and fire when ready," he climbed onto a little podium that had been designed for these occasions. From it he could see if there was any cheating.

The crowd went silent and he cleared his throat, "One, two, three, four, five, six, seven, eight, nine… Ten!"

I want the full truth," Inspector Smith demanded. "Now doctor if you please?"

"You know that she could have a negative reaction to this don't you."

"Doctor Marshal we have uncovered a plot to steal military secrets; do you expect me to leave it here?"

Josephine saw the hypo-spray coming towards her. She couldn't take much more of this, "No, please no!"

The doctor administered the injection and thirty seconds later Josephine puked all over the floor.

"Yew, well at least I'm not hungry anymore," David said.

"Clean her up and start again," the inspector ordered.

"I think we should give her a few minutes to recover." "Kenneth; get me some paper towels."

Kenneth ran out of the door, glad to be away from the smell.

"I want to puke again," Josephine said.

"I've never been any good with vomit," Mandy groaned.

"Get her into the bathroom until she's finished," Inspector Smith ordered.

It took an hour for Josephine to stop retching. By now it was deep into the night; Inspector Smith studied her from his side of the desk as she looked blearily up into his face.

"Who is Clarissa Clarke?" he asked.

"She is our mother."

Kenneth keyed that important piece of data into the computer, "Ah at last; the information I have indicates that this might be a code word for the operations director."

"How many people are working with you?"

"I don't know, it varies, we had Zeno but he was a traitor so we deactivated him."

"Deactivated probably means that they killed him."

"And of course we've got Lydia, she was supposed to move on but then she had to pretend to marry Bunion so we let her stay," Josephine's eyes began to roll; the doctor made sure she was sitting squarely in her seat.

"What is the purpose of your organization?"

"Purpose?"

"What does Clarissa Clarke's Traveling World of Wonders exist for?"

"To make money I suppose, that's quite important to most of us."

"And who exactly are your clients?"

"Anyone really, anyone who can pay the price of the ticket, now please leave me alone, I want to go to sleep," Josephine put her head on the desk and closed her eyes.

"Give her a few minutes," the doctor said.

"You see doctor, they really are mercenaries."

"Ruthless ones too," Kenneth added. "All they care about is money."

"I knew they weren't telling us everything; get the old man back in here, I want to interrogate him again."

"But sir I don't know if he'll be able to stand up to another dose of the truth drug," the doctor warned.

"You heard what she said, they're dangerous criminals, we have no choice," Inspector Smith said.

In a fast, continuous maneuver, Bunion swung around on his heel, aimed his pistol into the air and discharged it, turning some of the low mist into steam.

He stood still and faced Percy.

Percy aimed his gun carefully and slowly, but Bunion didn't flinch. Lydia dug her nails into her palms; a three second burst from a laser at this range would kill him.

Time hung in the air as Percy slowly moved his trigger finger; he fired the gun into Bunion's chest.

Bunion didn't dodge.

Smoke rose from his clothing before Percy moved his aim and wasted the rest of the charge into the air. Lydia ran up to Bunion, pushed him to the ground and rolled him over and over.

Percy stood above them, "My dignity is satisfied," he said.

"Are you hurt? Let me take a look," Lydia unbuttoned Bunion's shirt, his skin was red but the damage was minimal.

"What's this?" She picked up a mass of hot, black goop that was stuck to his clothing.

"That used to be the remote control for the time machine."

Josephine could hear something distant, like it was happening on another world. She opened half an eye and saw Zedekiah sitting on a chair next to her with the doctor standing over him holding the hypo-spray.

"No please I can't...."

"Hey the computer's crashed," Kenneth called out.

"What?" Inspector Smith said. "I thought all computer activity was routed through the Josephines."

"Not at the weekend, we use conventional computers when there's not much demand; they're cheaper to run."

"So what's wrong?"

"The whole network has crashed."

Josephine faded out of consciousness.

"Oh how about that? It just came back."

"Does it do that often?" Inspector Smith asked.

"I've never known it before."

"Now can we please get on?"

"Ohhh," Josephine woke up and vomited green bile all over the floor again.

The doctor examined her, "She's still reacting."

Josephine puked again as if to back up the doctor's statement; there was nothing left to vomit but her stomach hadn't got the message. She felt weak and woozy and she had a terrible headache. The doctor laid her on the bench at the back of the room while Zedekiah sat at the table facing the inspector.

"The truth drug, is that a standard interrogation procedure?" Zedekiah said.

"Of course it is; why do you ask?"

"Interesting."

"Doctor would you administer the drug now?"

"Doctor in your professional opinion, am I strong enough to handle this drug?" Zedekiah asked.

"Possibly," the doctor told him.

"And possibly not?"

"No."

"How would you feel if something happened to me as a consequence of a drug that you deliberately administered?"

"Well I ..."

"Would it bother you?"

"Well yes I suppose it would."

"Then as a health care professional sworn to do no harm, it is your duty to refuse to administer this drug."

The doctor looked up at Inspector Smith, "I'm afraid he's right," she said.

"Give the hypo-spray to me, I'll administer it myself," the inspector said.

"You can't do that, you're not qualified."

"Then I see only one solution to this situation, we'll have to take them downtown to the police facilities; we'll continue the interrogation there."

"No please, our time machine returns in a few hours."

"You won't be leaving in it anyway," the inspector signaled to the guards, "Take them away."

They dragged Josephine and Zedekiah out of the room, down the hallway and into the elevator where they pressed the ground floor button and the lift started to descend.

Josephine closed her painful eyes in concentration; suddenly an alarm sounded and the lift jerked to a halt.

"What's happening?" one of the guards asked.

"We're stuck between two floors," the other one said.

Josephine sank slowly to the ground but she kept concentrating. Another alarm started ringing; the sound seemed to be coming from all around them.

"That's the fire alarm."

All at once the elevator juddered into movement again.

"Hey why are we going up when we should be going down?"

The lift stopped and the doors opened but as the guards ran out to check the hall for fire they closed again with Zedekiah and Josephine still inside. The elevator moved upwards to stop again between floors.

"Are you controlling all this?" Zedekiah asked.

Josephine nodded her head.

"Are you all right?"

Josephine shook her head slowly from side to side.

"Can you see where all the guards are?"

"Yes I've tapped into the security system, the fire department is on its way; Inspector Smith will have to evacuate the building."

"They'll come for us."

"They can't see us, I took care of that."

"Good then maybe they'll be off our backs for a while."

"What's the time?" Josephine asked.

"Four a.m. we have four hours until the time machine arrives... if it does."

"If I can just stay conscious I'll be able to keep them on their toes until we can get out of here."

"Can you do that? You look awful."

"I'll have to; there's no choice."

Meanwhile the fire chief was not happy with Inspector Smith, "Why haven't you ordered everyone to evacuate?"

"Because there isn't really a fire; a rogue Josephine is causing this, we need to get in there and find her."

"Nevertheless we'll have to do our inspection; now please make sure there is no one in the building."

It took an hour to confirm that there was indeed no fire.

Josephine and Zedekiah spent most of it in a security blind spot, the dusty air ducting system on the fifteenth floor where Josephine spent her time lying down with her eyes shut as this was the only way that she could stand the enclosed space. Just as the fire department was leaving she made the network system crash again and while the inspector's men were trying to get it operational, all the Josephines turned up for work. It was five-fifteen on Sunday morning but they were convinced it was Monday.

Inspector Smith was angry, "Get me that Josephine and get the police."

But the police couldn't do anything because Josephine had turned up the temperature in the building, deactivated the security cameras, and locked all the doors.

"There's only one way to do this," the police chief told Inspector Smith as they stood outside the building, "we'll have smash all the locks and break in."

"Wait, you can't do that," the fire chief came running over.

"I thought you had gone," Inspector Smith said.

"We got another priority red call from your building; we're not allowed to ignore it."

"It's that Josephine, if you'll just let me in to capture her we could all go home."

"Nevertheless we'll have to check out the building again."

"We wasted a whole hour outside here while you did the first inspection."

"I know and I'm sorry but we are obligated to go by procedure."

"So do you want my men to break the main door down now?" the police chief asked.

As the men broke in they set off the burglar alarms, which wouldn't turn off because Josephine had changed the codes. It took until seven-fifteen a.m. to prize open all the doors so that the fire department could establish beyond all doubt that there was no fire and the building was safe.

"Have you found that Josephine yet?" Inspector Smith asked the chief of police as the firemen finally drove away.

"My men are searching for it now."

Suddenly there was a noise from up above them; it sounded like rotor blades; they looked up into the sky, "What the…?"

There was a sign on the bottom of the huge heli-plane that flew into view over the top of the building, 'International Terrorist Reaction Squad.'

Inspector Smith shouted into his earpiece, "WILL SOMEBODY GET ME THAT JOSEPHINE?"

Meanwhile inside the building Zedekiah and Josephine scrambled out of a cleaning closet.

"Are the people in the heli-plane searching for us?" Zedekiah asked.

"No and anyway their readouts tell them there's nobody in here," Josephine said.

"So why did they come?"

"They've had a tip off about Inspector Smith."

It was nearly eight o'clock before the inspector finally convinced the Terrorism Squad that he and his team were not international criminals. He sighed with relief as he watched the heli-plane leave, "Now at last we can get that Josephine, I want everyone up to the seventeenth floor immediately!"

Meanwhile Zedekiah looked at his watch, "The time machine is due in five minutes, we had better get into place."

They struggled up to the seventeenth floor and hid in an office, "There are men coming up the stairs," Josephine said.

"You disabled the elevators?"

"Yes."

"Are there any locked doors in their path?"

"No."

"Where are they now?"

"Floor fifteen."

Zedekiah looked at his watch, "We should make it; the time machine is due to arrive in less than a minute."

They ran out into the corridor, to the place where they were expecting it to materialize. "They're up to the floor sixteen," Josephine rubbed her eyes and massaged the back of her neck; she was dehydrated and her head was very sore.

"Thirty seconds," Zedekiah said.

"They knew we had to be here for eight o'clock."

"Ten seconds, nine... eight... seven... six...."

"They're up to the seventeenth."

There was a shout from down the other end of the corridor.

"Five..."

There should have been a faint buzzing noise.

"Four, three..."

A misty egg shape should have begun to materialize in front of them. Instead heavily armed security guards started running up the corridor towards them.

"Stop or I'll have to shoot," someone with a big, black laser rifle shouted.

"Two, one...."

Nothing!

Zedekiah and Josephine ran as laser bolts whizzed past their ears.

"What are we going to do now? I was sure that the Time Machine would come for us," Zedekiah said.

"It's here, I can sense it," Josephine shouted.

"Well where is it?"

"It must have tracked that ancient money, it thinks we're there."

"Where?" A laser blast singed Zedekiah's pony-tail and knocked his hat off his head; he didn't stop to pick it up.

"In the canteen."

"We've got two minutes or it'll leave without us."

They ran towards the elevators, twisting and turning to avoid the gunfire. A laser blast ignited the corner of Josephine's skirt but she let it blaze until they got inside.

One of men fired just as the doors were closing.

"Ahh," Josephine cried.

"He got you in the arm."

"I'm okay," water squeezed out of Josephine's eyes while she was beating the flames out of her clothing. The fire was out by the time they got to the top floor; they rushed up the last flight of stairs.

The canteen was locked with manual keys; "These doors are not linked into the computer system, I can't open them." They could see the time machine through the window standing by the counter in the canteen but they couldn't get to it.

"We've got twenty seconds before it disappears," a laser shot whizzed past Zedekiah's ear, "They've caught up with us, quick, we've got to get outside." As they ran around the building he was looking for a way to break the plate glass but it was impossible; he shook his head, "It's too late," he said.

The time machine had begun to disappear but they didn't have the leisure to stand and watch it because guards were chasing them across the roof.

"Quick, head for that bridge," Josephine shouted.

"The force-field isn't on."

"Keep running."

They raced onwards, still twisting and turning to avoid the laser fire. Josephine closed her eyes for a split second and the bridge glowed into activity just before Zedekiah ran off the side of the building. She hesitated, "I'm scared of heights."

"Just don't look down."

Josephine closed her eyes and ran onto the bridge; then she opened them again because she couldn't see where she was going. A laser hit her skirt and again it burst into flames; she looked all the long, long way down for a split second before another laser blast, whizzing past her, reminded her of that fact that she should be running.

Zedekiah and Josephine made it to the other side just before the guards could step onto it. Josephine closed her eyes again and the luminescent bridge disappeared. The guards came to a halt at the edge of the building. They fired across the gap but Josephine and Zedekiah were out of range.

Josephine patted out the flames of her blackened skirt.

Zedekiah stood there panting for breath, "What now?"

"Wait," Josephine said.

There was a faint buzzing noise and the time machine appeared in front of them.

"What did you do?"

"I programmed it to follow us."

"You can do that?"

"Apparently yes," Josephine and Zedekiah climbed in and closed the door. Josephine programmed their trip back to Zertza. "Oh!" she pointed to the control screen.

There was a message flashing all over it, 'Warning Batteries Nearly Exhausted.'

"What do we do now?" Zedekiah said.

Nobody woke up till lunchtime.

"I hate early mornings," Thomas said as he came yawning into the conservatory. Lydia, Sylvia, Isabella and Bunion had been sitting around the table, waiting for the Crown Prince to appear so that they could start their lunch.

The waiter served them all generous slices of melon.

"Isn't Percy here yet?"

"He said not to expect him," Isabella said, "he sent a message to say that he got so little sleep what with all the preparations for the duel, the hair alone took two hours, that he's decided to spend the day in bed. Do you think the duel will make the news?"

"Probably not; nobody died," Thomas said.

"I can't believe you people; you're treating the potential death of your fellow human beings as is it were entertainment," Lydia said.

"She was only asking if it'll make the news."

"Someone nearly died today. You could have lost Percy or I could have lost Bunion and yet you treat it like… it's nothing."

"Actually it got me thinking about joining the security forces. My father wants me to apply for the military, but perhaps I should be thinking of something closer to home, palace security should never have allowed the situation to escalate to that level and yet they were nowhere to be seen. What if there had been a genuine threat?" Isabella said.

"I've been saying that to father for such a long time," Thomas said.

"Oh Izzy it would be wonderful if you could guard us; you would be stationed here at the castle forever, we'd see you every day and I could make sure you got the most expensive longevity treatment; then you'd live as long as us," Sylvia said.

"Dizzy Izzy, a policewoman? That takes some stretch of the imagination," Thomas laughed. "So Bunion, are you ready for the big ceremony tomorrow?"

"Ceremony?"

"You're to be decorated as a Champion of the Royal House; I thought Sylvia already explained that to you."

"But we have to leave tomorrow."

"Oh please don't do that, you've been such a help to me, I couldn't possibly cope without you," Sylvia said.

"I think Isabella will do a great job; she won't let anything happen to you," Lydia said.

"Are you sure you can't stay?"

"We are due to transport out of here at one-thirty tomorrow."

"Then we'll have the ceremony in the morning; let's go swimming," Thomas said.

They played water volleyball and tag and then the young women sat in the Jacuzzi while the young men donned soft robes and played snooker.

"Henry asked me out," Sylvia announced coyly.

"He seems really nice," Lydia said.

"Percy seemed really nice too when I first met him, I'm going to be a little more cautious this time."

"Well you can rely on me to tell you if I suspect that there's even the slightest thing wrong with him," Isabella assured her.

"Take things slowly, let Percy get used to the fact that you are not with him any more before you go out with Henry in public, otherwise he could decide to fight a duel with him too."

"Oh don't worry I'll be discreet, I don't want anything to happen to Henry."

"Good," Lydia watched Bunion line up his snooker cue to take an awkward shot.

Chapter 16.

"We can't return to Zertza, there isn't enough juice in the batteries," Josephine said.

"So what are we going to do?"

"Get help and there's only one person I know of that is close enough in time."

"Who's that?" Zedekiah asked.

"Amos Narbandian."

The warning light on the screen flashed faster and faster as they tore through time and space and they breathed a sigh of relief when the buzzing noise wound down and they knew they were safely in Amos's time.

"What landing spot did you choose?" Zedekiah asked.

"Well I had to estimate the exact co-ordinates but if I got it right we should be in Amos's private quarters, I thought that would be the securest place," Josephine said.

Inspector Smith finally had to release Alex and his co-conspirators because of lack of evidence. All files that had anything to do with the presence of the time travelers had been mysteriously deleted. All that was left was the word of Inspector Smith and his two associates who insisted that a sinister ex-military organization called Clarissa Clarke's Traveling World of Wonders was stealing top-secret information and selling it to the highest bidder.

The only person who would listen to them was a man called Joseph Bridefield who worked as a secretary for the newly set up Temporal Commission, "Thank you for your useful information, I will make sure it gets into the right hands," he said.

Lydia looked out of the window of the pink room at the rain that was pouring down from the sky, "Do time machines work in the rain?" she asked Bunion.

"I don't know," he was dressed in a hastily altered white, military style uniform with gold trimmings and a peaked hat.

Lydia looked at the clock on the wall, "They're so late; do they do this deliberately?"

"They don't think about it that's all."

"We told them that our transport was coming at one-thirty and they said we would have the ceremony at half past eleven but its almost half past twelve."

"They assume that our transport will wait for us."

"But it won't wait and now that we don't have the remote control we can't change anything."

"You look very pretty."

"Thanks Bunion but I've only borrowed this gown from Isabella, I'm going to have to get changed before we leave and as good as you look in your uniform I think you should get changed too."

"Clarissa could invent a whole comedy routine based on this costume," Bunion said.

Thomas put his head round the door, "Everybody ready?"

The scent of tropical flowers rose from the big Jacuzzi. The man sitting in it was almost asleep after a very stressful day.

Suddenly through the steam he heard a buzzing noise somewhere above his head. As he opened his eyes he knew that he had to be dreaming. A strange egg shaped structure appeared out of the steam above him and floated there. He jumped out of the pool a split second before the thing dropped out of the air, falling heavily downwards with a great splash.

"What the...?" Amos Narbandian grabbed a white toweling robe and wrapped it around himself while a door flipped up and an old man and a Josephine with a raw wound on her arm and a burnt, ragged skirt got out.

The old man looked at him, "You must be Amos Narbandian," he held out his hand.

"Yes," Amos said.

"I'm Zedekiah Banes, I'm a Keeper of Knowledge, and this is Josephine, please could you help us get the time machine out of the water?"

"Okay...?"

It was an awkward structure to move because there were no hand holds, but as soon as they had set it onto the wet, tiled floor Josephine grabbed a line from inside the machine and headed for the nearest power point. "It won't fit, it's a bit different, oh no, I got it." The lights dimmed, "Sorry, I had to put it onto fast charge."

"Could you please tell me what's going on?"

Josephine looked at Amos but she found it hard to speak; this guy must be the best looking man in the universe and even in her weakened state she could appreciate that. When she did speak it was not what she had hoped to say, "I feel sick, where's your bathroom?"

Amos pointed the way, "Who are you people?"

"I told you I'm a Keeper of Knowledge; I come from eight hundred years into your future. We got hold of a time machine by using the information we found in your secret chamber and we went back in time to retrieve the Interference Project, which as you know was destroyed by the Time Guardians. Unfortunately we encountered a few problems, which is why my friend is feeling sick. We came here because we need to get back to Zertza but we're running out of power."

"I put that information about Zertza in the chamber only yesterday and you say you discovered it eight hundred years in the future? Why did you need to go back for the Interference Project? I've already gathered a lot of data, I was intending on taking it all down tomorrow and loading it onto the computer."

"We found very little information on your database; just the stuff about Zertza and a personal note that said that you thought that the Time Guardians were on to you."

"Something happens to me doesn't it? Please tell me, I want to know."

Zedekiah sighed, "Your girlfriend...."

"Amanda? We broke up today."

"Amanda finds you in your kitchen hanging from the ceiling, dead, with a suicide note written in your own hand by your side. Amanda never believed that it was suicide but well, the whole thing was covered up."

"What do you think I should do?"

"Get out of here as soon as you can."

"But they'll tail me wherever I go, if the Time Guardians want you dead, believe me you're dead."

"Well if it's any comfort to you, your organization lives on; in my day it is still the last bastion of truth in the Universe."

"The Time Guardians control everything even eight hundred years into the future?"

"Yes, I'm sorry to say that they do."

Josephine came back from the bathroom red eyed; she had bathed the laser wound, helped herself to a bandage from Amos's first aid kit and drunk a lot of water. "Believe it of not I feel a little better for that. Anyhow ready or not we have to go in fifteen minutes or the Time Guardians will track us."

"Can't you take me with you?" Amos said.

"There's no room, the time machine will only take two," Zedekiah said.

"We could do it if we had more power," Josephine said.

"But there's no room."

"There's enough cubic capacity for all of us but power's the problem; it would take a lot more energy to move the extra mass through time and space and the time machine isn't going to charge up in time."

"I've got power; I've got lots of it," Amos said.

"Anything portable?"

"There's the new fission generator, we use it for emergencies." Amos picked up a microphone, "Get me Gus... hey Gus I need that new fission generator, yes I know about the brown out, no I need it here, bring it to me immediately."

"Even if you come with us you'll probably die anyway, the Time Guardians are almost certainly right behind us," Zedekiah said.

"If I stay here I'm definitely dead; I'll take the chance."

"Then you had better get some clothes on."

Amos ran into his dressing room to make crucial decisions about what to wear. Only he could look great in that trademark frosted pink double breasted suit with the matching hat that looked so strangely similar in shape to the one Zedekiah had worn.

"Now write the suicide note," Josephine said.

"Huh?"

"If you fake your death no one will come looking for you."

Amos told the world that he had reached the top and realized that there was nowhere to go but down, he believed that the galaxy was ready to take responsibility for its own fashion choices and so he would leave them as a father leaves a child with his blessing.

"Does that sound cheesy enough?"

"Yes definitely," Josephine assured him.

There was a knock at the door and Amos answered it, "What do you want that for boss?" Gus asked.

"I'll tell you later," Amos grabbed the generator and closed the door in his face.

Josephine unplugged the lead from the wall socket, brightening the lights once more, and plugged it into the generator.

"I need a sample of your DNA, your hair will do."

"My hair?"

"Yes unless you have any other ideas, and I need a laser gun, you do have one don't you?"

"Well yes in a cupboard somewhere."

"And I need your jacket."

Amos took off his jacket to reveal a white vest that displayed his perfect torso and his muscular arms. He reluctantly cut off some of his hair. They fired the gun so that it scorched the hair and burned the jacket, and then they made a big burn mark on the wall.

"If all goes well they'll think you disintegrated."

"We'd better get going, there's not much time left," Zedekiah said.

"Is there anything else you want me to do?" Amos asked.

"Yea," Josephine said, "find me some painkillers."

Fitting three people into the little time machine was like playing a game of extreme twister. Josephine molded herself around the back wall; Amos squashed himself between her and Zedekiah, and Zedekiah bent his head at an acute angle until his neck really hurt, fortunately he didn't have Clarissa's problem with arthritis. He closed the door on the third attempt.

Josephine activated the co-ordinates and the machine left Amos's temple, and headed for Zertza.

Servants with huge umbrellas escorted Crown Prince Thomas and his friends out of the newer part of the castle and into the old, "We hold all the ceremonies in the old buildings, it stops the public having free access to our private quarters."

"It's for security reasons," Isabella said.

"We were thinking that after the ceremony we would all like to escort you down to the space port. It doesn't seem right to say goodbye to you here," Sylvia said.

"But it's pouring with rain; you'll catch your death."

"Of course we won't we'll be in the car, silly; what time did you say you have to check in?"

"We leave at one-thirty."

"Do you leave then or do you check in?"

"We leave at one-thirty so you see there's not much point in you coming down to the Space Port."

"But shouldn't you be checking in now?"

"Em, no it's a private flight; check in isn't necessary. Anyway we couldn't go without Bunion's medal could we?"

They walked into the massive, high vaulted Ceremonial Hall. It had stained glass windows and was ornately decorated in carved stone and dark wood and gold moldings.

"It's a pity you couldn't stay another day, my parents will be back tomorrow, they would have loved to have met you," Thomas said.

A large crowd of people had gathered to watch the presentation but the first row of seats was empty, except for Percy who was there early. This was the first time he had shown himself since the duel. Bunion walked up to him, "I want to thank you for what you did yesterday."

Percy looked at him, "You were faster than me; you could have killed me; I was merely returning the favor."

"You didn't have to do it," Bunion insisted, "thank you."

Bunion sat down in the pew next to him and Lydia sat next to Bunion. Thomas sat on the other side of Percy and Sylvia, and Isabella sat next to him.

"Why aren't we starting?" Lydia whispered.

"Oh we're just waiting for the other Champions to turn up," Thomas replied. "When I told the Chancellor that I wanted the ceremony for Bunion scheduled for today he decided that he might as well make the presentations to the others as well."

Lydia looked anxiously at the clock on the wall.

Amanda began to worry. Whenever they broke up Amos would apologize and plead with her to come back. But this time he never rang. Eventually she decided to go and see why. She discovered a burn mark on the kitchen wall, some singed hair, a piece of his frosted pink jacket and a laser pistol that had been left on its timer lying on the table facing the burn mark. Then there was the suicide note.

"This is a fake," she told the detective when he came to investigate. "There's nothing about me in it, I told him that he had been treating me unfairly and I broke up with him just to teach him a lesson, if this was a genuine suicide it would have been over me."

Despite Amanda's protests, the case seemed to be open and shut. All the evidence pointed to the fact that Amos had taken his own life. There was only one unanswered question.

"I brought a fission generator up to his apartment just before he..." Gus had to wipe his eyes, "I must have been the last person to speak to him. The thing is, it's missing and I haven't been able to find it."

He never did.

"What did the other champions do? Did they all fight duels?" Lydia asked Thomas.

"No of course not; two of them uncovered a plot against the Royal Family, one of them caught a horse when it was trying to throw the queen off its back and one is a guard who is retiring after ninety years of faithful service. He says he wants to devote more time to his wife and children. Ah here they all are now."

Four bedraggled men walked in the back door. They took off their rain capes, marched up to the front and sat on the opposite row. Finally a stately old woman placed herself in front of the old-fashioned wind organ that graced the back of the hall and the music began.

A man dressed in a black cape edged with red and gold took his place on the rostrum. He waited until the music had finished. "Friends we are gathered here this day to honor these men for the contribution they have made to the preservation of the safety and the honor of the royal family. A royal family, whose origins we all well know...."

The man then proceeded to describe in detail how Bellus had become a monarchy, how it had survived rebellions, murders and crop failures. How its distinguished forbears had strengthened their world politically, economically and socially. How its people had supported them in this endeavor and finally how the individuals that were to be honored today had added to this wonderful effort.

Lydia fidgeted; there were twenty minutes to go.

"And now for the awards themselves."

Lydia really hoped that he would call Bunion first.

"Would Mr. Martin Farrell come forward?"

Mr. Martin Farrell as it turned out, happened to have ninety year's worth of happy reminiscences of what it was like to be a guardian of the royal family.

Lydia stared at the clock....

The time machine materialized on Zertza. It was such a relief when Zedekiah was able to open the door and extrude himself out into the light and air.

But the relief was short lived; Bridefield and his henchmen had already surrounded the time machine.

"Impound that thing," Bridefield turned to Zedekiah, "you've been leading us an interesting dance Mr. Banes, it has been hard to keep track of you."

One of the henchmen went to climb into the time machine but the door slammed shut and it started to dematerialize.

Josephine leaned over and whispered to Zedekiah, "I programmed in a warning for Lydia and Bunion."

"Where do you think they'll go?"

"I don't know but they won't come here."

"Thomas, tell that man to put Bunion on next," Lydia whispered, "we have seven minutes."

Thomas duly did as he was told.

"I now call Mr. Em... Bunion... is there no other name?"

"I never had another one," Bunion said.

"Well Mr. Bunion would you step this way?" Bunion got up onto the platform. "Now Mr. Bunion would you like to tell the people what you did?"

"I did very little."

"It is said that you defended a maiden's honor."

"Yes."

The Chancellor was not satisfied with that answer. He took a long time trying to tease out every little detail about the incident, repeating most of them several times.

"Thomas, tell the man to give him his medal," Lydia whispered, "we've got ninety seconds."

Thomas looked a little puzzled but he nodded to the Chancellor.

"Oh yes well it gives me great pleasure to present to you, this wonderful medal that makes you... what planet are you from?"

"I don't know."

"Oh well this medal makes you an honorary Bellusian," the Chancellor finally pinned it onto Bunion's jacket.

The audience clapped.

"Bunion," Lydia shouted, "we've got sixty seconds."

Bunion jumped off the stage, grabbed Lydia's hand and ran down the center aisle to the door, "Hey where are you going? We haven't said goodbye," Thomas shouted.

"Thank you for everything," Lydia called back.

Thomas, Sylvia, Isabella and Percy ran after them. Bunion and Lydia hurried outside into the pouring rain; they raced down to the main courtyard.

"Don't follow us it's too wet," Lydia called back.

They raced to the spot where the time machine had left them five days earlier.

"Ten seconds," Lydia said.

"Ten seconds to what?" Thomas ran up beside her. There was a buzzing sound in the rain and something began to materialize in front of them, "What on Bellus is that?"

Lydia turned round to Thomas, "The word Bellus means war and you will be its king one day, promise me on your honor that you will be a king of peace."

Water dripped off the end of Thomas's nose, "Lydia why…?"

"Just promise me."

"Okay I promise."

"Promise me faithfully."

"I promise you faithfully that when I am king I will rule in peace," Thomas said.

Lydia hugged him, "Don't you ever forget," she said.

By now the time machine had completely materialized and the door had opened, "Time to go Lydia," Bunion said.

Sylvia hugged them both.

"You're very young, don't be in too much of a hurry to give your heart away; I won't be here to pick up the pieces next time," Lydia told her.

"Will we ever see you again?"

"One day perhaps."

Now it was Isabella's turn to hug them both, "You'll make a fine protector."

"Of the royal family?"

"Of everyone," Lydia said.

Percy hesitated but Lydia hugged him anyway, "You're all right, but you need to grow up and realize that you can't always get your own way."

"Time to go," Bunion said.

Their friends stood in the drenching rain and watched them climb into the strange craft and close the door, "That must be a time machine," Isabella said.

"Do you think so?" Percy asked.

"I'm sure of it."

"Do you think they came from the future or the past?" Thomas asked.

Percy ran his fingers through his ruined hairdo, "Do you think they came to change something?"

"We'll probably never know."

They waited for the little egg shaped vehicle to disappear.

Meanwhile inside the time machine the monitor flashed red.

"There's a message on the screen, it says 'Don't come back to Zertza; Bridefield is here.'"

"Cancel the co-ordinates," Bunion said.

Lydia hit the screen, "We're supposed to input an alternative destination; where shall we go?"

Out in the pouring rain Thomas stared at the time machine, "It's taking a long time to depart, isn't it?"

A black suited servant wielding a large umbrella, caught up with them. "Your Highness you shouldn't be out in this."

"Oh don't worry Mason, we won't be long we're just waiting for that time machine to disappear."

"That what? Your Highness, please tell me this is one of your little jokes."

"There it is, right in front of you, look," Thomas pointed to the egg shaped object with the raindrops bouncing off it.

"Your Highness if that really is a time machine we could all be in great danger, we must inform the Time Guardians; otherwise they might think that you were involved in this."

"No Mason we are not going to inform anybody, if the Time Guardians come here we shall simply deny any knowledge of it."

"But your Highness…."

"My word is final Mason, those people are our friends and one does not betray one's friends."

Meanwhile inside the craft: "There is only one place we can go; we made a promise," Bunion said.

"Yes you're right, I'd forgotten that." Lydia searched through the database for the right co-ordinates, selected them and pressed the 'start' button.

The buzzing started and the time machine disappeared.

Meanwhile Mason escorted Prince Thomas and his friends back into the Ceremonial Hall for the rest of the presentations. After they were settled in their places he slipped out of the back and made his way to the palace offices. His loyalty to the royal house was unquestionable, but sometimes in consideration for their safety he was obligated to disobey orders.

He sent a message to the Time Guardians.

It was dark, the stone floor hurt Clarissa's bones, everyone was hungry and above that they were very thirsty. There was no way to count the hours in this stinking cell. All they knew was that they had been there a very long time.

"I'm getting more memories; we were standing in the courtyard in the pouring rain watching Lydia and Bunion disappear," Clarissa said.

"Did they prevent the war?" Rosie asked.

Something clanged.

"Someone's coming," Annie said.

"Do you think they're bringing us water?"

A bright light shone through the bars, blinding its inmates, "Get up," the guard growled.

"Where are you taking us?" Zedekiah asked.

"You'll find out soon enough."

Geraldine helped Clarissa onto her feet, "Here lean on me."

"Where are we going?" Josephine held her head in her hands because it hurt so much that it felt as if it was going to explode.

"This way," the guard opened the cell door.

"What do you want us for?" Amos said as if he didn't know.

"Where's Bridefield?" Clarissa asked.

"In the yard with the firing squad."

Chapter 17.

Old men in black robes sat on plush, red leather benches in a wide semi circle in the high, vaulted room. A young man stood at the podium and his voice echoed into the microphone.

"Time travel has been with us for sixty years and in that time it has caused countless problems. This debate has lasted for many weeks and rightly so because what you distinguished gentlemen have come here to decide will affect mankind's future for all time to come.

"The evidence that you have seen laid out before you has proved conclusively that time travel is a very dangerous thing. I therefore urge you to outlaw it completely and to enforce such a ban with the utmost vigor. I also plead with you to punish all transgressors with the greatest severity, because the toleration of unregulated time travel has fundamentally interfered with the laws of causality. It has brought about time paradoxes, it has caused temporal crime sprees, it has caused confusion as people have tried to alter the future for their own personal gain and it has caused the suicide rate to soar as people find out the circumstances of their own deaths.

"When you vote, you must put a stop to this nonsense. No one must be allowed to change the timeline, not for any purpose however noble, because even the slightest alteration can have major and unforeseeable consequences. You must vote to outlaw time travel totally for the sake of all our pasts and all our futures."

The young man sat down, and a distinguished gentleman in a robe took the podium, "Thank you Mr. Bridefield, are there any counter arguments?"

There was a buzzing sound.

"What's that?"

The buzzing got louder and an egg shape began to materialize beside him.

"What's going on here?"

The egg shape solidified in front of the podium and the door opened. A dwarf dressed in a sodden white and gold military style uniform got out and a bedraggled young woman in a mauve chiffon dress followed him.

"What is the meaning of this?"

Lydia turned towards the distinguished gentleman, "I must apologize for our intrusion but you are about to make the worst decision in all history."

"How dare you?"

"I am sorry my Lord Goodrich but if you only knew what the future is going to bring, you would not be considering the steps you are about to take."

"Do you wish to pose a counterargument?"

"Yes my Lord I do."

"Someone, give her a microphone."

Lydia cleared her throat, "Bunion and I come from one thousand years into the future and our galaxy has lived under the protection of the Corps of Time Guardians for all that time."

"I thought this was a counterargument."

"It is my Lord because although the aims of the temporal laws are noble they have been enforced with the utmost ruthlessness. Instead of flexibility and reasonableness there is oppression and summary execution, and as a result of the arbitrary way in which the laws are interpreted mankind no longer indulges his scientific curiosity. He even shrinks back from what he already knows and his hold on the galaxy is weakening because the power of the Time Guardians has crushed his spirit."

"Do you have proof of the things you are saying?"

"Gentlemen we come from a future in which time travel is outlawed completely. Anyone using a time machine or trying to build a time machine, or trying to research anything that would be favorable to time technology faces the death penalty immediately and without trial."

"But that is only one possible future," Lord Goodrich said.

"Yes you're right; it is only one possible future. However if you do decide to deal severely with those who contravene the temporal laws, then even we who have traveled from the future to warn you about these things will be executed."

"Lydia," Bunion said.

"What?"

Bunion pointed.

"Bridefield," Lydia said.

"What do you want with Mr. Bridefield?"

"Bridefield has his own agenda my Lord."

"Are you accusing him of something?"

"In our day he, as leader of the Time Guardians is the main reason why the time laws are enforced with such brutality."

The air began to buzz again and the noise grew louder and louder until something egg shaped materialized next to Lydia and Bunion's time machine. The door opened and another Mr. Bridefield walked out of it followed by one of his guards. He bowed towards the Board of Governors and looked at Bunion, "You didn't really think that you could get away from us did you?"

"Whether we escape your clutches or not depends on these good gentlemen here," Bunion said.

"My Lords from my perspective you have already made the decision to ban time travel. These criminals are here to avoid the consequences of their actions. I came here today to show you just how efficient the Corps of Time Guardians is. We have recently apprehended a whole cell of terrorists who attempted to alter the timeline. I am happy to tell you that they have all been dealt with."

"You killed them? Please don't tell me you killed them." Bunion held Lydia tightly in his arms.

"The two people you have in front of you are the most culpable of all."

"Is that so?" Lord Goodrich said.

"Yes my Lord, they stand accused of contaminating the timeline."

"We didn't contaminate it," Lydia protested.

"You mean you didn't alter future history?"

"I admit that we did, but only for the best of reasons, we wanted to prevent a war that would have taken over half a billion lives."

"How do you know that your actions didn't have unforeseen consequences?"

"We don't know anything and we will not know unless we are allowed to return to our own time to see for ourselves. But we do know about Roberto Fettuccia, he saved a whole planet and yet you executed him anyway."

"What is going to happen to us?" Bunion wanted to know.

"What do you mean?"

"Are you going to kill us too?"

"Are you going to give us a trial?" Lydia asked.

"Or are you going to do what you usually do and line us up against a wall and blast us with a laser? Are you going to kill us for saving the lives of half a billion people?" Bunion asked.

"You have broken the law," Mr. Bridefield said.

"A law that doesn't exist yet; besides, if it is so dangerous to travel in time and space why are the Time Guardians allowed to do it? Have you really preserved the timeline? Do you know what consequences your own actions have had? Why can't people travel back in time to prevent disasters and lessen mankind's suffering?" Lydia asked.

"We have already spent many hours debating those issues; you are just wasting the Governor's time. My Lords these people are lying about the future to save their own hides. If you do not sanction the use of severe penalties in order to preserve the timeline you will leave it open to devastating abuse, it is essential that you grant us the power to uphold the law."

"But if things were monitored properly…" Lydia said.

"That is what the proposed Corps of Time Guardians is for," Bridefield countered.

"Lord Goodrich is everybody ready to cast their vote?"

"Have we heard all the arguments?"

"Yes my Lord."

"Have you got anything more to add? Anything we have not heard already?" Lord Goodrich asked Lydia.

"Only that I know that you men will do the right thing."

"Gentlemen please raise your hands if you are ready to vote."

Slowly, one by one each man lifted his hand.

"Those in favor of the prohibition of time travel itself, its technology, its research and the use of any temporal equipment, please raise your hands."

Slowly every occupant of every seat raised his hand.

"Motion carried. Now all those in favor of severe penalties for breaking the prohibition please raise your hands."

The old men looked uncomfortable.

"They're not convinced," Lydia whispered.

Some of the men raised their hands, and others who were not sure, hesitantly began to follow their lead.

"The vote's going the wrong way."

Bunion looked at Lydia and Lydia looked at Bunion, "We've got to cause a distraction."

"RUN," Bunion shouted.

Bunion and Lydia ran towards the large wooden door at the end of the room.

"Hey come back; restrain the prisoners," both Mr. Bridefields and their guard gave chase.

"We are not your prisoners, not until they take that final vote," Lydia shouted.

"These people cannot be allowed to get away."

"You can't legally stop us."

They could have run through the big, wooden doors and carried on running but they didn't, they circled back and raced around the vaulted room.

"Head them off; block their escape."

"This is total disrespect for the Council," Lord Goodrich shouted.

Lydia and Bunion scrambled over the benches that the Governors were sitting on, "We've got to get back to the time machine, we'll have to travel further back; we need more time to convince them," Lydia shouted.

Laser shots fizzed past the old men and scorched the polished, wooden floor. Lydia and Bunion ran down past the podium and scrambled gratefully back into the time machine.

"You must not escape," both Bridefields shouted

"You can't stop us, you don't have the authority."

Bunion caught hold of the door in order to pull it down but the two Bridefields grabbed it and forced it up again.

"We're not criminals," Lydia said.

"Nevertheless we cannot allow you to go...."

The two Bridefields raised their lasers and fired on them at point blank range. There was a gasp from the Governors who all peered over to see what had happened.

"Are they dead?" Lord Goodrich asked. "Well are they?"

The two Bridefields grabbed hold of Bunion and dragged him out of the time machine and laid him on the floor; his big, brown eyes stared sightlessly at the ceiling. "Take a good look at the body of a criminal"

"What about the young woman is she dead too?"

The two Bridefields picked Lydia up and dropped her beside Bunion. She lay there ashen in her ruined, lilac dress; she was beautiful even in death.

"Well is she dead?"

"Yes my Lord she is. This is an example of the effectiveness of the organization of men that will be formed once you have granted us the power to enforce the law."

Lord Cheltenham, an old man with white hair got out of his chair and came down to examine the bodies. He picked the medal off Bunion's chest and pulled out his glasses to read the inscription.

"Champion of the Royal House." He checked for a pulse and looked at his eyes with the experience of an ex-detective, which in fact he was, "He's definitely dead and so is the girl."

He checked the bodies over and looked up at the Bridefields, "These two were unarmed; why did you kill them?"

"You saw them; they were getting away."

"But you were holding the door; the time machine can't operate with the door open."

"They were dangerous criminals; I couldn't take the risk."

"Have they been convicted?" Well have they? What charges did they face?"

"None yet."

"And the other people they spoke of, their accomplices, the ones you killed, what were they convicted of?"

"They also tried to alter history."

"Yes, yes you've already said that, but what were they convicted of? Can I see the court records?"

"They're not available."

One by one the Board of Governors rose stiffly from their seats and crowded around the dead dwarf and his beautiful, lifeless companion.

"She was so pretty."

"We should have listened."

"It's not too late for us to change history; we could still modify the way that we were planning to enforce the time laws."

Everyone nodded their heads in agreement.

"I don't think it's a good idea to kill off our best scientists just because they know a little about time travel, do you?"

Everyone shook their heads in agreement.

At that moment Bridefield's power over the future weakened and the timeline reset itself. People who would have died because Bridefield viewed them as a threat, stayed alive.

Including....

A faint buzzing sound reached the ears of those that weren't half deaf. "Get out of the way, another of those things is about to land," Lord Goodrich said.

Another egg shaped vehicle materialized and two people, a man and a woman got out of it. "Who on Earth are you?"

"I am Joshua Lake and this is my wife Emily my Lord, here are our credentials," the man handed over some papers.

"Do you know where you are?"

"Yes my Lord."

"Do you know who we are?"

"Yes my Lord, I'm sorry, we didn't want to disturb you but we've lost our Josephine."

"What has that got to do with us?"

"She was special; she was designed to be the Temporal Judge, the real Time Guardian."

"What do you mean?"

"She has temporal memory; normally when a timeline alters those it affects are integrated so well into the new timeline that they have no memory of the former one and it becomes impossible to detect the alteration. Our Josephine is the first being that has ever been constructed with the ability to track the changes in the timelines. She can tell us how many alternative futures there are and which of them will benefit the human race the most. Also where mistakes have been made she can tell us what to do to fix them. But after you made your decision to prohibit time travel, Mr. Bridefield here... oh there's two of them... well he... they went about tracking down all temporal equipment and terminating all science projects that were even remotely related to time travel. We were scared and Josephine was only a vulnerable child; we had to protect her, so we hid her in the future on Zeltros Prime. The problem is that we've lost touch with her and can't get her back."

"Why haven't we had any information on this? Why didn't you tell us before?"

"We tried to see you but we weren't allowed, so we filed a report; we were assured it would be presented to you in detail."

"We read no such report," Lord Cheltenham told them.

"You say she's only a child?" Lord Goodrich said.

"The plan was to bring her back to this point in time after she had grown up."

"We're very worried about our Josephine, she's lost in time and she has no idea who she really is," Emily said.

"Bridefield, I think you had better give them back their Josephine," Lord Goodrich said.

"I can't, I executed her an hour ago."

Lord Goodrich spoke up, "Is everyone ready to vote?"

One by one all the old men put up their hands.

"I move that we put any laws on the manipulation of time in abeyance until we can sort this mess out; all in favor?"

Everyone, all together raised their hands.

Meanwhile, an hour earlier, old men in black robes sat on plush, red leather benches in a wide semi circle in the high vaulted room. Mr. Bridefield stood at the podium; his voice echoed into the microphone.

"This debate has lasted for many weeks and rightly so because what you distinguished gentlemen have come here to decide will affect mankind's future for all time to come."

There was a buzzing sound and something egg shaped appeared.

Lord Goodrich and Lord Cheltenham got out of it.

"What's going on?" Lord Goodrich demanded as he saw himself climb out of the time machine.

"Gentlemen we have a problem. Certain events are about to take place that we must prevent."

"You mean you want us to change the imminent timeline?"

"We want you to change it drastically."

"We are about to make a terrible mistake," Lord Cheltenham said.

"What do you want us to do?"

"We want you to arrest Mr. Bridefield, for murder!"

The buzzing noise started again and Lydia and Bunion's time machine began to appear, "These people have something to tell us; it is vital that we listen to them."

Chapter 18.

The Time Machine solidified and a beautiful girl and a dwarf, both in wet clothes stepped out. Lord Goodrich invited the girl to take the podium.

Lydia began to explain to the distinguished gentlemen what the future under Joseph Bridefield would be like.

After a while the air buzzed again and a third egg shaped object materialized out of the air; Mr. Bridefield walked out of it followed by one of his guards, "You didn't really think that you could get away from us?" he said.

"Whether we escape your clutches or not depends on these good gentlemen here," Bunion told him.

"Guards would you please arrest both Mr. Bridefields?" Lord Goodrich said. "I intend to keep them securely locked up so that they cannot chase the Josephine to Zeltros prime."

Just then the buzzing sound started up again, "Where did all these time machines come from?" the Lord Goodrich who had not got out of the time machine said.

The other Lord Goodrich jumped with excitement when Joshua Lake and a young woman with a cone head got out of a fourth time machine, "This man is the Josephine's father, his name is Joshua Lake."

"How does he know that?" Joshua asked.

"Because he met you here before, when I was lost on Zeltros Prime," Josephine told him.

"But you've never been to Zeltros Prime."

"I told you, time has been altered; that's why we had to come here."

"You really do remember previous time lines don't you," Lord Goodrich said.

"I do," Josephine said.

Lord Goodrich turned to the Board of Governors, "This Josephine has been built to track timelines; she remembers all the changes that come about when people attempt to alter time. She can tell us how many alternative timelines there have been, she can decide which of them will benefit us the most, and she can fix the mistakes; that's right Joshua isn't it?"

"Yes my Lord that's exactly right."

"Is everybody ready to vote?"

Everyone nodded their heads.

"I move that we ban the unregulated use of time travel and the unauthorized research into its technology, everybody in favor raise your hands."

The vote was unanimous.

"I also move that there will be no unauthorized punishments for transgressing the law, also that there will be no death penalties and that each individual case will be entitled to a fair trial."

The vote was unanimous.

"I also move that an advisory commission be set up in order to regulate all matters to do with the management of the temporal landscape and the preservation of the integrity of the timeline in whatever way fits the best interests of the galaxy and of mankind as a whole."

The vote was unanimous.

There was a pause but nothing happened.

"Is that it? Are you sure we've changed the future? Nothing feels any different," Lord Cheltenham said.

"I'm certain that we have," Lord Goodrich said.

They had integrated into the new timeline so well that they hadn't noticed that the older Bridefield had disappeared; in this timeline he had never been given authority to create the Corps of the Time Guardians and had never done the things that Lydia and Bunion had accused him of.

"Keep this person in custody," Josephine pointed to the original Mr. Bridefield, "whatever happens he has to be kept behind bars for the next three days or he could do untold damage to the future." She turned around to Lydia and Bunion, "Your job is done; you can now take your proper place in future history."

"Did we prevent the war?" Lydia asked.

"You prevented many injustices, more than you will ever know; everything is as it should be."

"When we get back to our own time will we remember anything?" Bunion asked.

"No but I will remember it for you."

Lord Goodrich shook Lydia and Bunion's hands, "Thank you for having the courage to come back to help us save the future."

"Your deaths saved my parent's lives," Josephine told Lydia.

"Deaths?"

"You've forgotten the old timeline already," Josephine hugged them as they said their farewells "I've set the co-ordinates, just press 'Start' when you're ready."

Lydia and Bunion climbed into the time machine and closed the door. Lydia stood bent over in her wet, ruined dress, Bunion stood in his damp military style suit, his big brown eyes looking up into hers, "We shall not see each other again," he said.

"That's not necessarily true."

"Our lives will take different paths; you have a destiny to fulfill Princess Stephanie."

"You knew all along didn't you? That's why you called me Mistress."

Bunion nodded, "We must say our goodbyes."

"Oh Bunion, how am I going to live without your wisdom and your patience and your tender heart?"

"You will not remember me and I will not remember you."

"But Bunion how could I possibly forget you?"

"We shall live in different worlds Lydia; you will have a good life and you will be happy."

"I couldn't possibly have a happy-ever-after without you Bunion," Lydia's glistening, blue eyes gazed into his wet, brown ones.

"Lydia I don't matter," Bunion pressed the 'start' button.

"Yes you do, you matter more than anything," Lydia stroked his hair with her delicate hands; she lifted his face upwards and bent down and kissed him properly for the first time.

The hairs on the backs of their necks stood up and the buzzing got louder and louder as the time machine went super-luminal, ripping through time and space. Finally it slowed down and eventually stopped.

The door opened and Princess Stephanie looked up at Prince Jason; it was their wedding day and they were in love. The crowd cheered as they stepped out of the time machine into the great flower bedecked Ceremonial Hall on Bellus. Prince Jason ran down the aisle to wait for his future wife while she took her father's arm.

Triumphant music came from the wooden pipe organ at the back of the Hall and two pretty young women picked up Princess Stephanie's long, satin train. As the wedding march played she started walking forward to take her place in front of the Chancellor. Prince Jason stood by her side.

The Chancellor cleared his throat and started to speak, "I remember watching Prince Jason and Princess Stephanie playing together when they were just small children. The little princess would pretend that her toy castle was a house and the young prince would defend it with his wooden soldiers. I remember thinking even then how right these young people were for each other."

Stephanie smiled; she remembered those sunny childhood days too. Each memory was crisp and clear almost as if it was brand new. But there were other memories, vague shadows of things that she wasn't sure of. They melted unnoticed like the time machine that had never been there, not in this new and happier timeline.

"And so dearly beloved we are gathered here today to witness the joining of this man and this woman in holy matrimony. Princess Stephanie what have you got to say to Prince Jason?"

Stephanie looked through her veil into Jason's face, "You are my whole universe; I could not live without your wisdom and your patience and your tender heart. It will be the greatest privilege in the worlds to be married to you."

"And Prince Jason what do you have to say to Princess Stephanie?"

Prince Jason smiled down at her, "I still remember first the day I saw you. You were three years old and I was six and I fell in love with you there and then. I am a man of few words Stephanie but I promise that every day I will tell you that I love you, I only hope that I can make you as happy as you have made me."

The Chancellor smiled, "If anyone has any legally binding objection to this marriage let him speak now or forever hold his peace."

The building was so silent that you could hear a pin drop.

"Do you Stephanie Taylor Winterburgh take Jason Dewberry Higham de Faye to be your lawfully wedded husband to have and to hold from this day forward in sickness and in health for as long as you both shall live?"

"I do."

"Are you sure?"

"Uh? Of course I am."

"I'm sorry I don't know why I said that; and do you Jason Dewberry Higham de Faye take Stephanie Taylor Winterburgh to be your lawfully wedded wife to have and to hold from this day forward in sickness and in health for as long as you both shall live?"

"I do."

"Who gives this woman to be married to this man?"

"I do," Stephanie's father said.

"Do we have the rings?"

"Oh yes, I have them somewhere, excuse me I'm sure... ah here they are," Timothy Banes, the best man picked them up off the floor.

Prince Jason lovingly placed a ring on Stephanie's finger and Stephanie placed a ring on Jason's finger.

"These rings are an outward and visible sign that these two people have pledged themselves to each other forever. I now pronounce them husband and wife."

The crowd cheered.

"You may kiss the bride."

Jason lifted the veil off Stephanie's face; he swept her up into his arms and kissed her tenderly. The crowd began to cheer.

"I've just had the strangest feeling that we've done this before, why would I get a sudden urge to dodge cabbages?"

Jason laughed, "I know what you mean; I had that feeling too."

The music started and the crowd cheered at full volume as the happy couple walked back down the aisle and out of the Ceremonial Hall into the bright sunshine that warmed the old courtyard. Some said that the courtyard was haunted but nobody could remember why.

Stephanie's parents and grandparents, King Luke and Queen Sarah and retired King Wentworth and retired Queen Alison joined Jason's parents and grandparents King Eric and Queen Susana, and retired King Thomas and retired Queen Philomena as they led all the guests to the grand ballroom in the modern part of the castle where the wedding feast awaited.

Josephine was one of the last to leave the Ceremonial Hall; she stood outside enjoying the sunshine.

"Excuse me but are you the judge?" a smartly dressed boy of about nine said to her.

"The Time Judge yes."

"Can you really remember all the different timelines? My mother says they interweave and that you understand how it all works."

"Yes that's true."

"Are you here to change something?" the boy had lively, intelligent eyes; Josephine liked him.

"No I'm just here to tell a story."

"Dillon, stop annoying that lady, I'm sure she doesn't want a child disturbing her peace and quiet," Percy Fopwais, the Lord Chancellor said.

"But grandfather you told me that I should have an inquiring mind."

"It's okay he's not annoying me in the least, I was going to tell the children a story later anyway," Josephine turned to Dillon, "Come and see me in the banqueting hall as soon as your parents dismiss you from the meal, and bring all your friends."

"Thanks for being so patient miss; now come along Dillon your grandmother's waiting for you."

The meal was perfect; the cake was beautiful and when the meal was finished and the speeches were over and before the dancing began, Josephine settled herself into a corner with those who wanted to listen to her story.

"Once upon a time there were two planets like Bellus and Bella only instead of being friends they were at war. The king and queen of one of the planets were so worried that people from the other planet would kill their beloved baby son that they turned him into a dwarf and entrusted him to their chief of security who at great self-sacrifice, changed herself into a wandering entertainer and took him far away from the war zone in order to keep him safe. Meanwhile the king and queen of the other planet had a beautiful baby daughter. They guarded her as best they could on their own planet, sometimes hiding her in monasteries and sometimes on desert islands."

Percy Fopwais and Mary, his wife of over a hundred years stood by and listened to the story for some time.

"She's telling a fairytale," Mary said.

Percy smiled, "There's always some truth in fairytales," as he listened to Josephine's story, puzzles from the past, things that he had wondered about for many years found their answer.

Eventually Percy and Mary were called away by Amos Narbandian who had been granted a three-day temporal visa in order to fit Princess Stephanie for her wedding dress. "I've been talking to your granddaughter; she wants to be married in green," he said.

"We have fervently tried to dissuade Juliana but she is adamant," Mary told him.

"Green is fine; we just have to choose the right shade."

"Do you think you could get another visa so that you could come and do our wedding?"

"I've got to come back to this time, I'm so popular; I've been fighting off beautiful women for most of the day, especially those daughters of Omar, there's so many of them."

"Stephanie invited them to the wedding; apparently they are looking for a husband for Olivia their eldest."

"She's gorgeous but she's not for me; wrong time zone."

"Have you met any of your descendants?" Mary asked.

"Actually that's the scariest thing of all. I don't marry Amanda I meet a girl named Cheryl."

"You found out the name of your future wife?"

"I saw some images of her; she doesn't seem to have much fashion sense."

"Perhaps she has deeper qualities that will attract you."

"Yea well maybe, but I've got all these descendants; there are Narbandians all over the galaxy."

"Did you find out the day of your death?"

"Yes but I've got two hundred and fifty years yet and I intend to have a great time," Amos said.

The grand ball started and Prince Jason and Princess Stephanie had their first dance together as a married couple. After that all the guests joined in until the ballroom was a swirling mass of color and joyful people.

But Josephine and the children didn't move until the story came to its conclusion, "You mean that Bunion and Lydia were really Princess Stephanie and Prince Jason all along?" Dillon Fopwais asked.

"Yes of course," Josephine said.

"Is this true?"

"Every word of it."

The kids had questions: "When the timeline changed what happened to everybody?"

"Why, most of them are here, look the beautiful Lady Isabella is on the dance floor right now. She retired from the security services long ago and married her sweetheart Zedekiah Banes. They have two children and three grandchildren. Their son is a doctor," Josephine said.

"What happened to the traveling circus?"

"It's playing right now at the celebrations at the old castle on Bella; only now it's called Richard Pargeter's World of Mystery and Illusion. Froggie is doing an aqua man routine at present and Grumpus's wife is the show's contortionist. She was never imprisoned for her human's rights campaigning because in this timeline all varieties of humans are equal."

"What about Jerry?"

"He was never kidnapped because there's no longer any need for a shady research business. He grew up with his parents and became a concert pianist."

"What about Roberto and Roslyn?"

"Roslyn married a good man and one of her descendants teaches at the Amos Foundation for Science and Technology. As for Roberto he has to stop drinking and decide what he's going to do with his life."

"Didn't you go into his future to see how he turned out?"

"His future is in his hands not mine."

"What about Natter?"

"He and Rosie met five months ago when she was singing at the Arpak games; she likes him even though he looks a bit strange; they've been going out ever since. She and Rosie have been separated for nearly ten years now and although they miss each other terribly they are both taking their own path in life. Rosie is an opera singer and Annie is a nurse; she enjoys caring for children and hopes to have some of her own one day"

"What happened to Zeno? Did they break him in pieces?"

"No of course not; there are many Zenos dotted about all over the galaxy; at present the one we know lectures in mechanical engineering at the Amos University."

"What happened to Kiii?"

"Well because of mankind's expansion of the galaxy, Aqua is at the crossroads of a trade route. It has had to adopt an open attitude, which means that all its inhabitants are prospering."

"What about the Jerome and Geraldine and the Keepers of Knowledge?"

"It has always been the mission of the Keepers of Knowledge to make sure that the Interference Project is kept updated; they have been the driving force behind most of the technological advancement down to our day.

"Jerome lives on Euphoria, which is a low gravity planet; he has a catering business and he and his wife and fifteen children have a pleasant house to live in.

"Geraldine is married to a man of her own species, they have a trucking business but she doesn't have any tattoos because the accident she was so ashamed of never took place."

"And what happens next?" Dillon said.

"Well that is up to all of you. You are the future; you must write your own story."

"Can't you just tell us what happens to us?"

"No because if I do I could change the way you live your lives and I'm only allowed to do that if something terrible is going to happen."

The children stood up and a little blonde haired girl with ringlets curtsied, "Well thank you for telling us the story, it was the best fairytale I have ever heard," she said.

"It was my pleasure," Josephine said.

"Yes thank you," all the children scattered to find their parents or to eat a little more cake.

Only Dillon stayed behind, "They all think that it's just a story don't they?"

"It is a fantastical tale."

"But it's more than just a fairytale; it's all true isn't it?"

"Every word."

"Your job is to take care of the timeline isn't it?"

"Yes that's right."

Dillon looked serious for a moment, "But what will happen to us if something happens to you?"

"The Temporal Commission is making arrangements to see that nothing does happen to me."

"You mean like body guards?"

"Yes something like that."

"Can I do that? I'd like to protect you."

"Dillon, you're only nine years old."

"I won't always be."

"Maybe I'll travel into the future and recruit you when you're older."

"I would love to protect the protector of time."

Josephine smiled at his bright-eyed enthusiasm.

"Would you like to dance?" Dillon asked.

Josephine held out her hand as the boy led her into the happy throng.

Stephanie looked up into her new husband's smiling face and Prince Jason gazed back into hers; his handsome brown eyes sparkled, "So Mrs. Dewberry Higham de Faye, are you happy?"

"I'm completely happy; you and I together, that's our happy-ever-after."

Meanwhile a thousand years in the past a lawyer slapped a court order on the sergeant's desk, "Release my client now," he demanded.

The sergeant looked up, "I have specific instructions regarding this man."

"They no longer apply, if you don't release him you'll be in contempt of court."

"He's helping the police with their enquiries."

"He can't help you to solve a crime that was never committed."

"Whether it was committed or not is a matter of debate."

"Nevertheless he can't be charged with something that he allegedly did in another timeline on the word of one Josephine."

"Well I don't know about that, I have my orders from Lord Goodrich."

"Who will also be in contempt of court if he doesn't agree to release my client straight away."

"Who did you get to sign your court order?" The sergeant looked at the name on the paper, "Oh Judge Stokes, he's a bit senile… is he still alive?"

"It doesn't matter whose name is on there, this is a legal document and it must be obeyed."

The lawyer was right. Not only could Bridefield not be charged with something he hadn't done, but the police didn't have the right to investigate something that had never happened, whatever the Lords said.

After Joseph Bridefield was freed he headed straight down to Dorian Industries. He had intended to close them down but now he needed them. There would have to be a change of plans.

Because one thing was for sure.

This story was not over.

Not by a very long way!

Other Publications by Pauline Jones:

Bridefield's Revenge: the exciting sequel to A Future Fairytale is due to be released in May of 2008. It opens out the story and shows the reader what our heroes are unwittingly fighting against. Meet the hairy inhabitants of Albacoria and the bat winged Urrahog. Find out why Joseph Bridefield is so intent on preserving the timeline. Now it is not just the fate of the Galaxy that is at stake but the future of mankind!

Paradox: the third book in the Future Fairytale series is due to be released early in 2009. Bridefield has decided that the only way to eradicate time travel is to use a time machine to prevent the events that led to its inception. Unfortunately for him, Daniel Dorian, the owner of the first time travel company has other ideas… big ones. Is it really possible to alter the past or are all timelines locked in a chain of cause and effect that cannot be broken? And what can Amos, the best looking guy in history, do about it?

The Dragons of Turanamek and Other Short Stories: This collection represents the best of Pauline's shorter stories. It includes time travel, fantasy and some humorous works. What would you do if you could travel in time? What are the odds that you would end up in a paradox?

An illustrated book of poetry is planned soon. Please check **www.cozyread.com** for all the latest news.

Also please visit **www.neweyesstudios.com**; for beautiful cards, photographs, paintings, calendars, and photo books.

www.ingramcontent.com/pod-product-compliance
Lightning Source LLC
Chambersburg PA
CBHW030405030726
47497CB00002B/480